For my Anglo-American grandchildren,
Charlotte and Frances Blau

FOR LOVE AND DUTY

MAISIE MOSCO is a Mancunian now living in London. A former journalist, she began writing fiction in the Sixties. Her early work was for the theatre. She is also the author of fourteen radio plays.

Her *Almonds and Raisins Trilogy* established her as a novelist of worldwide status. *For Love and Duty* is Maisie Mosco's eleventh novel.

MAISIE MOSCO

For Love and Duty

Fontana
An Imprint of HarperCollinsPublishers

Fontana
An Imprint of HarperCollins*Publishers*
77–85 Fulham Palace Road,
Hammersmith, London W6 8JB

Continental edition 1990
This edition published by Fontana 1991
9 8 7 6 5 4 3 2 1

First published in Great Britain by
HarperCollins*Publishers* 1990

ISBN 0 00 617999 1

Printed in Great Britain by
HarperCollins Manufacturing, Glasgow

'I slept, and dreamed that life was Beauty;
I woke, and found that life was Duty.'

ELLEN STURGIS HOOPER

Acknowledgements

My editor, Kate Parkin.

Stephen Mosco, for assistance
with research.

The characters in this book are
entirely imaginary and bear
no relation to any real
persons living or dead.

Prologue

THE BUSINESSWOMAN OF THE YEAR received the Award with an enigmatic smile. Applauding her from the luncheon tables in the flower-bedecked room were women who had succeeded as she had in a man's world, but there was to the recognition of her achievement a bittersweet flavour.

When eventually she left the hotel she was waylaid by journalists.

'Is it true that you're soon going to be seventy?'

'And that you've raised *two* families?'

'Are you now thinking of retiring?'

'Any tips for young women hoping to get to the top?'

She replied with her customary briskness and was about to make her escape when a Woman's Page reporter from one of the tabloids asked if receiving the Award was the realization of her dreams.

'Not exactly,' she said glancing at the gleaming statuette in her hand, 'and may we please leave it at that?'

But the question had opened the floodgate of memory and while the limousine awaiting her bore her to her home she saw herself again as a girl of seventeen on the day that love and duty changed her path . . .

PART ONE

1937 . . .

Chapter One

BELLA SAT holding her grandmother's hand, her mind not yet fully encompassing the tragedy that had overtaken the family. Her father's death in a flu epidemic, two years ago, had stunned them by its suddenness though he had lain for a week gravely ill. But this . . .

'How many times,' said her grandmother, 'did I warn your mam to be careful?'

Bella blotted out a picture of a heavy lorry, its brakes screeching. Of Edith Minsky's body crushed beneath the wheels.

'She'd run out of sugar and slipped out to buy some, while I minded the shop,' the old lady went on. 'Next thing I knew, the shop was full of neighbours and a policeman was telling me you had better be fetched home from school.'

The fishmonger next door had collected Bella, and the stench of his van returned to her now. Also the appetizing aroma of the stew her mother had put in the oven, which nobody could bring themselves to eat.

Later, Bella's uncles had arrived with their wives. Or Gran and I would be sitting in the kitchen, like we always do, Bella thought.

Instead, they were all seated in the room that Bella's mother had called the front parlour, though it was behind the shop, the polished mahogany china cabinet and starched white antimacassars a poignant reminder of the pride Edith Minsky had taken in her home.

Even the aspidistra had a well-cared-for look, Bella noted,

her gaze roving from the plant by the lace-curtained window to her parents' wedding photograph atop the cabinet.

Radiant is the word for how my mother looks in that photo, Bella thought. But that was before life knocked the stuffing out of her and I'm never going to let that happen to me. Mam was a lot better looking than I am, but she didn't have the brains, or the chance, to be what I'm going to be.

Bella's looks were those of her gran, who was her father's mother. A face whose only claim to beauty was hazel eyes with long dark lashes, and a figure that had at school earned her the nickname 'Boney'.

In the world Bella would shortly be entering, though, looks didn't matter, she was thinking when her Uncle Saul broke the silence.

'It was nice of that neighbour to take your little brother and sister home with her for the night, Bella.'

'It's that kind of neighbourhood,' said Gran. 'The twins were taken off our hands for the whole week of mourning when we lost my son.'

And no less bewildered by being whisked away now than they were then, Bella recalled. How was she to tell them that their mam was never coming back?

When the twins were born, Bella was twelve. Had she resented them? Oh yes. Which only child wouldn't resent two rivals for its parents' affection? How else could Bella have seen it? She had dealt with their howling presence by plugging her ears with cottonwool while doing her homework. By the time Joey and Sylvie were toddlers, they had seemed to understand that they mustn't make a noise while their big sister was studying.

Bella could remember them tiptoeing around with a finger to their lips. And now they were very dear to her. A pair of adorable five-year-olds who had not had their parents for long, their early childhood dominated by my education, she thought with a pang.

Looking back, it was as if Bella's getting a scholarship to Manchester High School was an accolade for the whole family, so rare an achievement was it for a girl from her background.

Bella's scholastic brilliance had been recognized at an early age and she had gone on to win a place at Oxford. Her father had not lived to know, but how proud her mother was when the wonderful news came.

'We forgot to congratulate you, Bella,' said her Uncle Saul as though he had divined her thoughts.

'If you'd been in when your mam rang up to tell me, I'd have wished you all the best then,' said Uncle Reuben. 'I meant to drop you a line, but you know how it is.'

When it came to her uncles, Bella certainly did. Though her mother was their only sister, they had rarely visited her, seemingly too engrossed in their own lives to spare Edith a thought. Only her death had brought them to Salford today, Saul from his trouser factory in Leeds and Reuben from his barber shop in Liverpool.

Both had arrived red-eyed with weeping. And tomorrow they'll shed more tears at my mam's graveside, thought Bella, some of which would be tears of conscience because they didn't do their duty by her after she was widowed, though duty shouldn't enter into it. Not with someone you love.

'It's October you'll be starting at university, isn't it?' Reuben went on. 'But by then, everything will be settled. Over and done with.'

Bella felt a chill settle in the pit of her stomach. 'Would you mind explaining to me what you mean?'

Her uncles exchanged a glance, then Saul fingered his silver watch-chain, and Reuben rested his arms on his paunch. They were seated side by side on the sofa, flanked by their wives whose corsetry had, as always, impelled them to choose upright chairs, the foursome reminiscent of a family portrait.

It was one that would imprint itself upon Bella's mind.

'The shop will have to be sold, won't it?' Reuben said to her. 'And Joey and Sylvie, who our sister was struggling to bring up on her own – well, Saul and me have talked it over and we're not going to let poor Edith down.'

Bella had not until then thought of the twins' future in practical terms. There hadn't been time. But her uncles were prising her out of her grief, away from her memories. Making her face up to realities that included the care and attention required by two little kids.

Bella listened in silence while they told her, as though it were a fait accompli, that Joey would live with Reuben and Sylvie with Saul.

Split up the twins? Not just to different houses, but to different towns.

'As for your grandma, Bella,' Saul added, 'when we mentioned the problem to the rabbi, after he'd helped us to make the funeral arrangements, he said that the Manchester Jewish Home for the Aged is our best bet if we can get her in.'

Bella sprang from her chair. 'My gran isn't a problem!'

'Well, your mam never made me feel like one,' Gran intervened, 'though I reckon in some ways I am. Nobody could've been a better daughter-in-law than Edith was to me. If it weren't for my bad health, I'd repay her by taking care of the twins myself.

'I'm still capable, though, of making us all some tea.'

A pause followed her dignified exit, the visitors avoiding Bella's eye and she glaring at them accusingly.

Saul cleared his throat. 'I didn't mean to upset her, Bella, but there's a lot to be sorted out and the sooner the better.'

His wife pursed her lips, hands clamped on the lizard-skin bag on her ample lap. 'Bella ought to be thankful that her Auntie Rosie and me aren't the sort to let our husbands' little nephew and niece be put in an orphanage.'

'Speak for yourself, Dolly,' her sister-in-law said. 'Me, I'm not asking for thanks.'

'But the way Bella's behaving, Rosie, anyone would think her uncles and aunties were her enemies!' Dolly exclaimed.

Another silence charged the atmosphere, while Dolly fiddled with her hennaed hair and Rosie with her imitation pearls.

The air in the small room was stifling and laden with the Evening in Paris scent drifting from Dolly's direction. Bella could hear her grandmother setting cups and saucers on a tray in the kitchen. The ornate clock on the mantelpiece was ticking relentlessly, as if reminding her that time did not stand still, nor could the clock be turned back. Telling her, too, that she had reached a crossroads in her life.

She surveyed her uncles and aunts and saw them for the kindly folk they were, allowing herself to imagine little Joey cradled against Rosie's motherly breast, and Sylvie being tucked up in bed by Dolly. Reuben wasn't as comfortably off as Saul, but neither twin would go short of affection and each would have the company of cousins to whom they would soon come to seem one of the family.

But, thought Bella, the twins won't have each other and they won't have me. It will be the end of *our* family. As for Gran . . .

Briefly, Bella envisaged herself in cap and gown, strolling through the college cloisters. Peering through a microscope in a laboratory, clad in a white coat. Conferring with her colleagues, years from now, about a scientific discovery that could help mankind. Receiving the Nobel Prize.

The dream disintegrated. She could not pursue her own ambition by turning her back on those she loved. Instead, she would carry on where her mother had left off.

Chapter Two

CASTING ASIDE the warnings of her uncles and aunts, Bella had, with the confidence of youth, given no thought to the practical problems ahead. She would take care of her grandmother and the twins. Cook, clean, and serve in the shop. It had seemed to her as simple as that.

She had not, of course, reckoned on the reality of two small children tugging at her skirt for attention, of the old lady's querulousness, of the boredom with which she herself was afflicted while waiting for a customer to select the exact shade of trimming with which to refurbish last year's spring hat, or to examine box after box of buttons before deciding that none was quite right.

Such was the nature of the business from which Bella's parents had made a meagre living. And always with a smile, Bella recalled on a sultry July morning, forcing herself to emulate them while one of the local dressmakers purchased some hooks-and-eyes and tried to decide if some odd lengths of coloured ribbons, piled on the counter, might come in useful.

In Edith Minsky's day, the ribbons would not have been heaped in a pile, but carefully arranged in a basket as were the remnants of lace. In that respect, Edith's tidiness had extended to the business. Buttons and buckles always replaced in their boxes and returned to the shelves, bobbins of thread, skeins of embroidery silk and of wool, needles for sewing and for knitting, all had their assigned places in Minsky's Haberdashery Store.

A posh name for a little shop, Bella had once thought. Not

until she found herself stepping into her father's shoes did it occur to her that he too might have been imbued with ambition. That had he lived, he might have gone on to expand the business, as her Uncle Saul had begun with one sewing machine in a back room and now owned a factory.

Though carrying on where her mother had left off was how Bella saw her new responsibilities, she sensed that the business as such had meant nothing to Edith, that it was to her just a means of supporting the family.

Bella, however, was her father's daughter. Why hadn't she realized it until now? That Len Minsky, who had taught her to read when she was four, and could add and subtract in his head faster than most could on paper, might have been anything he set out to be had boyhood poverty not dictated his life as her mother's death had changed the course of Bella's.

Edith, on the other hand, though not lacking in intelligence had harboured no personal aspirations, living entirely for her family and somehow muddling through to make ends meet after losing her husband.

'Muddling through' described it, Bella had thought while inspecting the botch her mother had made of keeping the books. Nor, it seemed, had Edith ever bothered to take stock, since no inventories covering the past two years were to be found; an insight into her mother's character that seemed to Bella incongruous.

How could a housewife as methodical as Edith was have been so haphazard in business matters? That running out of sugar had led to her mother's end was to Bella a painful irony. Even in hard times, and the thirties were no less so for the Minskys than for their neighbours, Edith had somehow managed to keep her larder topped up, priding herself that she had never in her married life needed to borrow so much as an egg.

The last time she had said so was on the Sunday preceding her death, after the fishmonger's wife borrowed a handful of raisins for the cake she was making for tea.

19

A poignant recollection causing Bella's eyes to sting with tears. But where would tears get her? She wrapped two remnants for the customer, who had finally decided that they *would* be useful, and kept a smile on her face.

'Your mam used to give me discount, love,' the tubby woman told her, 'on account of me being a regular customer.'

Discount on a card of hooks-and-eyes and a couple of ribbon ends? How had Edith made a profit? It was possible that she hadn't. That she'd just dipped into the till for her household requirements as if its contents were entirely hers to spend.

This was Bella's first week in the shop. A pile of bills from wholesalers still awaited her attention. And the puzzle that the books represented was daunting, to say the least. Nor had she yet established if her father, and afterwards her mother, had employed an accountant. If so, he must surely have washed his hands of Edith, Bella thought now.

'Your mam gave discount to all the regulars,' the customer revealed, while taking a handkerchief from the cuff of her floral print frock to mop the sweat from her face. 'What a muggy day it is!'

And for Bella one of revelations.

'The discount's why I always come here, instead of going to Lewis's trimmings department, in town,' the woman went on. 'Well, that and the convenience –'

'Did my father give discount?' Bella cut in.

'As a matter of fact he didn't.'

And it was his way, not her mother's, that Bella would run the business. 'Our prices are cut to the bone already,' she said, though she did not yet know if they were, or not.

'If that means I'm *not* getting discount, I might start going to Lewis's, where there's a much bigger selection,' the woman replied.

'But it would cost you your tram fare,' said Bella, 'wouldn't it, Mrs Baines?'

'I'm surprised you know my name. Though I've been a customer for years, I don't remember you ever helping in the shop. Like Elsie Mathers, who you went to Leicester Road

School with, used to serve in her dad's greengrocery,' Mrs Baines reminisced. 'Elsie's an assistant at Kendal Milne's now, her mam told me. A bit different from selling onions to the likes of me! Elsie always was a nice, refined lass, but she'd have to be to get a job where the toffs do their shopping.'

Bella returned to the subject from which they had strayed. 'The minimum amount for me to allow discount, Mrs Baines, is half-a-crown.'

'Two-and-sixpence! That's a quarter of my rent money, Bella –'

'But I, also, have to pay my rent, plus the overheads for running the shop.'

'You're a harder nut than your mam was,' Mrs Baines declared.

If Joey and Sylvie were to have the opportunity she had on their account eschewed, Bella would have to be, she thought while Mrs Baines handed her a shilling and received three-pence change.

The twins would not begin attending school until after the summer holiday, but already Bella was planning for their higher education, envisaging them scaling the academic heights that she herself had hoped to climb.

Meanwhile, she could hear them quarrelling and hastened to the kitchen immediately Mrs Baines departed.

'What's going on?'

Joey was punching Sylvie, and the little girl pulling his shock of black hair.

'I said I want my mam, and Sylvie called me a big baby!' Joey yelled. 'Why can't I have my mam, Bella?'

'Our mam's gone to heaven, hasn't she?' Sylvie said before bursting into tears.

'Could I please have a glass of water, Bella?' said Gran from her rocking chair by the window. 'What with the twins and the heat, I don't feel too well.'

Bella fetched the water, then gave her attention to the children, now sobbing in each other's arms. Only time would heal their hurt. Meanwhile, distraction was what they needed.

'If I let you help me in the shop, will you promise to be good? Sylvie can dust the counter, and Joey can fold up some lengths of ribbon and lace that I'm going to cut –'

'What are you going to do that for?' Gran interrupted.

'I've noticed that women can't resist a bargain,' Bella answered drily, 'and we're running out of remnants. We're not selling enough ribbon and lace by the yard, or even the quarter-yard, to be left with odds and ends.'

'Well, everyone has to count their coppers nowadays,' said Gran, 'what with so many men being on the dole for so long.'

'But they still manage to buy themselves a packet of Woodbines to smoke,' Bella countered, 'and their wives keep doing up the same best frock and hat they've had for years.'

'Like I used to, when your dad was a lad,' Gran recalled. 'We were living in Strangeways then.'

The twins had stopped weeping and were listening intently.

'Where's Strangeways?' Joey enquired.

'Can we go there?' said Sylvie. 'Why is Granny laughing?' she asked Bella when the old lady chuckled.

Gloom had reigned in the Minskys' home since Edith's death. But we can't go on that way, thought Bella, it's bad for the children.

'It struck me as funny, love, you wanting to go to Strangeways,' Gran told Sylvie. 'It used to be the district Jewish people wished they could get out of, where we all lived in cramped little houses, with black beetles for company and only a cold water tap.'

'I wouldn't like that,' said Joey.

'But we were thankful for a roof over our heads and a bite to eat, in those days,' said Gran. 'After what we'd escaped from, in Russia, all that mattered was we were somewhere safe.'

'Were there black beetles in Russia?' Joey asked.

'There might have been. But it's the Cossacks riding through our village on horseback that I remember. How it scattered the chickens, and raised great clouds of dust in summertime. And sent everyone rushing to bolt themselves inside their houses and hide their kids, 'cause they knew what might happen next.

'Many's the time my mother hid me and my sister in the laundry skip. Us at the bottom and a big pile of washing on top of us,' Gran recalled. 'We could barely breathe.'

'Why did your mother have to hide you?' Sylvie wanted to know.

'What did everyone think might be going to happen?' Joey continued the quizzing.

While Gran began telling them, Bella went to tuck Joey's shirt-tail where it was before his fight with Sylvie, and retied the blue bows in her little sister's pigtails, aware of a maternal feeling towards them that she hadn't expected would be aroused in her until she had children of her own.

Both resembled their mother, fresh-faced and with the refined features that Bella wished had been passed down to her. Much as she had loved her father, she could have done without inheriting his sallow complexion and a nose that just escaped being a beak.

'Why did the Tsar want the Jews to be Christians, Granny?' Joey interjected into the tale Bella had been told when she was their age.

'Didn't he *like* Jews?' asked Sylvie.

Everything you tell them leads to their wanting to know more, Bella thought, and there were times when she lost patience with their pelting her with questions. But their enquiring minds would single them out when they started school.

Nor did they forget Bella's promise to let them help in the shop, trailing behind her when she returned there after the family had eaten lunch.

'Our mam used to give us a *proper* dinner,' Joey complained, en route.

'Which you didn't always eat up,' said Gran who was accompanying them, none too sure that Bella ought to be cutting up ribbon and lace to be sold as remnants.

'I enjoyed the cheese and pickles we had today more than

that proper dinner Bella made us on Sunday,' said Sylvie. 'The cabbage was mushy. Bella doesn't know how to cook.'

'But I'll soon learn,' said Bella, 'like I'm having to learn about lots of things. Gran will give me some tips –'

'If you'd let me do the cooking, I wouldn't have to,' Gran cut in. 'Your mam never let me lift a finger, let alone a panful of veg on and off the stove. Not since I had that angina attack after your dad died.'

It struck Bella that Edith's pampering had turned Gran from an active woman into the semi-invalid that by now she herself thought she was, and that her frequent bouts of querulousness were due to time hanging too heavily on her once busy hands.

'From now on, the kitchen is all yours,' Bella said and saw Gran's face light with pleasure. 'I've enough to see to and think about. But you're not to wear yourself out making special meals for these two little monkeys, like Mam did!'

Bella handed a duster to Sylvie. 'After you've done the counter, you can climb on the ladder and give the boxes on the top shelves a good dusting. They've got cobwebs on them.'

'That's where the diamanté buckles and buttons are kept,' Gran recalled. 'In the twenties, they sold like hot cakes but they seem to've gone out of fashion. Or it could be that folk can't afford them any more.'

Nor had the shop bell rung to summon Bella since she went to find out why the twins were quarrelling.

Gran watched her pick up the scissors and begin snipping pieces from a roll of lace trimming. 'When your dad was a lad and I wanted to look nice for a Barmitzvah, or a wedding, I used to make a white lace flower to pin on my black frock. I had the frock for *his* Barmitzvah –'

And it seemed to Bella that most of Gran's recollections were, one way or another, attached to her dead son. Not just the family milestones that Barmitzvahs were. When Gran harked back even to something mundane, it was as if she was unable to do so without including him.

'It was the only good frock I'd got,' the old lady went on, 'made from a bit of black taffeta my sister bought at Flat Iron

Market. It was her who made me the frock, Bella, like she did the one I wore for your parents' wedding. And not too long after that she died giving birth to her first child, the baby as well.'

Joey stopped folding the lengths of lace and watched the cat lope into the shop from the living quarters. 'Is Whiskers going to die when her kittens are born?'

'If she does,' said Sylvie from atop the ladder, 'she'll have our mam to kiss and cuddle her when she gets to heaven.'

Both children's eyes had filled with tears.

'Show us how you made those lace flowers, Gran,' Bella said hastily, to divert them.

'There's nothing to it, Bella,' Gran said, selecting a length of lace and with the aid of some pins deftly transforming it.

'Well, not when you know how!'

'If you'll get me a needle and thread, I'll sew it up and you can have it. My dressing-up days are over, but it'd liven your grey costume, pinned to the lapel.'

'Never mind my grey costume,' Bella replied, 'that flower is good enough to sell. How would you like a part-time job, Gran?'

'If I can fit it in with my cooking,' Gran said with a smile. She watched Bella dismember a roll of satin ribbon, as she had the lace. 'Your parents would turn in their graves if they knew what you were doing! At this rate, Minsky's Haberdashery Store will soon be Minsky's remnant shop —'

They were interrupted by the entrance of a male customer. Or is he perhaps a wholesaler, come to demand payment? Bella wondered apprehensively. He was wearing a sober suit and carrying a briefcase.

'Good afternoon,' he said politely while removing his trilby hat.

Bella managed to smile. 'What can I do for you?'

'I thought there might be something I could do for *you*,' he answered. 'I was your father's accountant — and briefly your mother's, that's why I'm here. I heard that you'd taken over the business, Miss Minsky.'

While he expressed his condolences, Bella was aware of him sizing her up. Wondering, no doubt, if I take after my mam! But the books were the last thing Bella wanted to think about right now.

'Your mother was a nice lady. She didn't deserve to die so young,' he said finally, and Bella asked Gran to take the twins to the kitchen and give them some milk and biscuits. They had heard enough morbid talk for one afternoon!

'I didn't know if the business had an accountant,' she said when she was alone with the young man. 'What's your name?'

'Ezra Black.'

'It was kind of you to come.'

'To be truthful, your Uncle Saul rang up and asked me to. But I'd have called in anyway. I have clients in this district whom I sometimes see at their premises. It would have been churlish not to drop in and wish you luck.'

Bella would need more than luck to sort out the mess she had been left with, she thought while sizing *him* up. Though his appearance was somewhat owlish, he had nice grey eyes behind those big horn-rimmed glasses. She noted, too, that his sandy hair wasn't slicked back with brilliantine.

'You got fed up with my mother, didn't you?' she said. 'And I can't say I blame you –'

'I wouldn't put it that way, Miss Minsky,' he replied. 'It was just that I couldn't make her see that she was heading for trouble. You can't help someone who won't let you.'

'But you won't find me that way,' Bella informed him. 'That's if you're prepared to take me on?'

'Aren't you a bit on the young side for what *you're* taking on?'

'That doesn't mean I can't cope with it, Mr Black.'

He surveyed her again and wondered why at first he had thought her plain. There was something arresting about Bella Minsky, even in that drab grey coat overall. The way she held her head when she looked at you, slightly tilted. But most of all it was her eyes – now pinning him with a glance.

'Your parents used to call me by my first name. Why don't you do the same?' he said.

'I will if you'll stop calling me Miss Minsky. Are you going to be my accountant, Ezra? If so, I'll come to your office to see you –'

'Which your mother rarely did!' he said with a grin. 'I'll give you a ring to fix an appointment, Bella.'

'But it could be a long time before I can pay you,' she felt constrained to say.

'Who could know that better than me?'

'And you're still prepared to advise me?'

'It isn't every day that a chap gets the chance to help a maiden in distress!'

Chapter Three

IT HAD NOT TAKEN LONG for Bella to realize that drastic action was necessary to boost trade. She was not the kind to mark time and was coming to know herself a good deal better than she had before others became dependent upon her. Though she had switched from the academic to the material, the challenge to succeed remained.

Her shrewd judgement that even in hard times women could not resist a bargain led her to capitalize on that feminine trait. By the time the twins started school, Minsky's Haberdashery had held its first summer sale, a hectic week when Bella cleared out much of the old stock, including the diamanté buttons and buckles mouldering on the top shelves.

Later, she had instituted a special discount for dressmakers buying sewing items in bulk, and had set her sights on acquiring a button-covering machine.

As for the remnants her grandmother had disparaged, dress fabrics had joined the ribbons and lace now displayed in baskets outside the shop to allow passers-by to rummage, as they did in the cartons of imperfect pots and pans outside the local hardware store.

The fabrics, obtained from a manufacturer client of Ezra's who was glad to get however little for unusable lengths, were soon the main source of profit. Ezra, however, was horrified when Bella announced her intention of selling them too on Wigan Market.

'I can't let you do that,' he declared and received an icy glance.

'You being my accountant doesn't give you the right to tell

me what I can and can't do,' Bella informed him. 'Just one of the reasons I'm thinking of doing it is to help pay your fee. I'd probably make more in a day on a market stall than I do in a month at the shop. Shutting shop one day a week might seem unbusinesslike to you, Ezra, but –'

'How would you get the stuff to Wigan?' he interrupted.

'On the train, of course. You'd be surprised how much can be packed in the couple of old suitcases we've got in our attic. From the days when my mother used to take us on holiday to Blackpool,' Bella added.

Would such carefree times ever come again? Well, certainly not until the dole queues got shorter and people had more to spend, and even then not for Bella. But she would be able to send Gran and the twins to a nice boarding house near the North Pier. Like her dad had made sure his family got some sea air, though *he* couldn't leave the shop.

Ezra noted Bella's pensive expression. 'Let me put it this way,' he said carefully. He ought to've known she wouldn't take kindly to his laying down the law. 'Lugging heavy cases on and off trains isn't for you. Nor is shlepping the stuff from the station to the market.'

It's me he's thinking of, not the business, Bella registered. But she had sensed from the first that Ezra Black was a nice young man.

'Who do you think you are?' he went on with a laugh. 'Tarzan?' Right now, Ezra felt as if he were that muscular Hollywood hero, and Bella the heroine, Jane. Such was the protectiveness she aroused in him, though muscular he wasn't! He'd felt it on the day he first met her and joked about helping a maiden in distress. What he didn't know then, though, but had since learned, was that Bella Minsky was a highly independent and determined young woman.

'I haven't yet enquired when Wigan market day is,' she told him, 'but if it turns out to be Wednesday, I shall only lose a morning's trade at the shop, since it's half-day closing here.'

'Isn't that when shopkeepers do their buying?'

29

'In my case, what buying?' Bella answered. 'I'm keeping stocks as low as I can – like you advised – and the regular lines haven't suddenly begun moving faster.'

They were conversing in the shop and Bella surveyed with a smile her grandmother's artistic handiwork, a selection of lace and organdie flowers, displayed on a length of black velvet pinned to a wall.

'My gran's been kept busy making those. They're going very well and she's over the moon about it. In King Street, they'd fetch treble what we get for them, though. It makes you think, Ezra.'

'What does it make you think, Bella?'

'That prices aren't necessarily geared to the goods themselves.'

'Then you've learned something, haven't you?'

'But round here it can't be applied, can it? Even in good times, our profit has to come from turnover and when you don't get enough turnover you're in trouble.

'Like a cup of tea, Ezra? Unfortunately, I have time to make you some!'

'I had tea with the client I've just come from, thanks.'

'Have you many in this district?' Bella asked him, and received a rueful smile.

'I don't have what you could call many clients in *any* district, Bella. It takes years to build up a practice.'

'Then mightn't you have been better off staying with that firm you said you used to work for?'

Ezra shook his head. 'Both partners have sons in the practice. There was no future for me there.'

Bella studied the bespectacled countenance by now familiar to her. Not just familiar. Reassuring. 'Then why are you trying to stop *me* from doing what I think is best?'

'Best for who?'

Bella paused only to give him a withering glance before dashing from the shop to cover the baskets of remnants with waterproof sheeting, as rain began deluging from the bleak November sky.

'You're wet through,' he observed when she returned.

'Rather me than my goods. What the heck did you mean, asking me "best for who?"! I've a family to support, haven't I?'

'And it doesn't seem right,' said Ezra. 'You're only a kid.'

'I'll be eighteen on Sunday,' Bella retorted. 'My mother was a married lady at my age. And you couldn't have been that old yourself when you decided to set up in practice on your own.'

'I was twenty-five.'

Bella was taken aback. That meant he was going on thirty now, though he didn't look it. His round face lent him a schoolboy appearance, as if all that was missing was the Manchester Grammar School cap he had once worn.

His elitist education at that distinguished establishment was something that Ezra occasionally joked about. Bella, though, could not imagine ever seeing the time she had spent at Manchester High School in that light. It had opened her mind to a world she might otherwise not have known existed, instilled in her not just a thirst for scientific knowledge, but a love of literature and she would never stop being grateful for that. When do I now have time to read a novel, though? she was thinking when Ezra resumed speaking.

'Twenty-five isn't to be compared with eighteen, Bella. And a man has to have a target if he's going to get anywhere.'

'What makes you think it can't be like that for a woman?' Bella demanded.

She had taken off her coat overall to drape it over a chair to dry, and Ezra averted his eyes from her small, high breasts which the white jumper she was wearing emphasized. Even the lisle stockings she had on could not, he noted, detract from her shapely ankles.

'Why have you suddenly gone dumb, Ezra?'

'I was thinking of something I must do when I get back to the office,' he lied.

'In the middle of a conversation with me? If I'm that boring –'

'Boring,' he said with a smile, 'is the last thing you are!'

On the contrary, he thought, Bella's company was more stimulating than Ezra would have wished. Her effect on him too, and he'd better stop pretending to himself that she was just a kid. What she lacked in years, she made up for in brains and had matured in many ways since the July afternoon when she climbed the three flights of stairs to keep her first appointment with him, plonked the books on his rickety desk and said, 'Call this an office?'

Only her impish grin had stopped Ezra from telling her to go to hell and take the books with her. In effect, if not in words, what he had finally said to her mother.

Bella was regarding him impishly now, a quizzical expression in those beautiful hazel eyes.

'You'll never make your fortune if you stand gabbing with me all day,' she said.

'I'm not after making a fortune,' he replied. 'A nice house in Prestwich will suit me fine. That's what I'll have one day.'

And you'll live in it with me, Ezra silently added. It was then that he made up his mind he was going to marry Bella.

Chapter Four

By the spring of 1938, rumours of impending war with Germany cast a further cloud over a Britain not yet recovered from the decade's economic depression.

'If there's a war, will your young man be a soldier?' Sylvie asked Bella.

Kids are quick to sense their elders' anxieties, Bella thought. And the twins had big ears! 'Ezra isn't my young man,' she said.

'Then why have your cheeks gone red?' Joey enquired.

'It must be from the March wind, love.'

'And why are we meeting Ezra in the park?' Sylvie continued the badgering.

'If he isn't your young man?' said Joey.

'Because I told him I'd see him there. And I'm daft for taking you two with me!' Bella exclaimed. 'When I could have left you with Gran and had a Sunday afternoon to myself.'

'It was Gran who told us Ezra's your young man, and Gran doesn't tell fibs,' Sylvie declared.

Short of contradicting the latter, there was nothing Bella could say. Nor could she blame her grandmother for assuming what she did. Ezra's frequent presence in the Minskys' home was no longer solely professional, as it was last year when he and Bella had spent long evenings in the parlour, their heads together over nothing more personal than the books.

Waiting with the twins for a tram that would take them to Heaton Park, Bella cast her mind backward. When had she and Ezra begun courting? – as Gran would put it! Ezra's parents too, whom Bella had not yet met. But what it implies is something I'm not ready for.

Bella glanced down at Joey and Sylvie in the new reefer coats she had somehow managed to buy for them. They would soon need bigger shoes, as well.

'I'm cold. When will the tram come, Bella?' Sylvie asked.

Bella turned up the child's collar and adjusted her red beret more firmly on her head. 'When it does, we'll ride on the top deck,' she promised while tucking Joey's muffler snugly around his neck.

Berets and mufflers, like the jerseys and socks the children wore, could be knitted and Gran was a dab hand at that. But it still cost more to clothe and feed the family than Bella could afford. As for the gas and electricity bills –

Courting leads to marriage, Bella thought dispassionately, and if that's what Ezra has in mind for us, he must have shut his eyes to my circumstances. Not let himself see how things actually are for me.

There was another reason too for Bella's reluctance to accept that she and Ezra were courting. Fond of him though she was, something was lacking.

He had begun by inviting her to a dance at the Waterpark Club, an occasion that initiated Bella into the social activities enjoyed by young Jewish people in Manchester and Salford.

Though Bella had known that tennis was played there, and also at the Maccabi Club, she had not allowed pleasure to distract her from her studies. Nor, since leaving school, had joining a club as other girls did so much as entered her head.

It occurred to Bella now that there was only one girl whom she could call her friend. Those she had made at school had moved on. To Oxford, or Cambridge. Or to provincial universities. Including Manchester, but even going to college in your home town was in effect moving on.

Bella, on the other hand – well, I too am now immersed in the next stage of my life, but mine isn't going to lead to what theirs will.

She cast aside that unproductive thought and made a mental

34

note to give Connie Davidson a ring. They'd been pals since their elementary school days and had kept in touch after Bella got a scholarship to Manchester High and Connie failed to get a place at a high school.

Connie was at the club dance to which Ezra had invited Bella, and had welcomed her with characteristic warmth, Bella recalled when she and the twins were finally trundling along Bury Old Road atop a tram.

And my courtship with Ezra, if that's what it is, carried on from there. Though he had made Bella's birthday an excuse for the invitation, since then he had taken her to the pictures on Saturday nights, and to the functions that featured in the social scene.

Not until last week, though, did he pluck up courage to kiss Bella good night when he took her home. If Gran knew about that, she'd be waiting up for me from now on!

'Where in the park are we meeting your young man?' Sylvie asked.

'You'll see when we get there,' was Bella's irritated reply.

He was pacing beside the lake when they joined him.

'If you're thinking of taking a boat out, I hope you're a good rower!' said Bella.

She handed Joey the bag of crusts she had brought for him and Sylvie to feed the swans, and said when they had skipped off to do so, 'I hope you don't mind the kids coming along, Ezra.'

'Why would I mind?'

'Well, you weren't expecting this to be a family outing, were you?'

Ezra linked her arm and headed towards a bench. 'I've got nothing against kids, Bella.'

'But how would you feel about being saddled with two who weren't your own?'

He waited until they were seated on the bench before replying, 'You're jumping the gun a bit, aren't you?'

'If you say so.'

Ezra switched his gaze from the lake to Bella. One day he'd

35

buy her a better fur coat than the old grey squirrel she had on.

'All right,' he said, taking her hand, 'you're not jumping the gun. But time enough to discuss practical matters when I'm in a position to settle down.'

But *my* position, thought Bella, won't change until the twins are old enough to fend for themselves. She wouldn't desert them while they still needed her, and the same went for Gran. Whoever married Bella would have to bend his life as she had hers.

It was a lot to ask – and how many men would consider an ordinary girl like Bella Minsky worth it? Indeed, Bella wondered what Ezra saw in her.

Since our not seeing ourselves as others see us is not confined to our shortcomings, Bella was not to know that there was about her a je ne sais quoi that singled her out in a room full of pretty girls, though she had not yet learned to make the most of her appearance and still appeared plain at first glance.

Meanwhile, she kept her eye on Joey who had just unsuccessfully tried to climb the railing bordering the lake, and listened to Ezra's story of how his Viennese relatives had managed to get their daughter out of Austria at the eleventh hour.

'The next day, Hitler marched into the city,' he went on, 'and there's no knowing, now, if and when Gerda's parents will escape from the Nazis.'

'Why couldn't they come with Gerda?'

Ezra shrugged eloquently. 'If Britain would let in all those who want to come, Manchester would have even more Jewish refugees than are here already, and not just Manchester. There has to be some restriction for foreigners in normal circumstances, I suppose, but when people's lives are at stake – !

'You'll be meeting Gerda today,' he told Bella. 'My mother's invited you for tea, and Gerda is staying with us until a suitable home is found for her. She's only sixteen –'

'And your mother hasn't offered to give her a home?'

'My mother,' said Ezra, 'isn't like you. But I know you'll do your best to get on with her.'

Bella did not like the sound of that.

'My mother's a bit of a bossy-breeches,' he added with a grin.

And Bella's first meeting with her was to prove an unmitigated disaster. Mr Black, on the other hand, seemed a man of few words. Doubtless, thought Bella, he had long since stopped trying to get a word in edgeways.

In appearance he was as stringy as his wife was stout. Though Ezra could not be called fat, it was from his mother that he had inherited his round face, and the grey eyes softened by a gentleness absent in Mrs Black.

'You should get that squirrel coat remodelled, dear,' she said to Bella when they were all seated in the over-furnished living-room having tea.

'I like it the way it is,' said Bella, 'it was my mother's.'

'A hand-me-down is what it looks like, dear. That's what I meant. And my son is a professional man.'

Bella managed to smile. 'But it's me who's wearing it, not him.'

Mrs Black pursed her lips. 'And he's found himself a girl with a lot to learn.'

'True,' Bella responded, 'but I know what matters and what doesn't.'

'That depends on how a person looks at things, doesn't it, dear?' said Mrs Black. 'My son has told me all about the burden you've taken on. But meanwhile, he's being seen around with you. Tongues are wagging and some of them belong to his clients and possible clients. My Ezra could have any of the well-dressed young ladies in this town for the asking, not to mention their dowries. Their parents would be only too pleased to get an accountant for a son-in-law.'

'That's a bit of an exaggeration,' Ezra said awkwardly, and Bella glanced at the twins who seemed chastened into silence, as if they knew that the burden referred to was them. Nor were they partaking of the spread on the table.

'Your trouble, Ezra,' his mother answered, 'is you don't know your own value.' She returned her attention to Bella. 'But I'm sure that this young lady does.'

'Mine, or his?' Bella said coolly, though she was finding it difficult to control her feelings.

'What sort of smart alec remark is that?' said Mrs Black. 'Is she taking the mickey out of me, Ezra?'

'If she is, you deserve it, Mother! Now why don't we all get on with our tea?'

'I can't enjoy my tea, I can still smell the mothballs that came into the house with that coat.'

Ezra hastily changed the subject. 'Bella was hoping to meet Gerda. Where is she, Mother?'

'I let her go for a walk.'

Let her? thought Bella. The girl was lucky not to be offered a home by Mrs Black.

'I wouldn't mind having Gerda to live at our house,' Bella voiced her compassion for the young refugee.

'You haven't even set eyes on her!' Mrs Black exclaimed.

'But she needs a family, doesn't she? And we've got two spare rooms if you count the attic. She isn't a little kid who needs looking after, Mrs Black. And she could be a help to me in many ways.'

Ezra surveyed the two women in his life. His mother, briefly dumbstruck. Bella, eyes sparkling, as the impulsive suggestion she had just made set her thoughts racing. He loved them both, but their reaction to each other was even worse than he had anticipated. Another dilemma to add to those he had accumulated by falling for Bella.

Gerda arrived in time to join them at the tea table, her long fair hair awry from the wind and her expression far from happy.

'I called to see the committee lady who is finding for me a family,' she said after being introduced to Bella.

'And how does that look for me!' said Mrs Black indignantly. 'As if you can't wait to get away from here! Say something,' she demanded of her husband. 'Gerda is *your* cousin's child.'

It did not surprise Bella that his sole response was a long sigh. Then Gerda began weeping and Bella went to comfort her.

'I know how you must be feeling, love.'

The girl looked at her and tried to smile. 'How *can* you know?'

'It isn't that long since I lost my parents,' Bella told her, 'but yours aren't lost to you yet, remember. You still have hope. In the meantime, you're welcome to come and live in my home.'

'The committee will want to *see* your home,' said Mrs Black. It sounded like a threat.

Bella's gaze roved the room, taking in the several cut-glass vases, in which no flowers reposed; the silver on the sideboard; the beige leather three-piece suite, and the hideously patterned carpet that nevertheless smacked of money.

'They'll find it a lot different from this,' she replied, 'just a place behind a shop. But as my mother once said, it isn't where you live, it's who you live with that matters.'

Chapter Five

'HOW OLD WAS I,' Bella asked her grandmother, 'when my mam had that stillborn baby girl?'

Gran was shelling peas and paused with a pod in her hands. 'You'd have been about two, love.'

'So I might've had a sister who would now be Gerda's age.'

'And all the attention you're paying that girl, if Sylvie were older she'd be jealous.'

'But Sylvie isn't older, and I didn't have a companion while I was growing up,' Bella answered. 'I'm enjoying having one now.'

'You'd do well to remember, though,' said Gran resuming her task, 'that Gerda *isn't* your sister. Just a nice girl we're doing our duty by. Which is more than can be said for your young man's mother.'

But what had begun for Bella as a duty born of compassion was by now a labour of love. 'I felt drawn to Gerda the minute I met her,' she told Gran.

'Me, too. But you wouldn't catch me cleaning her shoes for her! She may've had a maid to wait on her in Vienna while she sat sketching, like she sometimes does here –'

'Two, as a matter of fact,' Bella cut in.

'But those days are over for her, maybe for ever.'

'Do you think Gerda doesn't know that, Gran, and it includes not having her parents, doesn't it? As for me doing things for her, she's still a schoolgirl, isn't she? I wasn't expected to do much for myself when I had a lot of homework to do.'

Remembrance of her mother at the ironing board returned to Bella. However tired she was, my mam always made sure

I had a clean blouse every day, to wear for school. Why shouldn't Bella do for Gerda what had been done for her? Treat the Viennese girl like one of the family.

Gerda had elected to continue her education and her understanding of English had proved good enough for her to enrol at Broughton High School.

Since she was not entitled to a free place, the fees had presented a problem which Mrs Black had not allowed her husband to surmount. Then Bella's Uncle Saul had come to the rescue – though his intention was far from that when he paid me that surprise visit, Bella recalled.

Saul had arrived at the shop one afternoon to find Bella packing her suitcases with remnants to take to Wigan Market the following day, and had said without preamble,

'It's a wonder your biceps aren't bulging by now, from all that stuff you carry!'

'Shall I roll up my sleeves, so you can see that they're not?'

'But what you're doing to yourself one way and another, Bella – When I heard you'd taken in a refugee girl, I said to your Auntie Dolly, "Has my niece gone out of her mind?" I thought the same when I heard about this market lark –'

'It isn't a lark, Uncle. It's one of the ways I make a living.'

'But you wouldn't have had to, if you'd let your Uncle Reuben and me do our duty.'

Saul watched Bella carefully folding lengths of fabric and placing them in the suitcases. 'Why not fill one case first and then begin on the other?' he said irrelevantly.

'I set out my stall one caseful at a time,' Bella told him, 'so I need the right assortment in each of them.'

Saul surveyed the shop, noting that Bella was making better use of the limited space than Edith had. Than her father had, come to that.

Saul wouldn't have given much for his late brother-in-law's chances of turning a tuppence-ha'penny suburban shop into a thriving business. Len didn't have the drive. Bella, though, was something else. Could be she takes after me!

Saul had once told Len that the wall beside the door was

41

wasted. Bella, he noted, hadn't needed telling. A boardful of those fancy flowers her grandmother made was now visible through the doorway – which Bella kept open, though her parents had not. And somehow she had managed to acquire a showcase counter, instead of that lump of wood that had made the place look dowdy and served only one purpose.

Saul had to admire her and said warmly, 'You get top marks for trying, Bella.'

'Have you come to check up on me, Uncle?'

'Well, someone has to, though I wouldn't have put it that way, love. And it doesn't make me happy to see you wearing yourself out. It still isn't too late to accept your uncles' offer.'

'Thanks. But if I didn't accept it at the time, I'm not likely to now.'

'I'd have thought you'd be *more* likely to now. When you said no to us, you didn't know what you were taking on. That's why I left it so long to talk sense to you again, Bella, though I felt like jumping into my car and driving here when I heard you'd taken that girl into your home –'

Bella sat on the lid of a bulging suitcase and forced the clasps into place. 'If I'd been born in Germany, or Austria, it would've been me who was homeless – or worse.'

Rumours about Nazi concentration camps were by now sending shudders through the British Jewish community.

'That's how we all feel,' said Saul. 'How could we not? And don't think I haven't given my whack to the refugee fund.'

Bella began packing the other suitcase, carefully selecting lengths from the skip in which she kept her stock. 'I've never thought you weren't a generous man, Uncle.'

'But *you* can't afford to be generous, can you?' he replied. 'It's all you can do to support yourself and the twins. Your gran, as well. I shouldn't think her pension goes too far –'

'Gran more than earns her keep,' Bella said hotly, 'so please don't imagine that she's sponging on me! That's what you thought about her for years, no doubt.'

'Not exactly. When your dad was alive, it was his duty to support his mother. But it wasn't my sister's duty,' Saul

42

declared, 'after she was widowed and still had kids to bring up. Edith was too soft for her own good and in some ways you're just like her, Bella.

'You could have been at Oxford now,' Saul went on, 'instead of doing what you're doing. But you couldn't bear the thought of your gran in an old folks' home – where she'd soon have settled down. Or of your little brother and sister missing each other, which they'd have got over in no time. Kids are hardier than you think.'

Since the twins now rarely mentioned their dead mother, and when they did it was without tears, Bella had already come to realize what her uncle was trying to tell her. But the reason she had made the decision she had went a lot deeper than that.

'Believe it or not, Uncle,' she replied, 'I'm getting a lot of satisfaction out of what I'm doing.'

'Aggravation and anxiety, too!'

'Nobody goes free of that,' she said, with a smile. 'All I've done is swap one set of worries for another. I used to get into a cold sweat in case I didn't pass my exams, and still would be doing if I'd gone to Oxford.'

'There was never any danger of you failing,' said Saul, 'but the same can't be said of the position you've put yourself in. If there's anything I can do –'

Bella almost said, No, thanks. But Uncle Saul wasn't short and his offer was sincere. 'You can lend me the money to buy a button-covering machine.'

'Consider it done.'

'And if you'd like to pay Gerda's school fees –'

'That, too, but don't tell your Auntie Dolly. She thinks education is a waste of time for girls.' Saul pinched Bella's cheek affectionately. 'Except when they're brilliant, like you.'

And look how I've ended up, Bella thought. 'I'll pay you back for the button-covering machine,' she said.

'Shouldn't you consult your accountant before you go borrowing?' Saul teased her. 'How's the romance going, by the way?'

By the way? It was one of the things her uncle had come to find out and when he got back to Leeds he would ring up Uncle Reuben in Liverpool and give him a full report! Bella's not letting them bring up the twins hadn't stopped them from keeping an eye on their dead sister's family.

'Did you and Uncle Reuben have a meeting to decide on your tactics?' she asked Saul drily. 'When I told him on the phone about Gerda coming to live with us?'

'We've had meetings about lots of things, since your mam died,' he revealed, 'and I can set your mind at rest about one thing, Bella. Your uncles will foot the bill for your wedding reception when the time comes.'

The only reply Bella could muster had been a stiff smile, she was recalling when Gerda's arrival from school returned her to the present. A present that still held no prospect of her uncles' expectations. Though Ezra had in the interim acquired a few more clients to swell his income, Bella's family responsibilities remained an insurmountable handicap to her becoming his wife.

Her uncles were probably hoping that love would eventually win the day and Bella let them take the twins off her hands, so she could live her own life. Maybe Ezra shared that hope, but it was unlikely to be put to the test.

Romantic love was the missing ingredient in Bella's courtship. Try as she would, she could not see Ezra in that light, nor did the kissing and cuddling to which they had by now progressed arouse in her any response. Instead, Bella had come to think that something was wrong with her, her pal Connie having revealed that her latest boyfriend had only to gaze into her eyes to render her weak with passion. Connie, though, had always been what was known as 'a devil with the lads', and had the looks to take her pick.

As Gerda has, Bella thought, watching the Viennese girl curl up in an armchair, her movements as sinuous as a cat's, one graceful hand toying with her hair.

Bella couldn't imagine Gerda, when her time came, not being set alight by a man's kisses, or by the touch of his hand on her breasts. If Broughton High weren't just a girls' school, we might be having trouble with Gerda already!

Almost a year had passed since Bella was moved by Gerda's plight to offer her a home. Since then, the girl had filled out to become the buxom young beauty she now was. The kind whom even another female could tell at a glance was made for love. Sensual from head to toe.

'How was school today?' Bella asked her.

'I am still not enjoying the algebra.'

'I don't enjoy shelling peas,' said Gran, who had just completed the task, 'but it has to be done.'

'Shelling peas is not a waste of time,' Gerda countered, 'but the schoolwork I am now doing –'

'Is *never* a waste of time,' Bella cut in.

'Even so, Bella, I am wishing that I had chosen instead a secretarial course.' Gerda's green eyes shadowed with distress. 'If it is not to be that I am one day reunited with my parents and return to Vienna, I should like to be of use to you in your business.'

'That's a kind thought, Gerda.'

'It was my hope to work with my father, though he already had three secretaries.'

Bella said wryly, 'What makes you think I'm ever going to need even one?'

It was Gran, now putting the peas on the cooker to boil, who replied. 'Nobody could live with you, Bella, without knowing you've the makings of a millionaire!'

'Not in the bank though,' Bella said with a laugh.

'Nor had Mr Marks, when he started his penny bazaar that ended up as Marks and Spencer,' said Gran. 'Or was it Mr Spencer?'

'I'm not too well up on that sort of history, Gran.'

'And you've a handicap they didn't have. You're a woman.'

One incapable of passion, thought Bella.

Chapter Six

BY THE SUMMER OF 1939, the 'peace in our time' triumphantly predicted by Mr Chamberlain on his return from Munich had given way to preparations for war.

So much for appeasement! Bella had thought when Hitler occupied Czechoslovakia. Only a fool would now believe that the dictator's aspirations would end there.

Her grandmother, mindful of shortages in the last war, began hoarding sugar, and the fishmonger, too old for military service, volunteered to be an air raid warden and was issued with a steel helmet. But not until gas masks were issued to civilians did the full import of what might lie ahead cause Bella to eye the twins anxiously.

'When we get home, can I put my gas mask on?' Joey asked excitedly, as the family took a short cut through Manley Park, the children skipping along with their newly acquired symbols of modern warfare packed in cardboard boxes and strung across their chests, as Gerda's was.

They had gone together to collect them and Bella was carrying her own and Gran's, the old lady's expression matching Bella's feelings.

'We can pretend there's an air raid, when we get home, can't we,' Joey prattled on.

'And have our evening cup of Ovaltine down in the cellar,' said Sylvie.

'War isn't a game,' Bella informed them, wishing she could add, but don't worry, there isn't going to be one. Plans were already in motion for evacuating children from the cities. How will Sylvie and Joey manage without me? But at least they'll have each other, which they wouldn't have if I'd let my aunts and uncles bring them up. And I'll visit them as often as possible, Bella's thoughts raced ahead.

The following day, Joey fell ill. When Sylvie went to prod him from his bed, so he would not be late for school, he was unable to raise his head from the pillow.

Once he would instinctively have asked for his mother, but his elder sister had long since become the mother-figure in his life. 'I want Bella,' he said.

'It's her market day, isn't it?' Sylvie responded. 'Would you like her to miss the train? What's the matter with you?'

'My head's hurting and I've got a stiff neck.'

'I'll go and ask Gran if you can have half an Aspro.'

Bella was putting on her coat to leave when Sylvie clattered downstairs, and returned that evening to find her grandmother applying cold compresses to Joey's forehead, the child on her lap while Gerda changed the sweat-soaked sheets.

Bella helped Gerda with the bed. Joey could barely keep his eyes open and had begun shivering.

'Stay with me, Bella,' he whimpered when she had tucked him up.

'I wouldn't dream of leaving you, love. But I think we'll get the doctor to take a look at you. Gerda can go and phone him.'

'He won't be able to come till after his evening surgery,' said Gran, 'and I wish I'd sent for him this morning, when Sylvie came to tell me Joey wasn't feeling well.'

'I'm the one she should have told.'

So rebuking was Bella's tone, her little sister was momentarily tongue-tied.

'It's me who takes care of you and Joey, isn't it?' Bella went on.

'But I didn't think –'

'Never mind what you didn't think!'

Sylvie cast an agonized glance at her twin, as though she were responsible for his worsened condition, and ran from the room.

47

'Now look what you've done, Bella,' said Gran. 'One thing I never did when your dad was a child was take my feelings out on him!'

With that, the old lady too made her exit, leaving Bella alone with a child who had never seemed more dear to her. Whatever Joey was sickening for, Sylvie was sure to get it, too. But she was more robust than he was. When they both caught measles, Sylvie was downstairs playing with her toys while Joey was still lying in bed with the curtains drawn.

Bella recalled her fear when she learned that measles could affect a child's eyesight. A fear that had proved unfounded and she mustn't let her imagination carry her away now.

Her imagination, however, could not have encompassed the shattering diagnosis. Her little brother had infantile paralysis.

Chapter Seven

WHILE JOEY LAY critically ill in hospital, Bella prayed every night for his recovery. Gran, who attended services on Sabbath mornings, prayed for the full recovery he was unlikely to make.

Why did you do this to Bella? the old lady would silently ask God in the echoing ambience of Higher Broughton Synagogue, where Joey would one day be Barmitzvah.

Would he walk to the Holy Ark whole and healthy, his head held high? Or drag himself along, his legs encased in the heavy calipers that were the lot of most children stricken by the dreaded disease for which there was no immunization, or cure. Be an object of pity for the rest of his life – and how would Bella live with that?

Though Joey was the one afflicted, it seemed to Gran that God had used him as an instrument to increase Bella's load, and she would sit with her gaze fixed unseeingly on the array of millinery atop the heads of the ladies on the opposite side of the gallery, her lips intoning the Hebrew words she knew by heart, her mind questioning God's will.

Was He testing Bella's strength? If so, Gran assured Him that this latest test hadn't been necessary, that her elder granddaughter would survive it as she had those preceding it, 'though she didn't seem to have much patience with her little sister nowadays.

Bella would have found her grandmother's private Sabbath monologues grimly amusing, though cyncism was not yet born in her. She was still the pragmatic girl she had always been, coping with her increasingly complicated lot and keeping her deepest feelings to herself.

When the incubation period ended without Sylvie's having contracted the disease, she was able to sigh with relief. But Joey continued to hover between life and death.

This too Bella kept to herself, mindful of her grandmother's heart condition, remaining adamant that she alone visit Joey.

It was a period in the Minsky household that none would forget, when Gran busied herself in the kitchen, Sylvie stayed out of Bella's way, Bella went through the motions of her everyday routine, and the tension of approaching war heightened while the sun went on shining in the summer sky.

It was also a time when Gerda proved that her wish to be of use to Bella was not just empty words, declining the holiday offered her by a schoolfriend whose parents had rented a house in St Anne's-on-the-Sea.

'How could I sunbathe and swim, while you are working so hard?' she said to Bella. 'I will go to the market with the remnants, if you will let me. Then you won't have to worry about perhaps getting home too late to visit Joey, as you did when the train broke down.'

'But I don't see you lugging suitcases,' Bella replied with a smile.

'Why would I lug them? I'll find a man to lift them for me. How else did I manage when I travelled alone from Vienna?'

Gerda instinctively made use of her femininity and would only have to eye a suitcase and look helpless for every male in the vicinity to leap to her aid, Bella thought. I, though, wouldn't know *how* to look helpless. Maybe it's time I learned!

Their conversation was cut short by Sylvie's entrance, on her face a timid expression that Bella failed to notice.

'I thought you were helping Gran make a new frock for your doll,' Bella said to her.

'Belinda is wearing the frock – look,' the child answered, taking the doll for Bella's inspection. 'We even made her a lace flower. Doesn't she look nice?'

'But Belinda would look even more nice if we brushed her hair,' said Gerda, 'and if you like, we can plait it. Like yours, Sylvie.'

Sylvie eyed Bella hesitantly. 'Could I please have some red ribbon, to make bows for Belinda's plaits?'

'Help yourself.'

It was Sunday morning, and Bella was tidying the shop after the Saturday rush when working girls spent some of their wages on haberdashery with which to enliven the dance frocks they would wear that evening. And nowadays, Bella had noticed, there was about them a careless abandon, as if they must make the most of the time left before all the boys went to war.

Since the careless abandon included their lashing out money, it was good for trade and Gran's lace flowers were, like fancy buckles and buttons, much in demand. When the old lady was not busy with domestic tasks, she was rarely without a needle and thread in her fingers, a thought that prompted Bella to say to her little sister,

'Don't ask Gran to make any more frocks for your doll. She has too much to do, and thanks to you, our dinner will be late and I'll have a rush to get to the hospital by visiting time.'

'Our dinner was in the oven before Gran started cutting out Belinda's frock,' the child answered, 'and –'

'Please don't argue with me, Sylvie! Now run along and let me get on.'

'Can't I help you tidy up, like I used to?'

'Not today.'

Gerda took Sylvie's hand and led her away from the counter. 'You and I shall go and plait Belinda's hair now, Sylvie, and then we'll lay the table for dinner.'

Bella then got a telephone call from her Uncle Saul.

'How's it going, love?'

'I'm getting by.'

'When didn't you? Would it help to get Sylvie off your hands for a couple of weeks? Our kids, as you know, always go to the Habonim summer camp. It's in Bedfordshire this year, and I'd be happy to treat Sylvie to a holiday if you'd like her to go with them. What do you say?'

Bella said yes without thinking twice. With Sylvie safely out of the way for a while, she would not have to worry about her as well as about Joey. At first, Sylvie had pestered her with questions about him. Now, though, she just gazes at me with eyes like saucers when I get back from the hospital. And the country air would improve Sylvie's appetite and return the glow to her cheeks.

When told at the dinner table of the treat in store for her, Sylvie displayed the opposite of enthusiasm.

'I won't know anyone at the camp,' she began.

'You'll be with your cousins, won't you?' said Bella, one eye on the clock. On Sundays, trams didn't trundle to town one after another, as they did on weekdays.

'I don't know them, either. I can't even remember when I last saw them.'

'It was when we all went to Leeds for your Auntie Dolly's nephew's wedding,' said Gran. 'Your cousins were brides-maids. They wore lovely taffeta frocks.'

'I don't remember,' said Sylvie.

Gran looked at Bella. 'Well, she was very little, wasn't she?'

Bella put down her knife and fork. 'Would you mind not aiding and abetting her?'

'Bella's sending me to camp because she doesn't love me,' Sylvie said tremulously.

'That isn't true,' Gerda replied when Bella remained silent.

'I'm not *going* to camp!' said Sylvie.

'Oh yes you are,' Bella told her.

Though Bella could not have known it, the exchange had set the pattern for her future relationship with her sister.

Chapter Eight

'ON THE DAY Joey was discharged from hospital, war was declared.

Gran was making tea for the ambulancemen who had transported her grandson, when Mr Chamberlain imparted his grave news to the nation, stilling her hand on the kettle as it did the tongues of his listeners.

'If the Duke of Windsor was listening, wherever he is now, I wonder how he feels,' said one of the ambulancemen when the broadcast was over.

His burly companion expressed the sentiments of many British citizens. 'How he feels is his own lookout! He shouldn't've put that Mrs Simpson before his country.'

The ambulanceman picked up his cap from the kitchen dresser and strode to the door. 'Thanks for offering us the tea, but we'd best be getting back. No time for loitering now there's a war on.'

'Will bombs be dropped on us today, Bella?' Joey asked from the armchair in which one of the men had gently deposited him, still wrapped in the blanket Bella had taken with her to the hospital.

'I shouldn't think so, love,' she said, forcing herself to sound cheerful.

'Then why were the ambulancemen in such a hurry?'

'It's how knowing we're now at war makes people feel, Joey. Now it's actually happened, they want to get on with winning.'

'And,' said Gerda intensely, 'if the British will accept an

53

Austrian in their military services, I shall volunteer to fight the Nazis.'

Bella, who felt like volunteering herself, said nothing. While other girls would leave home and put on uniform, she had no option but to remain where circumstances had anchored her.

The more so now, she thought surveying Joey with an aching heart. 'Let's drink that pot of tea you made for the men, Gran,' she said brusquely, 'we mustn't waste it now there's a war on.'

Then Sylvie, unduly silent, could no longer contain her rapture at having her twin back and went to hug and kiss him.

'Be careful you don't hurt him!' Bella cautioned her.

'I don't want people to be careful with me,' the boy said, 'I want them to treat me how they used to.'

It was not just Bella, but Gran and Gerda too who found it necessary to avert their eyes. Sooner or later, Joey would have to accept that things would never again be as they were for him.

In the weeks that followed, 'there's a war on' became Britain's most well-used phrase, though another, 'the phony war', would supersede it when time slipped by with no sign of the true meaning of war.

For Bella it was still business as usual. Meanwhile, Gerda found herself at present unacceptable to the Women's Services, and Ezra for active service due to his poor eyesight.

'They've offered me a commission in the Army Pay Corps, though,' he told Bella, 'where qualified accountants are needed. Shall you miss me?'

How could she not? Though going to the pictures and to dances had not crossed her mind while Joey lay ill, Ezra hadn't gone out enjoying himself without her, and was often waiting for her outside the hospital in the evenings, to escort her home.

He had sat with her in the kitchen night after night, when

Gran and Gerda had gone to bed, sensing that Bella stayed up late because sleep eluded her, silently holding her hand because he sensed too that she didn't want to talk.

Ezra was a man in a million, the sort who was there when you needed him and would never let you down. 'Of course I'll miss you,' Bella said.

'You won't have to. I was just testing you! I'm going to be stationed in Manchester. So we can go on doing our courting, can't we?' he added with a smile.

Was Ezra never going to lift his head from the sand?

Chapter Nine

WHEN MANCHESTER AND SALFORD were blitzed at the
end of 1940, changing the skyline overnight, Bella sat in the
cellar with Gran and the twins reconsidering her decision not
to allow Sylvie to be evacuated without Joey.

Joey's return to school had been greeted with sympathy
and helpfulness from his teachers and his classmates. Not all
parents had seen fit to send their children away to be cared
for by strangers, and many who had initially done so had
fetched them home when the 'phony war' stretched on.

But now everyone will want their kids to be where it's safe,
thought Bella when the cellar, despite her having had it
reinforced, reverberated from the bombing and a jar of her
grandmother's home-pickled cucumbers fell off a shelf.

'Don't you dare!' she said when Joey raised himself from
her side to deal with the damage. 'All you need is to cut
yourself on the broken glass –'

'I was going to get the broom and sweep it up – I forgot I
haven't got my irons on.' He looked down at his frail legs.
Bella had carried him to the cellar when the air raid siren
sounded.

'I wouldn't have let you if you *did* have them on, you could
lose your balance and tumble –'

'And I hope I get blown up tonight!' he said stridently. 'I
wish I were dead!'

Bella took him on her lap to comfort him, aware of Sylvie
silently cuddling her doll, and of Gran's distressed expression.

When hours later the all clear sounded and she returned
Joey to his bed, remaining with him until he fell asleep, she

could not bear to look at the cricket bat and ball he had once played with. But removing them from his room would be like telling him he would never again be like other boys.

Bella had let herself hope that eventually her little brother would adjust to his disability. She hadn't known he was eaten up by the misery he had unleashed in the cellar. Nor did she now know how to deal with it. Why hadn't she seen his no longer doing well at school for what it was? Not a temporary apathy, but a symptom of something much worse. He no longer cared.

Bella glanced at the ugly calipers propped beside the bed and had to stop herself from kicking them. She turned to tiptoe from the room, saw Sylvie standing in the doorway and hustled her to the landing.

'Why aren't you in bed?'

'I'm not sleepy and it will soon be time to get up. Gran's in the kitchen drinking tea with Mr Lewis. He's still got his air raid warden helmet on and he came to tell us there's no damage round here. But there's a lot in town –'

'I can see that from the flames,' said Bella glancing through the landing window at a distant sky that seemed livid with red weals.

'Mr Lewis thinks the fish market's been bombed and he's worried about where he'll get fish for his shop,' Sylvie prattled on, 'and he's heard that the garment district isn't there any more. Where was the garment district, Bella?'

'I'm too exhausted to answer your questions, Sylvie. Go to bed before I chase you there!'

'How can you, if you're too exhausted? And you got a shock when Joey said he wished he were dead, didn't you, Bella? But he's said it to me lots of times. And when I was at that camp, I wished you were dead for sending me away!'

Before Bella had time to utter, Sylvie was gone and her bedroom door shut. How could a child who looked the picture of innocence, the more so in her pretty pink dressing gown, have said something so hurtful to the big sister who had sacrificed so much for her?

Melodramatic though Sylvie's parting shot was, to Bella it was as though she and her good intentions had been pierced by an arrow.

All right, so she'd lied when she told Uncle Saul it *wasn't* a sacrifice. Lied to herself as well as to him. But get that word out of your mind, Bella. It isn't one that kids understand. Not until the twins grew up would they realize how raising them had affected Bella's life. Meanwhile, though, there were times like now, when Bella, still only twenty, felt ill-equipped for all she had undertaken. Times when she felt sorry for herself. But in my position, who wouldn't?

Bella left Gran to swap stories with Mr Lewis about the war they had thought the war to end all wars, which was doubtless what they were now doing, and went to shut herself away in her bedroom with her momentary self-pity.

The older generation still referred to that war as the Great War, but what would this one eventually be called? There must have been loss of life tonight, as there was each time London was blitzed. People unable to reach the air raid shelters in time. It was small wonder that families had begun making a second home on Tube station platforms.

Bella lay on her bed unable to sleep. Had Gerda reached a shelter in time? She had gone to a party and that had to be why Gran was sitting chinwagging with the fishmonger, though she must be dead beat. The old lady wouldn't rest until she knew Gerda was safe.

Despite Gran's warning to Bella not to grow too attached to the Viennese girl, she too had succumbed to the warmth that Gerda exuded. Though there were times when Gerda brooded about her parents, whose fate she would not now know until after the war, she was by nature comparable with a ray of sunshine, and sorely missed by the family after she had volunteered for the Land Army.

The Minskys' home was now a quieter place, no longer resounding with Gerda's laughter, or with her trilling voice drifting downstairs as she sang in the bath. Bella missed, too, the sisterly chats they had enjoyed while washing the supper dishes. And to Sylvie, Gerda was like a favourite aunt whom she now saw but rarely, the kind with patience to play games with kids, whom they run to when the dragon in their life ticks them off – and for Sylvie, the dragon is me! Bella thought, allowing her sense of humour to leaven her feelings in that respect. It was better to smile than to weep.

Bella found herself unable to apply that philosophy when later that day her grandmother did some plain speaking.

Bella arose after a couple of hours of unrefreshing sleep and tiptoed downstairs so as not to awaken the twins. Gran was busy in the kitchen.

'Is Gerda home yet?' Bella asked.

'No, but she rang up to tell us she's all right and to make sure that we are. Everyone at the party wanted to make calls, she said, so she went out to find a telephone kiosk and then had to stand in a long queue.'

'I didn't hear our phone ring.'

'With all you've got on your plate, Bella, I'm surprised you ever manage to sleep.'

'Have you been to bed, Gran?'

'Mr Lewis was still here talking my head off when Gerda rang up. After he left, I just sat in the rocking-chair thinking about Joey. I couldn't rest till I'd spoken to you about him. Pour yourself some tea, Bella. War or no war, I took the liberty of making myself a fresh pot.'

Bella did so and dropped a saccharine tablet into her cup. 'What Joey said in the cellar upset me, too,' she said with a wan smile, 'but we mustn't take it seriously.'

'We have to take seriously, though, how that little lad feels,' Gran replied, sitting down at the scrub-top table to begin peeling potatoes, 'and I'm sorry to have to say that you're the cause of it, Bella. Who but me is going to tell you?'

While Bella tried to recover from what felt like another arrow piercing her, her grandmother went on busying her hands as though it might help her say what she must.

'I know you're doing it out of love, Bella –'

'Doing what!'

'Turning that child into a namby-pamby. If he'd let you, you'd wipe his nose and his bottom for him. It isn't surprising that he thinks himself useless. Not just useless, *worthless*. The best thing for Joey, though he wouldn't take kindly to it and nor would you, is for him to live for a bit away from you, Bella. With folk who aren't heartbroken by what's happened to him. Who'd deal with him more – I can't think of the right word –'

Bella supplied it. 'Objectively? Only I don't agree with you, Gran. Joey has to be where he's loved.'

'Not if it's the sort of love that's damaging him,' Gran declared, 'and I don't think you're capable, Bella, of treating him differently from how you do.'

Was she? Could Bella let her little brother take the risks he was always wanting to take? Like getting in and out of the bath without help. Crossing the main road by himself, which she had made him promise never to do. If he fell and broke his legs, what then? And supposing that happened in the path of a car, or a lorry? He would end up crushed to death, like his mother.

Gran saw Bella shudder and divined her thoughts. 'You can't protect Joey for ever, Bella, and if you go on doing it –'

'Let me alone, will you, Gran!'

'But when are you going to come to your senses?'

It took Bella several days to do so, during which her grandmother said no more on the subject and Joey continued to display the anger evoked by his lot.

Gran's right, Bella thought. I was too emotionally involved to see the wood for the trees and I still *am* too involved to behave differently. A double purpose would be served if Joey were included in Bella's decision to evacuate Sylvie to a safer place.

But finding a family prepared to take a child with Joey's special needs would not be easy.

Chapter Ten

A SOLUTION to Bella's problem was found by Gerda.

'I mentioned to Jim and Martha that you want to evacuate the twins,' she said on the phone from Derbyshire, where she was stationed in the Land Army, 'and they'd be pleased to have them.'

'Haven't your farmer and his wife already got a houseful of evacuees?' Bella responded.

'Martha said she'll find room for two more. She is that sort of person.'

'But Joey needs special attention.'

'I thought you had begun to think positively,' Gerda replied. 'Was I mistaken?'

'Look – ! I've had a lecture from Gran and I don't require another from you!' Bella flashed. 'I might have babied Joey, but even if I hadn't he still wouldn't be like other children, would he?'

Gerda said coolly, 'I see no reason why a boy with calipers on his legs can't sit on a stool and milk a cow.'

Bella blotted out a picture of her little brother being kicked by the animal. 'Do the evacuees help on the farm?'

'Sure. After they've done their homework.'

'Where do they go to school?'

'There's a school in the village.'

'And I shouldn't think that any of its pupils end up at Oxford, or Cambridge,' said Bella. 'I'd be saying goodbye to that possibility for Joey, if I sent him to the farm.'

As for Sylvie, thought Bella, her talents seem to lie in other directions! That kid is a budding actress if ever I've met one. Well, she certainly knows how to make a scene!

'You can't think that far ahead, Bella,' said Gerda, 'there's a war on.'

And while it lasted, as Gerda had implied, your high hopes for the future must be set aside. 'Tell Martha and Jim I'm grateful for their offer and I'll accept it,' Bella said decisively. 'Have they any children of their own?'

'Unfortunately, no. They weren't young when they married. Martha used to be the village schoolmistress and Jim told me that it took him years to persuade her to swap that for being a farmer's wife. Love won in the end, though!' Gerda said with a laugh. 'Is it going to with you and Ezra?'

For love to win, I'd have to be in love with him, thought Bella. 'Well, I'm unlikely to rush into one of those wartime marriages,' she said.

'Me neither,' said Gerda, 'I'm having too good a time.'

If only that were Bella's reason. But she would have more *free* time when the twins were evacuated to the country. And what she would do with it . . . ?

The outcry when the twins learned of Bella's decision ended abruptly when she told them they were to live on the farm where Gerda worked.

'Why didn't you tell them that right away?' asked Gran.

'I didn't plan a strategy, Gran!'

Bella had got no further than mentioning a farm when Joey interrupted her with, 'What will I do if I'm chased by a bull?' And Sylvie had declared dramatically that she was not going.

'I was hoping they'd be brave,' Bella went on to Gran, aware of two pairs of dark eyes riveted to her, 'like their friends who've been evacuated had to be before they settled down and enjoyed being at the seaside, or in the country. But you two will have someone of your own there, won't you?' she added to the children with a smile.

'Gerda will tell us stories,' Joey said to Sylvie.

'And she'll kiss us good night,' said Sylvie, 'like she does when she comes home on leave.'

'I'm looking forward to it,' Joey decided, 'it'll be like a holiday.'

'Not quite,' Bella put in. 'You'll have to go to school and Gerda has to work hard on the farm. Now, what would you like for your tea?'

'They won't get asked that by the farmer's wife,' said Gran, 'and she'll wonder what sort of home they've come from, if they turn up their noses at what she puts before them.'

'What shall we do if it's bacon, or ham?' Sylvie asked.

'We'll tell her that Jews aren't allowed to eat it,' said Joey, 'and that we can't have meat that isn't kosher.'

'Gerda will have told her that,' said Bella.

'But if there's a river nearby, I can go fishing and fetch home our dinner,' said Joey, 'and Gerda can have some, too.'

Bella stopped herself from saying, 'Don't you dare! If you fell in the river, your calipers would weigh you down and you'd go under.' There was a glint in her little brother's eyes that hadn't been there since he was taken ill, and she must be thankful for that.

Chapter Eleven

THE DEPARTURE of the twins had initially left Bella with an aching void in her life. Only then had she realized the depth of her maternal feeling for them, that her being their surrogate mother worked two ways – she was missing them as much as they said on the phone that they missed her.

Bella was moved, too, to learn from Gerda that when Sylvie cut her finger with a breadknife, she had stared at the blood and said, 'I want Bella.' That it wasn't just Joey who instinctively turned to her.

But what was that farmer's wife doing, letting kids use a sharp knife? Bella's impression of Martha Dawson, whom she had met but once, was of a vague, grey-haired woman with a smile for everyone.

The farmhouse had looked spotlessly clean, but none too tidy. In the flagstoned kitchen, the young evacuees were helping themselves to bread and jam when Bella arrived with the twins, and Martha had told Joey and Sylvie to do the same. After which Bella had barely seen them.

Martha had taken her to see first where the boys slept, and then the girls' accommodation, two spacious rooms in what looked like a converted barn, with a bathroom that had seemed to Bella like a refrigerator on that bleak, February day.

She had stemmed her misgivings and had agreed with Martha that it was wisest not to visit the twins until they had settled down. When Bella said goodbye to them, they were helping the other children feed the pigs. An incongruous task for two Jewish kids! Bella's sense of humour had again come to her rescue.

When some weeks later she made her first visit, it was as though she were with two different children from those she had known, each of them engrossed in their own pursuits, and she, though they greeted her warmly, of no special importance.

Joey was scaling the trout he had caught in the River Trent, in readiness for the meal that Bella would share with him and Sylvie.

'Jim taught me how to fly-fish,' he said. 'And also how to play chess.'

'Which my wife taught *me*,' said the stocky farmer, 'and it used to be Martha who always check-mated me. Now, it's sometimes your brother, Miss Minsky. I haven't the sort of mind for chess, Martha says. But since Joey got interested in it – well, he can't be bothered playing snakes-and-ladders, or ludo, with the other kids!' Jim added with a chuckle.

'Does that make him unpopular with them?'

'Why should it?' Jim replied. 'Everyone has their own interests, don't they? And the things they're good at, that other folk aren't. In that way, kids are no different from grown-ups. Take your sister, for instance –'

Bella turned to look at Sylvie, who was bottle-feeding a lamb, beside the hearth.

'As you see,' Jim went on after pausing to relight his pipe, 'that little creature on Sylvie's lap is what you might call the black sheep of the family! The other little girls only have patience to feed the white lambs.'

'He didn't want to take his milk, at first,' said Sylvie, 'I think he was unhappy, but he's taking it from *me*.'

Perhaps, thought Bella drily, the lamb sensed in Sylvie the potential black sheep she sometimes seems! Bella's little sister would never be the kind to toe the line.

After lunch, for which Gerda and another Land Army girl joined the large gathering at the kitchen table, Bella found herself alone with Martha.

'Sorry I couldn't chat with you this morning,' the farmer's wife said, 'there was a lot to do in the dairy, after I'd got the dinner in the oven.'

'I don't know how you cope with it all,' said Bella.

'But somehow I do! It's only on a Sunday, though, I put a big spread on the table, Yorkshire pud and all that, and a fruit pie. The rest of the week it's just one course, but plenty of it. The kids don't starve.'

'They look brimming with health,' said Bella.

'And you should've seen some of them when they first came here,' Martha replied, 'neglected wasn't the word for it, poor little loves.'

This is a woman who should have had children of her own, thought Bella. 'All the same, I shouldn't like to have to cook for that lot,' she said.

'But as you saw, it's the kids who do the washing up. There're plenty of willing hands around the house, as well as on the farm – or Jim wouldn't have taken time off this morning to keep you company.'

Martha paused to hang up the tea towels the children had 'left lying around. 'It was Gerda who persuaded him to.'

'To keep me company?'

'No, to have an hour or two off and let her oil the tractor.'

'I can't imagine Gerda oiling a tractor,' Bella said with a smile.

'I couldn't imagine her doing any of what she does, when I first laid eyes on her,' said Martha, 'nor the other Land Army girl, Doris, come to that. To look at them, with their lipstick and powder – and Doris's fancy hairstyle – well, what use were those two going to be on a farm? Jim and I thought. It goes to show, doesn't it, that you can never tell by looking at someone what they're really like.'

Martha laughed and went to put another log on the fire. 'I got the impression, that day, that they weren't too confident themselves! Nobody knows what they're capable of until they try their hand at it.'

Bella's own experience was ample confirmation of that. 'Are Joey and Sylvie giving you any trouble?' she took the opportunity to ask.

'Not that I've noticed,' Martha replied, with one of her

vague smiles. 'My way with children is to let them get on with it and learn from their mistakes.'

But she isn't as vague as she sometimes seems, Bella thought. A lot more astute than I gave her credit for. What she's telling me is that she knows where I went wrong with Joey.

'The schoolmistress is very pleased with the twins,' Martha then revealed, 'and I'm enjoying giving Joey some science lessons. It's what he's mainly interested in, though he's just a little lad of nine.'

Bella felt a gladdening in her heart.

Chapter Twelve

THOUGH BELLA had been required to register along with other girls of her generation, her domestic responsibilities, including her grandmother, had exempted her from wartime service.

With the twins off her hands, she had volunteered to work in her free time at a Forces Canteen in the city centre, as her friend Connie did – though Bella suspected that Connie's reason for doing so was different from her own.

What could be a better hunting ground for a girl like Connie? Bella thought with amusement on a summer evening in 1942, while she and her friend poured tea and coffee at the canteen counter, Connie, as always, casting her predatory eye on the boys in khaki and blue.

'There are more ATS girls and WAAFs than usual here tonight,' Connie remarked later, returning from clearing tables, 'but not enough to go round. That corporal over there – don't let him see you look at him, Bella – asked could he take me home.'

'Shall you let him?'

'Well, he isn't bad looking, is he? But I said I'd let him know. Someone I really fancy might drop in just before we close.'

'And meanwhile, that poor chap will sit hoping all evening!' said Bella, caustically. 'You're terrible, Connie –'

'There's a war on, Bella.'

'You were terrible before there was a war on.'

'Or my wings might have been clipped while I was still in my teens. Like my cousin Nettie, tied down with a kid while her husband's having the time of his life in the Forces.'

'How do you know he is?'

'Aren't they all? The airman who took me home last time I was on duty at the canteen turned out to be a married man, and I didn't find out because he was honest with me. A slip of the tongue was how I found out.'

'Let's tidy the counter,' said Bella, 'before the next rush.'

While they did so, Connie said contemplatively, 'It's different for you.'

'What is?'

'You're courting. I'm not. I've still time to pick and choose. Did I tell you about the new Irish doctor who's come to work at our hospital?'

Connie was a medical secretary at Manchester Royal Infirmary, an exempt occupation that had spared her the factory work for which her sister had been recruited.

'No, but you told me about the Welsh one,' Bella answered drily.

'Unfortunately, the Irish one is too old for me, as well,' said Connie, 'but if you saw him, Bella, you'd fall at his feet.'

'That sort of thing I leave to you!'

'When I first started work at the Infirmary,' Connie said with a laugh, 'my mother thought her dream of getting a doctor son-in-law would come true! Now, she keeps telling me I've left it too late. All the young ones get drafted into the Medical Corps the minute they're qualified.'

She added regretfully, 'My job isn't as much fun as it used to be –' then glanced towards the canteen door and patted her auburn hair. 'Look what's just walked in, Bella !'

An airman whom even Bella had to admit was strikingly handsome had paused after entering, to take off his cap and smooth his hair.

'Just my luck,' said Connie, 'he's probably got a date with a WAAF.'

A moment later, he was at the counter bathing them with a smile that made him look even more like Connie's hero, Clark Gable.

'Could I trouble you girls for some change? I have to call someone up and I'm out of pennies.'

'You're Canadian, aren't you?' said Connie while changing the sixpence he handed her.

'How did you guess!'

'Well, for one thing you're wearing it on your sleeve,' was Bella's response to his playfulness, 'and no doubt you'll want coffee, not tea. Shall I get you a cup?'

'Don't mind my friend, she's super-efficient!' said Connie.

'But I don't have time for coffee right now,' he answered. 'I must go make that call.'

'You frightened him off, Bella!' Connie said watching him join the queue for the telephone. 'Why were you so sharp with him?'

'I didn't like the way he looked me over.'

'And it's a good thing Ezra wasn't here to see you blushing.'

The Canadian did not return to the counter, and Bella gave her attention to the tasks she was there to perform, cutting sandwiches for the horde of hungry young servicemen and women and pausing for a friendly word with those whom war had taken far from their homes, aware that something she preferred not to admit had this evening been stirred in her.

A familiar experience for Connie, no doubt, but not for Bella. And brought about by a man she might never see again, who could be posted away from Manchester before Bella's next stint at the canteen.

How shall you behave if you *do* see him again? she asked herself. The way that Connie behaves with men? Flirtatiously. Bella Minsky wouldn't know how to. She was, too, assailed by guilt because a stranger had aroused in her what Ezra, who loved her, could not.

Chapter Thirteen

IN THE MONTHS that followed, Bella made the most of the opportunity wartime was for those with the business acumen to take advantage of it.

Though she did not resort to the black market tactics with which some lined their pockets, she capitalized on the changing fashion scene as women began wearing hats with the day-length frocks they now wore for dances.

The cheap millinery with which she initially experimented was soon a staple line in the shop. Another was the headscarves every girl wanted after seeing a newspaper picture of Princess Elizabeth wearing one.

'What shall we do, Bella, when the wholesaler you get the scarves from can't get any more?' Gran asked one evening while they ate the nourishing soup she had made from the shinbone that came with their meagre meat ration.

'I've already thought of that, Gran. There are odds and ends of dress fabric up in the attic that wouldn't fetch much as remnants. Not too small to wear as a headscarf, though. All they need is squaring off and hemming. If you don't feel up to it, you can show me how to use your sewing machine —'

'And have you working all night, as well as the extra hours you put in at the canteen? Not likely!' said Gran. 'But there's nothing you wouldn't do, is there, Bella? You get more like Mr Marks — or was it Mr Spencer? — every day.'

Bella laughed. 'But I don't see me ending up owning stores like Marks and Spencer!'

Gran put down her soup spoon and surveyed the granddaughter she would not have thought capable of carrying the load she now did. A girl who was once so wrapped up in herself and her studies, she hadn't noticed that her parents were struggling to give her the advantages they hadn't had.

Well, she's had time since then to learn firsthand what struggling to support a family means, thought Gran, and could be that's what's changed her. Made her determined to do for her brother and sister what was done for her.

'How *do* you see yourself ending up?' Gran asked her.

'I'm courting, aren't I?' Bella said lightly.

'And don't think I haven't guessed what's holding things up,' Gran replied. 'It's me and the twins, isn't it, Bella? But if Ezra's willing to take on Joey and Sylvie, you needn't worry about where *I'll* live. I wouldn't be the first elderly woman to manage on a widow's pension and live on her own.'

Bella stopped eating and went to kiss her grandmother's cheek. 'I shall never let you do that, Gran. You're too useful to me! And when you qualify for your other pension, I shall take you out to celebrate.'

'Celebrating being old I can do without,' Gran added as they resumed their meal, 'though I can't say I'd like to be young again. Not with all I went through when I was.'

Bella interrupted her contemplation . 'After supper, I'll fetch some of that stuff from the attic and we'll begin cutting it up to make scarves –'

'With you,' said her grandmother, 'it's always back to business and no sooner said than done.'

'What would you say if I told you I'm thinking of opening a millinery shop?'

'Nothing would surprise me!'

'In business, Gran, you have to strike while the iron's hot. When I popped next door to buy our sweet ration, to send to the twins, Mr Beckwith told me his married daughter wants him and her mother to go and live with her, in Buxton, away from the air raids.'

'Nellie Beckwith's been trying to persuade them to do that since the Manchester blitz,' said Gran, revealing her prior

72

knowledge, 'but I don't see her dad giving up his business –'

'What he said to me, though,' Bella relayed, 'was the sweets and tobacco trade isn't what it was now there's rationing, and he might do it if his wife's arthritis gets much worse, so Nellie can help him look after her.'

'The poor woman can't even button up her own coat,' said Gran.

'And I'm as sorry for her as you are,' said Bella. 'But if a shop right next door to us becomes available –'

'You couldn't afford to rent it! Nor to fit it up for what you have in mind.'

'There's such a thing as a loan, Gran.'

Thus it was that Bella took her first step in the direction that would afterwards be her path. The worsening of her neighbour's condition hastened the availability of the shop, and Bella had no difficulty in securing a loan from her Uncle Saul, whose own fortunes had escalated along with the war.

By now, Saul had a second trouser factory to cope with orders pouring in from the military.

'If a man can't help his own, who then?' he said to Bella on the phone.

'But this won't be like the button-machine, Uncle. I'll pay you back with interest.'

'We'll talk about that when you can afford to pay me back, love, and knowing you, that day will come. Meanwhile, I've had some bad news, Bella, but don't tell your Auntie Dolly. I wouldn't have told you, if you hadn't rung me up –'

'Is it about my cousin?'

Saul's son, Walter, still a schoolboy when Bella's mother died, was in the army.

Her uncle's sorrowful sigh drifted over the line. 'Luckily, the War Office telegram came on a Saturday, or I wouldn't have been at home, and your auntie was at the hairdresser's. My lad is missing in action,' Saul told Bella, 'and I don't even know where. When he came home on embarkation leave, he didn't know where he'd be sent to.'

'They never do, Uncle. Security matters. That's why there are posters in the canteen I help in, reminding everyone that walls have ears. But the telegram you got allows us to hope. It wasn't one of the other kind and we must be thankful for that.'

Saul answered gruffly. 'Our family isn't a big one and it's a comfort to have a niece like you, Bella. I used to think you only cared about your nearest and dearest. And that you didn't realize how your Uncle Reuben and I felt about our dead sister's little kids, when we offered to bring them up.'

'But there's a lot I see differently now from how I did then,' Bella answered, 'and that includes you, Uncle Saul. If we'd lived in the same town, I'd have grown up feeling close to you. As things were –'

'You thought your uncles were neglecting your mother,' said Saul, 'but people get bogged down in their own lives, Bella.'

'I've found that out, too.' And if I'd gone to Oxford, how different my life would have been. I wouldn't have got involved with Ezra, who wants to turn me into a suburban housewife. Nor would I have met that Canadian.

Bella's remembrance of that brief encounter could be equated with a pebble being tossed into the placid pond her courtship was. Causing ripples that were still there.

When some weeks later she boarded a bus and found herself seated beside the man who had tossed the pebble she was momentarily tongue-tied. Would he remember her?

To her surprise, he did, and was again bathing her with that toothpaste-advertisement smile.

'I guess you're off duty today,' he said.

'Correct.'

'Are you always so unfriendly?'

Since Bella could not summon a suitable reply, she sat clutching her handbag and left the talking to him.

He said, with a laugh, 'The look you gave me that evening in the canteen, I wondered what I'd done to upset you.'

More than you know, thought Bella.

'It wasn't how the fair sex usually behaves with me!'

She had no doubt of that.

'And now you're giving me the cold shoulder again.'

Bella found her voice. 'I run a business, as well as working at the canteen. I don't have patience for flighty conversations.'

'And I guess that's me put in my place! Shall I go out the door and come in again?'

'You could hardly do that on a moving vehicle.'

'You sure do take everything seriously.'

'Believe it or not,' she told him, 'I'm known for my dry sense of humour.'

'Well, it goes missing when I'm around,' he replied. 'Are you headed for home? You live in Prestwich?'

'The answer to both questions is no,' said Bella, still unable to relax with him. 'I'm going to my boyfriend's home for tea, which I sometimes do on a Sunday.'

'The ones who appeal to me are always spoken for,' he said with chagrin. 'Is your boyfriend on leave?'

'He's stationed in Manchester.'

'Where you can keep an eye on him.'

'I don't have to.'

'That dry sense of humour you mentioned sure doesn't include *seeing* a joke!'

'I've a lot on my mind right now,' she said stiffly.

'I was beginning to think I had a bad effect on you.'

'You have no effect on me whatsoever,' Bella lied. 'I don't even know you.'

'Any chance of putting that right?'

Again she was tongue-tied.

'Of us being friends,' he qualified it and another of his smiles followed. 'I'm a nice Jewish boy from Toronto, and I haven't seen the Shabbos candles lit since I left home. I would sure appreciate an invitation to sit at your family's Friday night table.'

His tone was wistful and Bella turned to look at him, which she had carefully avoided doing.

'I haven't tasted kefulte fish since I left home, either,' he added with a laugh. 'Are you going to take pity on me?'

As always, Bella was wearing around her neck her thirteenth birthday gift from her parents.

'I didn't need to see your *mezuzah* to know you're Jewish,' he said when she fingered the charm. 'Your face has a biblical look.'

'Thanks!'

'I was paying you a compliment.'

'And compliments are your style, aren't they?' Bella said meeting his gaze. 'As for Friday night dinners, you must know as well as I do that every synagogue arranges hospitality like that for servicemen and women. Why haven't you taken advantage of it?'

'I didn't know I missed what I now know I do. And that has to be *your* effect on *me*.'

'I remind you of kefulte fish!'

'Did anyone ever tell you that you have remarkable eyes?'

'No, as a matter of fact.'

'Then let me be the first. They were what I remembered about you.'

Bella thought it more likely that he had remembered her because he wasn't accustomed to girls not succumbing to his charm.

'Are you stationed in Heaton Park?' she asked him.

'Which airman on this bus isn't?' he replied glancing around at the predominance of blue uniforms.

The spacious park, to which people had in peacetime gone to picnic in summer from all districts of Manchester and Salford, had been commandeered by the RAF and was now a transit camp for air crew trainees.

'I'm a physical training instructor,' the Canadian told Bella.

'And you weren't a sergeant when we met,' she remarked observing the third stripe now on his sleeve.

'I've just been made one,' he revealed.

76

'Congratulations.'

'It's no big deal, just what happens when you pass a course you get sent on. I was posted on mine the day after you were so shirty with me and it lasted till yesterday, or I'd sure have gone back for that coffee you offered to pour me –'

Bella averted her eyes.

'I guess if I were that boyfriend you mentioned, I'd hurry and put a ring on your finger before someone else does!'

What a smooth-tongued individual he is, Bella thought, as the bus reached the terminus and jerked to a halt. She couldn't wait to make her escape! – but was trapped beside him until all the airmen standing in the aisle had filed past.

When finally she alighted and he leapt from the platform to help her down, she felt like saying, 'Let go of me!'

'You're scowling,' he said. 'What have I done?'

Bella summoned the frigid manner of which she was capable when necessary and the words to match it. 'Why must you persist in attributing my demeanour to your effect upon me?'

'Did you eat a dictionary for lunch?'

'If I had one with me, I'd throw it at you! And the word I would use to describe you is "presumptuous".'

By then, she was heading away from the park towards the avenue where Ezra lived, her parting shot delivered over her shoulder.

'I guess I won't be getting that Shabbos supper invitation, then,' the Canadian called after her.

Bella halted and turned around. 'If you weren't the line-shooter you seem, you'd be welcome.'

'You have pretty hair,' he remarked, '*as well as* remarkable eyes.'

Bella took a scarf from her coat pocket and tied it around her head.

'There's no need to hide it from me!'

'In case you hadn't noticed, it's a windy day. I don't want to look a mess when I see my boyfriend,' Bella added though she could not have cared less.

'Lucky guy.'

'And there you go again with your flattery!'

'If that's what you think it is,' he answered. 'But as you said, you don't know me.'

'All right,' she said recklessly, 'you're invited for supper next Friday.'

She gave him her name and address, and he told her his name was Harold Diamond, but everyone called him Hal.

'Enjoy your tea,' he said as she departed.

Since Bella almost choked on it each time she was constrained to take tea with Ezra's mother, there was no chance of that. Nor, now she had re-encountered the Canadian, of kidding herself that what he had stirred in her had gone away.

On this occasion, strangers were present.

'I met these young ladies yesterday,' said Mrs Black introducing Bella to the two WAAFs seated on the sofa. 'They've just been posted to Heaton Park and they came to our Shabbos morning service.'

Though many local people, Jews and Gentiles, displayed such hospitality, Mrs Black was not one of them. What is she up to? thought Bella. Ezra's mother did nothing without some kind of ulterior motive. Try as she did to get on with her, the moment invariably came when Bella could contain herself no longer.

'You kept us waiting for tea,' she said now.

Ezra intervened with his habitual diplomacy, 'But there's no hurry, is there, Mother? It isn't as if you'd cooked a hot dinner –'

'Since when could Bella spare the time to have dinner with her "intended" and his parents?'

Bella saw the WAAFs glance at her hand and note the absence of an engagement ring. And if they hadn't sensed immediately that Mrs Black didn't approve of her, they knew now!

One of the girls gave Bella a wink and tried to lighten the atmosphere. 'If you've got any hot dinners going to waste, Mrs Black, you can count on Doreen and me!'

'You're welcome to join us next Friday night,' said Mrs

78

Black with a sidelong glance at Bella. 'Ezra always manages to be home from the Pay Office before I light my Shabbos candles.'

So that's it, thought Bella drily. His mother has made up her mind to elbow me out. To find him a girl without my encumbrances.

Mrs Black's next words seemed ample confirmation. 'Elaine and Doreen are pay clerks at the camp, Ezra, so you and them have something in common. When they told me yesterday that they could be stationed here till the war's over, I thought I'd start off by welcoming them to my home with a nice afternoon tea.'

'I can't tell you how lovely it is to be in a home that reminds me of mine,' said Doreen. 'I'm a Londoner,' she told Bella, as if her accent had not already done so.

'And I'm from Newcastle,' said Elaine.

'You don't sound like a Geordie,' Bella remarked as Mr Black entered with the teapot and his wife ushered her special guests to the table on which she had, today, laid her best silver and china.

'I was packed off to boarding school and came back talking like a toff!' Elaine replied.

'Elaine's father is a surgeon,' Mrs Black relayed, and Bella received another wink from Elaine, who seemed to have Mrs Black taped.

'And my mother can't wait to be a granny,' said Elaine, 'but she'll have to. I'm her only child.'

'Just like my Ezra,' said Mrs Black, 'and how your mother feels is only natural, dear.'

'But it was getting in the way of my social life,' Elaine answered, 'and I couldn't wait to get away from home.'

Doreen smiled at Mrs Black over her teacup. 'Elaine isn't like me.'

Mrs Black returned the smile and offered Doreen some more ginger cake. 'A person only has to chat to you, dear, to know you're an old-fashioned girl. What does *your* father do?'

'He runs the family business.'

'And what might that be?'

'Jewellery.'

Bella saw Mrs Black's eyes light up. Though a surgeon's daughter had snob value, the daughter of a London jeweller would bring with her a bigger dowry.

Since Ezra's expression had remained implacable, Bella had no idea what he was thinking. She sensed what Elaine was thinking, though – that she wouldn't come here again if she was paid to.

'It was nice of you to invite us for dinner on Friday, Mrs Black,' said Elaine, 'but I promised one of the other girls I'd go to the pictures with her.'

'On the Sabbath Eve?'

Elaine made use of a well-worn phrase. 'There's a war on, isn't there?'

'But the Sabbath is still the Sabbath,' said Doreen.

'And I can see,' said Mrs Black, 'that being in the Services hasn't changed *you*.'

'I haven't let it.'

As if, thought Bella, the war was for Doreen just a period of marking time while she did what she had been called upon to do. 'Stolid' was the word for her, for her appearance too. Pasty-faced and a bulky shape that uniform did nothing to enhance.

Elaine, though, was a petite blonde and as lively as her friend was dull. Making the most of her wartime experiences, instead of allowing them to wash over her.

'I got a lovely food parcel from my mother this week,' Doreen told Mrs Black.

'Your mother sounds my kind of person, dear. If my Ezra wasn't stationed in Manchester, I'd be doing the same for him.'

Mr Black stopped eating cake to make one of his rare contributions to the conversation. 'Lucky my son *is* stationed in Manchester, or he'd get food poisoning from chopped liver that's gone bad in the post.'

Mrs Black twitched the pearls encircling her fat neck. 'My husband is a bit of a joker, Doreen.'

If you appreciate *barbed* jokes, thought Bella, which seemed to be the sole weapon left in Mr Black's marital armoury. If he hadn't occasionally fired one at his wife, Bella would have assumed he'd stopped trying to prove that he still existed.

Mrs Black gave her full attention to Doreen. 'Can we expect *you* on Friday evening, dear?'

'I'm looking forward to it.'

Ezra's mother had chosen her candidate to replace Bella. Hadn't she noticed that her son had not shown the slightest interest in Doreen? In Elaine, either, come to that. Bella wanted to laugh. Her own involvement in the situation hadn't blinded her to the comedy it was.

Could the same be said of Bella's inviting Hal Diamond for Friday night supper? Not that Ezra, when she told him, would bat an eyelid. He was as sure of her as she of him.

Ezra, though, wasn't fully in the picture. And Bella was no longer sure of *herself*.

Chapter Fourteen

BELLA'S increasingly complicated personal life did not deter her from opening her millinery shop before the Jewish New Year, when even in wartime a new hat to wear for the Rosh Hashanah and Yom Kippur services was de rigueur.

With the aid of a shopfitter whom her Uncle Saul, a man with many contacts, had sent from Leeds, the transformation of the sweets and tobacco shop was swiftly completed, and Bella soon made aware that the range of hats that had boosted her takings in the haberdashery store would not do for the clientele she now hoped to attract.

'Haven't you got anything better?' was a question she became accustomed to hearing.

'What they mean by "better",' she said thoughtfully to her grandmother, 'is *model* hats, like they sell at Affleck and Brown, and Kendal Milne. If they can't get them from me, they'll go to town.'

'And where are you going to get those from in wartime, Bella? I should think the big stores are having trouble keeping up their supply.'

'I shall have to have them made, Gran.'

'They don't just have to be made, love. They have to be designed.'

Bella's reply was, 'I've been thinking it over and I know just the person to do that for me.' She opened the dresser drawer and took from it a sketchpad. 'Remember those fashion drawings Gerda used to amuse herself by doing? They were so good, I kept them –'

'But I don't remember them including hats,' said Gran.

'They didn't,' said Bella, bringing the pad to the table, where Gran was seated sewing the seams of a red jersey she had knitted for Joey. 'But Gerda's got what they call fashion *sense* – have another look at these sketches, Gran.'

'I'll take your word for it!'

'You think it's a crazy idea I've got in my head, don't you?' Bella said with a smile. 'But I've nothing to lose by giving it a try –'

'Except that you seem to've forgotten that Gerda is busy growing cabbages and milking cows!'

'All I'd need from her is some rough drawings and that wouldn't take her long.'

'But you'd still have to get the hats made.'

'Where there's a will, there's a way, Gran.'

'If there weren't, you'd invent one!'

While Gerda spent her free time designing hats – which she said would stop her from *turning into* a cabbage – Bella engaged her first employees. An advertisement in the *Manchester Evening News* had inundated her with replies from middle-aged women, milliners in their youth, who, as one reply put it, 'wouldn't mind earning a bob or two'.

Soon, Bella had acquired a team of workers minus the overheads of the hats being made on her premises. Her milliners would do what was required of them each in her own home.

When eventually the deep drawers were stocked, and Gerda's pièce de résistance in the centre of the window, Ezra stood with Bella in the elegant little shop surveying the gilt-framed mirrors, and the display of model millinery on stands.

'I've got to hand it to you, Bella.'

'Does that mean you didn't think I could do it? The carpet is a present from Uncle Saul, by the way – though how he can think of me while Walter is still missing . . .'

Ezra said after a pause, 'I think you could do anything you want to do, Bella. I always have and I hope it includes marrying me.'

He had finally proposed to her. And what a time to do it, thought Bella.

'I wouldn't expect you to give up your business.'

That's very nice of you! she exclaimed inside herself. 'Would you mind telling me what's brought this on?' she said mustering a smile. 'From my point of view, nothing has changed since that Sunday afternoon before the war, when we sat on a bench in Heaton Park and you told me I was jumping the gun –'

'Not about my feelings for you, though, and afterwards I admitted that, didn't I?'

'But what I actually asked you was a practical question, wasn't it? And I *still* have the twins and my grandmother to consider.'

'All right,' said Ezra, 'so nothing has changed, but something's been added. Whenever I come here, that damned Canadian's sitting with his big feet under the table.'

'My gran's taken a fancy to him.'

'Are you sure *you* haven't?'

Ezra picked up his officer cap and walked to the door.

'You just got here,' said Bella.

'But I can't stay. It's Friday night, isn't it?'

And Hal Diamond was as usual coming for supper. As Ezra had implied, Hal often dropped in casually, too – which Ezra himself had recently taken to doing.

'And my mother's invited Doreen's parents to join us,' he went on, 'they're in Manchester visiting their daughter.'

'Who's as welcome at your house as Hal is at mine,' Bella said pointedly.

Ezra looked taken aback. 'Me and Doreen? Don't be daft!'

'Tell that to your mother.'

'Are you saying my mother's a conniver?'

Bella was saved from replying by Gran's entering to ask how Ezra liked Minsky's millinery department.

84

'Minsky's millinery department?' he answered. 'We're looking at a brand new venture, aren't we, Bella?'

'Yes, as a matter of fact.'

'You don't seem to know your granddaughter as well as I do,' Ezra said to Gran. He turned to Bella. 'Tomorrow's when you launch the venture is why I came this evening. To wish you luck and give you a tip you might care to make use of. Continental fashion has a special cachet, and –'

'If you're going to suggest I tell my customers the hats are by a Viennese designer, I intend to,' Bella interrupted.

Ezra smiled ruefully. 'When weren't you one step ahead of me?'

'Thanks for coming to wish me luck, Ezra.'

'You deserve it,' he said before departing.

But he had not given Bella his usual farewell kiss on the cheek. Nor was the manner in which she had thanked him how a girl behaves with the man she's courting. As though we're strangers, thought Bella guiltily, and I'm to blame. She hadn't needed telling that though nothing had changed something had been added.

So successful were Gerda's designs – though Gran thought them outrageous – women who had formerly bought their model hats in town began patronizing 'Bella's' and it became necessary to employ an assistant in the shop.

Meanwhile, Ezra had said no more about marriage and Gran made a startling suggestion.

'It can't be very comfy for Hal, living in a Nissen hut in the park, can it, Bella? Why don't we offer the lad a civilian billet?'

While Bella digested her grandmother's words along with the baked cod she was eating, the old lady glanced around the cosy kitchen, at the firelight lending an added glow to the brass coalbox beside the hearth, the blue and white plates on the dresser shelves, the old leatherette sofa, and the brown chenille curtain trimmed with bobbles that kept draughts from entering through the back door.

'When you and I sit eating our supper like this, Bella, you wouldn't know there's a war on,' she said before switching her gaze to the blackout curtains shutting out the bleak November night. 'Well, not if it weren't for *them* – and I've been thinking what it must be like in winter for Hal.'

Bella took a little of the margarine from the dish that in peacetime held butter and carefully spread it on the boiled potatoes on her plate. 'For him and a lot of others,' she replied, 'and compared to what it must be like in the trenches, a Nissen hut is a palace.'

'All the same,' Gran persisted, 'plenty of airmen stationed at the park are billeted out, aren't they, Bella? Because there aren't enough huts to put them all in, Hal said.'

'He's been discussing it with you, has he! Putting the idea in your head –'

'Hal did no such thing. Having him here is my own idea,' Gran declared. 'Connie's next-door neighbour has airmen from the park lodging with her, doesn't she?'

And Connie hadn't failed to take advantage of it, thought Bella. 'But they're air crew trainees, waiting to be posted,' she said, 'they come and go –'

'I wouldn't like that,' Gran cut in, 'I'd worry about them getting shot down, after they'd gone from my life. But it wouldn't be that way with Hal and I'm thankful he's on the ground staff,' she added fervently. 'If anything happened to him, it'd be like losing one of my own.'

Only then did Bella realize how deeply Hal Diamond was entrenched in her grandmother's affections. It was Gran, not Bella, who had told him after the first Sabbath Eve he spent with them that he was welcome at her table every Friday night. Perhaps because there were tears in his eyes when he watched Gran light the Sabbath candles . . .

Remembrance of that evening returned to Bella. The pristine white tablecloth and the small embroidered one covering the plaited loaf. The brass candlesticks presented to Gran on her wedding day, and the wine goblet that Bella's parents had received on theirs. Hal in his uniform, looking devastatingly

86

handsome, and Gran and me wearing our best frocks like we do for Friday night supper even when it's just the two of us.

Wartime or not, Jewish tradition went on, and it could have been having that brought home to him that affected Hal Diamond when Gran covered her head with the bit of black lace she calls her Shabbos scarf and lit the candles.

And for Gran it was a treat to have a man present to bless the wine with the Kiddush prayer. She had taken Hal to her heart from then on, thought Bella recalling snippets of their conversation at the table – and me sitting there like a silent observer . . .

'Are you one of a big family?' Gran had asked Hal.

'No, but I had a wonderful sister and Bella reminds me of her some. After my father remarried, I left home for good.'

Bella had been left to deduce that his mother and sister were dead and he didn't like his step-mother.

When Gran asked him over the lemon tea what he did in peacetime, he replied, 'I tried my hand at a number of things and was just getting going as a travelling salesman when war was declared.'

To Bella, this had smacked of the rolling stone she sensed he was. And ostensibly, she thought returning to the present, it's Gran he drops in here to see and never without some goodies or toiletries from the NAAFI at the camp that civilians find hard to get. Or Gran wouldn't be smelling of Yardley's lavender talcum powder now and Bella of the Coty sandalwood soap he had casually handed to her last week.

'Ostensibly' was the key word. Though Hal was by now addressing the old lady as Gran, which Ezra never had, and Bella didn't doubt that he had grown fond of her grandmother, she was under no illusions as to what brought him here so often.

Bella would catch him looking at her and have to avert her eyes, as she had on the bus. And he continued to pass remarks about Ezra's good fortune, interpreted by Gran as the compliment any friend of the family might voice about her

87

granddaughter. A friend of the family was what Hal Diamond had become. But he hadn't fooled Bella.

Though her appetite had suddenly fled, she forced herself to eat her supper, mindful of the wartime posters illustrating a half-eaten meal and the words printed beneath it: If you didn't want it, why did you take it?

A caption equally applicable to other matters. If I don't want Ezra, why am I wasting his time? In some ways I *do*, but they don't include how I now know a woman can want a man. Ezra, though, was a man Bella felt safe with, comfortable too. He was straightforward and dependable and there was something about Hal Diamond that told her he was neither.

Which girl in her right mind would give up the sure thing for the unknown quantity Hal was? Yet nowadays plenty of girls were doing so, as if the escalation of the war had caused them to cast common sense to the winds and live for today.

'You've gone very quiet,' said Gran while removing their supper plates. 'And you haven't answered my question about Hal.'

'What makes you think he would be allowed to live outside the camp?' Bella stalled. 'That might only apply to airmen in transit –'

'He told me he could.'

'Who raised the subject on that occasion?'

'I don't remember. And why are you cross-examining me?' Gran added with asperity, bringing a dish of stewed apples to the table.

Bella sidestepped the question. 'Do you really want a man in the house to look after, Gran?'

'I'd be doing my bit for the war effort, wouldn't I? Like Connie's neighbour. And with the bedrooms we've got empty while Gerda and the twins aren't here, there's no reason for Hal to be in that hut.'

'The fact remains,' said Bella, 'that you've enough to do with just you and me. When Gerda was here she used to lend you a hand and you're not getting any younger.'

'Hal isn't the sort to let me wait on him and you know it,

88

Bella, he's kind and considerate. If you don't want him to live here, just say so instead of finding reasons including my age!'

When Bella remained silent, Gran served the stewed apples and said hopefully, 'We could put him in Joey's room, couldn't we?'

'Oh, no.'

'Why not?'

It's next to mine, Bella silently replied. 'It would mean shifting all Joey's things to the attic,' she said.

'Hal would do that for us. So what do you say, Bella? Yes, or no?'

Bella had a vision of herself leaving the bathroom wrapped in a towel and coming face to face with Hal Diamond on the landing, he wearing only his underwear and she having to drag her gaze from him.

'It wouldn't inconvenience *you*,' her grandmother declared as the vision dissolved.

'As it happens, it would. I'd have to remember to put on my dressing gown and all that, and when I'm in a rush in the morning, or tired out at night, why should I have to be bothered to?'

'If you'd said that at first, Bella, I'd have understood. Why didn't you?'

Because it's a lie. The truth is that what I just conjured up is altogether too intimate.

'But we could give Hal his own private quarters, couldn't we?' said Gran. 'Above the millinery department. The Beckwiths kept it so nice it wouldn't need decorating, and the bathroom's better than ours. Hal could use it without causing you any embarrassment.'

'All right, Gran. You can do your bit for the Air Force!'

But even with intimate encounters of the accidental kind unlikely, deliberate ones were capable of being engineered. There was a communicating door on the adjoining landings, as well as between the shops, which Ezra – of all people! – had suggested might prove useful.

Gran, from the goodness of her heart, had played puppeteer

with the strings of destiny no less than Ezra's manipulating mother was doing. There were no more objections to Hal Diamond's living here that Bella could reasonably have made and reason hadn't entered into it. Whether or not Hal was the potential wolf she thought him remained to be seen. She had put up a fight and lost, and so be it.

Chapter Fifteen

'DID YOU and Ezra go out and have yourselves a good time before the war?' Hal asked Bella while helping her clear the supper table.

'Yes, but it probably wouldn't be your idea of a good time,' she replied.

'My impression of Ezra is you could be right.'

'And what *is* your impression of Ezra?'

'That he wouldn't know how to show a girl a good time.'

Bella filled the washing-up bowl with water and dumped the plates into it, aware of Hal eyeing her stiffened back.

'Look – you asked me and I told you,' he said.

'And now you have, why don't you go out and have *yourself* a good time!' How dare he criticize Ezra, who had stood by her throughout her ups and downs.

Hal had by now dug himself still deeper into Gran's affections. So much so, that it was he, not Bella, who had managed to persuade her to spend a day in bed when she complained of breathlessness.

In the three months he had lived with them, Bella had contrived not to be alone with him, going directly to her room if she had been out at night and found him comfortably sprawled on the kitchen sofa when she returned.

That he had the good grace to make himself scarce if she returned with Ezra had surprised her. But maybe he can't bear the atmosphere, she thought uncharitably now. As I myself can't when I'm with the two of them.

Hal took one of the plates Bella had washed and began

drying it. 'The answer to what you just said to me, Bella, is my idea of a good time includes *you*.'

'Then you must change your ideas,' she said crisply, 'and find yourself a girl who isn't spoken for.'

'If I thought he was the right guy for you, I'd leave the field to him,' said Hal.

Bella turned to face him, her eyes blazing. 'Who are you to say who's right for me!'

'A guy you're in love with is who's right for you.' Hal put down the dry plate and picked up one from the draining board, continuing his mundane task as he said quietly, 'Yours has to be one of the longest courtships in history.'

'But there are problems I'm not able to surmount and I don't intend explaining them to you.'

'Whatever they are, if you were in love with Ezra you'd find a way. My impression of you, if you'd like that, too –'

'I wouldn't.'

'But I'm going to tell you anyways. I've never met a female like you, Bella.'

'And you're an expert on females, aren't you?'

'What a terrible impression *you* have of *me*. What do I have to do to correct it?'

'It isn't an impression, it's an instinct and instincts are usually right.'

Bella had resumed washing up and found herself being turned around.

'In that case, let's try one out,' Hal said before he kissed her.

Not only had she fought a battle and lost, she herself was lost. The strongest of all instincts was how Bella felt in Hal Diamond's arms.

The shrilling of the telephone interceded and Hal's next words returned Bella's feet to the ground.

'If that's Ezra, tell him you're busy tonight.'

'And so I shall be. Looking over Gerda's latest designs.'

'When do I get to meet Gerda? Don't Land Army girls get leave?'

'Not in the lambing season, it seems.'

'Hadn't you better answer the phone?'

'After I've told you that if you're looking for a convenient wartime liaison, you've chosen the *wrong* female.'

Bella turned on her heel and headed for the haberdashery, where the telephone was, her treacherous body still telling her what she would rather not know.

Chapter Sixteen

A WEEK LATER, Hal was again posted away on a course, a welcome respite for Bella. He would not return until after Easter, and relieved of the strain his presence was to her she gave her full attention to the seasonal boost in trade.

'You've lost interest in all but the millinery side of the business, haven't you?' said her Uncle Saul.

'I should think so, too,' said her Auntie Dolly whom he had brought to Manchester on a Sunday morning, to try on the model hats.

If my aunt knew Walter was missing, she wouldn't be sitting in front of a mirror admiring herself with that straw concoction on her head, thought Bella. Perhaps there was something to be said for the way Uncle Saul protected his wife, since her sitting wringing her hands would not change the stressful situation he himself was living with. Time enough for that if and when.

Strong character though Saul was, Bella's impression was that his wife ruled the roost. Bella could not recall a telephone chat with him that hadn't included, 'Don't tell your Auntie Dolly,' and on those occasions, she thought with a smile, it was himself he was protecting!

'We could do with a millinery shop like this in Leeds,' the plump little woman said.

'Maybe, after the war, Bella will open a branch there,' said Saul.

Bella was prohibited by her aunt's presence from saying that her first priority was to repay the loan he had preferred not to mention to Dolly. But I *can* make a gesture of my appreciation, she thought.

'That hat suits you very well, Auntie –'

Dolly slanted the brim further over one eye. 'You think so?' She took off the hat and tried on another.

'You're a hat person,' Bella told her, 'every one you've put on suits you.'

'What a saleswoman she is, Saul! But which of the two does my husband prefer?'

'If I tell you, you'll ask me what's wrong with the other one,' he replied.

Dolly gave him a withering glance and spent the next few minutes trying to decide between the straw hat and the ruched crêpe toque which had also taken her fancy.

'This one is definitely different,' she said to Bella trying on the toque yet again.

'I'm glad I'm a trouser manufacturer!' Saul exclaimed. 'For that you don't need patience and if Bella spends her days like this, I'm sorry for her.'

'Both these hats would match my outfit, Bella,' said Dolly ignoring the interruption.

'Then why not take the two, Auntie?'

Saul's reaction was, 'What is my niece doing to me? With two new hats in her wardrobe, my wife would be dithering about which to wear for the wedding we're going to. And with me standing dressed and ready to leave! Also,' he joked, 'I can't afford to buy her two new hats.'

'You're not going to,' said Bella, 'they're a gift from me.' And the heck with the toque being my most expensive model.

'I can't let you do that,' said her uncle.

But Bella was already packing the straw hat. Were it not for Uncle Saul and his contacts, how would she have acquired the necessary boxes in wartime?

Dolly brought the toque to the counter and kissed Bella warmly. 'Everyone should have such a nice niece! A clever one also, that's why I'm surprised that you're still dabbling with the bits and bobs your dad made his living from, Bella.'

'But sooner or later,' said Saul, 'she'll shut that side of the business down.'

Bella tied up the box with ribbon, an expense she had thought worthwhile. To the women who were now her customers the packaging mattered as much as the hat. 'As a matter of fact, I've considered doing that,' she told her uncle, 'but I doubt that I ever shall. How my dad earned his living wasn't just dabbling to him.'

Bella kept to herself the thought she had once had. That her father had probably hoped to build Minsky's Haberdashery Store into something he could be proud of.

'What you said, though, doesn't make business sense,' Saul declared, 'and that isn't like you.'

'What I should have said,' Bella qualified it, 'is I shall never dispense with that side of the business entirely. There are items my dad sold, and that I still do, that wouldn't disgrace a model hat shop-window,' Bella added as a long-ago day returned to her.

'I've only been to London once in my life,' she went on, 'when my dad took my mam and me with him to the Jewish ex-Servicemen's annual parade at the Cenotaph.'

She paused reminiscently. 'A lot of men used to take their wives and children along. There was a special train and everyone took sandwiches. To eat on the way to remember those who'd given their lives for Britain in the war to end all wars, only it didn't turn out to be,' Bella said with feeling.

Saul's expression shadowed and she knew he was thinking of his son. 'Get on with your story, Bella –'

'There isn't much to tell. We had time to spare after the parade, before the train brought us back to Manchester, and we went for a walk in the West End. Because it was Sunday, it was very quiet, not at all how I'd expected it would be. Well, except for Piccadilly Circus.

'One of the women with us said she'd like to see Bond Street, and that was how I came to go there.'

Bella saw herself again as a little girl, warmly dressed against the November sleet that had begun to fall, a scarlet beret on her head matching the remembrance poppy pinned to her coat.

'I'd never seen shop windows like those I saw there,' she recalled, 'and the one that relates to what I said, Uncle, was a milliner's with just one hat on display. But there were a few fancy buckles, too, and they were what caught my dad's eye. If a Bond Street milliner can stock them . . .'

Bella collected herself and smiled. 'In wartime, though, what's the point of thinking ahead? And meanwhile I'll make do with what my gran still calls Minsky's millinery department.'

When again her grandmother complained of breathlessness, Bella had a word with the family doctor.

'If I suggested she visit your surgery for a check-up, she'd behave as though I'd insulted her,' Bella told him on the phone.

'But I'd rather she took that attitude than consider herself the invalid she once did,' he replied. 'I'll drop in for a cup of tea, Bella, like I sometimes do with my elderly patients who are too independent for their own good. Your gran isn't the only one I have to handle with care!'

The tactic he employed with others did not work with Gran.

'You don't look too good yourself,' she answered his observing her pallor when the tea was poured and he seated opposite her.

Bella wanted to laugh. It would take a more practised conspirator than the kindly doctor to hoodwink Gran!

'With your young partner gone to the army, you must have even more work to do,' Gran went on, 'so how come you've time for tea-parties?'

'I wouldn't call this one,' he hedged. 'Where's the cake?'

'Gran hasn't baked this week, she hasn't felt up to it,' Bella put in helpfully.

'Which the doctor already knows!' Gran flashed. 'Or he wouldn't be here. Who do you two think you're fooling?'

'In that case, I may as well take your blood pressure.'

'And next time you drop in for a cuppa while you're passing and want me to believe it, leave your medical bag in your car,' said Gran while reluctantly rolling up her sleeve.

She turned her attention to Bella. 'If this is your way of proving I'm not well enough to have an airman billeted here, it's your fault if my blood pressure is sky high!'

'As a matter of fact it isn't too bad,' the doctor eventually pronounced. 'May I listen to your heart now?'

'Could I stop you?'

Her grandmother's expression when the stethoscope was strategically placed told Bella what the old lady had not confided. That she feared the symptom that had slowed her down must be taken seriously, putting paid to the active life she enjoyed.

Instead, the doctor said cheerfully, 'There's plenty of life in you yet!' He finished his tea and added with a twinkle in his eye, 'If there's no cake when I drop in again, I shall want to know why.'

Bella walked with him to his car. 'Was that the truth you told Gran?'

'Give or take that she's a year or so older than when I last examined her and the human body can be likened to a machine subjected to wear and tear.'

The doctor smoothed his thinning grey hair, his expression reflective behind the pince-nez that lent him a scholarly appearance. 'When it comes to heart patients, Bella, there are those who sit in a chair waiting to die and others determined to live to the full even if that shortens the odds.'

He put his bag in the car and unbuttoned his jacket before getting in. 'I used to think your grandmother was one of the former, but something changed her. Could it have been you?' he added with a smile.

'All I did was aid and abet her.'

'A good thing you did. Any chance of your getting her away for a few days, Bella? Easter weekend is coming up and a change of air would do her good.' The doctor turned the ignition key and appraised Bella's weary appearance. 'It would do you no harm either. You've too much on your shoulders,' he said before departing.

But little chance of lightening my load, she thought. Since opening 'Bella's' she had given up her market stall, but organizing the making of the hats was even more time-consuming.

If Gerda weren't in the Land Army and I had the capital, there would be no stopping us, Bella reflected returning to the shop. But the time Bella was hoping for could be far in the future. In London, people still spent their nights in the Tube stations while German bombers continued their onslaught. Nor was there yet any sign of the promised 'Second Front' that would sweep the Allies to victory.

Meanwhile, the twins had been gone from home for two years, during which Gran had not seen them. To do so, thought Bella, would be as good a tonic for her as the fresh air the doctor had recommended.

That evening Bella rang up Gerda.

'You've disturbed the designer at work!' Gerda said jokingly.

'What you're doing for me, Gerda, is no laughing matter. Where would I be without you?'

'Knowing you, Bella, you'd have found someone. There's an expression that Martha sometimes uses that makes me think of you. She talks about some people always falling with their bottom in butter.'

That was not how Bella would describe her own vicissitudes! 'If I came to see you and the twins next weekend, Gerda, and brought Gran, could you find us a place in the village to stay the night? We'd come on Sunday and stay over for Easter Monday since the shop will be closed –'

'I could ask at the pub.'

'I don't see Gran staying there!'

In the event, they stayed at the vicarage.

'Don't you go telling the doctor I puffed and panted my way up all those stairs,' said Gran after they had been warmly escorted to an attic room and Bella was unpacking an overnight bag.

The rest of the guest accommodation in the spacious old house, which seemed badly in need of repair, was occupied by young mothers with their babies to whom the vicar and his wife were playing wartime hosts.

'I won't tell the doctor if you'll lie down and rest for a while,' Bella replied.

Gran grudgingly obliged but did not rest her tongue. 'The vicar said something about showing us round his church –'

'Well, it'll be full of flowers, specially decorated for Easter. I expect he's very proud of it,' said Bella.

'All the same, your great-great-grandfather, the rabbi, would turn in his grave, Bella, if we so much as crossed the threshold.'

'But there's one God for everyone, Gran. And I sometimes wonder where He is.'

Since Gran had continued delivering her Sabbath morning monologues to God, though they were now about the lives being lost in the war, she remained silent.

'I expected you to tell me to go and scrub my mouth out for taking God's name in vain, as you did when I was growing up,' Bella said while laying their hair-brushes on the chintz-flounced dressing table.

Gerda had told them to leave the overnight bag at the vicarage, which was in the village and close to the railway station, before taking the bus to the farm.

The Easter Sunday service was over by the time they arrived and the vicar's wife, wrapped in a floral-patterned overall and flustered from serving lunch to the evacuee mothers and their little ones, had nevertheless personally escorted them to their room. Nor could the vicar have been more friendly.

'I should like to think that the rabbi-ancestor of mine you just mentioned, Gran, *wouldn't* turn in his grave if we entered a church.'

'But if he were to, you couldn't blame him,' Gran replied. 'He died in an Easter pogrom, when Russian Jews were being massacred, and the village priest didn't let even the children hide in his church. The only survivor was my father, just a little lad at the time, but which child would forget hiding down the well, under the bucket and hanging on to it like he was to his life? It was him who told me.'

Bella said after a silence, 'But that was a long time ago. And if I'm offered a hot-cross-bun for breakfast tomorrow, I shall show my appreciation of the welcome we've received here by eating it.'

Gran's arrival at the farm was greeted ecstatically by Joey and Sylvie, who were pacing the yard waiting for them.

No, Joey's walking would never again include pacing, thought Bella, but he had come on a ton since she last saw him and was inches taller. Sylvie, too. What were those little bumps under Sylvie's blouse? My kid sister has already begun developing breasts! Me, I was still flat as a pancake at the age of eleven and I'm not too well-endowed in that department now.

Bella's reunions with the twins were always emotional for her, if not for them. But two years was a long time in a child's life. That they no longer hugged and kissed her was understandable. Martha is now their mother-figure, Bella accepted without resentment as the farmer's wife emerged from the dairy.

'We'd like you to meet our grandmother,' Sylvie said with a poise beyond her years.

'We're very proud of her,' Joey added.

'Anyone'd think I was the Queen Mother!' said Gran with a chuckle.

'With your snowy hair and that hat you have on, you put me in mind of Queen Mary,' said Martha. 'Is your hat one that Gerda thought up?'

Gran laughed. 'Turbans were thought up before Gerda was born and I've had mine for years. Where *is* the famous hat-designer?' she enquired jokingly.

'Busy with her sketchpad, I don't doubt,' Martha replied, 'since Jim's given everyone Easter Sunday off.'

Gran eyed Martha's apron. 'Everyone but the woman of the house, you mean!'

'I'd just popped into the dairy to steal some cream for our tea.'

'The twins,' said Gran surveying Joey and Sylvie, 'look as if they get cream for every meal. Is there time for them to take me for a walk before tea?'

Bella stopped herself from saying that Joey didn't go for walks and nor should Gran. A moment later, he and Sylvie were escorting Gran through the gate and she telling them how being in the country reminded her of her Russian child-hood.

'While we've a moment alone together,' said Martha, 'I'd like a word with you about Joey, Miss Minsky.'

Bella went with her to sit down on the bench outside the dairy, feeling as if the sun shining down on the farmyard had briefly been blotted out. 'What's wrong, Mrs Dawson?'

Martha took in Bella's anxious expression. 'Why do you assume that something's wrong?'

'Things haven't exactly gone right for Joey, have they?'

'The same could be said of some of the other kids, and especially in wartime,' Martha replied absently pleating her apron and glancing to where her young charges were playing in a field.

'See that lad in the blue shirt? His dad won't be coming home from the war. And the little girl in the gingham frock hasn't had a visit from her mam since she arrived here.'

'Doesn't her mother write to her?'

'If you can call the occasional picture postcard from Black-pool, or wherever, that. All I can do, though,' said Martha, 'is give the child a stable home life while she's with me and hope it'll stand her in good stead.

'According to little Nancy, there were lots of "uncles" visiting her house before the war – her dad is a merchant seaman – and she wasn't allowed in her mother's bedroom.'

Martha added briskly, 'What I'm trying to tell you, Miss Minsky –'

'Isn't it time you called me Bella?'

Martha appraised the young woman beside her, whose confident manner made her seem older than she was. Since she'd had the millinery shop, Bella Minsky had smartened her appearance. She wasn't the sort to visit a farm in high heels and a tight skirt, but her tan costume had real leather buttons and she was wearing a felt hat that completed the country-outfit appearance.

Martha had from the first felt uncomfortable with Bella, though she couldn't put her finger on why. And it was possible that Joey might never be a match for his elder sister, though that couldn't be said of Sylvie, Martha thought now.

'All right, Bella,' she said, 'and perhaps I should put what I have to say to you this way – there's more than one kind of handicap a child can have and they're not all physical, as what I told you about those two kids illustrates. Joey's is and he's making better progress than Nancy and Richard. As for you assuming that something is wrong, it's quite the opposite.

'You know that Joey and Sylvie took the high school scholarship exam – well, it's too soon to know the results, of course, but I thought it'd please you to hear that the schoolmistress expects Joey to pass with flying colours. She says she's never had a pupil like him and that doesn't surprise me,' Martha declared.

The same had been said of Bella, but she had feared that Joey's chance of a scholarship would be diminished by his removal to a village schoolroom.

'Thanks for telling me,' she replied, 'and also for the extra tuition Joey's received from you. It wasn't just limited to your encouraging his interest in science, Gerda told me.'

Martha smiled. 'But he's that good at arithmetic, I had trouble keeping up with him! I've a feeling the teachers at the high school in Derby will have the same trouble.'

'How will he get to Derby?'

'The same way lots of other children do. On a train.' Martha paused before adding, 'If that sounded a bit sharp, it's because I seem to've wasted my breath.'

Gerda emerged from the farmhouse in time to watch Martha's stiff-backed departure.

'What did you say to upset her, Bella?'

The sort of thing I can't help saying and thinking, no matter how I try. 'We were talking about Joey.'

'And you're still obsessed by him, aren't you?'

'I wouldn't put it that way.'

'But others would. Do yourself and him a favour, Bella, don't let Joey know it. Shall we now discuss your other obsession?'

'What, in your opinion, is that?'

'Your business, Bella. You never take time off to enjoy yourself. When did you last listen to some music? Or read a novel? Or sit holding hands with the man you're supposed to be courting?'

Supposed to be was right. 'Since you and I aren't living under the same roof now,' Bella replied, 'how can you know what I'm doing and not doing?'

'I know *you*. You're only twenty-three, Bella, but you're not like other girls. It's as if something is driving you.'

'I still have to raise and educate the twins, don't I?' Bella managed to smile. 'Now may we please change the subject?'

Gerda was leaning against the dairy wall, looking lovely as always, thought Bella, the jodhpurs and pullover that were Land Army uniform enhancing her voluptuous shape and the sunlight making her hair look like crinkly corn.

'I must come soon and meet the airman who's billeted with you,' she said. 'Maybe he'll give me some Canadian cigarettes!'

Bella blotted out remembrance of Hal Diamond's kiss. "About your refusal to be paid for your designs, Gerda – I can't let you go on working for nothing. You could be earning far more than I can afford.' Bella paused reminiscently. 'When I think back to your saying you wished you'd opted for a secretarial course – well, I hadn't seen your sketchpad then. Had you yourself no idea of how talented you are?'

Gerda said lightly, 'When you were a schoolgirl, Bella, did

you know you had a talent for business? At home in Vienna, I used to sometimes draw the outfits I saw in my mother's fashion magazines, to amuse myself –'

'But your parents never thought of sending you to art school?'

Gerda laughed. 'They would have fainted at the mere idea! And it certainly didn't enter *my* head. My upbringing was such, Bella, that I never questioned what was planned for me as it was for the girls who were my friends, whose parents were my parents' friends.

'A finishing school in Switzerland,' Gerda went on, 'after which I would have been introduced to a selection of suitable young men.'

'Were you looking forward to what was planned for you?'

Gerda dropped the stub of the cigarette she was smoking and ground it out with the heel of a muddy boot, her expression unreadable.

'You once said you'd hoped to help your father in his business,' Bella prodded her.

'But he would have fainted at that idea, too,' Gerda said with a wan smile. 'What does it matter now, Bella, if I was looking forward to my future or not? I am fortunate to *have* a future. Possibly my parents are dead, and many of my friends, too.

'Nor does it matter now if you were looking forward to going to Oxford, Bella,' she added, 'which I know you were.'

'It was a lot more positive than that,' Bella told her. 'I knew what I wanted to be.'

Gerda's response was, 'You're a positive kind of person. I'm not, I live my life like I play the piano –'

'By ear, you mean! But life isn't a musical instrument,' said Bella.

'I sometimes think that for you, it's a cash register,' Gerda replied.

'Are you saying that all I live for is money?'

'Not for the money itself. For what you can do with it for those you love. But where do *you* come into it, Bella?'

'I don't have time to consider that aspect. And since you mentioned money, we're back with your refusing to be paid for your designs, Gerda.'

'All right, Bella. If it will make you feel better, put whatever you would like to pay me in the bank for me. I don't require it now.'

Gerda's rare seriousness dissipated into laughter and she took Bella's hand to pull her from the bench. 'Come, I'll show you what Martha calls my rogues' gallery! I don't need the Canadian cigarettes I joked about, Bella. I get plenty of American ones from the Yanks at the camp close by.'

Gerda took Bella to the cluttered room she shared with the other Land Army girl. The walls were plastered with photographs of GIs, and the dressing table piled with cartons of Lucky Strikes.

She switched on the radio, tuned in to the American Forces Network, and said while Frank Sinatra crooned 'Come Out Wherever You Are', 'Camel cigarettes are very strong, so Doris and I don't accept them.'

Bella was looking at the photographs. 'You can certainly afford to be choosy. You're incorrigible, Gerda!'

'But I can't help being me, like you can't help being you.'

Chapter Seventeen

REFRESHING THOUGH the brief country interlude was for Bella, she returned home feeling chastened by Martha's words. As for what Gerda had finally uttered – it was as if she'd said, 'You're your own worst enemy, Bella.'

Maybe I am, thought Bella, watching her young assistant carefully arrange some hats in a drawer. I don't *have* to drive myself the way I do. The business is ticking over nicely and Uncle Saul isn't breathing down my neck for repayment of his loan.

'Which models do you intend putting in the window this week, Miss Minsky?' the girl enquired.

'I haven't decided, Amelia.'

'Would you mind if I made a suggestion?'

'Go ahead.'

'Why don't we have a black and white display? I was thinking about it over the weekend –'

'Oh, were you!' Bella said with a smile. For a kid of sixteen, Amelia wasn't short of smart ideas. 'How many black and white models have we in stock?'

'I'll have a look –'

'I happen to know that we only have two, Amelia, and I'm surprised that you didn't. One of your jobs is to check the stock.'

Bella added when the girl looked crestfallen, 'It was a good suggestion, though, and one that tells me you're interested in the business. That's something I value, Amelia. So don't go volunteering for the Services the minute you're old enough!' she joked.

'I wouldn't leave you unless I had to, Miss Minsky.'

Though Bella could not have known it, she was always to have that effect upon her employees, an asset more valuable than she could then have realized. Her combination of firmness and encouragement was doubtless responsible. But there was about her too a quality that inspired loyalty.

Meanwhile she allowed Amelia to dress the shop window under her supervision, noting the girl's enthusiasm, and the carefree manner in which she chatted of this and that. Was I like that at her age? It seemed too long ago to remember. But Bella's enthusiasm nowadays was born of necessity. And how can I possibly be carefree? she thought when a phone call from Ezra interrupted her musing.

'Was it a nice weekend, Bella?'

'I always enjoy visiting the twins and Gerda, and Gran had a lovely time. How was *your* weekend?' Bella enquired.

'Terrible! My parents had a real ding-dong.'

'Your father is incapable of that,' Bella answered.

'Not any more, it seems! He came out of his shell and told my mother he's giving the house to me and taking her to live in a rented flat in Blackpool.'

'Can he afford to give up his business?'

'He doesn't intend to, he'll travel back and forth, he says, like another optician he knows has been doing for years. Say something, Bella,' Ezra demanded after a pause.

'I can't. I'm too stunned.'

'So was I,' Ezra told her. 'But when I came to, I began to see what this means for *us*. Dad's always been sympathetic about the position we're in, Bella. I think he wants to make things easier for us and so he has. Even by taking my mother where she can't get at us!

'We'll have a home big enough to accommodate the twins and your grandmother,' he went on. 'It would have been years before I could have bought a house that size, in that district.'

'But there's always been room for you in my home,' Bella responded.

'And how would it have looked – me moving in behind the shop with you and your family?'

'There's a strong streak of your mother in you, Ezra,' Bella said icily, 'and I've just learned the true reason for our lengthy courtship.'

'In the meantime,' he retorted, 'that Canadian Romeo is living in your home! Well, you're now going to have to choose between us.'

'Choice doesn't enter into it,' Bella replied. 'Even if I'd never met Hal Diamond, I should now know that I can't marry *you*.'

The end of Bella's courtship was as if a weight had been lifted from her.

Her grandmother kept her thoughts to herself until she heard Bella humming a tune while watering the aspidistra.

'I gave that plant a drink yesterday. And if your cheerfulness is anything to go by, you ought to've broken it off with Ezra a long time ago. Why didn't you, if that was how you felt about him?'

Bella fingered one of the plant's shiny leaves. All she'd told Gran was that she had decided that Ezra wasn't the right man for her. But you used what he said on the phone as an excuse to break it off, didn't you, Bella? Grasped it with both hands.

'It wasn't how I felt about him, Gran, but how I *didn't* feel about him. There was always something missing.'

Gran went on dusting the parlour furniture, her habitual Sunday morning task. 'Something that's liable to go missing from the happiest of marriages,' she declared, 'when the couple comes down to earth.'

'But if it isn't there to start off with,' said Bella, 'I'd never know what being in love is like.'

'Is that so?' said Gran.

'Why are you looking at me like that?'

'I'd have to be blind, deaf and dumb, Bella, not to have noticed what's going on with you and Hal.'

'Nothing is going on.'

'Is that so?'

'Will you please stop saying that!'

'You were never able to fool me, Bella, and you're blushing as if you were still a schoolgirl. There has to be a reason and I don't need telling what it is.'

Gran sat down on the piano stool and gazed into space. 'I was madly in love myself once. But it wasn't your grandfather. It was before I was introduced to him. In my day, in Russia, Jewish girls had their husbands chosen for them by their parents —'

'Didn't they even supply you with a few different boys to choose from?'

Gran shook her head. 'Your grandfather came from a different village and we only met once before our wedding day.'

'That's terrible!' Bella exclaimed.

'I thought so myself,' said Gran, 'and perhaps he did, too. We never discussed it.'

'What sort of man was he?' asked Bella. He had died long before her birth, and Joey was named after him.

'Quiet, like your dad was,' Gran told her. 'Kind and considerate, as well. When God took him from me, I thanked Him for giving me a good husband though I didn't have him for long.'

'And what was the boy you were in love with like?'

Gran smiled. 'The sort they call "the life and soul of the party". My parents would never have picked *him* for one of their daughters. He used to play the violin at weddings and make eyes at the bride,' she added wryly.

'I heard, after I'd left the village for your granddad's, that he'd married a baker's widow from Kiev and gone to live over her shop. He wouldn't have gone short of women to make eyes at in a bakery!'

'But his wife,' said Bella, 'would soon have put a stop to that.'

'I wish her luck,' said Gran. 'It's a long time since I've

110

thought of him, Bella, and how I see it now is – well, there are some men who are like that and they'll never change.' Gran paused before adding, 'I think Hal's that sort.'

Bella, too.

'If I'd realized before he came to live here that you were already falling for him, I would never have suggested it.'

'You're warning me, aren't you, Gran?'

'And you're a sensible girl.'

In every respect but the one that matters.

Chapter Eighteen

BY THE TIME Hal asked Bella to marry him she was pregnant.

They had become lovers on the night Hal returned from his course, Bella casting convention aside, fired by the passion of which she had once not thought herself capable.

Whatever comes or goes, I'll have this to remember, she had thought while his sensuous mouth devoured her and she shamelessly allowed it. Nor, as night after night they made love in his room above the millinery shop, did she let herself think of the future.

Hal's eventual proposal was humorously couched and some-what self-deprecating. 'Could you bear to have me around permanently, Bella?'

They had just eaten Sunday lunch and he had settled Gran in a deckchair in the back yard, while he and Bella dealt with the dishes.

'You're very domesticated,' she stalled. Though the moment she'd hoped for was here, the problem that followed in its wake would have to be faced.

She then learned that there would not be one.

'If you'll marry me, I'll forget about going back to Canada after the war,' Hal said. 'We'll all live happily ever after behind the shop.'

Bella felt like whooping with joy though she was gripped by emotion.

Hal dried a saucepan and hung it above the cooker with its companions. 'I'd miss my own country, Bella, but there's no one I care about there.' His expression briefly shadowed. 'Not any more.'

How could Bella be in love with a man she knew so little about? She stemmed her misgivings. He had told her in their intimate moments that he'd never known true happiness until now and that was enough.

'Will you have me, Bella?'

After she had said that she would, she shared her secret with him.

Hal's reaction was, 'Sit down and put your feet up.'

'That isn't necessary at this stage!' Bella said with a laugh. 'But I now have an idea of the fusspot husband you're going to be –'

'How long have you known you're pregnant?'

'Long enough to be getting morning sickness.'

Hal enfolded her in his arms. 'Why didn't you tell me?'

'And have you think I'd trapped you into marrying me?'

Hal said after kissing her tenderly, 'But you couldn't have hidden your condition from me much longer. Nor from Gran!'

They glanced through the window to where the old lady was enjoying the July sunshine, beside her the sweet-scented flowers she had planted in a barrel, and the rest of the yard a repository for empty cartons from the shops not yet collected for wartime salvage.

'One day,' said Bella, 'Gran will have a real garden to sit in.'

'Meanwhile, though,' said Hal, 'I suggest we try to avoid her finding out what you kept from me. What would you say to a quick wedding?'

'Yes, please and not just for that reason.'

They were married by special licence the following Sunday, the rabbi assuming as older people did that in wartime young men in uniform couldn't wait and their girls required no persuading.

Gran had said no more about Bella's being sensible. Instead it was as if, having warned her granddaughter, she had accepted the inevitable.

Gerda kept Bella company in the synagogue ante-room where brides awaited their bridegrooms for the traditional lowering of the wedding veil before the ceremony.

It was their first opportunity for a private word since Bella rang up the farm to deliver her news and Gerda said now, 'I'm still finding this hard to believe!'

'That for once in my life I'm playing things by ear, like you do? The answer, Gerda, is I've fallen in love and for the moment nothing else matters. You look beautiful in that green frock, by the way –'

'Martha gave me all her clothing coupons so I could buy it, or I'd have had to wear my shirt and jodhpurs! But "beautiful" is the word reserved for the bride on her wedding day and it's the right one for you, Bella.'

Bella eyed her own reflection in the mirror provided to put the finishing touches to her appearance and saw a tall slender young woman simply clad in beige, her sole adornment the tea rose anchoring the veiling to her hat.

'Beautiful I've never been,' she said drily, 'but there does seem to be a glow about me today.'

'There'll be even more of a glow about you tomorrow,' Gerda said with a wink.

'Tomorrow I'll be back in the shop!'

Chapter Nineteen

WHEN EZRA'S ENGAGEMENT to Doreen was announced in the *Jewish Chronicle*, Bella privately wished him the undiluted joy her marriage was. Bella sometimes felt like pinching herself to make sure she wasn't dreaming that all had come right for her.

That idyllic quality came to an abrupt end when she fell off the haberdashery stool while reaching down a box and that evening lost the baby she was carrying.

From Gran she received a lecture instead of sympathy. 'If you'd rested after you fell, you might not have miscarried.'

'I've a business to run,' Bella replied from the depths of her misery. 'I can't shut up shop and pamper myself.'

'Which would you rather lose, Bella? A child, or a bit of trade?'

'That isn't a fair question. Would you mind fixing my pillows, Gran. My back is aching and I'm weak as a kitten.'

Gran said while doing so, 'But that wouldn't stop you from working tomorrow, would it, if the doctor would let you. I'm beginning to think I should have warned Hal about *you*, before he burned *his* boats, instead of the other way round! He'll be up to keep you company after he's seen the doctor out – and more fool him!'

Left to digest her grandmother's words, Bella lay gazing at the ceiling. Would Hal be as hard on her? The baby she'd lost was his, too, and they had not yet had time alone together.

When he joined her she wept in his arms and he stroked her hair. 'I won't climb on stools the next time,' she promised him.

Bella dried her eyes and sipped the tea he had brought her. Hal's expression seemed unreadable. 'What are you thinking?'

'That the next time shouldn't be too soon.'

'Did the doctor say that?'

'No.'

'Then why are *you* saying it?'

'Your business is just taking off, isn't it?'

'And you think I'm putting that first.'

Bella added after a silence, 'If you'd worked like I have, Hal, you might see things differently.'

'Is that some kind of crack?'

There was now a glint in her husband's eyes that she had not seen there before. 'No,' she replied, 'it's a statement of fact.'

'Including that unlike you I'm not an achiever.'

How can this be happening? Bella asked herself. I love him and he loves me, but suddenly it was as if a wall of glass had arisen between them.

'There's still time for you to be one,' she said. 'How would you fancy working with me, after the war?'

'*For* you, you mean.'

'I said *with* me.'

Again Hal's expression was unfathomable.

'Did you ring up Gerda yet?' Bella asked him. 'If she can't get leave to stand in for me while I'm out of action –'

'I did and she was upset to hear you'd miscarried.'

'But can she come?'

'She said she'd call back. Now try to get some sleep.'

Hal took the cup and saucer from her, kissed her cheek, and left the room.

Sleep? With all Bella had on her mind? Yesterday she hadn't known that the business was coming between her and Hal. But she knew now.

Gerda arrived the next day with a bouquet of chrysanthemums, and butter and cream from the farmer's wife.

'I appreciate the Dawsons sparing you at harvest time,' said Bella after Gerda had embraced her.

'With those two, *people* always come first,' Gerda replied.

'This time of year is busy for me, too,' Bella said, 'it's when my Jewish customers buy new hats to wear for Rosh Hashanah –'

'As my mother and her friends did in Vienna,' Gerda cut in. 'You'll never change, will you, Bella? When Hal rang up to give me your message, I thought, How can Bella be thinking of business when she's just lost her baby?'

'If I told you my heart is aching would you believe me?'

'I'm sure it is, but you're not lying here wringing your hands.'

'It wouldn't bring the baby back.'

'Not only do you fall with your bottom in butter,' said Gerda, 'you're very good at picking yourself up.'

'I've had to be,' Bella answered, 'and since a fall brought on my miscarriage, you might have spared me that tasteless remark. Thank you, though, for rushing to my side when I need you.'

'You gave me a home when I needed one.'

'For which you've repaid me by designing the hats.'

'But you'd have got where you are now without me,' Gerda declared. 'You're that sort of person, Bella. It isn't just the need to support the twins and your grandmother that's driving you, though you might think so. What you're driven by is ambition and I'm sorry for Hal.'

'What has he been saying to you?'

'Nothing. He doesn't have to. I tried to tell you that day we had the chat in the farmyard. When there was still only yourself to consider. But you're now a married woman and your husband must feel he's married to a dynamo –'

'This is all I need!' Bella exclaimed. 'I thought you'd come to my rescue, Gerda –'

'I have and you can instruct me about the shops in a minute. I happen to think that what we're discussing is more important. If you go on as you are doing, Bella, you could soon find your marriage *beyond* rescue. The twins sent you their love, by the way.'

'Their love will never be by the way to me.'

'And *I* wouldn't be your friend if I didn't speak my mind.'

Chapter Twenty

THOUGH BELLA could not metamorphose from the person she was into the one others would prefer her to be, there were times when she was conscience-stricken on her husband's account. Times, too, when she felt as if she were *two* people. The loving wife and the businesswoman forging ahead.

Hal had said no more since the confrontation that followed her miscarriage and she was now pregnant again. More than a year had since slipped by, but only when their shared passion blotted it out was Bella able to fool herself that the barrier that had arisen between them was not still there.

In the interim, her impulsive friend Connie had joined the ATS, to get away from home.

'So how's married life?' Connie quipped when she returned on leave.

'Married life,' said Bella, 'isn't a joke.'

'Well, the question certainly didn't raise a smile from you! Any chance of us having a night out together while I'm home?' Connie asked. 'Would Hal mind?'

'I don't have time for nights out,' Bella answered, 'and I'm sure you don't go short of them where you're stationed.'

Connie had dropped in to the shop unannounced and was seated on the stool in the haberdashery, admiring her khaki-clad legs. 'On duty I have to wear horrible thick stockings – only officers are allowed to wear silk ones. I got these from a GI who got them from one of the WAACs at his camp – I didn't enquire how!'

'You're having the time of your life in the ATS, aren't you?' Bella answered while tidying the counter. 'And you've chosen the wrong day to visit me. My assistant's got flu and Gran will have to help out if I get customers in both shops at once.'

'You're married, but nothing has really changed for you,' said Connie. 'For me, though – well, sure I'm having a good time. But where I'm stationed, it's as if something is hovering over us. Everywhere you look there are American tanks and jeeps and nobody has to tell us it's in readiness for the Second Front.

'It isn't until you see with your own eyes all that equipment,' Connie went on, 'that you realize that when the Allies *do* invade, the lads you're dancing with tonight could be maimed or dead this time next week –'

Connie collected herself and said drily, 'But I shouldn't be depressing a mother-to-be! Any news of your cousin Walter?'

'Only that Crete was where he went missing. If Uncle Saul didn't have his business to think of . . . '

'And how's business with you?'

'I'm thinking of opening another shop.'

'Have you told Hal yet?'

'No, as a matter of fact.'

'That doesn't surprise me,' said Connie, 'but when you do, I'd be interested to know how he reacts.'

'He won't try to stop me,' Bella predicted, 'he just lets me get on with things.'

'That's very nice for you in one way,' Connie replied, 'but in another – well, what kind of man is that?'

The entrance of a customer in the millinery shop saved Bella from having to reply. Connie's question was one to which she herself was seeking the answer.

When I let myself think about it, she reflected that evening while standing in a queue at Salford Bus Station, her ankles swollen from being on her feet all day, the December sleet dampening her coat, and guilt that she was not taking care of herself suddenly assailing her.

Guilt on Hal's account, too. She had left him to spend the evening alone while she pursued business matters that could not be dealt with during the day, since she could not leave the shops.

Why should I have to feel guilty about that, though! That wouldn't be how a business*man* would be feeling. But for me – well, Gran had summed it up the first time she compared Bella with the founders of Marks and Spencer: 'You've a handicap they didn't have, you're a woman.'

And the handicap isn't just biological, Bella thought now. Which wife would make her husband feel he was neglecting her because he wanted to get ahead and did what he had to do? Though Hal had never put it into words, Bella could not have been unaware that he saw himself as taking second place.

She had told him over supper of her plan to open another shop, his reaction as passive as she had come to expect, nor did he raise any objection to her going to view a property this evening.

She was now on her way back from doing so, part of her despite her personal misery bristling with excitement – the shop could not be more ideally situated, between a hair-dresser's and a pharmacy in a wealthy suburb on the south side of town.

The opportunity had to be grasped, but Hal would not share her elation. Instead he would give her another of the smiles that masked his private thoughts.

Not only was her husband's Canadian background still a mystery, so was Hal himself.

Bella felt herself being jostled forward in the bus queue, the odour of damp clothing all around her and her shoulders aching from carrying the bag of millinery materials she had yet to deliver to one of her outworkers. Bella didn't allow those middle-aged and elderly women to cart heavy packages back and forth.

Tonight, though, she felt chilled to her bones. And again guilt was gripping her. Gran always retired early and this wasn't the first time Hal must make do with his own company. She would put off delivering the stuff till tomorrow and go directly home, give her husband a pleasant surprise.

A surprise of another kind awaited Bella. Music was drifting from the kitchen as she made her way there from the shop and the smile died on her face when she opened the door.

Silhouetted in the firelight was a frozen tableau that could be entitled 'Caught in the Act'. Gerda on the hearthrug, breasts spilled forth from her unbuttoned blouse and Hal straddling her.

Bella switched on the light and wanted to avert her eyes, but did not allow them the dignity of scrambling to their feet and fixing their clothing unwatched.

'We weren't expecting you back for a while and I guess we had too much to drink,' said Hal.

Unnecessarily on both counts. His speech was slurred and Gerda had begun giggling. On the table was a bottle of Vat 69, the two glasses beside it heightening the aura of intimacy.

'I haven't seen that brand of whisky before,' Bella remarked. How could her mind be functioning when the rest of her was numb?

'It's hard to get,' Gerda said through her giggles.

'Which can't be said of you. Do the GIs pay you with liquor, as well as with cigarettes? And would one of you mind switching the wireless off?'

Hal obliged and sat down on the sofa.

'Bella never did like Henry Hall and the BBC Dance Orchestra,' Gerda spluttered as if it were a huge joke.

'But their signature tune is "Here's to the Next Time",' said Bella, 'and what could be more fitting for *you*?'

'Don't be horrid to me on my birthday,' Gerda pouted. 'I wanted to celebrate it with you, so I hopped on a train though you forgot to send me a card.'

'She didn't,' said Hal, '*I* forgot to mail it.'

'Then I apologize to Bella. For everything. Bella must forgive us for what the whisky did.'

'I don't hear my husband asking my forgiveness.'

'Would there be any point?'

'No, as a matter of fact.'

'Don't be silly,' said Gerda.

'It's you who's been silly,' Bella replied. 'If you hadn't proved yourself unworthy, I'd have taken you into my business after the war and made you a partner.'

'Only Bella,' Gerda said to Hal, 'could bring business into this.'

Bella felt the first stirring of the child in her womb as she gazed with contempt at the man who had fathered it and the girl she had thought her friend.

'Get out of my life,' she said to them, 'I never want to see either of you again.'

PART TWO

1950 . . .

Chapter One

SEATED WITH HER FAMILY at the supper table on a Sabbath Eve in the autumn of 1950, Bella was assailed by déjà vu.

Her daughter's rapt expression while Gran lit the candles had reminded Bella of Sylvie at that age, and her son was sitting where Joey used to sit.

'Like history repeating itself, isn't it?' said Gran divining Bella's thoughts. She watched the children spooning their chicken soup and added her favourite cliché. 'Oh, how time flies!'

And here I am, Bella reflected, destined to raise another set of twins on my own. If I'd known on the night I prefer to forget that I was carrying two babies, would I have booted their father out? Or been impelled to swallow my pain and my pride?

Since that question was now purely academic, Bella brushed it aside as she did her erosive yearning for the man who had let her down. She had not heard from Hal since he passed her on the stairs without a word after packing his kitbag, the slamming of the door a moment later lending finality to what she had steeled herself to do.

Gerda had not bothered to wait for him, but had fled immediately, shame written on her face. Nor had her subsequent pleas softened Bella's attitude. Instead, it was Gerda whom Bella blamed, her mind returning to the Viennese girl in school uniform, who even then had exuded the sexuality that had cut short Bella's marriage.

Gran interrupted her thoughts. 'I wasn't just referring

to twins running in our family, when I mentioned history repeating itself. What I meant –'

'I know what you meant, Gran. But little piggies have big ears.' Bella glanced at the children who were listening with interest. 'Finish your soup, Leonard. You, too, Edith.'

She had called them after her dead parents, and Edith bore a strong resemblance to her namesake, fresh-complexioned and dainty. Leonard was the image of his own father. Even at the age of five, thought Bella, there's something about his smile that tells me he'll be a devil with the girls when he grows up.

'Uncle Joey said he'd send me a picture postcard from Oxford,' the little boy said.

'And Auntie Sylvie told me I could go to London to see her,' said his sister.

'We'll all go to visit them,' Bella promised.

'If you can spare the time from business!' said Gran.

'For this I shall *make* time,' Bella declared.

'And for your own sake, so you should,' Gran replied. 'Would either of them be where they now are if it weren't for you? You deserve the pleasure of them showing you round the colleges they're at.'

Briefly, Bella's expression had lit with pride, and why wouldn't it? thought Gran. It wasn't just how she had scrimped and saved to give her brother and sister their chance, or how she'd sacrificed her *own* chance of being what she wanted to be. It was how she had put her whole heart into her hopes for them.

When Joey got a scholarship to Oxford, and Sylvie to the Royal Academy of Dramatic Art, though Gran was pleased for them, she was overjoyed for Bella. How many rewards of the kind that really matter has my elder granddaughter had? Instead, Bella had experienced let-downs that were enough to stop her from believing in anyone ever again.

Meanwhile, though Gran couldn't see Joey not appreciating all Bella had done for him, she wasn't too sure about Sylvie – nor any too pleased on her own account to have a granddaughter who's going on the stage! When word got around, the other ladies would be tut-tutting about it at the Sabbath morning service.

Bella cleared the soup plates from the table and went to help Gran dish up the next course. 'We'll visit Joey and Sylvie before I open my next shop.'

'And when will that be, Bella? You've just forked out money to buy a motor car!'

'A second-hand one.'

Gran said while carving the chicken, 'I still can't believe who taught you to drive it.'

'Ezra doesn't hold the past against me, Gran, or he wouldn't have agreed to be my accountant again, after he was de-mobbed. He's a happily married man now.'

Gran kept her doubts in that respect to herself.

'Ezra was always a good friend to me,' Bella went on, 'and he still is.'

'And it's you who needs reminding of the size of little piggies' ears,' said Gran.

Again the children were listening intently.

'Did Sally Black's daddy really teach you to drive, Mummy?' Edith asked.

'And don't you think it was kind of him to offer?' Bella said with a smile.

'But if you run the car into a lamppost, like I thought you were going to the day after you passed your driving test, it will be Sally's dad's fault,' said Leonard, 'and I'll tell Sally that.'

'I'd rather you didn't, Leonard,' said Edith, 'Sally's my best friend and I don't want her to be upset.'

Bella had forgotten that Ezra's child was in the same class at infants' school as her children. Nor was she sure that Ezra's wife knew about the driving lessons he had volunteered when she bought the ancient Vauxhall.

Though Doreen was never less than pleasant to Bella when they encountered each other, she had yet to invite her to her home. As if, thought Bella now, she sees me as a threat because I haven't a husband – and Ezra has to play down his friendship with me.

'Can I invite Sally for tea on Sunday?' Edith asked.

'Of course,' said Bella.

'Can I tell her to bring her tricycle?'

'Why not?'

'She's got a doll's-house, too,' Edith prattled on, 'and a swing in her garden that her grandparents in London bought for her. When I went to her house, I had a lovely time –'

'That's why she's your best friend, isn't it?' said Leonard.

'No, it is not!'

'I wouldn't go to play at Edwin's house if he didn't have a train set,' said Leonard.

'Then you'd better not do so again,' Bella interceded sharply. There were tears in her gentle daughter's eyes.

'I like Sally,' said Edith.

'Well I don't,' said Leonard, 'she's a horrid fat girl, like Edwin's a horrid fat boy.'

'We don't choose our friends according to what they have, or haven't,' Bella informed her son. 'And looks don't matter, Leonard. It's the person inside who does and I think Sally and Edwin are lovely children.'

Leonard's response was, 'I wish I had a granddad to buy me a train set.'

Bella stopped herself from revealing that the twins had a grandfather in Canada. If she told them, they would pepper her with questions she was unable to answer.

While the meal progressed, Edith subdued as always after a tiff with her brother, and he sulking, Bella reflected that in some ways her own position was similar to Connie's. Her friend had predictably been a GI-bride. Connie's disillusion, though, was effected on the other side of the Atlantic, where she had chosen to remain with her child when her marriage, as she had put it in a letter, 'hit the rocks'.

So enthusiastically Americanized did Connie now seem, Bella would have been surprised had she returned to England and her situation differed from Bella's in two important respects. She did not have to earn her living, since her husband was supporting her and her little boy, and the child had contact with his father.

Though Hal was still legally tied to Bella, and had known she was pregnant when they separated, he had not offered financial support. Nor had Bella contacted the Canadian authorities in that respect. She would do nothing to help him establish a parental right over the twins.

'Go on with what you were saying about opening another shop,' Gran said while they ate the lokshen pudding she had served for dessert. Why did I let myself hope that with another set of kids to bring up, Bella would settle for what she now has? It isn't in her to stand still. It never was.

Bella watched the innocent cause of her lost business opportunity in 1944 begin eating their pudding. Determined though she then was to go ahead with her plans, learning of her twin pregnancy had put paid to it, reminding her yet again of the biological handicap inherent in being a business-*woman*.

Whence would come the designs for the hats in the shop she already had, she had not immediately considered, too disheartened to prod herself from the despondency into which she had descended.

It was her young assistant, Amelia, who had prodded her out of it. 'I'm sorry to hear that Gerda can't work for you any more, Mrs Diamond, but our stock is running low and Easter bonnet time won't be long in coming. Why don't you design the hats yourself, like some of the milliners up the road do?'

That was the day when Bella decided to revert to her single name, though her children would bear their father's, she recalled, reliving her conversation with Amelia. After I'd told her that Hal and I had split up and she tried to hide her distress on my account.

If the girl had put two and two together about Gerda's coincidental disappearance from the scene, she had hidden that, too, showing only her concern about who would now design the hats and eventually making the suggestion she had.

'From now on, I shall be known as Miss Minsky again,' Bella had said, while Amelia averted her eyes from the bulge under her frock. 'But you can call me Bella, like the customers do.'

'Can I really?'

'Why not? We're friends, aren't we?' And there's more integrity in this ordinary girl than in Gerda's sort for all her talk of being my friend, Bella had thought.

'As for me designing hats, though,' she had gone on, 'the milliners you mentioned aren't just shopkeepers, Amelia.'

'Nor are you.'

'If that's a compliment, thanks. But unlike them, I'm not trained to make hats.'

'That doesn't mean you couldn't put your ideas on paper,' Amelia persisted. 'Your drawings wouldn't have to be perfect and you could write notes at the side –'

'Saying: That fuzz at the side is supposed to be a feather? Or that where I've put the bow is the back, not the front?' Bella answered with a smile.

'As long as the outworkers understand, what would that matter?' said Amelia. 'Gerda once told me that it's the ideas, not the sketches, that count and that was the hardest part for her. Coming up with them, I mean.'

Would it be any less difficult for Bella? More so, perhaps. But she wouldn't let the departure of that treacherous little bitch beat her!

The next day she had begun visualizing hats to enhance the current garment fashion, setting them on paper however roughly, and she had never looked back.

Now, her children were of an age when she was again able to step forward. Though war work had claimed Amelia when she reached the age to register, she had afterwards returned to 'Bella's' and would be trusted to manage the shop while Bella herself built up a clientele on the south side of the city.

Six years late, but without a man to prick my conscience

and slow me down, Bella thought, and by chance the premises she had viewed that wintry evening were again vacant.

'Who says opportunity never knocks twice!' she said after telling her grandmother.

'But who would have run the store you've already got, if you'd branched out then?' Gran wanted to know.

'You still think of "Bella's" as Minsky's millinery department, don't you?' Bella said with a laugh. 'As for what you just asked, I hadn't got around to working it out.'

'But like I once said, if there isn't a way you'll invent one!'

'If you're not inventive in business, Gran, you don't stand a chance.'

'When you open your new place, I'll keep an eye on the haberdashery, if you like,' Gran said casually.

Too casually. Bella had always known why her grandmother referred to 'Bella's' as Minsky's millinery department. Gran's as sentimental about the business my dad began on a shoe-string as I am. And right if she thinks I'm neglecting it.

'I'd be pleased if you did,' Bella replied, 'and I'll employ an assistant, don't worry.'

'The worrying I leave to you!'

'We've finished our pudding. Are we getting another dessert, too, like always on Friday nights?' said Leonard.

While Gran peeled a pear for Edith, Bella fetched from the refrigerator the jelly she had made for Leonard.

'This lad and his fads,' said Gran.

'It isn't my fault if I don't like fruit. Edith doesn't like jelly.'

'But her not liking jelly doesn't put your mother to extra trouble,' Gran told him, 'and it's time she stopped pandering to you, Leonard.'

'He always gets the chicken wings and I have to have the legs, but I don't mind,' Edith put in.

Bella tried not to notice the smile on her son's face, though 'smug' was the word for it. Is it Leonard's fault that I absolutely adore him? It was neither child's fault that they didn't have a daddy, but Edith seemed less in need of compensating, as Sylvie had when she and Joey were orphaned. The special place Joey had in Bella's heart was created long before illness struck him, evoked by the vulnerability she had detected in him.

And Leonard has only to look at me appealingly and I give in. The lecture she'd given him this evening was rare indeed.

'I'd rather have raspberry jelly than strawberry,' the little boy said.

'And I'm sure your mother will remember that!' Gran exclaimed. 'Like she reminds me every Friday, as if I didn't know, that you won't eat chopped liver with onions in it. There was none of this nonsense when she was little,' Gran went on, 'nor her brother and sister. If they didn't like something with onions in it, a portion without onions wasn't made specially for them.'

Bella said stiffly, 'If you'd like me to deal with the chopped liver in future, I will.'

'It isn't the trouble I'm put to, Bella. When did I ever mind that for my family? – though I mind *you* being put to it, with all you have to do.'

Gran waited until the children had consumed their extra dessert and gone to look at their picture books, beside the hearth, before lowering her voice and continuing her homily. 'That lad has you in the palm of his hand, Bella, and it'll be your fault if he grows up thinking the world revolves around him.'

'Thank you for telling me!'

'When, if ever, shall you come to your senses, Bella? Give your attention to what really matters? Instead of being driven by ambition.'

'That's the word Gerda used about me!' Bella flashed. 'And it seems you don't understand me any better than she did –'

Gran surveyed the striking woman of thirty her grand-daughter now was, the streak of silver in her hair telling its own tale, and wondered how long it would take her to fully understand *herself*.

134

Chapter Two

'THERE'S A TELEGRAM-BOY getting off his bike outside the shop,' Amelia observed while she and Bella were selecting hats for the window display.

Bella put down the floppy, ruched velvet beret she had just picked up. The 'New Look' inspired by Dior at the end of the forties had been superseded by voluminous coats which her hat designs must enhance.

'I hope he isn't bringing you bad news,' said Amelia.

Even in peacetime, the sight of a uniformed lad bearing a yellow envelope was not associated with glad tidings. While the boy stood cheerfully whistling and Bella's fingers fumbled to open the envelope, her imagination centred as always on her brother. Joey's overcoming his disability to the extent he had seemed too good to be true –

The boy watched her read the telegram. 'Any reply?'

'No. I'll reply by phone.'

Amelia noted her dazed expression. 'Is it all right for me to give him a threepenny-bit from the till?'

'Please do.'

Bella collected herself and said when the boy had departed with his tip, 'I shall have to go to London, Amelia.'

'How long for?'

'I don't know.'

Bella's imaginings could not have stretched to the message she had received: 'Your husband is with me and ill. Sylvie.'

Hal wasn't in Canada as she had supposed. Instead, he was with her sister. A twofold shock for Bella. And why had Sylvie sent a telegram when she could have rung up?

A question that did not remain puzzling for long, though Hal's being with Sylvie still was. When Bella went to ring up Sylvie, she found that her own telephone was dead. Since this was Monday morning and she had not made any calls over the weekend, Sylvie could have been trying to reach her for a couple of days.

Bella hastened to the nearest call box, reported that her line was out of order, and tried to get through to the pay-phone in the house Sylvie shared with other drama students. As usual, the number was engaged.

Though Sylvie had not worded the telegram as a summons, its urgency was implicit. As was Bella's need to know what was going on! – and how it had come about. Sylvie was still a schoolgirl evacuee when Bella's marriage broke up and she hardly knew Hal; it wasn't possible that he had kept in touch with her. But she was now the headstrong young woman Bella had long ago sensed that one day she would be.

Bella showed the telegram to her grandmother and left her to digest it while she went to pack a bag.

'I wouldn't have expected you to leave the business and rush to Hal's side,' Gran said when Bella returned downstairs and was putting on her coat. 'Isn't tomorrow the day you sign the lease for your new shop?'

'I'll phone Ezra from the station and ask him to get it held over until I get back.'

'Good old Ezra,' said Gran cryptically.

Bella was checking that she had enough money for the train ticket and paused to look at her grandmother. 'What was that supposed to mean?'

'Ezra's always there when you need him, isn't he?'

'He's a nice man.'

'But you didn't appreciate him when you should have.'

Bella snapped her handbag shut. 'I don't live in the past, Gran, where would it get me! And it isn't Hal's side I'm rushing to, it's Sylvie's.'

*

136

Bella had expected her second visit to London to be as exciting as the trip she recalled from her childhood. She had looked forward to showing her children the sights, as her parents had shown them to her, and Bond Street would now have been a feast for her adult eyes.

Instead, she was trudging alone up the grimy incline from the platform at Euston Station and beset by anxiety. Briefly, too, her confidence had deserted her. Scared to travel by Tube in case you get lost? she chided herself in the taxi queue. You consider yourself an independent woman. But that's in your home town. Once you step out into the wider world, you're a lot less sure of yourself.

If Mr Marks – or was it Mr Spencer! – had been like you, he'd have got no further than the penny bazaar Gran once mentioned, Bella's introspection continued when she was finally seated in a cab and on her way to West Kensington, the hubbub of the capital on a working day all around her and fumes from the heavy traffic drifting to her nostrils.

She wouldn't like to drive a car in London! And how difficult it would be to start at the bottom and make your name here, in this vast city with its thronged pavements and an atmosphere of everyone hurrying to wherever they were going.

Is that what you're after, Bella asked herself, making your name up north? Not exactly. But the clientele she hoped to attract to her new shop included the sort of women whose pictures you saw in *Cheshire Life*, to whom the label was as important as the hat.

Bella gave her mind to this while her eye took in the wartime damage visible here and there, the streets that seemed an endless stretch of plate glass windows, and others whose architecture had remained a testament to the past.

She did not waste time contemplating what she would find on her arrival at Sylvie's bedsitter, her capacity to live her life on two levels enabling her to muse on a business matter en route to a situation that would surely have rendered most women incapable of coherent thought.

By the time the taxi reached Kensington High Street, she had decided that an imposing 'B' would be her label. Black on white, and the label made of silk to enhance the model hat image.

'Comin' to live in bedsit land, love?' the driver asked when they had arrived at her destination and Bella was paying him.

'No, I'm just visiting.' *One* way of putting it!

The blue-jowled man gazed regretfully at the dingy façade of a once well-kept terrace. 'These used to be 'omes for the gentry, but things've changed since the war and it 'asn't taken long!'

Bella glanced at the house in which her sister lived. Its brass doorknob looked as if it hadn't been polished since war was declared. The windows could do with cleaning, too. 'It would take several servants to keep one of these houses the way it should be,' she remarked.

'And nobody wants to be one any more,' said the driver. 'Everyone wants to better theirself.'

Bella then found herself a captive audience while the driver enlarged on his theme.

'They didn't turn up their noses once,' he said with feeling while handing Bella some change, 'pickin' and choosin' about 'ow they earn their livin'! But while the war was on, everyone pulled together. We 'ad to beat the Jerries 'n' the Japs, didn't we?

'It's them who'll be pullin' together now, though, to get back on their feet, and the Japs'll soon be up to their old tricks,' he declared with disgust, 'cornerin' the market with cheap goods. The victor could end up the vanquished!'

Bella watched the taxi hurtle down the street as if propelled by the driver's wrath. She turned to survey the house. Was Sylvie's bedsitter the one with knickers and stockings drying on a hanger suspended from the window? If so, Gran would have a fit, though it wouldn't surprise Bella. A girl who could grow so far from her roots as to want to be an actress was liable to discard other aspects of her conditioning.

But why am I standing here? Putting off the moment when I'll see Hal. Bella steeled herself for the encounter, mounted the flaking stone steps, and pressed the bell beside a card on which was printed her sister's name.

A buzz preceded the opening of the door. She stepped inside and saw Sylvie standing at the head of the stairs.

'Am I glad to see you, Bella! I've had the most terrible time –'

'I'm here now, love, and you can tell me all about it. Don't bother coming down. I'll come up.'

'There isn't much to tell,' Sylvie said when Bella joined her on the landing and they had hugged each other. 'Just that I ran into Hal in the West End and you wouldn't believe what he was doing –'

Oh yes I would and there was probably a woman hanging on his arm.

'He was selling shoe-laces in the street.'

‧ That *was* a shock.

Sylvie went on with her tale. ' "Can't you get a job?" I said to him, but he couldn't answer me for coughing. All he was able to do was give me the lovely smile I remembered from when I was a kid –'

Bella remembered it all too well.

'And I knew I couldn't just leave him there,' said Sylvie. 'He's still my brother-in-law, isn't he? And the father of my nephew and niece.'

Not to mention of my children, thought Bella.

'I hadn't realized your family feeling was that strong,' she said.

'Compared with yours, you mean?'

'What sort of crack is that?'

'It isn't a crack. But what *you* said was a reminder, wasn't it?'

'Of what?'

'Of everything you've done for me and I don't need reminding. As for my family feeling,' Sylvie harked back, 'what else but that would have impelled me to bring Hal home with me, instead of leaving him to the fate you probably think he deserves.'

'I wouldn't wish it on anyone to have to stand on the pavement selling shoe-laces.'

'Does that mean you'll consider taking Hal back? I promised him I'd try to persuade you to. He's still in love with you, Bella.'

'But what makes you think I'm still in love with *him*?'

'Well, you haven't replaced him, have you? Which could be because you're too wrapped up in your business – Gerda agrees.'

'She's still in touch with you?'

'But too busy to see me often. She works for a millinery manufacturer who's also her boyfriend.'

'How very convenient for her,' Bella said tersely, 'but I'm not here to discuss Gerda. Is there no place but this smelly landing where we can talk privately?' she added as the odour of boiled cabbage drifted from below.

'I'm afraid not and I must say my smartly dressed sister looks wrong for this setting,' Sylvie answered leaning against the drab wall, hands thrust in the pockets of her crumpled corduroy slacks, 'Drama students, though, don't dress conventionally.'

'Did I mention your clothes?'

'I can sense your disapproval a mile off, Bella, I always could and our lives are now poles apart, aren't they? Me doing what I'm doing and you still tucked away where you've always been.'

Sylvie appreciates all I've done for her, but only on a material level, thought Bella, or she couldn't have made that hurtful remark. But she was only five when you turned down your chance to go to Oxford and you didn't include in the bedtime stories you told the twins the one about the girl who wanted to be a scientist and became a businesswoman on her little brother's and sister's account.

'I haven't finished telling you about Hal,' said Sylvie. 'When I got him back here, he looked feverish and I put him to bed on my divan. I intended sleeping on the floor, but I was up all night putting cold compresses on his forehead and making him drink lots of tea, like Gran used to give us when we had a high temperature.'

'How long has he been here?'

'Since Saturday.'

'And how is he now?'

'He seems a little better. And how dispassionate *you* sound! More like a district nurse here to give him treatment than the woman who once shared a bed with him –'

'That's enough, Sylvie!'

'I just can't understand how you tick, Bella, and I never could. This morning Hal coughed up some blood,' Sylvie went on. 'That was when I decided to ring you up, but I couldn't get through. Your husband needs looking after –'

'And you think that's sufficient reason for me to take him back?'

Bella switched her gaze to a stained glass window through which wintry sunlight was adding an uncharacteristic halo to Sylvie's tangled black hair. Gone was the little girl with the neat pigtails, in her place the budding actress who seemed to think that living in London for a few months had endowed her with the wisdom to talk down to the woman who had raised her.

'The least you can do, Bella, is take a look at Hal. If you won't take responsibility, he'll have to go into a hospital. I'll call a doctor –'

'You ought to have done so, anyway.'

'When are you going to stop telling me what I ought to've done and what I ought to do!' Sylvie simmered down. 'Look – you could just take him back temporarily, couldn't you? Until he's recovered –'

'And how would that affect my children?' Bella asked quietly.

'I hadn't thought of that.'

'Then maybe you ought to.'

'There you go again!'

Sylvie stalked towards a door at the far end of the long landing. As she often had to her room in her childhood, Bella recalled while following her. Would that she were still playing with her doll, instead of with my life!

The doll had not been ejected from Sylvie's new life, Bella noted on entering her sister's bedsitter and could not but find the sight of Belinda, somewhat the worse for wear and propped on the mantelpiece, a poignant reminder of times past.

The same could not be said of Bella's reaction to seeing her husband. Hal was lying back against a mound of colourful cushions, on his face the smile that had led to her downfall.

'You're looking good,' he said surveying her.

'Compliments,' she replied, 'were always your style.'

'I didn't ask Sylvie to send for you.'

'Who else was there for her to send for?'

'That doesn't have to be your problem.'

'You're no longer my problem in any respect.'

But Bella's treacherous heart was telling her otherwise, her body, too. Whatever she had anticipated it wasn't this. That the unkempt man lying in her sister's bed was still capable of casting his spell over her.

'How are my kids?' he enquired.

'When did you learn of their existence?'

'I told him yesterday,' Sylvie interceded.

'It was a surprise to find out I had two,' said Hal, 'when I was expecting only one.'

'Physically,' said Bella, 'it was I to whom that word applied, but you didn't give a damn about me. Not then, or since.'

'Would you believe me if I said there hasn't been a day I haven't thought about you?'

'No.'

'That's what you said when I asked if you'd believe me if I begged your forgiveness.' Hal turned to Sylvie. 'Your sister is a hard woman.'

'I've had to be. But except for you,' said Bella, 'it was never my own survival I was fighting for. Now, my children enter into it. What sort of father would you be to them, if I took you back?'

Hal held her gaze. 'A better one than mine, in the ways that matter, was to me.'

'You make him sound like a monster.'

'That's a good description for a guy who neglects his wife and kids in order to become the tycoon my father is,' Hal answered. 'He was too busy to come to the hospital when my mother lay dying and ticked me off for leaving the office to sit with her.

'That was when I told him to train someone else to take over his business. I never went back to the office and if he saw me now, he'd say I'd got my just desserts.'

Bella had never before heard Hal speak with such intensity. And she had learned more about him from what he had just said than in the time they had lived as husband and wife.

You're *still* husband and wife, Bella, and like you, Hal is the product of his background, complete with scars though he didn't let you know they were hurting.

A paroxysm of coughing then gripped him and Bella went to mop his fevered brow and hold his hand. He was her children's father and, heaven help her, the man she hadn't stopped wanting.

'I can't take Hal home till he's fit to travel, Sylvie,' she communicated her decision. 'Meanwhile, will you please do now what I told you that you ought to've done?'

'On this occasion, willingly.'

Bella watched her sister leave the room to call a doctor. But it isn't willingly that I'm taking Hal back. I'm doing what my old enemies, love and duty, impel me to do and there's no guarantee things will turn out any differently from when duty didn't enter into it. When what I felt for Hal was undiluted love.

Chapter Three

HAL'S RECOVERY was speedier than Bella had anticipated, the new wonder-drug, penicillin, serving to stem his respiratory infection.

If penicillin had been discovered when I was a child, she thought when they returned to Manchester, I wouldn't have lost my father. And seeing my kids with theirs . . .

Edith and Leonard were captivated by their Canadian daddy, pelting him with questions. Their mam momentarily forgotten! Bella registered drily, surveying her husband seated on the kitchen sofa with a child on either side of him.

'How are you feeling?' she asked him.

'As if I've been transported to heaven on a magic carpet, I guess.'

'I wouldn't call the mucky train we travelled on that!'

Nor would Bella call what she had returned to 'heaven'. Amelia had tried to cope in her absence, Gran helping out in the haberdashery as she had promised. But wedding orders requiring Bella's special attention had accumulated in her absence.

Bella glanced at the clock.

'If you have things to do, don't worry about me, I'm fine,' said Hal.

If? Bella had not yet called Ezra to let him know she was back and available to sign the lease for her new shop. Some of her outworkers were awaiting designs and materials, and the hats they had completed must be examined by Bella's critical eye. And Amelia had made an appointment for a bride-to-be and her mother to discuss their requirements with

Bella later today. A time-consuming prospect, as Bella knew from experience, and one that demanded diplomacy about imposing her own ideas. Profitable though special orders were, Bella was finding it increasingly difficult to slot them into her schedule.

What schedule? There's no time to plan my days, *or* my nights. I just get on my skates first thing in the morning and keep going until I drop.

Bella glanced at Hal, who would take no more kindly to it than he had years ago, though he had kept his thoughts to himself. And I've much more on my plate now than I had then.

Hal, though, will have to accept that I've taken him back on my own terms.

There was from the first an element of self-preservation on Bella's part. Life had too often presented her with setbacks. Nor would she ever again fully trust her husband. There was, too, the maturity with which she had approached their reconciliation. The second chance she was giving Hal would not be allowed to impede her business intentions.

'Mummy doesn't usually have afternoon tea with us when we get home from school,' Edith told Hal while Bella cleared the table.

'Nor will your daddy,' said Bella. 'He'll be working, like your friends' daddies do.'

'But today is special for us, isn't it?' Edith said snuggling closer to Hal. 'Leonard and I have only just *got* our daddy.'

Bella went on with her task, brushing cake crumbs from the table before washing the dishes. Gran had made an excuse to go upstairs, leaving Bella and her family alone.

An hour had slipped by since Bella and Hal arrived home, during which the twins had remained glued to Hal's side as though they feared he might disappear from their lives as suddenly as he had entered them.

It will take a while for them to stop feeling that way, thought Bella. When they had asked her why they didn't have a daddy, she had supplied a simplification of the truth that had led to another question: *Why* didn't you and Daddy get on with each other? To which the only suitable answer was that they were too young to understand.

Bella had telephoned them each day from London, telling them only that she would return with a lovely surprise.

'I'm so glad that you and our daddy get on with each other again,' Edith said to her now.

Let's hope it lasts, Bella silently replied.

'Tell us some more about Canada, Daddy,' Leonard was saying when she made her exit to the shop.

Chapter Four

THOUGH SYLVIE had slept in a friend's room during Bella's stay in London, Hal's illness had prohibited their making love.

Or I might have been pregnant now, Bella thought when they returned home. The caution tempering her still wanting Hal had not then included contraception. Passion would have carried me away – on the brink of opening another shop.

Hal was constrained to cool his ardour on their first night in the bed where their children were conceived, and Bella hers.

'If you knew how I've longed for you, Bella –'

'But I didn't let myself long for you.'

'You were always a woman with will power.'

Bella removed his hand from her breast. 'Except where you were concerned.'

'That sure doesn't apply now.'

'What applies now,' said Bella, 'is common sense. I've a business to run. And raising two sets of twins is more than enough for one woman. Tomorrow I'll make an appointment to be fitted with a Dutch cap.'

'What in the hell is that?'

'Well, you don't wear it on your head! One of the brides whose headdress I designed told me about the gadget she intended getting for her other end. Young girls nowadays are much more clued-up than I was –'

' 'I prefer you the way you were,' said Hal while stroking her thigh.

Again Bella removed his hand.

'I am sure getting the brush-off tonight!'

'Only because one thing leads to another and I can't take the risk.'

Bella got out of bed to pour him some of the lemonade Gran had made for him.

'What I could use right now is a Canadian Club on the rocks!'

'But the doctor said no alcohol for the moment and plenty of fluids while you're recuperating.'

Bella watched him sip the drink and afterwards straightened his pillows.

'Thanks for looking after me,' Hal said.

'I don't require or expect gratitude from those I love,' Bella replied.

'Then you do still love me?'

'Would I have taken you back if I didn't?'

'Come back to bed.'

They lay for a while silently side by side, Hal with his hands safely behind his head, the lamplight casting a glow on his face and his expression pensive.

'I've had time to do a lot of thinking, Bella –'

'And I'd be interested to know where you did it.'

'I've always been something of a mystery to you, haven't I?'

'But your children won't let you be one to them. They'll want to know all about you.'

'And that's going to be difficult.' Hal added after pausing, 'There are things I just can't talk about, Bella.'

Did he think she didn't know that?

'You used to tell me about your childhood,' Hal went on, 'the way people do. But I don't want to remember mine. Or what came after it. When I said what I did in London, about my father, it was like going through it all over again.'

'But you must have happy memories of your mother and your sister,' Bella said gently.

'Sure. But my father figures in those memories, too, casting a blight over them as he did over his family!' Hal calmed down and added, 'While I was briefly back in Toronto, I learned that he now has another son. My half-brother sure has my sympathy.'

'Are you sure you're not jealous of him?'

'Jealous of the new heir to my father's business? That kid doesn't yet know what he's in for. I sent him a gift, by the way. No reason to ignore his arrival because our father's the kind of guy he is.'

'Did you receive an acknowledgement?' Bella asked.

'From my father's secretary, the same one who sent my mother flowers on the anniversaries he was never there to celebrate with her: 'Ross thanks you for the beautiful pewter tankard.'

'But he won't appreciate it till he grows up,' Bella said with a laugh. 'You could have thought of something more suitable for a little boy.'

'On the contrary,' said Hal, 'I gave a lot of thought to what to send to *that* little boy. He'll still have the tankard when he's old enough to think for himself and maybe he'll question the picture of me presented to him.

'And if you're wondering why a gift-wrapped package didn't arrive here when it should have, Bella, I bought a teddy bear then decided not to send it. That it would seem no more than an empty gesture from the guy who let you down.'

Given Bella's feelings at the time, the teddy bear would surely have been dumped in the dustbin. 'Did that reasoning also account for your not offering financial support?'

'I haven't held down a regular job since I was demobbed,' Hal replied, 'and that's the truth.'

'Wasn't that the case, too, before you joined up?'

'I'm sure getting the third degree!'

'And while I'm grilling you there's something else I'd like to know,' said Bella. 'Were you having an affair with Gerda behind my back?'

'I'm surprised to hear you mention her name.'

'Believe it or not, I think of her often. She was like another sister to me. That made what she did even harder to take.'

'The answer to your question,' said Hal, 'is no. What Gerda

told you that night wasn't a lie. Does that make her less of a sinner from your point of view?'

'No. But it does you. If Gerda drank too much whisky and felt horny – her expression, not mine – she could have gone out and picked up a man at a Services club, like she was in the habit of doing. It didn't have to be my husband.

'I don't blame you for succumbing to Gerda's wiles, Hal, though I did at the time,' Bella went on. 'Any man would, she's a beautiful girl –'

'But unlike you, the kind who'll look dumpy when she's older,' Hal opined. 'She'd gained weight from comforting herself with Hershey bars when I last saw her –'

'When was that?'

'For a while we cried on each other's shoulder,' Hal confessed. 'What else would you expect? I had a hole in my life and so had she. But what happened between us that night never happened again, and not too long afterwards I was posted south.

'I never saw Gerda again. Nor did I think that you and I would ever lie in bed together discussing her! It's a waste of our valuable time.'

'On the contrary,' said Bella, 'it's cleared the air. We're not starting afresh with a clean slate, Hal. The present is invariably built on the past and there's our children's future to consider as well as our own.'

'What are you leading up to, Bella?'

'I once asked you to work with me, after the war – remember?'

'And I said no, thanks.'

'But you weren't yet the father of twins and I'm hoping you'll now change your mind.'

Hal said after a silence, 'If I did, what would my function be?'

'Do you know anything about book-keeping?'

'My father made sure of that!'

'If I could leave that side of things to you,' Bella told him, 'it would be a load off my shoulders. Also, I'll need someone to manage the haberdashery when I open my new shop.'

'And you won't stop with *that* shop, will you?' said Hal.

On his face was the enigmatic expression Bella remembered. But she wouldn't let that cold glass wall arise between them again. The way to avoid it was to involve Hal in the business.

'If we pull together,' she declared, 'we could end up with a string of suburban shops and one in town. And buy a nice house for our family to live in long before then.'

'Did you repay your Uncle Saul's loan yet?' Hal enquired.

'With the interest I promised him, though he didn't want to take it.'

'He's a helluva guy.'

Bella's expression shadowed with distress. 'But his son didn't come back from the war and it shattered him. You can never tell what people are made of until they're put to the test.'

'Are *you* putting *me* to the test, Bella? Trying to find out what I'm made of? – by taking me into your business. If so, let me save you the trouble. Like I once told you, I'm not the stuff achievers are made of.'

Bella turned to look at him. 'How can you know till you've tried?'

'I know because I don't *want* to try.'

'You achieved promotions in the Air Force,' Bella reminded him.

'But like I said to you when we re-met on that bus and I'd just got my third stripe, getting it was no big deal. You were on your way to Ezra's for tea, I recall –'

'And he's back in my life, as friend and accountant,' Bella supplied. 'You'll find him as helpful to you in the business as I do, Hal.'

'I haven't said yes to your proposition, Bella.'

'But I'm hoping you will.'

'If I do, don't expect me to strive the way you do.'

'All I ask, Hal, is that you do what you have to and accept that I'm the opposite of you. Would you care for a chaste cuddle?'

Bella said when they were holding each other close, 'There's more to marriage than sex and romance. You talked about the hole in your life, Hal. How I'd describe the one in mine, without you, is an aching void.'

Hal silenced her with a kiss which but for their children's entrance might have weakened Bella's resolve.

Edith was weeping piteously. 'I dreamt that my daddy had gone away.'

'And she woke me up,' said Leonard, rubbing his eyes. 'You're never going to go away, are you, Daddy?'

Bella exchanged a glance with Hal and saw that tears had sprung to his eyes, as they had the first time he watched Gran light the Sabbath candles. But this was a moving moment for both of them, and another meaningful milestone that would engrave itself upon Bella's mind.

She watched Hal get out of bed, swoop up his son and his daughter and deposit them beside her.

'The children can sleep with us tonight, for a special treat,' he said.

Our first taste of our own family life, thought Bella when the lamp was switched off, and long may the sweetness last.

Chapter Five

THE TRIP TO OXFORD that Bella had promised her children did not take place until the spring of 1951. By then, Hal was managing the haberdashery, and Bella's new shop had begun making an impact among the affluent women on the south side of town.

Joey's decision to remain in Oxford over the Easter break had stirred uneasiness in Bella. Since the college recess included the Passover period, her brother would not be present at the family Seder. How could he do that to Gran? Though he had said on the phone that he had a great deal of studying to do and Bella believed him, her instinct told her it had to be more than that.

On Easter Saturday, she telephoned him. 'As you can't manage to come home, Joey, we'll come to see you.'

'When?'

'Tomorrow.'

'You might have given me more notice, Bella.'

'Does that mean you'd rather we didn't come?'

'Of course not. But –'

'But what?'

'Never mind. How long will you be staying?'

'I must be back here by Monday night, to open the shops on Tuesday – like the time Gran and I visited you and Sylvie at the farm. Had you forgotten?'

'That was a long time ago.'

And my brother, like my sister, now seems concerned only with his own new life. Bella stemmed her hurt.

'I'll try to book you in at the Randolph,' said Joey.

153

Seemingly he's forgotten too that I'm not made of money!
'A small, private hotel will do.'

Bella was left feeling that being at Oxford had removed
Joey from the real world. Though the same went for Sylvie
vis-à-vis drama college, this had been for Bella less of a
shock. Even as small children the two had displayed marked
characteristics foretelling the adults they would become. It
had not surprised Bella that Joey had followed the path events
had prohibited her from taking. As she already knew that
her daughter was a potential scholar and that her son was
not.

'Have the kids ever had a real vacation?' Hal asked as he
drove his family south.

'Last summer, we went to Blackpool for a week with
Granny,' Edith replied from the back seat.

'But she didn't feel well enough to take us on the sands
every day,' said Leonard, 'and I'm glad she hasn't come with
us.'

'That's a dreadful thing to say,' Edith rebuked him.

'He's only a little boy,' said Bella.

'I'm only a little girl, but I wouldn't say what Leonard did.
I wouldn't even think it, Mummy.'

'Well, you're a goody-goody, aren't you!' said Leonard.
'But you're not the one our mummy loves best.'

'Our mummy loves us both best. I asked her and she said
so.'

Hal saw, through the driver's mirror, Leonard stick out his
tongue at his sister. Something would have to be done about
that boy. 'There's plenty of love to go round, kids,' he said.

But it isn't evenly distributed, he thought, or Edith wouldn't
require the reassurance she was always seeking from Bella.
Did Bella know how plain her partiality towards Leonard was?
Probably not and it's equally probable that she hasn't admitted
it to herself. My wife is a clever woman, but as capable of
blinding herself to what she'd rather not see as anyone else.

As they left the lush Cheshire countryside behind, heading
towards Stafford, Hal glanced at Bella – unduly silent

today – elegant as always, in a fawn linen suit and a deceptively simple straw hat that said a lot for why she was making her mark so swiftly where it counted.

Though Hal had mentally raised his eyebrows at the price she was prepared to pay for labels that were just a bit of silk with her initial embroidered on them, he did not doubt that in business Bella knew what she was doing.

And Bella's designs were classier than those Hal recalled seeing in the shop in Gerda's day. When Bella's first set of twins were still schoolkids – this was how she sometimes referred to Sylvie and Joey, and why wouldn't she? A mother was what she'd been to them and whether they realized it or not, she still was.

Was it Joey she was preoccupied by now? Worried about his opting not to come home for the college vacation?

In Hal's opinion, there was more reason to worry about Sylvie. Ill though he was then, he couldn't have failed to note that the bohemian atmosphere, and the weirdo young people dropping by her place at all hours, wasn't a suitable set-up for a nice Jewish girl.

If that's what being a drama student can do, I hope my daughter doesn't take after her aunt, thought Hal. It hasn't taken long for me to begin thinking like a family guy! But Edith shows no sign of following in Sylvie's footsteps in any respect. Except when Leonard riles her, she's a placid little girl – and too easily hurt.

Sylvie, though, had in her childhood received the same treatment from Bella that Edith sensed was *her* lot, Hal continued reflecting. The first time he had visited the farm with Bella, he'd known which twin was her favourite. An impression that time had done nothing to change.

But Sylvie had proved herself more resilient than Hal felt his daughter was. There's a good deal more than just Leonard's behaviour that something must be done about, Hal thought, but discussing this with Bella would cause trouble between her and me.

What people shut their eyes to, they don't want to be told

and that doesn't just apply to family matters. Hal had made it clear to Bella that he wasn't the sort of guy to spend his days striving for the moon. Life is too short! Okay, she'd accepted it. But doesn't she realize that talking business every evening bores me stiff? That it's enough that I'm cooped up in a shop, day in, day out, watching the clock until closing time –

Hal's ruminating was cut short by Edith's plaintive voice. 'I feel sick.'

'Try not to throw up till we get you out of the car, honey,' he said pulling up beside a grassy verge that bordered the highway.

'And don't do it over me!' said Leonard.

But Edith already had. Over herself, too.

'Please don't be cross with me for spoiling my frock, Mummy –'

'Who cares about your frock?' said Leonard. 'Look what you've done to my trousers!'

That's the difference between them, Hal registered as he and Bella got the children out of the car, the suitcase too, to change their clothing. And this is family life, he thought wryly. Would he be without it? No, you had to take the rough with the smooth and he counted himself lucky. If being penned behind a counter was the price he had to pay, there was a price for everything.

Bella's girlhood visit to Oxford, when she had come for her interview at Somerville, could not but return to her when they drove through the city, the gracious architecture of the colleges all about her enhancing the atmosphere of the historic seat of learning in which her brother was equipping himself for the bright future denied to her.

Did Joey realize how fortunate he was? Bella doubted it, since she had made it possible for him to take following his inclinations for granted, and for Sylvie too.

Neither had been made to see how their elder sister had

156

striven to give them their chance in life. You don't say to youngsters, 'Look at what I'm doing for you and never forget it.'

But Bella too had taken everything for granted, until the rude awakening that had followed her mother's death. Only then had she seen her parents as a man and a woman who had put their children before themselves.

Hal slowed the car in the stream of traffic filtering along the high street and Bella absently noted a woman pedestrian wearing an over-adorned spring hat – that my clientele wouldn't be seen dead in! Another part of her mind remained with her brother and her sister, scenes from their childhood and the endless struggle her own life then was returning to her like lantern slides flashed on to a screen.

If I required a reward, though, Bella reflected, what Joey and Sylvie have achieved would be more than enough. Whether Sylvie would make it as an actress remained to be seen. It was now up to her. But Bella had no doubt that Joey's determination to work in the field she herself had once aspired to would not falter.

Was his own disability the reason for his opting for medical research? Bella had felt unable to ask him, as she was still unable to glance at his legs without a pang. If immunization against poliomyelitis had been available in the thirties, Joey would not have been struck down. Nor had a vaccine yet been developed and when Leonard, or Edith, complained of a headache Bella was terror-stricken. But there was still a multitude of diseases that medical science had not yet succeeded in conquering . . .

What am I doing selling hats? thought Bella. Catering to feminine vanity, when I could have been helping to save lives. Put that way, how futile my life seems. 'Could have been' will echo in my ears no matter what I achieve in the work that Fate imposed on me.

'Okay, kids,' Hal said when they had left the high street and he was following the route supplied by Joey, 'we'll soon be there. Your uncle has found us a place close to downtown, so we can leave the car there and walk to see all the sights.'

Bella turned round to smile at the children. 'Some of the beautiful buildings we drove past are colleges. One day, you two might be students here, like Uncle Joey is,' she added though there seemed little likelihood of that for Leonard.

She's mapping out their future for them, thought Hal. As my father did for me and look how that turned out. 'For God's sake, Bella! They're only six,' he said.

'And I like Blackpool better than Oxford,' said Leonard, 'but Uncle Joey said we can go rowing on the river. Can we, Daddy? He said it's where they practise for the boat race and he laughed when I asked if he was in the team.'

Bella winced on her brother's behalf. Joey often joked about his disability, but what was that but veneer?

'That was a daft question to ask him,' Edith told *her* brother.

'And you're a clever-breeches! Can we go rowing or not, Daddy?'

It was Bella who replied. 'Since we're here to spend time with your uncle, we shan't do anything he is unable to do, Leonard.'

'It isn't fair!'

'Nor,' said Bella, 'is it fair that Uncle Joey isn't able to enjoy many of the activities that others do.'

'But that isn't my fault, is it?' said Leonard.

'Be quiet! I don't want to hear another word from you!' Hal exclaimed while turning the car into a leafy avenue.

Silence was maintained by all until he had halted the vehicle outside a shabby, Edwardian villa.

Meanwhile, Bella had taken her compact from her bag and was powdering her nose.

'It's only the landlady you're about to meet,' Hal said to her, 'not one of your fancy customers!'

'She happens to be a friend of my brother's. Didn't I mention it?'

Her tone was too offhand and she knew darn well she hadn't mentioned it.

Bella went on, 'Joey told me when I had a word with him,

after you did, that every guest-house he tried was full over the holiday weekend. But this lady – she only takes students – kindly offered us the chalet in her back garden where her husband used to work.'

'What is a chalet?' Edith enquired.

Bella snapped her compact shut. 'You'll find out in a few minutes.'

'Why did her husband work in one?' asked Leonard.

'Your uncle said he was a professor, and I expect he needed somewhere quiet to escape to, with the house full of students.'

'But it doesn't strike me as suitable accommodation for us and the kids,' said Hal.

'I wasn't going to let that stop me from visiting my brother.'

From finding out what's going on, you mean, thought Hal, and a girl is probably at the centre of it. Why else would a first year undergraduate elect to spend his vacation in college? But if Bella feared that some delectable damsel had seduced her brother, she would have to learn the hard way that Joey was no different from other lads and it was up to him not to let satisfying his urges take precedence over what he was here for.

When finally they had made their way up the mossy, paved drive and Bella had pressed the doorbell, Edith showed signs of wanting to retreat, her expression somewhat apprehensive.

'That place in the garden might be full of spiders,' she said as the door opened.

'Did I hear someone mention spiders?' said the woman greeting them with a smile. 'My husband had some unique specimens, but he willed them to a museum, I'm afraid –'

She ushered them inside. 'Since I'm not expecting other visitors, you must be Joey's family. Please make yourselves at home. Joey will be along shortly, he's in the bath.'

Bella found herself swept along as if by a tide from a small, panelled hall into a large, chintzy sitting-room, its walls lined floor to ceiling with books, during which the woman went on talking.

'There was rather a late party here last night and Joey

stayed over,' she answered Bella's unasked question: Why was Joey taking a bath here?

'I'm sorry only to be able to offer you the chalet,' she said, 'but you'll find it quite comfortable. It was my husband's retreat, you see –'

Bella had been right about that.

'And he was always happiest with lots of greenery around him. While he was writing his books, I sometimes didn't see him for days. Well, except when I took him his meals. Please don't wait for me to invite you to sit down, I'm not that kind of hostess,' she added with a smile that lent charm to her pudgy face.

Bella and Hal put themselves side by side on the window seat, but the children remained standing, fascinated by an ambience totally foreign to them.

'We've got a lot of books in our house,' Edith told the woman, 'but not as many as you have.'

'Have you learned to read yet, my dear?'

Edith nodded shyly.

'I taught the twins to read when they were four,' said Bella, 'as I did Joey and his sister. Have you any children?'

'Unfortunately not.'

Which put paid to Bella's suspicion that she had a daughter and Joey had fallen for her.

'Joey didn't tell me your name,' Bella said, 'or what the charge for the chalet will be.'

'Charge, my dear? I wouldn't dream of it, you're my welcome guests. And my name is Beth.'

'Beth what?' Leonard asked.

'Beth Watson,' she answered with a laugh as Joey entered the room.

'Widow of the late lamented Professor Henry Watson,' Joey added before greeting Bella and the children with kisses and his brother-in-law with a friendly slap on the back.

Joey looks the masculine equivalent of radiant, Bella registered. Oh yes, there had to be a girl in his life and how happy Bella was for him. But why hadn't he just said so, instead of prevaricating about why he was spending his vacation in Oxford?

While Beth kept the conversational ball rolling, Bella's second deduction was that the girl's home was in Oxford, or she wouldn't be here during the Easter break. The third was that she wasn't Jewish and Joey keeping his love affair a secret because of that.

Though he may have confided in Sylvie, to whom Bella was coming to think nothing was sacred, telling the sister who'd raised him was a different matter. As for Gran, who kept a strictly kosher home and despite her advanced years still walked to and from the synagogue every Saturday, since riding on the Sabbath was forbidden – Joey's having a gentile girlfriend would break her heart.

Bella did not close her shops on the Sabbath, doing so would considerably reduce her income. But she could not have contemplated what still was for most Jews the major sin: Marrying out of the faith. And if Joey was truly in love with this girl –

Bella stemmed her racing thoughts. Though her instinct told her that something was afoot and Joey seemed unable to meet her gaze, she mustn't let her imagination leap that far ahead! Get herself worked up about a student romance that was as likely to peter out as to last.

'Do your children like lasagna?' Beth enquired.

'I don't know what it is,' said Leonard.

'Nor did your uncle before we met,' Beth replied exchanging a smile with Joey, 'and I've told him it's time he visited Italy, and not just for the food. My parents left me a tiny apartment in Bellagio,' she said to Bella and Hal.

'On the shores of Lake Como,' Beth went on, 'and across the lake are the mountains. They lent the apartment to Henry and me for our honeymoon and it couldn't have been a more romantic setting. Not that Henry didn't forget I was there if he spotted an interesting creepy-crawlie!'

'But why did your husband *want* to collect creepy-crawlies?' Edith asked.

'To study them, my dear. He was what is called an entomologist. That's a nice new word for you to remember.'

And Edith won't forget it, thought Bella, though it had doubtless gone in one of Leonard's ears and out the other. 'Bellagio sounds delightful,' she bridged the brief gap in the conversation.

'Perfect for you and me to have a *second* honeymoon,' said Hal with a smile.

'When would I have time for one?' Though Hal could have applied for a short leave, Bella's business commitments had deprived them of a *first* honeymoon, she was recalling when Beth changed the subject.

'Did you design the hat you have on?'

'Yes, as a matter of fact.' Why can't I relax with this friendly woman? What is it about her?

'It's very nice,' Beth pronounced, 'though it wouldn't suit *me*.'

'My mummy makes special order hats,' Edith informed her. 'Well, she doesn't make them herself, her workers do, after she's drawn them a picture – and you could have one made that would suit you. Couldn't she, Mummy?'

Beth laughed. 'What you have here is an embryo saleswoman!' she said to Bella. 'As for the second honeymoon your husband mentioned, you'd be welcome to borrow my little apartment any time other than July and August. That's when I take my holiday.'

'And Beth has kindly invited me along,' said Joey exchanging another smile with her.

'How nice for you,' said Bella, but her brother continued to avoid her eye.

'For me,' Beth declared, 'there is nowhere like the Italian lakes.'

'But you should see Lake Ontario,' said Hal nostalgically.

'Perhaps we shall, one day,' Beth said to Joey. 'Henry had no interest in travelling other than in search of exotic specimens for his collection,' she told her guests, 'and . . . '

But Bella was no longer listening. We? My little brother

162

and this faded rose? No. It wasn't possible. Even Bella's too fertile imagination had to stop short of that.

Until then, Bella's preoccupation had allowed her to do no more than register Beth's appearance. She was the sort of middle-aged woman you would pass in the street without noticing her. Greying fair hair done up in an untidy bun. Shapeless, though her clothes were the floppy sort that could lend that impression. And wearing unfashionable glasses that kept slipping down her snub nose.

You are out of your mind to leap to the ridiculous conclusion you have! Bella told herself. And if you're not, then your brother has to be out of his!

'Well, Joey,' Bella said collecting herself, 'your niece and nephew are on tenterhooks to begin their sightseeing. Shall we go?'

It was Beth who replied. 'We've made an itinerary. But first I must give you lunch.'

'Thank you, but my husband and I were thinking of buying crisps and sandwiches and lemonade, and picnicking by the river,' Bella said politely.

'But on Easter Sunday, people will be queuing to buy refreshments,' said Beth, 'and we can eat alfresco here. I've made a vegetarian lasagna which Joey and I find just as delicious when eaten cold.'

'And wait till you taste Beth's salad dressing,' said Joey.

'I've never heard of salad dressing,' Leonard responded.

'Nor had your uncle,' Beth said, yet again.

Hal got up from his seat and went to tousle Joey's hair. 'I guess college has opened up a whole new world for this guy!'

College? thought Bella. The professor's widow was more like it! Did the discoveries she was helping Joey make include bed? Ridiculous *wasn't* the word for it, *bizarre* was – and Bella could think of less polite adjectives! The two had just shared the sort of intimate glance she remembered sharing with Hal when they first became lovers.

'We'll leave immediately we've eaten,' Beth said while

leading the way to a cheerful kitchen redolent of garlic, through the open French window and on to a terrace overlooking a garden resembling a jungle.

When eventually they were all seated at the ancient wood table, the lasagna and a huge bowl of salad before them and Joey pouring Chianti, Beth said, 'We forgot to bring the orangeade for the children from the fridge –'

'I'll get it,' said Bella, 'and would you mind if I made myself some tea?' I'm suffering from shock.

'You'll find tea in the blue canister,' Joey told her.

'And the sugar is in the red one,' said Beth.

How would Bella get through the rest of today, and tomorrow, with that incongruous couple before her eyes? If Hal hasn't tumbled to what I have, he is less perceptive than I thought.

Taking a punt on the Isis was, to the children's delight, included in the itinerary, young couples waving from the river banks as the boats glided by – and my brother sharing a cushion with that woman, thought Bella with distaste, while my husband – and he, too, is now avoiding my eye! – wields the pole.

'I've never known a longer day,' she said when the twins were finally tucked up at either end of a shabby sofa in the chalet and Hal gathered her close in the rusting brass bed the professor had shared only with his thoughts.

'I know how you feel,' Hal answered, 'but there's nothing you can do that wouldn't make an enemy of your brother. You have to let it ride.'

'And what if Joey can't get himself out of her clutches?'

'There's no such thing.'

'Is that the voice of experience?'

'How wouldn't it be? And I have to tell you that if Joey doesn't extricate himself, it'll be because he doesn't want to and he won't be the first guy to find happiness with an older woman.'

*

164

Joey and Beth were side by side in the bathroom brushing their teeth, which would have told Bella how deeply entrenched their relationship already was.

Some months had passed since Joey came with a friend to one of the Sunday evening gatherings Beth had continued giving after her husband's death and had found himself warmed by the easy, open-house atmosphere.

'That house is like a homely oasis in cold academia, Chris,' Joey had remarked as they walked back to their college rooms.

Chris had replied, 'It isn't just the house, it's Beth. My cousin was one of Professor Watson's students and I remember him telling me that the prof's wife was a bit of a legend. That people of all ages took their troubles to her – though I've drawn the line at that!'

'I gather the professor was somewhat eccentric.'

'Not if you don't think that preferring insects to people is strange,' Chris said drily. 'Beth took it all in her stride, though. She has an amazing sense of values. I once broke a glass while helping her clear up and needless to say my apologies were profuse. "Anything that money can replace isn't worth worrying about," she said to me.'

'Maybe,' said Joey, 'she was hinting that you should pay for the damage!'

'When you get to know her, you'll find out that she means what she says,' Chris answered, 'and that applies, by the way, to her telling you to drop in on a Sunday evening whenever you're at a loose end. If she hadn't liked you, Joey, she wouldn't have said it. I've never known anyone with such an enormous circle of friends.'

But were they *true* friends? Joey had wondered, turning up his coat collar against the chill autumn wind as they entered the college cloisters. Like Chris Bennett, who would include me in all his socializing if I'd let him and hang the possible inconvenience of missing the last bus because poor Joey Minsky can't run for it.

Joey had long ago learned that fair weather friendships were likely to feature large in his life. Nothing had changed in that respect since his schooldays. If you couldn't run with the pack, the others were sorry for you, but Joey didn't want that. What he wanted was unattainable: To be like everyone else.

'Feeling exhausted?' Chris asked when Joey slowed his pace.

'It *was* rather a long walk.'

But one that Joey had found himself repeating the following Sunday evening, when Chris had a date. And again and again, when Chris's dating Helena Partridge became a steady relationship.

'You're becoming one of the regulars, Joey,' Beth greeted his fifth appearance.

'I'm surprised that you notice who's here, there's always such a crowd,' he replied.

'I'm kept so busy, that is sometimes true. But it doesn't include you.'

'Well, I'm very noticeable, aren't I?'

'If you're referring to your disability, I noticed it only once, Joey. The first time you came and then just briefly. A moment later I was thinking, What a wry sense of humour this lad has.'

'Especially about himself.'

'But I imagine there's the other side of the coin, too, and if you ever feel like talking about it, you know where to come.' Beth added when Joey handed her a box of chocolates, 'Thank you, but there's no need for this and I'm fat enough!'

Joey had replied to her self-deprecation with the diplomatic silence he would have accorded any overweight middle-aged woman, and had spent the rest of the evening listening to a couple of biochemists discuss the research programme in which they were currently involved, thinking to himself that one day he would be similarly engaged, and exchanging an occasional smile with Beth as she mingled with her guests.

During the Christmas vacation that had followed, Joey's thoughts had several times strayed to Beth and the façade she presented to the world.

Everyone wears a public mask, he had reflected, and I should know! Is Beth in her private moments as desolate as me in mine? How could she not have been even when her eccentric husband was alive? When for a split-second her mask sometimes slipped, her expression had told Joey that she was lonely in the midst of a crowd.

'I missed you,' she said when he next saw her.

'And I you.'

She had greeted him with a hug, as she did Chris, whose girlfriend was with him.

'What a nice lady,' Helena said when Beth left them to hang up their coats and returned to the sitting room, 'so lovely and casual and I find that refreshing. Don't you, Joey?'

'Sorry, Helena – what did you say?'

'I was expressing my reaction to meeting Beth.' Helena ran a comb through her coppery curls and added teasingly, 'Joey seems miles away, doesn't he, Chris? I wonder who the girl is?'

'Someone he met while he was home in Manchester?'

'Sorry to disappoint you,' said Joey, his light tone belying his private confusion. Me getting an erection when a woman old enough to be my mother hugs me? But she wasn't just *any* middle-aged woman. She was Beth. And he shocked by his response to her physical proximity when she had hugged him.

Later, when they exchanged a glance across the room, he found that she had only to look at him to produce that same effect and made an excuse to leave early.

The following Sunday, Joey stayed away from her gathering and Chris afterwards told him that Beth had asked if he was unwell.

'That's *one* way of putting it,' said Joey.

He and Chris were seated beside the hearth in Joey's rooms, Chris smoking his pipe and Joey gazing moodily into the fire.

'Want to tell me what ails you?' Chris asked quietly.

'If I did, you'd burst out laughing.'

'Try me.'

'I think I'm in love with Beth.'

'Love isn't a laughing matter.'

'Is that all you're going to say? Nothing about me losing my mind?'

'That, my dear chap, is exactly what love is.' Chris puffed his pipe thoughtfully. 'A form of madness notwithstanding the object of one's adoration. Logic doesn't enter into it. Nor does the path of true love necessarily run smoothly –'

'Does that refer to you and Helena?' Joey cut in.

'I'm happy to say I've encountered no pitfalls so far,' Chris replied, 'but let me remind you, Joey, of our tender age, that neither you, nor I, is yet sufficiently experienced to know what true love is.'

'You're too damned sensible for words!' said Joey. 'But that doesn't seem to be the case with me –'

'As a matter of fact,' said Chris, 'I was thinking about my parents' experience vis-à-vis what we're discussing. My father, as you know, is a Jew and my mother a Protestant –'

'And it must be your mother you look like,' Joey interrupted surveying his friend's markedly Aryan appearance.

'Be that as it may, my Jewish grandparents never accepted her, or me,' Chris revealed. 'My father, of course, knew that they wouldn't, though he doubtless hoped that they would eventually. That's what I meant about logic not entering into it, Joey.'

A contemplative silence followed while Chris relit his pipe and Joey absently eyed a pile of books on the table, the rain lashing the windows heightening his personal bleakness.

'I'd have the problem your father had even if Beth weren't an older woman and I wanted to marry her,' Joey said.

'Marriage,' said Chris, 'is far in the future for both of us. How could we possibly afford it!'

'Meanwhile,' said Joey, 'if Beth knew how I feel about her, she'd bar me from the house. I have to stay away from her, Chris.'

Two weeks later, Joey received a brief note from Beth: 'What have I done to deserve it? I prefer to know.' To which Chris's reaction was that Joey owed Beth an explanation for seemingly dropping her.

'It would have to be a lie,' said Joey.

'Not necessarily,' Chris countered, 'young chaps have been known to get crushes on older women whom they admire –'

'How I feel isn't a *crush*!'

'But that's how Beth would construe it if you told her the truth and it's preferable to your telling her nothing,' said Chris. 'If you weren't special to her, she wouldn't be so hurt.'

Joey learned *how* special after steeling himself to call at the house that afternoon.

Beth's welcoming embrace proved too much for him and he could not stop himself from kissing her. Their progress from the hall to her bedroom had seemed like a fantasy come true.

'I love you, Beth,' were the only words he had spoken.

'And I you.'

The rest of the afternoon was his initiation to sexual communion, Beth's unloosed hair spread upon the pillow and her velvety thighs enveloping him.

'We must keep this a secret,' she had said before he departed.

'Why?'

'Because it's that kind of world, my darling, and I shall still be in Oxford when you have gone.'

'I'm never going to leave you, Beth.'

She had smiled and brushed his fingertips with her lips. 'Time will tell.'

Though Beth might have anticipated the opposite, time had served only to deepen their relationship, Joey reflected emerging from his remembrances and watching her add a handful of fragrant crystals to the bath water.

'After all that sightseeing, a nice hot soak will do you good,' she said. 'Me, too.'

'I used to share the bath with my twin sister when we were little,' Joey recalled when they were lying opposite each other, 'but it wasn't like this! Did I tell you how beautiful your breasts are?'

'Frequently, but I don't mind hearing it again. I don't think

Henry really noticed them. Is the water relaxing your legs, darling?'

'That's what Bella used to ask me at bathtime. After I got polio and she stopped economizing on hot water so I could have the bath to myself, which pleased Sylvie as much as it did me. We used to quarrel about which of us had the end without the taps and who got to use the sponge first –'

'But I shall *always* let you have the end without the taps,' Beth promised, 'and I'll buy you your very own sponge,' she added with a laugh.

'Bella, though,' Joey revealed, 'had to count her pennies in those days. My childhood was different from yours, Beth. Nannies and all that were just something I read about in the Christopher Robin poetry book that Bella bought for Sylvie and me.'

'*When We Were Very Young,*' Beth supplied the title while soaping her shoulders. 'I had that book too and my nanny used to read it to me. You're very attached to Bella, aren't you?'

'How could I not be?'

'And she to you,' said Beth. 'She doesn't like *me*, though.'

Joey did not argue about what he too had sensed. 'She will when she gets to know you.'

'But that is unlikely to happen, my darling. She's guessed about *us*.'

'What makes you think that?'

'Your elder sister is an astute woman, and equipped with the sixth sense all women are endowed with. I couldn't have failed to note her reaction when you weren't around to receive your family and I let slip that you were in the bath and had stayed here overnight. There was another, though I don't think it was more than mentally raising her eyebrows, when at some point it became plain that you and I had the house to ourselves –'

'It was when you apologized for being unable to offer without their permission the rooms your lodgers aren't occupying during the vacation,' Joey recalled.

'Then you did notice?'

'All right. I did!'

'And your sister's expression when you said you'd be spending the night here again,' said Beth, 'was enough to tell me she had no intention of getting to know me. Bella thinks I'm a cradle-snatcher,' she added wryly.

'But she'll have to accept that I'm not her baby brother any more.'

Chapter Six

JOEY'S WEEKLY LETTERS to Bella never failed to mention Beth. And equally pointed is my never mentioning her when I write to him, Bella thought. As though we're engaged in tactical warfare – and what but that is it? I want Joey to give up this woman and Joey knows it without us having exchanged a word on the subject.

'It isn't as if Beth is attractive,' Bella said to Hal, handing him Joey's latest epistle while they ate breakfast.

'But you know what they say about the eye of the beholder. There's also the one about all cats being grey at night,' Hal added while spreading marmalade on his toast, 'and Beth might be a wildcat in bed.'

'Distasteful though I find what that conjures up,' said Bella, 'I'd be relieved if it was the explanation. That she's just using Joey and he her for as long as it suits them to.'

But Bella had the feeling that there was more to it than that.

Hal cut into her reflections. 'I've thought of a way I could be really useful to you in the business, Bella. Remember me telling you I was once a travelling salesman in Canada? Since I know the ropes, why don't I go peddle your hats on the road?'

Though Bella no longer doubted that Hal loved her, many were the women he would encounter on the road and in that respect she couldn't trust him. There was, too, another reason for turning down his suggestion and Hal's not seeing it for himself proved how little thought he gave to the business.

'I'm not running a factory,' she said, 'nor a warehouse. A hat with my label on it is an exclusive model. Does Norman Hartnell peddle his gowns on the road?'

'Who in the hell is Norman Hartnell?'

'He designs clothes for some of the Royal Family.'

'I knew you had big ideas, Bella, but I guess I didn't realize *how* big!'

'This has nothing to do with the size of my ideas,' she replied, 'it concerns the nature of my business. As Gerda once said to me, I know where I'm going. And what you suggested isn't the way to get there. It would cheapen my label and –'

'You don't have to explain to me,' Hal interrupted, 'you're the boss. And *I'm* putting in for a transfer from the haberdashery.'

'The haberdashery is where I need you.'

'You don't need the haberdashery.'

'It isn't losing money.'

'Nor is it making much and I'll tell you for why. You're not interested in it,' said Hal. 'You don't have time to be.'

But you do, Bella silently replied. When Hal had told her he wasn't an achiever and had no wish to be one she hadn't realized what that meant in practice. That outside shop hours he never gave his work a thought and showed little enthusiasm when he *was* working.

'Why not offload that side of your business and have done with it?' he went on.

'It's possible that one day I shall, but not yet.'

'You're the boss,' Hal said again.

A remark to which Bella could supply no suitable answer. Instead she got up and kissed his cheek. 'Will you take Gran her breakfast, Hal? I'm already late. Get her to spend the morning in bed, if you can – the money for the cleaning lady is on the dresser, if Gran isn't up before she leaves. And if you could nip next door to pick up the fish from Mr Lewis, it would save Gran the trouble.'

Hal masked his mixed feelings with a laugh. 'Anything else?'

'Only that I love you.'

But love, thought Hal, could be a trap.

Chapter Seven

WHILE JOEY was sunning himself in Italy with Beth, his twin spent her vacation on a Greek island.

'This is something my sister has never done,' Sylvie reflected to her girlfriend when they were picnicking on a pebbled beach, the Mediterranean shimmering in the midday heat.

'Got herself sunburnt in Mykonos, you mean, while consuming stuffed vine leaves and Fetta cheese.'

'Bella has never even had time to get herself windburnt in Blackpool,' Sylvie replied, 'and time is the crux of what I just said, Tess. My sister's never known what it's like to feel young and free. And it's my fault. Well, mine and my brother's. If she had let our uncles bring us up —'

'That was *her* decision, wasn't it?'

'But it doesn't alter the sacrifice she made for Joey and me. If she'd thought of herself and let us go, we'd have turned out very differently from how we have. In my case, my uncle and aunt would have squashed my inclinations to go on the stage. Bella, on the other hand . . . '

Tess bit into a ripe tomato and wiped some seeds from her chin with the back of her hand. 'I should like to meet Bella. Does she know of my existence?'

'Only that I've moved in with a sculptress I met at a party. Sharing your studio is cheaper than renting my bedsit was, I said. I could hardly have told her the truth.'

Tess surveyed Sylvie with quizzical grey eyes. 'That you've gone off men, you mean, and I'm responsible.'

'If that's how you want to put it.'

'I just want you to be clear about yourself, Sylvie, and that includes that you're different from me. One pointer to that is that you were with a chap at that party —'

'But I soon lost interest in him.'

Tess brushed a strand of hair from her brow and topped up the wine in their Bakelite beakers. 'I, though, could never have *been* interested in him in the way we're discussing. In my teens I knew a boy who was good company and looked like Adonis, but I couldn't bear to have his arm around me when we went to the pictures. All I wanted from him was friendship.

'It wasn't until I left home for art school, and a girl lent me a copy of *The Well of Loneliness*, that I knew what I was,' Tess went on, 'and it was a relief to find out. That girl was my first lover. She'd recognized in me a mirror image of herself. Lending me the novel was her way of telling me.'

'Okay,' said Sylvie, 'she was your awakening and you were mine.'

'With the big difference I mentioned,' said Tess, 'you didn't grow up feeling yourself some sort of freak.'

'Do you feel like one now, in another way?' Sylvie asked her.

'Not in the least.'

'Me neither.'

'But that doesn't change what I'm trying to tell you, Sylvie. That you're not a born lesbian and I've known others like you, who but for a chance meeting would have stayed on the heterosexual track.'

Sylvie said after a pause, 'Are you telling me this because you're fed up with me?'

'If I were you'd know and vice versa,' Tess answered. 'I'm telling you because you have a choice, Sylvie. Marriage and children and all that. I didn't.'

Tess gazed pensively along the shore to where some fishermen were mending their nets beside an upturned boat and a woman had just fetched a straying toddler from the sea, yelling at him in Greek. Meanwhile another of her several young children began heading seaward and it was necessary for her to chase after him.

'I shouldn't like to be chasing kids in this heat,' Sylvie remarked, 'and it makes me realize what a trouble to Bella my brother and I were, though she took us no further than the park.'

'But I should have liked to have children,' said Tess. 'And what you've been saying about your sister today doesn't fit my impression that you don't really like her.'

Sylvie picked up a pebble and dusted off the sand. 'You can love and respect someone, Tess, *without* liking them and that probably applies, too, to Bella vis-à-vis me – but minus the respect! I've never been able to talk to Bella. It was always as though she was preparing her answers before I'd got my words out.

'When I look back, it was as if there was a different set of rules for Joey than for me, and that began before he got polio. He was her favourite and he still is. But given Joey's liaison, Bella can't go on thinking that he's the good twin and I'm the bad one!' Sylvie added drily. 'Though she would consider me marginally the worst of us if she knew about you and me.'

'What do you make of your brother's affair?' Tess asked handing Sylvie half of the orange she had just peeled.

Sylvie ate a slice of the fruit contemplatively before replying, 'Joey's needing a mother-figure in the forefront of his life has to account for it. When we lost our mum he went on clinging to Bella's skirt for a lot longer than I did. While we were evacuated during the war, the farmer's wife replaced Bella –'

'For you, too,' Tess interrupted.

'But I don't require mothering now. It doesn't surprise me that my brother still does. What I'm saying, Tess, is that Beth is filling that need and Joey's sexual needs too. What could be a happier situation for him?'

'Put like that,' said Sylvie, 'it might help Bella to understand.'

'Why are you so concerned about Bella?'

'The day may come when you and I require her understanding.'

Chapter Eight

BY THE MID-FIFTIES, Bella had opened a shop in Leeds and had moved her family to a semi-detached house in Prestwich.

Were it not for the down-payment required for the latter, her business expansion would have included Liverpool. But Gran had taken precedence. In summer, the old lady now had a patch of lawn on which to sit in her deckchair and a laburnum to shade her from the sun, and in winter she could gaze through the window at a scene more pleasant than empty packing cases piled against a backyard wall.

If this is what being an achiever means, Hal doesn't know what he's missed, Bella sometimes thought. The pleasure she had given Gran was a high reward. Hal, though . . . Well, Bella would always associate the sole occasion on which her husband had displayed some business acumen with the death of George VI.

'Better order in some black ribbon, I guess,' Hal had said, 'he was a good king and people will want to wear mourning armbands on his funeral day. They'll be doing the same in Canada.'

'Good idea,' said Bella.

'Approval fom the boss!' he replied.

'That joke is beginning to pall,' she told him, 'if it *is* a joke.'

'What else would it be?'

Your way of saying you're not enjoying a situation you're responsible for, she had wanted to retort. Instead she had let it pass, since her husband lacked the incentive she was unable to provide.

Gran returned her to the present. 'How old are you now, Bella?'

'Old enough to have children at high school!'

'When it comes to people's ages, including my own, I lose count,' said Gran, 'but it seems like yesterday to me that you were seventeen.'

A turning point in your life as well as in mine, Bella thought.

'And you got me going again,' Gran went on, 'instead of keeping me wrapped in cottonwool, like your mam did. If you hadn't, Bella – well, I wouldn't have lasted as long as I have.'

Gran was now nearing eighty and increasingly frail. But to Bella she had seemed an old lady when still in her fifties, as women of that age did in those days. Gran's generation hadn't tried to stay young. How different it was now, Bella reflected visualizing some of the older ladies for whom she designed hats.

'I've a lot to thank you for, Bella,' said Gran.

'And I you. Who was it who took over the household and let me get on with building the business?' Bella answered with a smile.

'But I'm not up to doing much more than a bit of cooking now.'

'That's more than enough. Do you get lonely while the rest of us are out all day, Gran?'

'I've my wireless set, haven't I?' Gran replied. 'And my memories to keep me company. I reckon I'm lucky to have a family coming home to me. The twins tell me all their doings at school, while they have their afternoon tea, just like Joey and Sylvie used to. But it's not often I get to have a nice chat with you.'

For once, Bella and her grandmother had the house to themselves. Leonard and Edith, their end of term examinations over, were each spending the night at a friend's home and Hal was out playing canasta.

When did my husband get interested in cards? Bella absently wondered. But you don't keep a record of things like that. Or notice your kids growing older. Bella's were now eleven, and the years rush by so fast, before I know it they'll be old enough to drive and wanting to borrow my car!

'I thought I'd see Joey and Sylvie married before I go,' Gran said with a sigh, 'but I'm giving up hope. All Joey seems interested in is test-tubes! And travelling all over the place, like Sylvie does with that troupe, won't find her a suitable husband.'

Bella laughed. 'Don't let Sylvie hear you call the repertory company she's joined what you did! You make it sound like a circus, Gran, and her a trapeze artiste.'

'She might as well be, the upside-down life she lives,' said Gran caustically. 'As for Joey, it can't be that no girl will have him, though it's possible that his being disabled makes him think otherwise.'

Gran had voiced Bella's private explanation for her brother's continuing relationship with Beth – for whom the post-graduate work Joey was now doing was fortuitously centred in Oxford. Bella couldn't blame Fate for that, though. Joey's brilliance had secured him the opportunity to do what he had set his heart on and Bella was happy for him on that account.

Sylvie, though, talented as she was, was prey to the precariousness of her profession. And for her there would not be the rewards along the way that Joey would experience, each minor breakthrough an achievement in itself.

Gran prodded Bella from her reflection. 'How is Minsky's haberdashery department doing?'

They were drinking lemon tea in the modern kitchen to which her grandmother would never grow accustomed and the question she had just asked was another indication of her affection for the past. What else but that *was* the haberdashery?

Bella put down her cup and kept her tone casual. 'It's Hal you should be asking, not me, Gran.'

'When I do, he tells me it's doing fine.'

'There's your answer then.'

'And I'm glad you never gave your dad's shop up, Bella.'

'It was quite a concession on your part, Gran, to refer to it as a department!' Bella said lightly.

'A person has to move with the times, don't they?'

Bella had to laugh.

'But your dad will be waiting for me when I get there,' Gran went on, 'and I'll be able to tell him you kept *his* business going.'

But only a sentimental fool would, thought Bella, and in business that doesn't match the rest of me.

'I can remember the day your dad *opened* his shop,' Gran said with a faraway look in her eyes, 'and how he stood behind the counter like a ship's captain about to set sail.'

She collected herself and finished drinking her tea. 'But you're a different sort of captain from what he was, Bella, capable of sailing a lot farther than he might have got.'

'Would you please stop talking about ships, Gran, and tell me in plain language what you're trying to?'

'Only that your dad would be proud of you, and he'd understand why, if you let the haberdashery go. I shall tell him everything when I see him.'

'Meanwhile,' said Bella, 'you're still in the land of the living and it's past your bedtime.'

After her grandmother had retired, Bella went to sit in the living-room, recalling how the parlour behind the shop was used only on special occasions, like the relic of a bygone era it was.

Only her mother's china cabinet had accompanied the family to their new home. And little by little, thought Bella, our way of life has changed. Including that Hal and I spend less time together than we used to.

When did that begin happening? A question in the same category as when did Hal begin playing cards and for Bella equally unanswerable. How it seemed to her now, though, was that her husband was part of a circle of married men whose wives too enjoyed whatever their own pursuits might be.

But the diversion Hal had found for himself was preferable

to infidelity. Confident though Bella was that he loved her, there were times when a picture would rise before her of Gerda spreadeagled beneath him on the hearthrug. Would the memory of that be with her till the day she died?

A more material reminder of the female she had thought her friend was now to be seen in department stores, stylish but mass-produced hats bearing the label 'Gerda'.

The slut must have wheedled that millinery manufacturer boyfriend Sylvie mentioned into giving her her own label, Bella was thinking uncharitably when a telephone call from Ezra cut short her musing.

'Everything all right?' she asked him. Edith's friendship with his daughter, Sally, had continued as they grew older and it was at Ezra's home that she was spending the night.

'Fine,' Ezra replied, 'but you know what a fusser my wife is! Doreen wants a word with you –'

'And my husband needed no encouragement to dial your number!' Doreen joked when he had handed her the receiver.

Half-joked, thought Bella. Doreen is as unlikely ever to forget how Ezra once felt about me as I am to forget Hal's transgression.

While Doreen rambled on before coming to the point, Bella recalled the few occasions on which she had visited the Blacks. The first time was a house-warming party, when they moved from the home gifted to Ezra by his father to the more fashionable Whitefield where a Jewish golf club was the centre of the social scene. The last time was in 1953 and before Bella and her family had acquired a television set. Doreen had given a Coronation Day party, plying her guests with food while they watched the young queen being crowned. And I, Bella recollected, kept catching Doreen watching *me*.

Doreen finally asked the question that was the reason for calling Bella tonight. 'Does Edith's hay fever medicine have to be kept in the fridge? Edith said no, but I thought it best to check with you.'

'With Edith that isn't necessary,' Bella answered drily. 'Leonard, on the other hand –'

'Say no more,' Doreen cut in. 'Couldn't-care-less is what I'd call that boy.'

'He has his compensations,' said Bella.

'If you mean his winning ways, I'm keeping my daughter well away from him!'

Doreen's final remark was another of her half-jokes, thought Bella after replacing the receiver, and there's no doubt that my son is in more respects than his looks a replica of his father. The natural charm and the lack of interest in achievement.

Though Leonard was not Edith's intellectual equal, he had passed the 'eleven-plus' examination and was now a pupil at Stand Grammar School. Edith, like Sally Black, had won a place at Manchester High, as long ago Bella had, her end of term report confirming her diligence.

Leonard's report, though –

Again the shrilling of the telephone bell cut short Bella's thoughts.

'I expected Hal to answer the phone,' said Sylvie, 'you're usually busy doing your designs or whatever in the evenings.'

'But Hal is out and I'm having the night off,' Bella replied. Why does Sylvie have the knack of rubbing me up the wrong way?

'I'm not cast in the next couple of plays we're doing,' Sylvie said, 'and –'

'Why is that?' Bella interrupted.

'You sound just like you used to when I had to tell you I wasn't top of the class!'

'Well, I care about you, don't I?'

'But why must the people you care about have to come up to your expectations?'

Bella was left to digest that question while Sylvie asked another.

'I want to make it in the theatre, Bella. Of course I do. But if I don't, shall you care about me any the less?'

'You should know the answer to that.'

'But it doesn't stop me from feeling that if I fail I'll have let you down.' Sylvie returned to the subject from which she had digressed. 'Since I've got some time off, I'm thinking of coming home for the weekend and bringing a friend.'

'Male, or female?' Bella enquired. 'Gran is longing for you to bring a nice Jewish boy home and tell her you're getting engaged. Do you ever meet any?'

'There's one in the company as it happens, but we're just platonic friends. Sorry to disappoint Gran, *and* you,' Sylvie said flippantly, 'but it's only Tess I'm thinking of bringing home.'

Bella's first impression of Tess was of a quietly spoken young woman, her appearance anything but arty. Instead, she was clad in a simple summer frock – unlike Sylvie whose outfit was, as always, as colourful as her personality.

Sylvie had arrived with her arms laden with flowers and Tess with a gift from her studio, a small modern sculpture about which Gran was duly polite, but which Bella thought indicative of Tess's talent.

At the Sabbath Eve supper table, Tess was intrigued by the ancient ritual, listening carefully to Hal's translating for her the Hebrew blessings, and remarking that she could not imagine a family bound by such tradition ever breaking up.

Later, while they sat drinking lemon tea, so sensible was her conversation Bella asked herself, What is Tess doing with my madcap sister?

A question answered all too graphically the following morning, when before leaving for work she opened the door of the room they were sharing and saw them asleep together in one of the twin beds.

Bella closed the door soundlessly, returned to the kitchen with the tray she had taken upstairs for them, added sugar to one of the cups of tea and swallowed down the hot, sweet beverage prescribed for shock.

'I guess your nice idea was foiled by them still being asleep and you not wanting to disturb them,' Hal said from behind his *Daily Express.*

Bella decided to leave him in blissful ignorance and never had she more appreciated the meaning of that phrase. I, though, am reeling as I was that day in Oxford – and much good piling sugar in my tea did then!

If Tess were the stereotype lesbian, Eton cropped and with a penchant for mannish clothes, and Sylvie a girl who had never dated boys – Bella stemmed her whirling thoughts since she could make no more sense of her sister's having a female lover than of her brother's incongruous affair.

Chapter Nine

A DECADE that Bella was glad to put behind her ended with her grandmother's death on New Year's Eve.

Gran had closed her eyes in her chair by the fire never to reopen them. Thus it was that 1960 began for the family with a funeral gathering.

While covering the mirrors, a ritual required in a Jewish house of mourning, Bella relived the scene in the parlour that had preceded her mother's funeral. Herself and Gran huddled close together. Her uncles and aunts grouped as if for a family portrait. Uncle Saul fiddling with his watch-chain before their plans for Joey and Sylvie were put to her.

If I'd known how my brother and sister would turn out, would I have let them go? No, the blood tie that had impelled Bella to undertake what she had was no less strong now. Though there were times when she had cause to think there was but a hair's-breadth between love and duty, it was the former not the latter that still gave her sleepless nights on their account.

Her husband, for whom Gran's going must seem as it did to Bella like the end of an era, was gazing pensively through the window at the windswept garden.

'I guess I'll never stop thinking of that laburnum as Gran's tree. I'd have liked to have said goodbye to her.'

'Me, too, Hal, but for her it was a good way to go.'

'Your grandmother was a remarkable woman.'

'There's no need to tell me that.'

'But I want you to know how *I* valued her. I never knew either of my own grandmothers, they died before I was born.'

Another snippet from Hal's other life, thought Bella, dropped briefly into the conversation as always. When did I begin thinking of the past he can't bring himself to talk about as his other life?

'She was a real friend to me,' Hal went on, 'and I hope our son appreciates the great-grandmother he had. Our daughter sure does, did you hear Edith sobbing in her room?'

'Edith is more emotional than Leonard.'

'But what's the betting that Leonard shed a silent tear because Gran died at an inconvenient time for him? He'll have to miss out on the party he was going to tonight.'

'Why have you got such a down on Leonard?'

'That's how you'd see it, I guess. Leonard can do no wrong. Edith, though –'

'Is her daddy's girl,' Bella cut in, 'and that could be why Leonard turns to me for comfort.'

'Are you sure the picture you're painting is the right way round?'

The silence that followed was bristling with hostility and Bella decided to speak her mind.

'You set the pattern for your relationship with Leonard when he was little,' she said crisply.

'What I actually did,' Hal replied, 'was try to set right the damage you'd already done. But I didn't succeed. He's still the selfish kid he was then, except that he's learned to coat it with charm.'

'*You*, my love, are the expert on charm!'

Bella turned on her heel and left the room.

Custom decreed that only males witness a burial and Bella was constrained that afternoon to remain at home in an atmosphere heavy with the unspoken matters that stood like a barrier between her and the two seated alongside her.

Though other women were present, neighbours and acquaintances, ladies to whom Gran had been a familiar figure at synagogue services, Doreen and her daughter, who was holding Edith's hand, it was for Bella as though she were on an island with Sylvie and Beth.

In the four years since Bella made her shattering discovery about her sister, Sylvie had risen to playing leading roles in prestigious productions. And each time I see her, she looks more striking, Bella observed. There was a glow about her skin that make-up couldn't achieve. Radiance was the word for it – and who am I to pass judgement on her being what she is? I should be thankful that my sister is happy. My brother, too.

Why can't I be? Bella ruminated. Because Joey has tied himself to a woman too old to give him children. And Sylvie's lesbian relationship would render her a social outcast if it were known outside her own unconventional circle. Childlessness would be *her* lot, too.

And your lot is disappointment, thought Bella. Though the initial shocks and the revulsion accompanying them were long gone, a bitter aftertaste had lingered on.

Bella had reckoned herself as good an actress as her sister when four years ago she had plastered a smile on her face and got through the rest of that weekend without letting Sylvie and Tess suspect that she knew their secret.

Since Sylvie had not brought Tess home with her again, Bella had not been required to repeat the charade with the two of them. Only with her sister, adding another layer of strain to their inability to communicate.

What chance is there, Bella thought now, of me talking to Sylvie about her and Tess? She would cut me off with a single sentence: 'You wouldn't understand.' As she had since her childhood.

It wasn't that way with Joey, he couldn't have been closer to me. But Bella hadn't tried hard enough on that other shattering weekend and there must have been moments when her feelings were written on her face. As they doubtless were when Joey walked in with Beth today. What both would have read in Bella's expression was: That woman is not welcome here.

But Joey could not have thought otherwise and before Gran's funeral day ended Beth's presence was explained.

The tradition of visiting the bereaved had ensured that the family would not be alone until after evening prayers for the departed had been said. Those who had afterwards kept them company had now left and Bella had risen from her chair to go and make a pot of tea when her brother stopped her short.

'Beth came with me because we're getting married, Bella.'

She turned to look at him and could not stop herself from saying, 'A fine time to let me know I've lost you as well as Gran.'

In the fraught pause that followed Bella was aware, as if an outsider looking on, of Leonard gently returning her to her chair, of Joey putting his arm around Beth's podgy shoulders, that Edith was seated on a stool at Hal's feet, and of Sylvie's rebuking gaze.

Another family cameo I shall never forget, Bella thought with the part of her mind that was recording it.

Then Leonard broke the silence. 'My mother is exhausted,' he said to Joey, 'and this is hardly the time to make a wedding announcement.'

Hal found his voice. 'For a kid of fifteen, Leonard, you have too big an idea of yourself! It isn't for you to elect yourself the family spokesman.'

'If I may be allowed to reply to what my sister said to me,' Joey intervened, 'her equating my marriage with losing me is how she sees fit to interpret it.'

'But you have more than one sister,' his twin reminded him, 'and I'm happy for you, Joey.'

'Me, too,' said his niece.

Bella watched Sylvie and Edith kiss both Joey and Beth, and Hal shake their hands and wish them '*Mazeltov*'.

While Joey explained to Beth that *Mazeltov* was the Hebrew expression of congratulations, Bella remained in her chair, Leonard's comforting hand on her shoulder. All right, so he's his mother's boy, she thought emotionally, like his sister clings to her dad. A situation not uncommon in families, but in ours it's coming to feel like two alliances on either side of a painful divide.

'It isn't that I don't wish you luck, Uncle Joey,' Leonard then said, 'just that I don't like seeing my mother upset.'

'I understand, Leonard,' Joey replied.

'And would that our sister were capable of displaying understanding,' Sylvie said theatrically.

Bella remained silent, recalling the assortment of pretty girls at the synagogue service Joey had attended with the family when he came home for Rosh Hashanah. And the *right* girl would love him enough not to mind his disability, she was thinking when Beth addressed her.

'If it would help for me to become Jewish, I'm prepared to do so, Bella.'

'Beth didn't tell me that until we were on our way here,' Joey added, 'and I told her it's less important now Gran is gone.'

'Which has to be why you made your announcement today,' Bella said coldly. 'You've been waiting for Gran to die.'

'What a terrible way to put it, Mum,' said Edith, 'you know perfectly well what Uncle Joey meant. And you can't say that waiting so long to get married, so he wouldn't distress Gran, wasn't a sacrifice.'

'You don't know the meaning of the word "sacrifice",' Bella informed her.

'Is that a reference to the one you probably wish you hadn't made?' Joey enquired.

Bella saw him exchange a glance with Sylvie, and managed to smile. 'I've had reason to subject myself to some soul-searching on that score, and while I wouldn't say I have no regrets, believe it or not I'd do the same again.'

She turned her attention to Beth. 'As for you converting to Judaism, we needn't concern ourselves about my brother having a child born out of the faith.'

'I'm not as old as I look and I'm pregnant,' Beth said wryly.

The proverbial pin could have been heard dropping.

Shock number three for *me*, thought Bella, but it has its

191

good side. For Leonard and Edith, though – what would they think of their uncle sleeping with a woman he wasn't yet married to?

'So when's the wedding?' Sylvie asked them.

'Before we get down to discussing that,' said Joey, 'I must tell you that Beth's condition is something else she told me about on our way here.'

Beth didn't use it to seal the knot, Bella reflected, and I have to respect her for that. Nor would she be the first family bride pregnant on her wedding day. That distinction remained Bella's.

'You must take good care of yourself,' she said to Beth. 'Now, if everyone will excuse me, it's been a long day.'

'You still haven't given me your blessing,' said Joey.

Bella turned in the doorway to look at him and knew that he would not be truly happy without it. 'If Beth would like me to, I'll design her wedding hat,' she said mustering a smile. Right now, that was the best she could do.

Chapter Ten

IN THE MID-SIXTIES, Leonard dropped out of college and left home to find work in London.

'You wouldn't have let Edith do it,' Hal said to Bella after their son's departure, 'you'd have put your foot down.'

'Like *you* tried to, you mean, and where did it get you? If we'd *both* blown our tops, Leonard would still have gone and years could have passed before we saw him again. Like that row between you and your father that you once mentioned –'

'My father,' said Hal, 'is devoid of normal human feelings and that's all I intend saying about it.'

'But returning to your comparison between Edith and Leonard, she's at university. His was just a commercial course and he wasn't really interested in it.'

'What in the hell is that boy interested in except enjoying himself?'

'We must give him time to find out.'

An all-too-familiar strained silence followed, while Bella sipped her tea and Hal ate the kippers that were his Sunday breakfast.

'I miss Leonard terribly,' Bella said with a forlorn smile. 'It will take me a while to get used to not having him around.'

'Believe it or not, that goes for me, too,' Hal replied, 'on both counts. And in one way, he's gone up in my estimation. Though a lot of kids are leaving the nest nowadays, to make their own way, I wouldn't have thought Leonard had the guts.'

Something that could be likened to a fever had arrived along with the new music blaring from radios and record-players countrywide and had taken the young generation in its grip.

'Remember when Leonard bought his first Beatles record,' Bella reminisced, 'and we heard it thumping through the ceiling? Now, even Edith has a picture of John Lennon in her room.'

'*Even* Edith?'

Bella went on eating her boiled egg. 'You know what I mean.'

'No. I don't and I'd like you to tell me.'

She put down her spoon. 'Can't we enjoy a leisurely breakfast together, once a week, without all this?'

'All what?'

'Which question would you like me to answer first!'

'In order of appearance will be fine.'

'And please don't remind me of my actress sister. The way she worked to get where she was – I still can't believe what she's done.'

At the height of her career, Sylvie had turned her back on the West End stage to join one of the small experimental theatre groups now mushrooming in seedy venues.

'I am never going to fathom her!' Bella exclaimed.

'Did you ever try to?'

'Since she was five years old and it continues to be like butting my head on a brick wall. As for what I said about our daughter – well, Edith reminds me of my mother.'

'Since I didn't know your mother, you're going to have to elaborate on that.'

'In a nutshell,' said Bella, 'she did what she had to and bent over backwards to keep people happy. But the main reason Edith reminds me of her is she hasn't an adventurous bone in her body.'

'Wouldn't you say that could be to her advantage?'

'But there's so much she's going to miss,' Bella said regretfully. 'When I got a place at Oxford, I wouldn't have chosen to live with relatives even if I'd had any there.'

Bella resumed eating her egg which had had time to congeal.

'But Edith's living with Joey and Beth is typical of her. She probably spends her free time taking little Hannah for walks!'

The new member of the family, named after Gran, was now four, and her resemblance to Bella another poignant reminder that blood was thicker than water, come what may.

If it weren't, I *would* have gone to Oxford, she thought now. Done my own thing, as the American jargon that's crossed the Atlantic along with the rest would put it. Instead, though Sylvie's doings, professional *and* personal, remain a source of anxiety to me, I'm watching Joey make the most of his life on both fronts.

ι Hal had said that night in the chalet that Joey wouldn't be the first man to find happiness with an older woman and so it had proved. Nor could the research in which he was engaged be more fulfilling. A new drug that doctors were prescribing for migraine was the result of years of work by Joey and his friend, Chris Bennett, and a customer's mentioning that she was taking that drug a proud moment for Bella.

She refilled her teacup and switched her mind to business. 'About the Liverpool shop, Hal –'

'Do we have to discuss work on a Sunday?'

'Since you're going there tomorrow to pick up the books, yes if you don't mind.'

A substantial offer from a chain of wine merchants had finally persuaded Bella to put business before sentiment, the money exchanged for the lease of the haberdashery premises enabling her to open her fourth branch. But ornamental buckles now featured in the window displays of all her shops, her private memorial to her father.

Closing down the haberdashery was a relief for Hal, thought Bella, but what his function in the business now was would be hard to define. He made himself useful and she must be thankful for that.

'The Liverpool shop is lagging behind,' she told him, 'and I'd like you to chat with the manageress. If I didn't have some wedding orders to see to in Leeds, I'd go to Liverpool myself –'

'I can tell you why Liverpool's lagging behind without talking to the manageress,' Hal interrupted. 'Firstly, she's wrong for that location. Secondly, so are the hats. It's Beatles City, isn't it? And teenagers aren't the only ones affected.'

Hal paused only for breath. 'Last time I called there, some young women were giggling at the hats in the window and I got the impression they thought them *old* hat, as you English would say.'

'Not about *my* designs!' Bella retorted.

'I knew you weren't going to like this,' said Hal, 'but I still had to tell you. If you don't move with the times, Bella, you're going to get left behind, and these are *some* times. Those young women I mentioned had on skirts a lot shorter than you'd let Edith wear and theirs weren't the only thighs I saw gleaming above knee-high boots that day.'

'All right, so the mini-skirt is in! I could hardly not have known that.'

'And while it's getting shorter and shorter, you're still designing hats that couldn't look anything but ridiculous worn with it,' Hal summed up his comments.

While Bella was thinking this over, her husband removed a kipper bone from between his teeth. 'Instead of devoting yourself to your high class suburban shops in Manchester and Leeds, Bella, you should be opening your eyes to the changing scene and the branch in downtown Liverpool is a good place to start. Put the right stock and a trendy young manageress in there is how *I* see it.'

'You'd have made a good business consultant, Hal.'

'But I wouldn't have wanted to be one.'

To how many other lucrative occupations does that apply? Bella wanted to say. But where would it get her? Hal was personable and bright, attributes he could have capitalized on. Instead he was an appendage in his wife's business and seemingly satisfied.

'If you're going to continue branching out,' he went on, 'your designs have to be more "with-it".'

'With what?'

'And your not knowing that expression proves it. There's a whole new language out there, Bella, but where you spend your days you don't hear it. If you don't buck up your ideas, your model hats will soon be museum pieces.'

'Thanks for being concerned about me,' she said keeping her tone light.

'I wouldn't want the family achiever to go bankrupt,' he replied with a smile, 'and now the business meeting is over, let's go back to bed.'

'Mums and dads aren't supposed to do that sort of thing.'

'But the kids aren't here and I guess it's time we stopped calling them kids.'

'And what does that make *us*?'

'Young enough to do what we're going to and then some,' said Hal taking her hand and leading her out of the kitchen.

'Not having to repress my Sunday morning urges is an advantage of the twins being away from home,' he said on the way upstairs.

'I can think of another.'

'We don't have to stand in line for the bathroom.'

'There's that, too,' Bella said with a laugh, 'but the one that occurred to me is that the parting has helped you appreciate your son.'

Chapter Eleven

LEONARD WAS WORKING in a West End boutique, his sartorial elegance an advertisement for the velvet jackets and frilled shirts he sold to young men whose hair was as long as his own.

In his lunch break, he would saunter to one of the coffee bars where the music was more important than the menu and the atmosphere vibrant with youth. Home was never like this! – a reflection that included sharing a flat with one of his colleagues; and the plethora of dolly-birds from whom he could take his pick minus the repercussions of being seen with a *shiksah* in his home town.

A chap had to have his fling before settling down and Leonard would have liked to have discussed it with his dad, man to man. Me and Dad *talking*? he thought while combing his hair in readiness for his lunchtime foray. That'll be the day! The minute I get a word out he shouts me down.

Even Edith, though, hadn't managed to get Dad to open up about his youth. Dad never mentioned Canada if he could help it. It was from their mother, not their father, that Leonard and Edith had learned that they had a Canadian granddad and an uncle of their own generation.

The revelation had come on their tenth birthday. After Dad began weeping while we cut our cake, Leonard recalled, and he left the room.

While making his way along Carnaby Street, the sights and sounds of the sixties all about him, that very different scene returned to Leonard. The moment of silence before Edith and

I found our tongues. And Mum cautioning us when we did.

'Please don't ask Dad, when he comes back, what's wrong,' she whispered, 'and let's keep our voices down while we talk about it. He's sitting in the parlour and hasn't shut the door.'

A conspiratorial atmosphere had then enveloped the three of them. Gran must have been ill in bed at the time, since she wasn't part of this memory. One that together with other childhood recollections of his father seemed no less mysterious now than it had then. How wouldn't he have been cloaked with mystery for Edith and me? Leonard reflected. Appearing in our lives out of the blue when we were five, like the happy ending to a fairy tale.

Some fairy tale it had turned out to be!

Leonard simmered down as he had too often had to while living under the same roof as his father. Though Leonard was prepared to admit that he hadn't been the easiest of kids to raise, he had tried to make a friend of his dad in the recent past. But it's as if he has me weighed up for what he thinks I am and won't give me the chance to prove I'm not.

Mum, on the other hand, hadn't kicked up a fuss when Leonard dropped out of college to come to London. Instead, she had backed him up, telling him it was his life and he must make the most of it – which she was helping him do by supplementing his wage packet on condition that he kept it to himself.

If his mother weren't the person she was, Leonard would have thought she was scared of his father. Since it wasn't fear that made her handle Dad with kid gloves, what was it?

It was as though Bella would go to any lengths to preserve the boat she had once thought sunk: Her marriage. Did Leonard's dad realize how lucky he was to have a wife like her?

On the surface he seemed to, but who could know what went on in Hal's mind? Like his past he was anything but an open book. Maybe Leonard would visit Toronto one day and play detective. Learn all about Hal Diamond from the man who had raised *him*.

Meanwhile, all Leonard had to go on was the little his mother had revealed years ago.

'His children's birthdays can't but remind your dad of his own childhood, and it wasn't a happy one,' she had said to explain Hal's emotional exit. 'You've got a Canadian granddad, by the way.'

'And nobody told us!' Leonard remembered exclaiming.

Again his mother had put a finger to her lips. As if my dad was ill and I mustn't disturb him, Leonard thought now.

'Dad isn't to know that I've told you now,' she had gone on quietly, 'it's just that *I* think you should know.'

Bella had then mentioned the young uncle from their grandfather's second marriage, before adding, 'There are things you're not old enough to understand and even if that weren't so, your father's wish to keep some things to himself would have to be respected.'

Not if it includes me never meeting my granddad, Leonard resolved returning to the present. But generous though his mother was, she wouldn't fork out for a trip that could overturn his dad's apple cart. Leonard would have to borrow the necessary and Aunt Sylvie was his best bet.

When Leonard told Edith of his intention, she advised him against it. Parted though they now were by their separate pursuits, they had continued to celebrate their birthdays together and Edith had come up to London to dine with her twin.

'Since this is our twenty-first, I thought we'd splash out,' Leonard said when they were seated opposite each other at the White Tower, Edith wearing the simple black frock she kept for special occasions and Leonard resplendent in a maroon velvet suit.

Edith fingered the strand of pearls around her neck. 'My gift from Uncle Joey and Aunt Beth.'

Leonard showed her the silver cigarette case they had sent him and lit a cigarette. 'I might buy myself a matching lighter with the birthday cheque from Mum. What will you do with yours?'

'Put it away for a rainy day,' Edith said with a laugh, 'like I always do.'

'For someone as careful as you,' said Leonard, 'a rainy day is never going to come!'

. 'But the same can't be said of you. And our birthday money is from Mum and Dad.'

'In a manner of speaking,' Leonard replied, 'but let's not spoil our evening by going into that.'

It was then that he expressed his determination to delve into their father's past.

'If I were you, I'd let well alone,' said Edith.

'And the way you put it describes the atmosphere we were raised in,' Leonard declared. 'You're a "peace at any price" person, Edith, but from my point of view it wasn't exactly peaceful. It's Mum though, not us, who is still living with the strain. I don't think she knows much more about Dad now than what she told us when we were ten.'

'And if it's for her sake you're thinking of going to Toronto,' Edith answered, 'don't do it, Leonard. What I ought to have said to you was leave well *enough* alone. Our parents love each other and nothing is perfect. Mum doesn't know that Dad is a gambler and we decided not to tell her when you found out –'

A hiatus in the conversation followed while a waiter took their order, Edith raising her eyebrows when Leonard opted for smoked salmon and sole with fresh asparagus.

'Today is our coming of age,' he reminded her when they were again able to talk privately, 'and what does my sister celebrate with? A tomato juice and an omelette!'

'I like tomato juice and I'm sure the omelette will be delicious.'

'That isn't the point, Edith, what is it that you can never live just for today, can you?'

'You on the other hand spend money as if there's no tomorrow.'

'And tonight we're going to toast our birthday with champagne,' Leonard said as the wine waiter approached.

'But please don't expect me to help you pay for it.'

Edith said after the champagne was ordered, 'I sometimes wonder, Leonard, how you and I can be peas from the same pod! We don't resemble each other in any way,' she added surveying her brother, 'and the height you've grown to you're more like a runner bean than a pea!'

They fell companionably silent, despite their differences as close now as they had always been.

'About Dad's gambling,' Leonard harked back after the first course was served and the Veuve Clicquot poured, 'a flutter on the horses is nothing to get worked up about. I wish that were the *only* thing he'd kept from Mum!'

'Am I to gather from that that you lay the odd bet yourself, Leonard?'

'I have better things to do with my money.'

Edith glanced around the elegant restaurant. The well-dressed diners matched the affluent ambience. If this was the life that her brother aspired to he would have to stop living for today. Splashing out was Leonard's idea of 'better things to do with his money'.

'What *I* wish, Leonard, is that whoever told you they'd seen Dad at the bookie's had kept their mouth shut,' Edith said with distress.

'It was just a casual remark, love, not an attempt to make mischief –'

'But why did you have to tell *me*? I could've done without knowing.'

'And that's your attitude about Dad's past, isn't it?' Leonard raised his glass. 'Here's lookin' at ya, kid!'

'But *you* look more like Clark Gable than Humphrey Bogart.'

'Like Dad, you mean? Well, there's nothing I can do about that. Many happy returns, Edith.'

'And from me to you.'

They clinked glasses.

'We've come a long way together,' Leonard said with a laugh, 'and long may it last!'

They went on with their meal and chatted of this and that, Edith registering how different their lives were.

'Mixing with the gentry, are you!' she said drily when Leonard mentioned that some of his dates were débutantes.

'Nowadays,' he replied with a grin, 'it's more a matter of them mixing with our sort. The Beatles have made Northern accents fashionable. If you fancy meeting some of my crowd, we can go on to a party tonight.'

'No, thanks. I'll take the late train to Oxford and you can go on to the party. I've an essay to finish and it could take me all night.'

'Keeping your eye on the ball as always,' Leonard said affectionately.

'But I have met a chap I rather like.'

'About time! When am I going to meet him?'

Edith laughed. 'If you're that keen, come to Oxford on Sunday evening. He drops in at Aunt Beth's gatherings.'

'From what you've told me about them, I don't think they're for me! You must bring him up to town some time.'

'If I can detach him from his work. He's an American, by the way.'

'And Jewish, I hope?'

'Yes, as a matter of fact.'

They shared a laugh, recalling their mother's frequently employing that reply as the conversation stopper it was.

A moment later their rapport was shattered.

'About me going to Toronto —' said Leonard.

'Do us all a favour and forget it.'

'Mum doesn't have to know.'

'What if you found out something she *should* know?'

'I suppose I'd have to tell her.'

'That's why I don't want you to go.'

'This is something I have to do for my own sake.'

'Then you're even more self-centred than I've always thought you.'

'And thank you for making my twenty-first birthday an occasion I prefer to forget.'

Chapter Twelve

SOUND THOUGH Hal's rare business advice seemed, the sixties fashion scene was affecting only one of Bella's shops.

That has to be due to where the Liverpool branch is situated, she thought while driving to Leeds with her designs for another wedding order. In the midst of the boutiques that had mushroomed in the city centre as they had in Manchester, pop music blaring from their doorways combining with rails of outrageous garments to tempt young people inside.

Nowadays they had money in their pockets and couldn't wait to spend it. It was as if the Beatles and Mary Quant had between them set going some sort of crazy roundabout and all the kids had leapt aboard.

Though some of their mums too had opted for mini-skirts – if the style had crossed the Atlantic that would certainly include Connie! – there would always be a market for elegance and Bella would continue to cater for it. Her clientele wouldn't dream of going hatless as many women now did and for them it had to be a model hat.

But I'd be daft not to capitalize on the young scene while it lasts, Bella decided. Leonard had told her on the phone that there was a shop in Chelsea specializing in trendy hats for girls who didn't buy their headgear from department stores.

Where cheap replicas of Gerda's designs for the young must be selling like hot cakes, Bella thought before blotting out remembrance of Gerda and her treachery.

It was not just business that had stood in the way of Bella's acquiring women friends, or that none had crossed her path who might have filled that gap. It's my inability to reveal myself to someone who might let me down and what is friendship but two-way trusting?

I'd have done anything for Connie and she for me and that still goes, Bella reflected. Though the Atlantic is now between us, our friendship hasn't faltered since the day it began – two little girls hiding together in the cloakroom so nobody would see them crying for their mothers on their first morning at school, Bella recalled with a smile.

There wasn't much to smile about, though, in the letter she had received from Connie today, written in a hotel in Reno while Connie awaited her second divorce, in company, she had said, with other women in a hurry to rid themselves of their husbands.

Bella swerved the car to avoid some sheep that had strayed on to the moorland road and returned her mind to business.

Hal was right about the Liverpool shop and she would introduce some trendy hats too into her suburban branches. Designs that would appeal to girls like Sally Black, who when Bella last saw her was wearing one of the butcher-boy caps made popular by the new young role model, Twiggy.

In my day, Bella recalled, it was Lana Turner and her sweater-girl look and Connie had the figure for it, but I didn't. As for Hal's advice, Bella was pleased that he was showing an interest, but doubted it would last. And the suggestion he had made over breakfast this morning, that she open a hat boutique in Manchester city centre, was just Hal talking off the top of his head, with no thought to where the necessary capital would come from.

Bella would not build her business on bank loans and was doing very nicely, thank you. But how could her husband know her feelings in that respect when they so rarely discussed business? Hal lowered a mental shutter at the end of his working day. For Bella – well, she wouldn't be where she now was if she hadn't eaten, slept and dreamt business. Which didn't mean she hadn't had to make all their domestic decisions too.

Hal learned to lean on me, she reflected, and I didn't notice it happening. Like his going out to play cards, the pattern was established while I just got on with what I had to do. Does that make me a bad wife?

Bella shrugged off her misgivings and began mentally designing the trendy hats that would bear her label. By the time she reached Leeds she was impatient to set down her ideas on paper, but that would have to wait until this evening, after she and Hal had eaten dinner and he had gone to his own pursuit.

Dealing with the wedding order that had brought her to Leeds did not take as long as Bella had anticipated and she decided to visit her relatives whose home was just a short drive from her shop.

Her Uncle Saul, now in a wheelchair, greeted her with his habitual words, 'Look what I've come to!'

'And let it be a lesson to Bella,' said her aunt. 'Money can't buy good health and you can lose your health piling it up.'

'Hard work never killed anyone,' Saul retorted. 'I went on working when I knew my son wouldn't be coming back, didn't I? Then I thought, What am I doing it for? How many meals a day can a person eat? How many clothes can they wear?'

'Didn't I say that to you?' Dolly demanded. 'While our children were still young I used to say it, when you came home from the factory dead beat. And I went on pleading with you, didn't I?'

'But Walter always wanted to come into the business and it was *his* future I was thinking of.' Saul fumbled for his handkerchief and dabbed his eyes. 'Until there was no need. And even then I couldn't keep away from the office.'

'With you, work was a habit!' Dolly exlaimed.

'A man could have worse habits! And in the end I sold out, didn't I? My daughters have married well, what would they want with trouser factories? What I got for the business, I invested for my grandchildren,' he told Bella.

'But how often do they come to see you?' said Dolly.

Bella watched her aunt pour tea into the fragile china cups

which, like the silver teapot, had once been kept for special occasions. Since losing their son, not only had her aunt and uncle's relationship undergone a change, Dolly had emerged as a very different woman from the one whom her husband had thought it necessary to protect.

Gone was the vain female Saul had years ago brought to Bella's shop to try on hats. Though Dolly was well-dressed as always, in a tailored, grey dress, a cameo brooch pinned to the collar, it was plain that her appearance was no longer her major concern, and her attitude to her possessions that they were to use, not to treasure.

As if, thought Bella, Uncle Saul's accident brought her up short. They had just moved into this house, the kind of home that Dolly had long coveted, when Saul fell down the marble staircase injuring his spine beyond repair.

But seemingly it hadn't occurred to Dolly that Saul's incentive to work as he had had included her own acquisitiveness.

'Is either of your children thinking of joining you in your business?' Dolly enquired handing Bella her tea.

'I shouldn't think it's entered Edith's head! But it isn't impossible that Leonard might eventually.'

'What's wrong with now?' said Saul. 'You could use another pair of hands and it's been like that for you for years. You don't have to tell me.'

That my husband doesn't pull his weight, Bella silently added. Uncle Saul was too astute not to have divined it. 'I have very reliable employees,' she said.

'But they can't be like one of your own,' Saul replied. 'It was what I was looking forward to with Walter, having someone who'd care as much about the business as I did.'

Dolly returned to the lesson to which she had earlier referred. 'You should take some time off, Bella, while you still have your health and strength. Don't let it be with you and Hal like it was with your uncle and me. I had to go on holiday without him, and now he's free to go with me I'm pushing him in a wheelchair.'

Dolly offered the biscuits and continued her homily. 'Be like your Uncle Reuben, Bella, who was satisfied with one little barber shop and is now enjoying his retirement.'

'People can't choose who they take after,' said Saul, 'and Bella takes after *me*.'

'If I didn't know that would I be saying to her what I am?' Dolly replied. 'And I'm sorry for her if she's going to kill herself building a big business for a son who might not take it over. There are more ways than one of what you plan for never happening.'

That last bit refers to herself, too, thought Bella. Uncle Reuben and Aunt Rosie were, as Dolly had mentioned, enjoying the autumn of their lives if a good deal more modestly than Dolly had anticipated sharing hers with Saul. In a tiny bungalow in Blackpool, where they could stroll together on the North Pier, or sit reading in one of the seafront shelters when it rained, content with their lot as they had always been.

Uncle Reuben, like Hal, wasn't an achiever and had limited his striving to that required to provide the necessities and simple pleasures of life, fortunate in his choice of a wife since Aunt Rosie was the opposite of acquisitive.

'If Leonard doesn't come into my business, it won't upset me,' Bella told Dolly.

'Then what are you working so hard for? The shops you already have aren't enough for you? If we'd never had a son Saul would have done no differently than he did,' Dolly declared, 'and I sometimes think the two of you were born with the same disease!'

Its name was ambition. Bella could no longer deny that what Gerda and Gran had said years ago in that respect was true.

'My niece could've been anything she set out to be and so could I,' Saul informed Dolly, 'if that's what you're calling a disease. In my case it was poverty that put me behind a sewing machine when I was fourteen, or I'd have ended up a solicitor with a big practice instead of a manufacturer.'

'And we all know what stopped Bella from being a scientist,' said Dolly, 'but it makes not a hap'orth of difference to what I just said.'

'Once *you* get a bee in your bonnet, there's no getting it out,' said Saul, 'but it isn't you who suffers the sting and this isn't the only bee!'

'If I'd stung you with a few of my bees when I should have, instead of humouring you –'

Only paralysis stopped Saul from springing from his wheelchair. 'Did you hear that, Bella? Humouring me, she said, when all the time it was the other way round. Me giving in to her every whim!'

While her uncle and aunt continued their habitual bickering Bella's gaze roved the room; the Chinese carpet a mellow gold in the late afternoon sunlight; tastefully arranged sofas and chairs; the lacquered cabinet filled with curios, and the framed watercolours enhancing the walls.

But this lovely home, thought Bella, is a prison for two people now serving the sentence life has meted out to them.

'More tea?' her aunt asked.

'My niece has more important things to do than linger at *your* tea-parties,' said Saul when Bella declined and rose to leave. He then spilled his own tea and it was necessary for Dolly to deal with the damage.

'I'll see myself out,' said Bella.

They paused only to kiss her goodbye and tell her to come again soon.

'Tea-parties?' Dolly was snorting as Bella left the room. 'I don't even bother baking any more. Nobody expects me to.'

'Because you're burdened with me.'

'I never said that.'

'But your sourpuss face stops us from getting visitors. And my niece will stop coming if you keep holding me up as a bad example to her, like you did today!'

But who ever learned from the experience of others? Bella reflected, their voices echoing stridently in her ears as she closed the front door behind her. People were the victims, or beneficiaries, of their own personalities. Which of the two Bella was, she wasn't sure.

Chapter Thirteen

LEONARD'S DELVING into his father's past was prohibited by his inability to finance the necessary trip to Toronto.

'You haven't yet repaid the twenty pounds I lent you some months ago,' said his Aunt Sylvie, 'and I hope you're not turning into the cadger your dad thinks you.'

Leonard had not known his father's low opinion of him included that. 'I'd forgotten I owed it to you –'

'No doubt,' Sylvie cut in crisply, 'but that's your trouble, Leonard, and it's high time you got your act together.'

'The last person I'd expect to be lectured by is you.'

'And why is that?'

'For one thing, you're not suburban. And for another, you've never talked down to me.'

'Nor am I doing so now,' Sylvie replied. 'I'm just making clear that money borrowed must be repaid, to which I might add that one's relatives and friends aren't there to be taken advantage of.'

Sylvie paused to glance around the airy studio room. 'I could live here for free, Leonard – Tess's sculptures are in great demand, as you know. As opposed to the offerings of my theatre group! But I insist upon paying my way.'

Leonard eyed the powerful bronze study of two women embracing that dominated the room. 'Is that supposed to be you and her?' Oh God, why had he said it? But he couldn't unsay it and his aunt was riveting him with one of the actressy glances she was known to employ offstage when necessary. Contemptuous described this one.

'If that was a jibe, Leonard, I've developed a thick skin, or I should be badly scarred by now.'

'It wasn't.'

'Then I must hope that it wasn't the preamble to some kind of subtle blackmail.'

'What?'

'A broad hint that you won't communicate to your mother what you've divined about Tess and me and it would be nice if in return I were to let you have the cash you came for.'

Leonard was momentarily speechless. 'Is that what you think of me?'

'It's difficult to *know* what to think of you,' Sylvie said appraising him, 'there are so many different sides to you, Leonard. But the side of you I've seen most of since you came to London is, I'm afraid, the lounge lizard and that too was there in embryo when you were a child. As the little boy who wants to please everyone is still there.'

'I doubt that my father would say that includes him.'

'Well, he saw through you, didn't he?' Sylvie replied. 'It took me longer to do so. And my sister, heaven help her, is never likely to.'

Sylvie rose from the colourful floor cushion on which she was reclining and went to gaze thoughtfully through the window at the walled garden, where Tess was seated beneath a beech tree moulding a plaster figure.

'Please go on with what you were saying,' Leonard said stiffly, 'I'm finding it most interesting.'

'Your mother's interpretation of your moving from job to job, as you have – not to mention your periods of unemployment – is that you're feeling your way and finding your feet. It isn't mine.'

Sylvie turned to look at him. 'You didn't even mention what the large amount of cash you now need is for –'

'Something very important,' Leonard interrupted, 'but I wasn't given *time* to tell you. As it happens, I came here thinking you were the only person who would understand.

How wrong I was! I wouldn't take a loan from you now, Aunt Sylvie, if you begged me to.'

Leonard was gone before Sylvie had time to utter. The front door banged shut and she was left with the memory of his face having paled, and the intensity of his expression.

Did Bella realize what a complex son she had? Probably not. It's as though my sister has tunnel vision, unable to see what is happening around her while she goes on forging ahead.

Impulsively and with love in her heart, Sylvie dialled Bella's telephone number.

It was Hal who picked up the receiver. 'How's my actress sister-in-law doing?'

'I was thinking of Bella and felt like chatting to her.'

'When did Bella have time to chat?'

'On a Sunday afternoon I was hoping to find her at home.'

'But it's now when she sees her accountant,' said Hal ruefully.

'And I bet Ezra's wife feels just like you do!'

'With bells on,' Hal said with a laugh. 'I guess Doreen hasn't forgotten what was once between her husband and my wife.'

'But you have?'

'I never saw it as a big romance, Sylvie, just as a waste of Bella. But with the benefit of hindsight . . . '

'Yes?' Sylvie prodded him.

'I did her no favours by coming on the scene. I'll tell her you called, Sylvie.'

Sylvie replaced the receiver and imagined Hal doing so in an empty house, afterwards roaming restlessly from room to room awaiting Bella's return. Tunnel vision was right! Or was it that Bella didn't see what it didn't suit her to see? – as applicable to her son as to her husband.

I've never understood her, nor she me! Words Sylvie had said to herself all too often, as Bella doubtless had the other way round.

Meanwhile, keeping her private life a secret from Bella was

a burden Sylvie must continue to carry. Nor could she direct Bella's attention to her husband's inner loneliness and the precarious path her son was treading.

From me it would seem like an accusation.

Chapter Fourteen

IN THE SWELTERING SUMMER OF 1969, Edith married the young American she had met at one of Beth's gatherings.

Though the thesis Keith Rosenberg was writing had still to be completed and time was of little importance in the ethos in which he worked, Bella knew that sooner or later he would achieve his doctorate and her daughter be whisked away to the United States.

'Edith will make an admirable academic wife,' she said to Hal with mixed feelings the morning after the wedding.

'Edith,' he declared, 'is the sort to adapt to whatever is required of her and that includes her husband's requirements, I guess. If she'd married a medic she'd fit in with his unsocial hours.'

'Fortunately, though,' said Bella, 'historians are able to live a normal family life.'

'And Keith's a lucky guy.'

Bella watched Hal spread marmalade on his toast, in his eyes the quizzical expression that said more than words.

'But you're not?' she answered.

'I got no more and no less than I bargained for, and the same goes for you I guess.'

Bella could think of no suitable reply and continued eating her egg. Why do our potentially contentious discussions invariably take place at breakfast? – and on days when rushing off to work can't be used as an excuse to escape.

Though this was Monday, they were spending the morning at home recovering from yesterday's celebrations, which had included in the evening entertaining those of Keith's relatives who had flown from Pittsburgh to be at his wedding.

'Keith's mum is a nice lady, but a bit of a mother-hen,' Bella said with a smile.

'He's her one and only, isn't he?'

'And she wept buckets at the ceremony!' Bella replied, the scene beneath the marriage canopy returning to her.

Keith's portly father red-faced from the heat, under his top hat casting anxious glances at his wife sobbing into her handkerchief, her ample bosom encased in bright blue lace and heaving with emotion. Hal, strikingly handsome in formal dress, never removing *his* glance from his daughter. Keith, ginger hair flaming under the white *yarmulke* he had chosen to wear, towering over his diminutive bride and she a vision of filmy loveliness, Bella thought with pride, in her simple and decorous gown, orange blossom anchoring her veil.

'Our daughter must have been one of the few brides nowadays opting for an old-fashioned wedding dress,' Bella said. 'Most of the girls I design headdresses for want something sensational to go with their sixties frocks and, believe it or not, one of them fancied wearing a beret!'

'That wouldn't have taken much designing –'

'I made her a satin one and covered it with white sequins,' Bella recalled. 'Since she'd made up her mind to be married in a mini-dress, I didn't waste my breath trying to talk her out of it.'

Hal helped himself to more toast. 'That couldn't have been a Jewish wedding, the rabbi wouldn't have allowed it.'

'Nor was it a church wedding,' Bella told him, 'and the girl's mother – I made her hat – was very upset about it. She said that a lot of young people are getting married in register offices these days and their parents don't like it.'

'There's plenty going on these days that *Jewish* parents don't like,' Hal answered. 'One of the guys I play cards with has a daughter who's living with her boyfriend, to make sure he's the right one for her.

'If she decides he isn't, she'll try living with her next boyfriend, I thought, and where will it end? I felt even more thankful,' Hal went on, 'that Edith is the girl she is. She knew what she wanted from life and she's found it. Edith will stay happily married to Keith and on all counts.'

Which can't be said of you and me, thought Bella.

'I don't have to worry about her,' Hal said, 'and from here on she won't need me. If there was anything I could do for my son I would, but there isn't.'

'You could try being kinder to him.'

'Instead of trying to counteract the effects of *your* sort of kindness. If you think I don't know you send him money, you must think me a real *shlemiel*. On his sporadic earnings, Leonard would be wearing rags and tatters, not the expensive gear he shows up in when he does us a favour and pays us a visit,' said Hal.

'And what you've just said accounts for how you are with him?'

'What else? Well, it did before I washed my hands of the layabout he's become. Why didn't he take a ride back to London with Sylvie?'

Leonard had not yet risen from his bed.

'Is he unemployed again?'

Bella drank some tea and kept her tone level. 'Yes, and there's something I haven't got around to telling you.'

'I don't think I want to hear it.'

'But you're going to. After you hit the hay last night, I went to Leonard's room for a chat. He wasn't himself at the wedding –'

'Nor did he kiss his sister goodbye when she left for her honeymoon, an unforgivable oversight.'

'Most of the chatting was done by me,' Bella went on. 'I've never known Leonard less talkative, or seen him looking more downcast. But things haven't exactly gone right for him in London –'

'*Your* way of putting it,' said Hal.

'I'm concerned for our son's welfare and I'm sure you are.

What I've done, Hal, is ask Leonard to come into the business. I suggested it might help him decide if he spends some time at my elbow and that's what he's going to do.'

Chapter Fifteen

Sylvie's fear that Bella was due for an awakening materialized sooner than she had anticipated, nor could she have envisaged the terrible form it would take.

After Edith returned from her honeymoon, Hal took his own life.

Considerate to the last, Bella thought with the part of her mind that was functioning as if from afar. He didn't mar Edith's two weeks of bliss in Cornwall and ensured that it wouldn't be me who found him.

The woman who cleaned a neighbour's home each morning, and Bella's in the afternoon, had gone as usual to the garage where the bucket and mop were kept, to find Hal seated in his car with the engine running.

Leonard was now accompanying Bella to work as she had suggested and the police had located them at the Didsbury shop. Not until she saw the ambulance parked outside her house did Bella emerge from her trancelike state while her son drove home.

The cleaner was sitting stupefied in the kitchen when they arrived and was still there some time later, the house now all too silent after the police had departed with their notebooks and the ambulance with its grim burden.

'Could you drink a cup of tea, Mrs Diamond?'

Bella shook her head.

'Shall Leonard fetch you a drop of brandy?'

She glanced at her ashen-faced son. 'It would do *him* no harm to have some. You, too, Peggy.'

'No, thanks,' said Leonard, 'I couldn't swallow it down.'

'One of the policemen fetched me a drop from the cabinet before you got here,' said Peggy.

Bella had not until then noticed the glass on the table.

'But isn't it just like your mum, Leonard,' Peggy went on, 'to be thinking of others instead of herself, and oh the shock she's had!'

One that neither tea, nor brandy, could repair. Until today, Bella hadn't known the real meaning of the word 'shock'. Or was it that everything was relative, that major matters seemed in retrospect of minor significance compared with this?

'It was the same when your great-gran died,' Peggy was telling Leonard. 'I remember your mum making sure those who'd travelled to the funeral had a meal, though she didn't eat a morsel herself. That was nearly ten years ago, but as the old lady was fond of reminding me, time has a way of flying.'

And there are moments, thought Bella, when you wonder what the way you spent it was all about. This was one of them.

Peggy's kindly countenance crumpled with distress. 'I still can't believe what's happened,' she said dabbing her eyes with a corner of her flowered apron. 'Poor Mr Diamond was the cheerful sort and I reckon he must've had a brainstorm while he was driving to work that made him come back home and do what he did.'

On the contrary, Hal had carefully planned it and something he had said the morning after Edith's wedding returned to Bella:

'From here on she won't need me. If there was anything I could do for my son I would, but there isn't.'

The note he had left for Bella implied that she had *never* needed him: You'll get by without me. Remember me with love.

The pain that Bella had kept at bay suddenly engulfed her, but it was her private pain and there were things to do. 'We must phone Oxford and London, Leonard, and get in touch with the rabbi. I'll make the calls while you run Peggy home.'

'I'm not leaving you, Mum.'

'And I don't need running home,' said Peggy, 'the fresh air will do me good. I'll be here for the funeral tomorrow, Mrs Diamond.'

'It won't be tomorrow, there will have to be an inquest.'

The *family* inquest that took place in Bella's living-room on the eve of Hal's funeral proved more harrowing than the formal enquiry.

It was Bella who began it, her thoughts as oppressive as the sultry weather and her gaze fixed upon a framed photograph of Hal.

'Why did he do it!'

'A good question,' said Sylvie, 'and since Keith and Beth have gone for a walk, an opportunity to let some skeletons out of the cupboard.'

'Forget the skeletons,' said Joey, 'let's talk about contributory factors.'

'And if anyone present knows why my husband decided not to go on living, now's the time to tell me,' said Bella.

'But if you'd seen it for yourself,' said Sylvie, 'and done something about it, Hal might not have made the decision he did.'

Edith, seated on the arm of her father's favourite chair, raised her voice. 'I agree.'

'Well *I* damn well don't,' said Leonard, 'and how dare the lot of you sit here and tell my mother she's responsible for my father's killing himself!'

'Don't include me in that,' said Joey, 'I did say contributory factors. Bella can't be held totally to blame.'

'Is that supposed to ease my conscience?' she asked him.

'What conscience?' said Edith. 'You just went on doing your own thing, Mum, without even thinking of how it affected Dad.'

Bella smiled wanly. 'You're wrong about that.'

'And balance what you just said against how Dad took Mum

for granted,' Leonard told his sister, 'then add to it that if he'd been the breadwinner when we were kids, we would probably have starved.'

'We wouldn't have starved,' said Bella, 'but the breadwinner wouldn't have brought us any cake.'

Edith burst into tears. 'I can't bear this – Dad isn't yet in his grave and – well, all *I* want is to remember that he loved me.'

'But that's never going to be good enough for me,' said Leonard, 'nor will it be for Mum.'

Leonard went to stand with his back to the hearth, the moustache he had grown heightening his resemblance to his father and for Bella painfully so.

'We weren't sitting by his deathbed holding his hand, were we?' he went on to his sister. 'He took his leave of you and me as suddenly as he walked into our lives. Mum knew damn all about him when she married him, but he wasn't born the day before she met him.'

'Is that why you wanted to go to Toronto? Were you hoping to find out something that would make you seem Mr Perfect by comparison?'

Edith turned to Bella, who was still taking in what she had just learned. 'I tried to talk Leonard out of it, Mum, I didn't want him to go.'

'But I've no intention of going to *my* grave,' said Leonard, 'not knowing who Dad was. And Aunt Sylvie now knows why I needed the money she refused to lend me.'

It seemed to Bella then that she had gone on living her everyday life unaware that a web of secrets was being woven around her.

'Any more revelations?' she asked stridently.

'I shouldn't be surprised if Hal had gambling debts,' said Joey, 'and that could have been the final straw.'

'Gambling debts from playing cards with friends?'

'It depends upon the friends,' said her brother.

'And Dad also liked a flutter on the horses,' her son now told her.

Bella rose to gaze through the window. This must be how it felt to think you were treading solid ground and find instead that it was shifting sand. 'How could you have known what you just revealed, when I didn't?' she said turning to look at Leonard.

'I found out by accident, Mum.'

'And when he mentioned it to me, we kept it to ourselves in case it might worry you,' said Edith.

A web of secrets was right and Bella felt like the proverbial fly trapped in it.

'Everyone knows how much you have on your plate, Mum,' Edith capped it.

'That,' said Sylvie, 'has always been my sister's trouble. Marching through life, her eye on the target, without bothering to glance from side to side. I suffered a lot from that while I was growing up, though Joey didn't.'

'Well, not in the way you did,' Joey put in, 'since my rehabilitation was an adjunct of Bella's target. If I'd let her, she'd have moulded me as she has her business.'

What Bella was hearing was as if her sister had slapped one of her cheeks and her brother the other. 'I see,' was all she was capable of saying.

'But it's somewhat late for you to begin seeing, isn't it?' said Sylvie. 'Nor need you tell us you meant well. That goes without saying, Bella. And I now have a *personal* revelation to make. If secrets can be equated with skeletons in the cupboard mine is overdue for an airing, though my nephew already knows.'

'As I have for a long time,' said Bella.

'Uncle Joey and me, too,' Edith added, 'your relations aren't daft, Aunt Sylvie.'

'Have the lot of you been discussing Tess and me between yourselves!'

'Edith and I did have a word about it,' said Joey, 'on the way back to Oxford from that exhibition preview Tess invited us to, wasn't it, Edith?'

'And Aunt Beth wasn't with us, it was while Hannah had

chicken-pox,' Edith recalled. 'We decided that if you wanted to play let's pretend it was fine by us,' she told Sylvie.

'As for me,' said Bella, 'I shall never understand your way of finding happiness, Sylvie —'

'Any more than you did mine,' Joey cut in.

'But I wish Sylvie and Tess well, as eventually I did you and Beth.'

Bella managed to smile at her brother and sister, though her own partner was gone from her. *Remember me with love*. What but that and their children had held them together until suddenly it wasn't enough for him?

Sylvie came to kiss her. 'You might be seeing more of me from now on.'

'I'll look forward to that.'

'So long as I can bring Tess.'

'If I haven't made that clear, then let me do so now, Sylvie. And if I may, I'll take advantage of your hospitality when I come to London.'

'When will that be?'

'When I'm free to come.'

'You might just as well say never!'

'On the contrary,' said Bella, 'I'm thinking of selling the business.'

'But you won't,' said her brother, 'we know you.'

'Or could it be that you *think* you do?' Bella replied, mustering another smile. 'The truth is that none of you really knows me and there's nobody in this room for whom I haven't willingly bent my life.'

'Which you didn't for my father,' said Edith.

'He preferred to bend his to suit me and I let him, it's as simple as that, Edith.'

'And the answer to why Dad ended it all could be in Canada,' said Leonard. 'How can we know the sort of memories he lived with, when he never talked about them? Or that they didn't eventually become unbearable?'

'I shouldn't construe that as *more* than a contributory factor,' Joey advised.

'Could you stop thinking like a scientist just for the moment, Uncle? My father was flesh and blood, not one of your laboratory specimens. If he were here now, I'd want to hold him and comfort him for everything I didn't give a thought to while he was alive.'

Leonard sat down on the sofa and put his head in his hands.

'But I must be the one who goes to Toronto,' said Bella.

'If either of you goes, I'm finished with you,' Edith told them vehemently. 'Why can't you respect Dad's wishes now he's dead, Mum, like long ago you told Leonard and me that we must?'

'Leonard has already given you his reason. Mine is that I have to go on living and I shall know no peace till I lay the ghost your father's past was to me for twenty-five years.'

Bella paused to steady her tremulous voice. 'I must now ask you to respect *my* wishes, Edith.'

'In this case, that's easier said than done.'

'Nevertheless I shall go to Toronto after I've sold the business.'

'A minute ago you were only *thinking* of selling it,' said Leonard.

'But I've now made up my mind.'

Though her inner dynamo was no longer functioning, for Leonard's sake Bella might have continued forging ahead. But her Aunt Dolly's warning had returned to her: 'Don't build up your business for a son who might never take it over.'

A stunned silence had followed her announcement and Bella surveyed the four whom she had raised, scenes from their childhoods rising before her like snapshots in a family album.

To them, designing hats and making money had seemed her raison d'être and they must now accept that they had not really known her. Did she really know herself? The girl burdened by love and duty with responsibilities beyond her years was now a woman of forty-nine.

What she would do with the rest of her life remained to be seen.

PART THREE

1970 . . .

Chapter One

BELLA EXPERIENCED no difficulty in finding a buyer for her thriving business. Though the price was decreased by her refusal to stay on as designer, money was the least of her concerns.

Spirited as she had seemed during the family confrontation, that was but a mask for her bruised feelings and her own contribution to her husband's ending his life continued to haunt her.

Alone in the house, she lay night after night staring into the dark, memories allowing her no sleep. Her own radiant image in the mirror on her wedding day. Hal's quizzical expression when she entered Sylvie's bedsitter where he was lying ill. Her return with him to Manchester and his meeting his children. His joy and theirs. The tenderness and the passion when he and Bella finally consummated their reunion. And the day he had said that he wasn't an achiever, but would not try to stop Bella from being one.

Nothing and nobody could have stopped me, she reflected on her last night in the bed they had shared.

The house too was sold, together with all but one item of furniture, to a newly-wed couple from Newcastle delighted to acquire a ready-made home.

Bella had smiled wryly when the young man mentioned that he was being transferred to Manchester and worked for Marks and Spencer, recalling her grandmother's favourite success story – but what was success to Bella now?

His wife had been disappointed that the china cabinet was not for sale. Sylvie had wanted that memento of her childhood, revealing a sentimentality Bella had not known was in her.

Bella, though, wanted to discard reminders of the past and made her way to the lumber room early the next morning to do what she had not yet brought herself to do.

If Edith had known her father's Air Force uniform was still hanging in a cupboard, she would have claimed it and hugged it to her breast crying her eyes out. But Bella's daughter was now expecting a child and had already done too much weeping over morbid matters.

Bella had difficulty in containing her own emotion as she carried the uniform downstairs. In different circumstances, Edith's baby, should it be a boy, might one day have pranced around delightedly wearing his grandfather's Service cap, she was thinking poignantly when a faded photograph fell from the jacket.

She retrieved it and saw that the jacket lining was undone at the hem. Hal had had a secret hiding place. But what was one more secret among the many?

He had shown Bella snapshots of his sister, and one of his mother when she was young. Who was the girl in the photograph he *hadn't* shown her, but had kept for so many years? The name of a Montreal photographer was stamped on the back of it, though he had never mentioned that city, heightening Bella's feeling – shared with her son – that in Canada she would find important pieces of the puzzle. Not just of Hal's committing suicide, but of the enigma he himself was.

Impulsively, Bella decided to pack the uniform and give it to the father-in-law she had not met, who did not yet know his son was dead. If he didn't want it, let him be the one to dispose of it.

The doorbell prodded Bella from her churning thoughts. Seven a.m. was too early for the milkman to collect his money even when the customer was moving out that day. Unless he feared that Bella had done a moonlight flit –

The early caller was Ezra. And who else would it be but

the man who had stood by Bella since she took over the haberdashery when she was seventeen?

We've both come a long way since then, she thought recalling the shabby suit that Ezra had worn, and how she had brightened her old grey costume with one of Gran's lace flowers for their first date.

Ezra was now a prosperous man, and the fruits of Bella's labours invested as he had advised, allowing her to be what she had never been. A lady of leisure.

'It's nice to see you smile,' said Ezra, 'and I shouldn't think the couple who've bought the house and furniture would mind us using the sofa. Aren't you going to ask me to sit down?'

'By all means do. You can't help being the perfect gentleman, can you!'

'Or I might make use of the sofa for a different purpose,' he muttered as they settled themselves side by side. 'I'm still in love with you, Bella, which doesn't mean Doreen isn't a good wife.'

'Is that what you came to tell me?'

'I came to tell you that wherever you are in the world you can count on me.'

'I'll bear that in mind if I row with Sylvie and haven't enough cash to stay in a hotel if she kicks me out!'

Ezra's double chin wobbled with emotion. 'Please don't make fun of me, Bella, and what I just said isn't a joke. You won't be staying with your sister for long and then you're off to Canada.'

'After which I'll spend some time with Connie, in New York.'

'What shall you do after that?'

'Who knows?' Bella replied. 'I'm free for the first time in my life and I could turn into a social butterfly.'

'Never!'

'How do I know till I've tried it? Would it add to your anxiety if I told you that Keith's parents have invited me to stay at their holiday apartment in Florida?'

'How wouldn't it?' he said regarding her solemnly through the owlish spectacles he still preferred to those with modern frames. 'You could encounter someone on your travels who would land you in trouble all over again. And what bothers me also is you no longer have a home.'

Bella ignored the addendum. 'What you're saying is you don't trust my judgement.'

'Not when it comes to men, or you'd have married me instead of letting us both in for what we could have done without.'

Bella kept her tone light. 'You said Doreen is a good wife to you, and your corpulence proves she knows the proverbial way to a man's heart –'

'But not the recipe for happiness,' Ezra cut in. 'That, I'd have had with you though you didn't love me. It would've been enough that *I* love you.'

'But not enough for *me*,' Bella told him.

'As you said about the social butterfly life, how can you know till you've tried it?' he replied.

'It hasn't worked for *you*, has it? Marrying someone you didn't love because there were qualities that you admired in her.'

'That my mother admired in her!'

'You too,' said Bella, 'if you're prepared to admit it. This seems to me a time when nothing less than honesty will do.'

'The parting of the ways, you mean.'

'I hope that in spirit we shall never come to that, Ezra, and I want you to know how highly I value you. But it's time you stopped deluding yourself that we'd have been happy together.'

Ezra glanced at the uniform which Bella had laid on a chair and briefly it was as if the man who had come between them was there in the room.

'Were you happy with Hal?'

'Since I was in love with him till the day he died, the answer is a qualified yes. He made me miserable, too, as I'm sure I did him, but what we had together was worth it.'

'From the expression now on your face, you don't have to convince me,' Ezra said gruffly. 'Promise me you'll take care of yourself, Bella, and remember what I said about counting on me.'

'If I lose my umbrella in Timbuktu I'll dial your number.'

Ezra glanced at his watch and rose. 'And if I don't get home with the bagels soon, Doreen will start ringing up hospitals! I know her.'

'Don't be too sure of that,' Bella said from the depths of her experience, 'or you could be in for some surprises.'

'Meanwhile, if she rings up to make sure you're really leaving town, don't bother telling her I was here! She's never stopped being jealous of you.'

It struck Bella then that she was what her sister called an offstage character in Ezra's and Doreen's married life. Ever between them and again the present was built on the past.

Bella took the photograph that was part of Hal's past from the folds of his jacket and put it into her handbag, wishing that she had remained ignorant of its existence.

Chapter Two

'HOW DOES IT FEEL to have burned your boats?' Sylvie enquired when Bella arrived in London.

'Somewhat unreal.'

'There's something I must tell you that will bring you down to earth. Leonard is in trouble.'

'Is it a girl?'

'That kind of trouble is usually phrased the other way round. Leonard is in with what *you'd* call a bad lot, Bella, though I am more tolerant. Plenty of people in my world smoke pot.'

They were drinking coffee in the kitchen and Bella put down her cup. 'Oh my God.'

'You didn't fall apart when you assumed it was a girl,' Sylvie remarked, 'and I knew you'd react as you have. I still had to tell you. Leonard is your son, not mine, for which I'm grateful!

'The police raided a party he was at – the neighbours are probably fed up with the thumping that passes for music nowadays. And cannabis has a distinctive smell. Anyway, somebody gave the police the tip-off.'

'Are you telling me my son is in jail?'

'No. But that could be the outcome. They all had to make statements and Leonard was the one who'd supplied the pot, which makes him in the eyes of the law a pusher.'

'Would you mind explaining that? I'm new to the language!'

'Pushers sell drugs. Leonard hadn't just brought the stuff along to share with his friends, like Tess and I take a bottle of wine to parties,' said Sylvie, 'though that's what you'd no doubt prefer to believe.'

'I'd prefer not to believe *any* of this! But why are you so sure Leonard didn't do that?'

Sylvie topped up their coffee cups and returned the percolator to the hotplate before replying. 'In some ways, you've lived a sheltered life, Bella. It will take you some time to get used to the real world. Leonard left home in the mid-sixties and we're now into a new decade –'

'What is all this leading up to?' Bella cut in.

'Though I can't respect him, I have more sympathy for Leonard since we had the family showdown. He's what the Americans call a mixed-up kid –'

'But no longer a kid, he's twenty-five,' Bella said crisply.

'All the same,' Sylvie countered, 'it's easy to understand how someone like him could get caught up in the drug scene, since whatever he's looking for he has yet to find.'

'You're frightening me to death, Sylvie!'

'What I'm actually doing is trying to help you face the facts. After Hal's suicide,' Sylvie went on, 'Leonard began dropping in here again. I'm his link with home, aren't I? On his last visit, he told me what I've told you and didn't deny what he's accused of. His appearance in court is scheduled for later this week and he asked if I would accompany him.

'My answer was that I'm not the archetypal aunt, nor am I prepared to transform my appearance for that role and put on a performance for the magistrates. I told Leonard he must get *his* act together and that includes standing on his own feet. But that's never going to happen, Bella, while you go on encouraging him to think the world owes him a living.

'Before the family showdown, I wouldn't have said that to you,' Sylvie added.

'But you're not pulling your punches now!'

'With Leonard I never did and I left him in no doubt that you would learn from me what you have. He wasn't too pleased.' Sylvie gazed contemplatively at the bowl of tangerines on the table. 'Your son has never applied to himself the rules he sets for others. Nor does he see in himself the traits he inherited from his father along with the charm.'

'Perhaps he'd rather *not* see them.'

'You agree they're there?'

'I've always known it, Sylvie.'

'Then why didn't you try to knock them out of him?'

'You'd have to be a mother to understand.'

'And that, I'm unlikely to be!' Sylvie said drily. 'But give me the child and I'll show you the man, as the quotation would have us believe and it makes sense, Bella. All of us are products of our childhood – and by and large you didn't make too bad a job of Joey and me.'

They shared a smile of rapport that once would not have been possible.

What Sylvie called the 'family showdown' had seemed to Bella more like an inquest, as if the relationships she had taken for granted were suddenly no more and everything questionable. But mine with my sister is now a good deal happier, she thought while they sat together in companionable silence, wintry sunlight streaming through the window and Tess's cat curled up by the fire.

With my daughter the opposite describes it, Bella was thinking when Sylvie asked if she intended visiting Edith before leaving for Canada.

'You seem to have read my thoughts, Sylvie, but another fact I have to face is that my daughter doesn't want to see me. She hasn't been to Manchester since Hal's funeral. Nor has she invited me to stay with her, though she knows I haven't been short of free time.'

'I don't like the sound of that.'

'But there's nothing to be done about it. When Edith said if I go to Toronto she's finished with me, she meant it.'

'Your daughter has high principles,' said Sylvie, 'would that the same could be said of your son. And I consider myself fortunate to be learning about motherhood second-hand!'

*

Bella steeled herself to accompany Leonard to court and was beset by a sense of unreality throughout the proceedings.

Since Leonard was a first offender and his mother's presence implied the respectability of his background, he was let off with a stern warning and a heavy fine.

'You look like a schoolmarm in that get-up, Mum!' he said with a grin as they emerged from the building into a rainstorm.

Though unwilling to do so herself, Sylvie had advised Bella to dress for the part and she had on a dark grey coat, a matching velour hat set primly on her head.

'Schoolmarms nowadays, Leonard, are just as likely to wear mini-skirts.'

'The mini's on its way out. Didn't anyone tell you? And the maxi is in.'

'And if that's a portent that the seventies will see young people regaining their common sense, I must hope that will include you, Leonard.'

'Going to play the heavy-handed mother, are you? Does that mean you're not going to take me for a celebratory lunch?'

Leonard took Bella's arm to help her stride over a puddle. How like his father he was, solicitous and kind, but with too many of the same failings, as Sylvie had unnecessarily said. Any way of making enough money to get by on would have done for Hal as for Leonard. And Joey's assumption that Hal had left gambling debts had proved correct.

How he would meet them didn't seem to have entered his head, but considering possible consequences was no more Hal's way than it was his son's.

'The cab rank is across the road,' said Leonard.

'But a bus will do me fine. Are cabs your usual way of getting around London?' Bella asked tartly.

'It depends on how I'm fixed for cash,' Leonard replied.

'And you never know how you'll be fixed from one day to

the next, do you?' They had halted at a bus stop and Bella tilted her hat to the rakish angle fashion demanded.

'Now you look like my mum,' Leonard said with the smile that had never failed to soften her heart.

Nor did it now, but Bella would not let herself succumb. 'A celebratory lunch, you said, Leonard. Would you mind telling me what there is to celebrate?'

'I could've been put behind bars, but I wasn't.'

Bella would not forget standing on Hammersmith Road in the rain fearing for her son, passers-by jostling her and the roar of traffic in her ears. If Leonard went through life with the attitude he had just expressed, what was to become of him?

'You've just given me cause to wish I hadn't put in an appearance in court on your behalf,' she told him. 'It strikes me, Leonard, that being behind bars is how you're one day going to learn your lesson. Your being a first offender was just a technicality, wasn't it? And please don't lie to me.'

'All right, so the other times I didn't get caught! And you have my promise that I won't take the chance again.'

When eventually they were seated aboard a bus, Leonard asked Bella how she was enjoying her retirement.

'It isn't the usual sort of retirement and I'm not ready to settle for a rocking-chair!'

'You never will be, Mum, and like the rest of the family I'm wondering what you'll end up doing.'

Bella told him that she had toyed with the idea of applying for one of the university courses available to mature students.

'That doesn't surprise me, Mum. You were cheated of your chance of going to college when you were young and your sudden decision to sell the business – what you said at the family trial – well I got the impression you were telling us you'd made sure each of *us* had our chance and now it's your turn.'

We each have our own nomenclature for that catalystic occasion, thought Bella whilst eyeing the shocking-pink hat the woman seated in front of her was wearing, its style as outmoded as that sixties colour now was. Joey had afterwards referred to it as the 'family fracas'. And Edith no doubt recalls it as the night family treason was committed and her mother the traitor.

'*Was* that what you were telling us?' Leonard prodded her.

'In a manner of speaking, yes,' Bella answered, 'though going to college is unlikely to enter into it.'

'Why not? You've the brains for it,' said her son.

'But my chance to do what your Uncle Joey's now doing is long gone. There's no way to get back the lost years.'

'So forget science, just enrol for a course that would fill in your time and that you'd enjoy.'

Bella's response was, 'Where would that get me?'

'You're never going to change,' Leonard said with a laugh. 'But its time *you* did and we'll be discussing that over lunch.'

'As a matter of fact, Mum, I've a business proposition to put to you.'

'Oh yes?' Bella said warily.

'There's an in-place restaurant up for sale near to where I live –'

Bella didn't let him launch into the persuasive tactics she knew would follow. 'If it's an in-place, why is it up for sale?'

'I heard they've had staff problems.'

'But you can't envisage that happening to you. Added to which, what do you know about running a restaurant, Leonard? There's a good deal more to it than dispensing bonhomie to the customers. What would you do if your chef walked out on you? Send for *me*? As for the buying in, can you tell if a melon is ripe by feeling it?'

'Judging by the underripe melon we sometimes got given at home, nor can you.'

'But I'm not thinking of going into the restaurant business. If it's what you really want to do, Leonard, find a restaurateur who'll let you work your way up from the bottom, so you can learn the trade. When you're ready, come back to me with your proposition.'

239

'By then, the place I fancy owning will've been sold. But thanks for the lecture.'

It would take more than a lecture to bring Leonard down to earth and again Bella feared for him.

That evening Joey came up to London to dine with his sisters.

'We ought to have arranged this for when Beth could have come,' Bella said when the three of them were seated at the table enjoying the baked halibut Tess had cooked for them before going out to meet a friend.

Joey and Sylvie exchanged a glance, then Joey put down his fork. 'We wanted you to ourselves, Bella. Since you're going away and nobody knows for how long, Beth and Tess thought that perfectly understandable. My daughter sends you her love, by the way.'

'And how is *my* daughter? If it were left to her to keep me up to date, she could already be living in the States and I wouldn't know.'

'Edith is blooming,' Joey replied, 'and the up-to-date news is that Keith has completed his thesis.'

'Thanks for filling me in, Joey.'

'You don't deserve what's happened between you and Edith,' he said sympathetically, 'but it still isn't too late to set things right.'

'You could call off your trip to Canada,' said Sylvie.

'Is delving into a dead husband's past more important than losing a living daughter?' said Joey.

'That might seem a simple choice to you,' Bella answered, 'but I lived with that past for twenty-five years of my life and Hal ended his by his own hand. He will never be laid to rest in my heart if I don't lay the ghost.'

A pause followed during which Sylvie toyed with her food, Joey sipped his wine, and Bella surveyed them. 'Is this why you wanted me to yourselves?'

'Not entirely,' said her brother.

'What's next on the agenda!'

'Your future,' said her sister.

'My future is nobody's concern but mine.'

Joey ladled some more lemon sauce on the remains of his fish and resumed eating. 'That wasn't your attitude the other way round.'

'And the boot is now on the other foot,' said Sylvie, 'it's our turn to worry about *you*.'

Despite her irritation, Bella could not but find the situation moving. Unreal, too.

'As I said to you in another respect,' Sylvie went on, 'in some ways you've led a sheltered life.'

'But you're now a woman of means about to set forth on your travels,' said Joey, 'and what's happened has made you vulnerable.'

'To put it bluntly,' said Sylvie, 'you're fair game for some man with an eye to the main chance to con you. We had to warn you.'

'This,' said Bella, 'is beginning to feel like a two-pronged attack!'

They watched her fling down her napkin and leave the table.

'The boot really is on the other foot,' Sylvie said to Joey, 'it used to be me marching off in a huff.'

'And I can't say I'm enjoying exchanging roles!' Bella exclaimed from the window bay.

'When you get back, if you fancy settling in Oxford, Beth and I would be delighted,' Joey told her, 'and we'll help you house-hunt.'

'I was about to suggest that Bella might make her home in London,' said Sylvie.

Again Bella was moved, but the irritation was still there. 'Where you can keep an eye on me!' she said to them drily.

'If that's how you care to put it,' Joey replied. 'We owe you a lot, Bella, and speaking for myself, I love you and I'm not one to welch on my duty.'

If this was how being on the receiving end felt, Bella would not like it to be her lot for the rest of her life.

Chapter Three

'BELLA'S FLIGHT to Toronto was her first time aboard a plane. And you considered yourself a sophisticated woman, she had thought while the Air Canada stewardess helped her fasten her seat-belt.

An illusion already dispelled by her stay in London, which had left her with the impression that she had spent her life tucked away in a quiet corner of the world, though Manchester was a busy provincial city.

The sheltered existence Sylvie had referred to seemed the more so when Bella emerged uncertainly from the terminal at Toronto's Lester B. Pearson Airport where a colourful throng of international passengers headed for the taxi rank.

While she waited in the queue behind an Arab couple, her eye absently admiring a passing hat – would Bella never stop noticing hats? – she steeled herself for what she was here to do and that included telling Mr Diamond the manner of his son's dying.

Bella would not spare her father-in-law the details! A surge of anger evoked by *his* contribution to the enigma Hal was hardened her resolve. The makings of her husband's suicide had begun long before he met her, causing him to shut the door on his early life. Only from time to time had he briefly opened it, allowing Bella a glimpse inside.

Had he not, I would now be calling all the Diamonds in the telephone book, she thought later in the hotel room she had reserved for only one night. But Hal had once mentioned the name of his father's company and the street where its head office was situated. Bella's intention was to take a cab there and beard the lion in his den.

Her son had been surprised that she didn't intend taking the opportunity to sight-see in Toronto and also of seeing Niagara Falls. That's the basic difference between Leonard and me, she reflected after showering and donning the bathrobe provided by a hotel whose luxury she had barely noticed. For Bella this was strictly business, if not in the commercial sense.

For Leonard, though, there had to be a pleasurable aspect to everything. If he'd been the one to make this trip, he might afterwards have stayed on this side of the Atlantic and never been heard of again! An exaggeration perhaps, but in essence what was he already but a rolling stone?

As his father was before meeting me, Bella thought wanly. Would Hal have taken his own life if he'd shared it with a different woman? With the passage of time she was coming to view their marriage objectively and the picture of herself this presented was one she would rather not see.

Sexually virile though Hal was to the end of his days, there were more ways of emasculating a man than chopping off his balls, as he himself might have put it, and more ways of being a man than the ability to do the necessary in bed.

It would take a much stronger character than Hal Diamond was, to feel himself the equal of a woman like Bella. He had not let that inequality matter, but that wasn't to say it hadn't damaged him.

Bella stemmed her painful thoughts and selected one of the deceptively simple hats that were her style to wear with her black suit, carefully appraising herself in the mirror after putting it on.

Her chic appearance would not disgrace the man who had married her and given his low opinion of his son, it was possible that Mr Diamond was in for more than one shock.

In the taxi taking her to her father-in-law's office, Hal's uniform in a parcel beside her, she absently surveyed downtown Toronto, alive with the everyday activities of a thriving city. It was here that Hal had spent his unhappy childhood, while his mother grew more and more frail and his father went ruthlessly from strength to strength.

As he'd continued to do, Bella had thought when she told the cab driver where she wished to be taken and he replied that Diamond Enterprises now operated from the Diamond Building.

'Whoever gave you that address must have got it from their old address book!' he said now with a laugh.

No, from his memories, thought Bella. 'I never went back to the office after my mother died,' Hal had said, and years later had allowed Bella another glimpse of that day, in which was included the name of his father's company and the street he had stumbled along in anguish after losing his mum and cutting himself off from his dad.

Such was the jigsaw puzzle Bella was left to put together and how few were the pieces. Her daughter's accusing face rose before her. But nothing could have stopped Bella from doing what she had to do.

The driver had pulled up outside the imposing entrance of a towering edifice, its powerful structure in keeping with Bella's preconception of the man she was about to meet.

'You've forgotten your package, ma'am,' the friendly Canadian said when she had paid him.

Bella picked up the parcelled uniform and managed to smile, feeling that she was delivering to Mr Diamond all that remained of his son. Would he treasure it , or tell her to go to hell and take Hal's uniform with her?

She made her way across the echoing foyer, past potted palms and white leather sofas, to a reception desk that matched the rest.

If Gran had seen this, she'd have cited Diamond Enterprises as an example of where she thought I was heading, not 'Mr Marks, or was it Mr Spencer?' And if Leonard were here, he'd be thinking himself on to a good thing.

The ash blonde seated behind the sleek expanse of glass and chromium plate gave Bella a plastic smile. 'May I help you?'

'I'm here to see Mr Diamond and he isn't expecting me.'

'Mr Diamond doesn't see anyone without an appointment.'

'I think he will make an exception when you tell him that Mrs Hal Diamond wishes to see *him*.'

'Are you a relative?'

'Yes, as a matter of fact.'

'I'll let him know you're here.'

A moment later, Bella was instructed to take the direct elevator to the executive suite.

A young man of around her son's age was waiting there to receive her.

'Please forgive me for not coming down,' he said politely, 'some people were with me when I learned of your arrival and I had to hand them over to a vice-president. I'm Ross Diamond,' he added shaking her hand.

The baby brother to whom Hal had sent a gift was now grown up and in the business. He escorted Bella into an office reminiscent of those she had seen in Hollywood films.

A window spanning an entire wall afforded a panoramic view of the city. Bleached maple panelling enhanced the impression of space and light. Bella's high heels disappeared into the shag-pile carpet and her gaze was drawn as if by a magnet to the oil painting hung behind the desk.

'My father in his prime,' said Ross Diamond.

But for Bella, it was like looking at a picture of her husband.

'It's your father I'm here to see.'

'You're a little late for that,' he replied, 'my father died three months ago. But please sit down, you and I have a lot to talk about and I've cancelled the rest of my schedule for today.'

He waited for Bella to do so, then put himself in the club chair opposite hers. Though it had crossed her mind that her father-in-law might by now be dead, she had not let that possibility deter her.

As though the trip itself was a pilgrimage I had to make because I loved Hal, she was reflecting when Ross Diamond said, 'I should tell you that my father asked for your husband on his deathbed.'

'My *late* husband.'

'I'm sorry to hear that.'

'Are you?'

'Hal was my brother, wasn't he?'

'But I doubt that the picture of him presented to you by your father was an endearing one.'

'How could it have been? Can I get you a drink?'

'No, thanks.'

'But I guess I'm in need of one!' Ross went to open a cocktail cabinet discreetly housed in the wall panelling. 'One person I never expected to meet was my brother's wife if he had one.'

'Do *you* yet have a wife?' Bella asked while he poured Canadian Club on the ice he had shovelled into a crystal tumbler.

'I haven't had time to find one.'

Given whose son he was and his being in the business, that didn't surprise Bella.

'Dad had a coronary in the office when I was still a school-kid.' Ross revealed. 'That didn't stop him from going ahead with his plans for this building. His second heart attack was shortly after I came into the business and Mom didn't have to ask me to do everything I could to lighten his load.'

Had Bella been capable of smiling even sardonically at that moment she would surely have done so, as the scenario her father-in-law's personality had decreed for his sons appeared before her. Hal's defection was self-preservation and Ross had spent his adult life preserving their father.

Though no situation was quite that simple, it was the core of the matter that had brought Bella to where she now was.

'Now, though,' Ross went on, 'Mom keeps telling me to slacken off.'

'That sounds like good advice,' Bella said noting his weary appearance.

'But I guess working too hard gets to be a habit.'

'One I once shared,' she told him, 'but habits can be broken.'

'First I'd have to want to.' Ross swirled the liquor in his glass and gazed at it contemplatively. 'I guess I'm too proud of what my dad achieved to let him down.'

'Like your brother did?'

He met Bella's challenging glance. 'There's no arguing with that.'

'In your opinion,' Bella replied, 'and you hold it against Hal.'

'If you'd like to know what I really hold against him,' Ross said with feeling, 'it's the way he just walked out and never came back, after all the scrapes Dad had got him out of.'

'Like what?'

'Like Hal's first marriage.'

Bella was glad that she was sitting down.

Ross eyed her expression. 'He didn't tell you about it?'

'No, as a matter of fact.'

'Typical!'

'How dare you speak of Hal in that tone,' Bella retorted, 'your picture of him is even more incomplete than mine. I lived with him and we raised two children together. You, on the other hand, never met him. His not telling me what I've just learned from you is typical only of his painful inability to talk of the past.'

Bella found that she was trembling. And she now knew who the girl in the photograph was and why Hal had kept it. He must have loved her very much.

'I'd like that drink you offered me now,' she said to Ross.

'What'll it be?'

'I think a sip of brandy is called for.'

'And I'm sorry for shaking you up. How old are your children?' Ross asked while pouring the drink.

'They're twins, a boy and a girl, and they're now twenty-five.'

'That isn't a boy and a girl, it's a man and a woman,' he said with a smile, 'though my mom still refers to me as a boy and I'm pushing thirty.'

But his appearance would always be boyish, thought Bella

as he handed her the glass, the cowlick he kept brushing from his brow enhancing that impression as did his deep blue eyes and his fresh complexion.

'It's weird I guess to find out I have a nephew and niece of my own generation,' he said. 'And my father died thinking he had only one grandchild.'

'From Hal's first marriage, I presume?' Whatever Bella had expected it hadn't included any of this.

'And if your legs can still carry you,' said Ross, 'I'll show you a photo of her. The family gallery Dad kept on his desk isn't my idea of office décor, but I hadn't the heart to change anything when I moved in here.'

But the day you impose your ideas on your father's will equate with Hal's escape years ago, thought Bella. Like her husband – who had also been someone else's – this lad had a personality all his own and that day had to come.

She followed Ross behind the desk on which some framed photographs stood beside a vase of yellow chrysanthemums.

The brittle step-mother Bella had visualized from Hal's brief reference to his father's second marriage turned out to be a fair-haired woman with a gentle smile.

'You look like your mum, Ross.'

'And the picture in the filigree frame is Hal's mother.'

'May I take it for my children?'

'Please do and they might like to see what their half-sister looks like, if you'd care to take them her photo too.'

Bella doubted that Edith, her daddy's girl, would want to see it.

'The one at the end of the row is Hal's sister,' said Ross, 'she married an Australian and lives in Melbourne.'

Bella switched her gaze from the pretty face she was studying to the photograph Ross had pointed out. 'Henrietta is alive?'

'Hal told you she was dead? Well, I guess that figures,' said Ross.

'Hal wasn't a liar!'

'He just didn't tell you the whole truth.'

248

'What he actually said was that he'd once had a wonderful sister and I *assumed* she was dead.'

'My brother sure left you to do a lot of assuming,' said Ross as they returned to the sitting area. 'Henrietta was several years older than him,' he went on, 'and my reading of this is that he respected her and knew his taking off was the end of their relationship.'

But like so much else it was only a reading, putting one's own interpretation on the snippets of information available and filling in the gaps as best one may.

'But when they flew in for Dad's funeral,' said Ross, 'Henrietta's husband told me she's never recovered from Hal's disappearance. And I have to tell you that my dad spent a fortune trying to trace him. The enquiries came to a dead end in Detroit, though.'

Detroit, like Montreal, was a city that Hal had never mentioned.

'Hal worked there in an automobile plant in 1939, but after that the private eye came up with zilch.'

'1939 was when Hal joined up,' Bella informed him.

'Hal served in the war?'

'That was how we met.'

Remembrance of herself and Connie behind the canteen counter, and a Canadian airman who looked like Clark Gable walking in, returned to Bella.

'I brought his uniform to give to your father,' she told Ross. 'If you'd care to have it, it's yours.'

'Thanks,' he replied sounding subdued.

'It hasn't got a pilot's wings on it, Ross. Hal wasn't a hero, but nor was he quite the weakling you seem to think. If you're wondering why I qualified that, in some ways he *was* weak, but they didn't get in the way of our personal happiness.'

'My dad would've been pleased to know Hal had a wife like you,' Ross answered, 'he never stopped worrying about him.'

'Did Hal's first wife come from Montreal?'

'How could you have known that?'

Bella took the faded photograph from her handbag and

showed it to him. 'The name of the studio, stamped on the back, told me.'

'I never saw a picture of Pauline before, but her daughter sure looks like her, and Pauline and Jeanette could probably feature in that famous book of records you have in your country,' Ross declared, 'as the only mother and daughter to have taken the veil and be together in the same nunnery.'

A silence followed while Bella digested what she had heard and Ross got himself another drink.

'Pauline is French Canadian,' Ross said returning to sit opposite her. 'Hal met her when he was waiting on tables in her father's restaurant. I guess they must have been crazy about each other to elope like they did. Pauline was only sixteen and when they got back, her father called mine and between them they got the marriage annulled.'

'*If you knew what my father did to me* . . . ' Hal had once said. But Bella could not have interpreted that as anything approaching the reality. After which there was no likelihood of his ever returning to the fold.

'It can't have been the first time that's been arranged between a Catholic and a Jewish family,' Ross opined, 'but in this case it was followed by what I've already told you. Pauline couldn't have known she was pregnant and the next day she was shut away to repent in the convent and Hal banging on the gates.

'If that sounds to you melodramatic,' Ross went on, 'it's what her father told the detective doing the trace, though that was a year or so later. He also said Pauline's little girl was being raised in the convent. When Dad heard that, according to my mom he hit the roof and called his partner in crime in Montreal, demanding to know why he'd kept secret that Marvin Diamond had a granddaughter.'

Bella glanced at the oil painting of that powerful but misguided man and could well imagine him doing so. But he too had suffered the consequences of his own actions. Gone to his grave without being reconciled with his elder son.

'Dad didn't get to see a picture of Jeanette, though, till the one on his desk arrived out of the blue in the sixties,' Ross continued. 'It came with a note from her other granddad, saying it was taken the day before she became a Bride of Christ.

'Dad couldn't have failed to get the message. Till then, he'd let himself hope that one day Jeanette would breeze in and say, "Hi, Gramps," but he finally had to accept that was never going to happen. He'd have had to take on the whole Catholic Church right up to the Pope to get *that* marriage annulled and he still wouldn't have succeeded.'

'But our religion, too, played its part in the tragedy,' said Bella.

'With that I have to agree.'

'Was that why you referred to your father and Pauline's as partners in crime?'

'I had a lot of respect for my dad, but don't get the idea I think he was perfect,' Ross replied, 'and I guess why I referred to Hal's first marriage as a scrape was I was raised seeing it that way.'

Bella said after a pause, 'The same could be said of the way you see Hal.'

'But I'm never going to get to meet him now. And I'm glad to know he had some happiness with you,' Ross added quietly.

'If I weren't certain of that, what you've told me would be unbearable.'

'I haven't yet mentioned that now I know of their existence, there'll be legacies coming to your son and daughter. A clause in my father's will directed that should it be learned that his elder son had children, they were to receive between them –'

'I don't wish to know the amount,' Bella cut in. 'It concerns Edith and Leonard and I'll leave you their addresses. It's possible that my daughter will refuse to accept the money, given the rift between your father and Hal. They were very close.'

Leonard, though, would accept it with alacrity and it would slip through his fingers with equal speed.

Bella was tempted to spare Ross the knowledge of how Hal had died, but thought better of it.

When she told him he paled visibly.

'That might help you understand why I had to come here,' she said, 'and I myself understand a good deal more than I did before we had this talk.'

Bella glanced at the pewter tankard on the desk. 'Hal would've been pleased that you kept his gift, though I shouldn't think he expected you to fill it with pencils when you grew up!'

'Dare I invite you to dinner tonight?'

'Am I so formidable?'

'I can't make up my mind!'

She gave him a warm smile and watched him put the framed pictures of Hal's mother, and of his other daughter, into a padded envelope for her. 'You're a nice lad to have for a brother-in-law, Ross. But you and I have put each other through enough for one day, much as I appreciate your invitation.'

Bella had to smile wryly when Ross handed her the envelope. Beside the company name was an embossed lion. But she had come too late to beard the real one in his den and would never know how that confrontation might have turned out.

'What sort of business *is* Diamond Enterprises?' she enquired while Ross walked with her to the elevator.

'Hal didn't even tell you that? And you didn't ask him?'

'The best way to put it,' Bella replied, 'is that I trod carefully because I sensed a minefield. And I wasn't wrong.'

Ross paused to remove a wilting leaf from one of the exotic plants that lined the broad corridor.

'My dad used to take care of these himself, he had what they call green fingers in the horticultural sense as well as for making money. I'm not a natural successor to him in either sense, but I do my best!

'I'd have liked to be a concert pianist,' he added, 'but whether I'd have made it wasn't put to the test.'

Another like me, thought Bella, and the world must be full

of people cheated by circumstances of following their natural bent.

'Diamond Enterprises,' Ross said as they resumed walking, 'is what you would term an entrepreneurial company, with a range of interests including the jewel that happens to be the family name and with which my father began building his empire.'

'Dealing in diamonds?'

'In a small way. When Hal was born, Dad didn't even have an office. I guess fathering a son was his incentive.'

Bella thought of her Uncle Saul who had slaved on *his* son's account, though personal ambition too had spurred him on. Men like Saul Lazarus and Marvin Diamond were doubly driven if they had sons to step into their shoes.

'I'd like to think my birth was a shot in the arm for Dad after Hal's walking out,' said Ross.

'How could it not have been?'

A son needed to feel loved by his father and sometimes reassurance was required. Where did that leave Bella's son?

'My mom would adore your hat,' Ross said irrelevantly as they reached the elevator. 'Do you have time to meet her? And for me to show you Toronto? Could we fix something up for tomorrow?'

Now he's found me, he doesn't want to let me go and Bella felt equally drawn to him. 'I'm booked on the first flight to New York, Ross. But perhaps you'll visit me in England some time.'

'I'd sure like to, only you didn't give me your address.'

'Right now I haven't one. When I'm settled I'll let you know.'

'Did you have to sell your home? Didn't Hal provide for you?'

So concerned was he, Bella placed a hand on his arm. 'I sold my home for no other reason than to try to put Hal's suicide behind me. That doesn't mean I'm ever going to forget him.'

'And you must come back to Canada, it's a beautiful country.'

But for Bella it would remain the place she associated with the past that had haunted her married life.

That night she lay thinking of Hal and Pauline, Hal hammering on the convent gates, the girl within, and wept for them both.

Rest in peace, my love.

Chapter Four

CONNIE WAS WAITING for Bella at Kennedy Airport, attired in crimson pants and a white cashmere sweater that emphasized her curves.

'Welcome to America, Bella! And do I have a lot to tell you.'

'When didn't you?' said Bella as they embraced affectionately. 'Being with you is like a breath of fresh air, Connie.'

'I guess the opposite goes for this fair city! Is this all the baggage you have? You sure travel light, Bella.'

'It's as well I do since they wouldn't let me take the luggage trolley any further than customs. Shlepping a suitcase doesn't match my expectations of New York.'

'Nor will lots of things,' said Connie with a smile, 'wait till you see Broadway. I'll take the case and you can tote the hatbox. You must be the only woman outside the British Royal Family who still travels with one.'

Bella remarked as they left the terminal building, 'You don't feel British any more, do you?'

'After living here so long and three American husbands, the answer has to be how could I? Is the hat you have on one of your designs, Bella?'

'Yes, as a matter of fact.'

'Oh how that reply takes me back!'

They shared a laugh.

'Remember that night in the canteen?' said Connie. 'It was me who fancied Hal and you who got him. How was Toronto?'

'It helped me understand the man I married.'

'And I have to say you seem much more tranquil than

when we last spoke on the phone,' Connie replied. 'Me, though, I'm never going to understand *any* man and I no longer expect to, which will save me a lot of disappointments.'

Bella eyed her friend's profile, the jawline as firm now as in her twenties. 'That facelift you had certainly did the trick.'

'And you should think about getting one while you're here, Bella. In this country it's no big deal.'

'My face was never my fortune, Connie!'

'While your brains were doing what they did for you, it didn't have to be. But whatever you got for your business won't last for ever,' said Connie, 'and at your age your best bet is a husband who can keep you.

'If you think I'm speaking ill of the dead, I'm not,' Connie went on, 'you were crazy about Hal and him about you, that made up for his shortcomings. But it doesn't come twice in any woman's life, I'm here to tell you. And I sometimes have to laugh because the only guy I'd have married for love though he didn't have a penny, never proposed to me.'

'You were in love with your first husband,' Bella reminded her.

'Sure, but he wasn't just a handsome GI, he came from a wealthy family and I knew that when I said yes to him.'

They had begun threading their way through the car park and Bella clamped a hand to her hat as the wind tried to tear it from her head. 'Which of your hundreds of boyfriends was the one you just mentioned, Connie?'

'A guy I had an affair with after my second marriage broke up.'

Connie set down Bella's suitcase beside a gleaming white Cadillac.

'This is *your* car?'

'Part of my last divorce settlement along with the penthouse I'm now living in.'

Connie had replied as casually as if Bella had asked what time it was. Getting married and unmarried with affairs in between has become her way of life, thought Bella. But what sort of life was that?

'Do they have penthouses in London?' Connie enquired while putting Bella's luggage in the car boot.

'I wouldn't know and that won't be what I'm looking for wherever I finally settle,' Bella said with a laugh.

Connie's response was one now all too familiar to Bella. 'Wherever you finally settle? I don't like the sound of that.'

She too was concerned about Bella's future and once again Bella was moved and irritated simultaneously. 'I need time to sort myself out,' she answered.

'That, I can understand.'

They fell silent until they had left the airport behind and joined the traffic heading towards Manhattan, each immersed in her own thoughts in the comfortable atmosphere true friendship allows.

'Any chance you might settle in London?' Connie asked.

'My sister would like me to.'

'If you do,' said Connie, 'could be you'll have me around the corner.'

'You're thinking of returning to England?'

'It all depends.'

'There has to be a man involved in this!'

'And he happens to be British. If I marry him, I'll never have to worry about money again.'

'If you *stay* married to him,' said Bella. 'Has he popped the question?'

'Not yet. But he wants a wife, not just an affair and then goodbye, I can tell,' said Connie. 'And his first marriage lasted till his wife died – if that isn't a good reference, what would be?'

'Believe it or not,' said Bella, 'among our age group in the country you were born and raised in, most couples manage to stay married.'

'For better or worse, you mean!'

'What I actually mean, Connie, is that it's only the young-sters who seem to approach matrimony thinking that if a husband or wife doesn't come up to expectations, they can cut their losses and get a new one.'

'Is that some sort of crack about *me*, Bella? If so, I have to tell you I've really tried and it hasn't been easy.'

There was now a hint of weariness in Connie's voice, her middle-aged good-time-girl aura briefly gone and it occurred to Bella that her friend yearned for stability in more ways than the financial.

'This British guy I've met is a little older than I'd like for my next husband,' Connie said contemplatively while overtaking a dented Ford that was holding up its betters, 'but you can't have everything and that should be your policy too, Bella.'

'I appreciate your concern, Connie, I really do, but would you please stop planning my future for me? The last thing I'm looking for is a husband –'

Connie then whizzed past a truck with barely an inch to spare.

'And if you go on driving as recklessly as you are doing, I might never get to see your penthouse!' Bella exclaimed.

'I was always the reckless one of the two of us,' Connie said reminiscently, 'but in some ways we seem to have swapped places. When you called up to tell me you'd made a spur-of-the-moment decision to sell your business I thought, That isn't like Bella –'

'You weren't the only one!'

'Okay, so you did what you felt like doing, but I don't see you turning into a gipsy,' said Connie. 'I agree it's too soon for you to think of remarrying, you're not a divorcee. But if I hook Victor, I'll be in England to help you manhunt when you're ready.'

'Thanks for the warning,' said Bella. 'How long have you known Victor?'

'Long enough,' Connie replied.

Bella would not have been surprised if she had met him only last night and had sized him up immediately as a suitable candidate for husband number-four.

'Has your son met him?' she asked.

'Don't even mention my son! "Just send me an invitation to the wedding, Mom," is Warren's attitude.'

'Given that Victor would be his third step-father, that doesn't surprise me.'

'But it's hurtful to *me*.'

Connie returned to the subject from which they had digressed. 'I met Victor while I was vacationing in Palm Beach and so was he. With all I have to spend my alimony on, I couldn't afford to stay in that pricey place for more than a week, but Victor was there for a month.'

Bella had to laugh. 'What better recommendation could there be than that?'

'Well, he sure showed me a good time with no expense spared,' said Connie, 'though I got the impression his heart wasn't in it.'

'How long ago did he lose his wife?'

'He said it was last year, but don't get the idea he was using me as a shoulder to cry on,' Connie replied, 'Victor isn't that kind of guy.'

'Has he any children?'

'A daughter who works with him in his business, he said, and one he didn't say much about, so he could be having trouble with her. What he did say, though, was that even the best of daughters couldn't take the place of the helpmate a wife is.'

'That doesn't sound like a description of you!'

'But I'm not letting it put me off. How do I know till I've tried it?'

Bella's new attitude to life, but she wouldn't be quite as reckless as Connie continued to be, she thought while admiring the Manhattan skyline.

'I'm looking forward to seeing all those skyscrapers lit up,' she said to Connie, 'and could we take a walk in Central Park this evening?'

'If you want to risk your life, go right ahead,' Connie answered, 'me, I'm not risking mine! It's dangerous to go walking in the street at night here, Bella, and nobody in their right mind would set foot in Central Park after dark. New York is full of muggers, didn't you know?'

'I don't think I've heard that word before –'

'Okay, but you now know what it means,' said Connie. 'A girlfriend of mine was mugged at knife-point outside her own front door last week. And when you and I go shopping for groceries, Bella, make sure your gold chain and *mezuzah* are tucked out of sight. Mine were snatched from my neck in broad daylight.'

'How can you bear to live here?' Bella asked her. The picture of violence Connie was painting made Bella glad that she lived in England.

'Like it says on my car sticker, I love New York.'

Connie, though, seemed able to smile and shrug it off.

'And I have a lot of friends here,' Connie added, 'some of whom you'll be meeting at my place tonight.'

'I'm not in the mood for parties, Connie.'

'Did I say it was a party? Just a few people dropping by is all and Victor will be one of them. Tomorrow he flies back to London, so tonight is my last opportunity to have you look him over and give me your opinion, Bella.

'Also for me to let him see I have a social life and am not just sitting here waiting for him –'

'You're no less crafty than you always were!' Bella cut in with a laugh.

'But a long way it's got me,' said Connie again briefly revealing her inner bleakness. 'To tell you the truth, Bella, when Victor said in Palm Beach that he intended rounding off his vacation with a stopover in New York and would call me, I didn't expect him to. How often do guys say what they mean, or mean what they say?'

'You're the expert,' said Bella, 'not me.'

'And Victor has to be the exception that proves the rule,' Connie replied. 'Okay, Bella, so he's never been to New York before and electing myself his sightseeing guide, which I did, could prove worth it, though my feet are killing me.

'Yesterday we took in the Museum of Modern Art, Chinatown and Little Italy,' Connie went on, 'and the day before was just a little gentle exercise by comparison! A boat ride to see the Immigrants' Museum, or whatever it's called, that's housed in the Statue of Liberty.'

'I had no idea the statue wasn't a solid structure,' said Bella.

'But if I let you talk me into taking you there,' said Connie, 'I'm sure not giving a repeat performance of the one I gave to kid Victor I'm as supple as I look, which entailed climbing with him up God knows how many steps to see the view from the lady's head!'

Connie waited for Bella to stop laughing before adding, 'Which I have to say Victor accomplished without even puffing or blowing – a recommendation in another important respect,' she said with the saucy smile Bella remembered from their youth.

'I appreciate your taking time off from your current man-catching project to meet my plane,' said Bella.

'And I seem to remember you meeting mine on the day you'd opened a new shop, when I flew in for my mother's funeral,' said Connie, 'but ours is that kind of friendship and will be, I guess, till one of us is kicking up the daisies, which can never be said with certainty about marriage.'

The occasion to which Connie had referred was the last time they had seen each other, yet each was thinking now that it was as if it were yesterday.

'Who'd have thought we'd get sentimental about each other in our old age!' Connie said collecting herself.

'There's still some time to go till we're in that category,' said Bella, 'and I'm amazed you've survived to *middle* age, the way you drive.'

'If I didn't, in New York I'd never reach my destination,' said Connie after thumbing her nose at a man who had removed a fat cigar from between his lips only to yell through his car window that she was a crazy bitch.

They were approaching Greenwich Village, where Connie lived, and were soon caught up in a traffic jam that defied even her intrepid ability to somehow extricate her vehicle.

'This is worse than London,' Bella remarked.

'And it isn't even rush hour!'

When eventually they moved on if at a snail's pace, Bella at last began to believe that she was in New York, though there remained the sensation that she was being driven through a film set. The children, black and white, playing handball behind high, wire netting. The cop chatting to an aproned man in the doorway of a bakery. The small park seeming like a green haven, to which a statue lent grace. The assortment of restaurants and bars and of people hurrying by clutching paper bags piled high with groceries.

'Don't they provide plastic carrier bags in your supermarkets?' she asked Connie.

'That's what I wish when a tomato topples off my groceries and hits the sidewalk! And we've just gone by the famous Bleeker Street, by the way,' Connie told her, 'where I met the guy I mentioned having an affair with.'

'You met him in the street?' said Bella. 'Thanks for telling me what it's famous for!'

'I dropped my handkerchief and he picked it up.'

'You're kidding me!'

'No, it's true, and would you mind not ribbing me about that particular guy?' Connie requested quietly as she turned the car into a tree-lined avenue of tall, terraced houses. 'If he'd asked me to, I'd have scrubbed floors for him.'

'But not for long,' Bella replied with a smile.

'Here's where I live,' Connie said pulling up half-way along the terrace.

'I wouldn't have expected to find penthouses here,' Bella remarked.

'Big apartment blocks are what the word conjures up,' said Connie, 'but mine is at the top of a brownstone. These homes were built for Wasps,' she added as they mounted the broad steps to the front door. 'Not the stinging kind!' she said noting Bella's confused expression. 'Just the abbreviation for White Anglo-Saxon Protestants, some of whom see themselves as America's aristocracy, and would lock up a daughter seen having a casual cup of coffee with a Jew or a black.

'My son didn't believe that till he dated a Wellesley College girl when he was at Harvard and she made no secret of why she couldn't invite him to the coming-of-age party her parents were giving for her at their home on Beacon Hill.'

Connie said when they had entered the small but elegant lobby and were riding upward in a tiny lift, 'I sometimes think that's why Warren is so determined to succeed and he's sure getting there in Wall Street. That he's proving to himself that you don't have to be a Wasp.'

Incentive of another kind, thought Bella.

'But why should Jews have to prove themselves?' Connie added.

'*Feel* we have to, you mean,' Bella replied, 'and that's a somewhat complex question to discuss with Victor if you run out of subjects!'

The lift opened directly into Connie's split-level apartment and Bella paused on the upper level, surveying her friend's good taste.

Pale apricot walls and a matching carpet were the setting for simple modern furniture that did not seem out of place in a living-room dominated by an old-fashioned fireplace and the far from vast space had been cleverly used, an intimate dining area provided by one of the wide alcoves flanking the hearth, in the other a pair of cinnamon-coloured armchairs and a leather-topped wine table.

'This is absolutely beautiful, Connie!'

'But I can't take the credit for it. I used an interior decorating firm, like everyone I know does and it cost me a fortune,' said Connie. 'I wanted them to take out the fireplace, but they refused to. I also requested drapes and they said no to that, too.'

'I should think not, with that view,' said Bella feasting her eyes on the church steeple rising above some treetops, 'and the fireplace is lovely, do you ever light a fire in it, Connie?'

'If I did, who would clear out the ashes the next morning? I can afford a maid only once a week and she doesn't always show up!'

'Then why not fill the hearth with plants? Bella suggested.

'It didn't occur to me. I'm not artistic like you.'

Bella laughed and took off her hat. 'If you'd seen my so-called drawings you wouldn't have said that!'

'Which reminds me,' said Connie, 'Victor is in the same business you were, though he has a factory, not shops. I think he said his company label is "Gerda" and that was his wife's name.'

Thus it was that Bella learned of Gerda's death and it was as if the years had returned her full circle from the night she was forced to rethink her life and start afresh, as she was again doing now.

Though she had felt herself pale, Connie had not noticed. Nor would Bella have expected her to remember the name of the Viennese girl she had befriended, or that the girl had designed hats for Bella's first shop. It was too long ago and too much had in the interim happened in Connie's own life for her to recall the finer details of Bella's.

When later they were in the kitchen preparing lunch together, Connie chattering as always, and Bella washing lettuce, she was thankful that she was facing the sink and Connie unable to see her expression.

Between them, Gerda and Hal had hardened her, but she had gone on loving her husband and despite Gerda's treachery was now grieving for her, remembrance of the lovely girl who had been to her like a sister bringing tears to her eyes.

There's something I've never told you, she wanted to say to Connie. I didn't tell even my grandmother why my marriage suddenly fell apart. Instead, I plastered over the wound, but it has never healed. How could it when the other woman was Gerda whom I'd have trusted with my life?

Bella had been unable to speak of that hurt and Connie had not pressed her for reasons. Nor Gran, though the coincidence of Hal's departure and Gerda's suddenly deserting the family could not have escaped her.

Gran, as Hal had said on her funeral day, was a truly remarkable woman. It was she who had eventually cleared out Gerda's room and packed her clothing, requiring no more from Bella than that she carry the suitcase up to the attic. It had still been there years later when the family moved from behind the shop to their new home, but Hal had evidently seen Gerda's initials on the lid, since it was he who had emptied the attic, and he had not brought it downstairs with the battered old cases Bella had once packed with remnants to take to the market.

Now, a bizarre twist of fate had brought Bella face to face with that painful episode in her past.

'You and Victor will have a lot in common to talk about,' Connie said while garnishing a mound of cottage cheese with pineapple.

And this evening could present Bella with another minefield in which she must tread carefully.

Victor Lang was a charismatic silver-haired man whose searching gaze caused Bella to wonder how he had failed to see through Gerda. If he had, he was unlikely to have stayed married to her, Bella was thinking while Connie introduced them.

'At last!' Victor said as they shook hands.

Bella glued a smile to her face. 'That sounds ominous. What has my friend been saying to you about me?'

'I'll leave him to tell you,' said Connie before departing to greet some newly arrived guests, 'and I guess I'd better put out some more pretzels and nuts. In New York, you can't ask a few people to drop by without everyone bringing someone!'

Bella glanced around the crowded room, aware of Victor appraising her. Did her smile look as false as it felt?

'To set your mind at rest,' he said drily, 'Connie told me only good things about you. And the same went for my wife. Does the name "Gerda" ring a bell for you?'

An *alarm* bell better described it. 'Yes, as a matter of fact.' But Bella knew that *this* conversation would not stop short there and added lightly, 'What a small world it is!'

'My feeling exactly,' said Victor, 'when Connie mentioned your name and that you're a milliner.'

'Technically, I've never been one,' Bella replied, 'just a woman who found herself having to design hats though she can't draw for toffee and it paid off.'

'I gathered from my wife that anything you set your mind to would have paid off,' Victor answered, 'and she told me before she died that she had never recovered from losing your friendship.'

Bella held his glance. 'If that is an accusation, I have no reason to defend myself. Shall we leave it at that?'

'An accusation it wasn't,' Victor said quietly, 'just me voicing Gerda's regret. Though she didn't tell me what had caused the rift and I didn't ask, she left me in no doubt that she had done something that hurt you deeply, which you were unable to forgive.'

Bella changed the subject, her gaze roving the room. 'Connie told me she has lots of friends, but I hadn't realized just how many!'

More guests had arrived and were jostling by to get to the dining alcove, where Connie had set the tray of canapés she and Bella had prepared, now supplemented by hastily opened packets of cocktail snacks.

An assortment of women, some casually clad and others as though they had dressed for a special occasion, added shrillness to the buzz of conversation. And it's possible, thought Bella, that for Connie and those of her pals currently between husbands, every opportunity to meet a man was a special occasion.

Connie's garb, in contrast to Bella's black wool frock, was a pink chiffon kaftan through which her shape was seductively visible.

'Can I get you a drink?' Victor asked.

Bella glanced at the improvised bar, a table by the window where Connie's friends were helping themselves to white wine. 'No thanks, I'm not much of a drinker.'

'Something else we have in common,' said Victor, 'as well as my wife and the millinery business.'

'I'm no longer in business.'

'Connie didn't tell me that and it would certainly have surprised Gerda. Shall we find ourselves a quiet corner?'

Bella found herself being steered to the alcove in which the two armchairs were handily placed for a tête-à-tête.

'That's better!' said Victor when they were seated opposite each other. 'And I hope you don't mind my monopolizing you. If you knew how often Gerda mentioned you . . . '

Seemingly, Bella had been an offstage character in Victor's married life, as she still was in Ezra's. So deeply entrenched in Gerda's conscience that I existed for her husband too, Bella thought while he told her that he had fallen in love with the girl who came to work for him after the war and together they had built up the business begun by his father.

'How did your father get into the millinery trade?' Bella enquired.

'By marrying my mother,' Victor replied with a smile, 'but calling what they had a business is something of an exaggeration. What it actually was, was a backstreet room where my mother and a few other women made the hats, with a table in a corner that my father called his office.'

Give or take the details, not dissimilar from how Bella had begun. She, though, had had to ferry the designs and materials, and the finished hats, back and forth between her workers' homes and the shop.

Victor observed her reminiscent expression. 'Gerda told me that your early struggles were a lot like mine. I'd gone straight from school into the army,' he went on, 'looking no further ahead than surviving, which was the attitude of most of us called up after Dunkirk, though studying law was what I'd had in mind.

'When I was demobbed, my father said, "How about taking over the business?" "What business?" I said and he said, "Your mother and I have had enough." '

Victor added after a pause, 'My wartime experiences had knocked the spots off me and agreeing to my father's suggestion seemed a lot simpler than applying for a university place and studying for exams.

'By the time Gerda came into my life I'd emerged from my apathy, but without her designs the business wouldn't have taken off the way it did.'

'Nor would mine,' Bella said stiffly, 'and I've remained grateful to her.'

'But she was then part of your family, wasn't she? And as she was always saying, she owed you a lot. There was no reason for her to put in the hours she did to help *me* get going, I was just her employer. Unless, as I sometimes thought in those days, she was using work to get something out of her system. Later, when we'd married and she spoke of her rift with you, I wondered if that had accounted for it.

'When I first met Gerda, she struck me as a girl without a care in the world and how wrong I was. It was some time before she told me her parents had died in the camps and that the only relatives she had left were some distant cousins in Manchester with whom she'd lost contact. I got the impression they didn't give a damn about her.'

Though that wasn't true of Ezra and his father, it certainly was of Mrs Black, Bella recalled with distaste.

'The day she came for her interview,' Victor went on, 'she had on an old belted raincoat and a schoolgirl beret, and I thought, What can a kid like this know about designing hats? She looked about sixteen, and I remember her bursting out laughing, though I've no recollection of what I'd said. I think that was when I fell in love with her . . . '

Bella could believe it, as she would have if he had said he'd fallen in love with Gerda while he watched her sketching, crinkly blonde hair falling carelessly over one eye, or reaching something down from a shelf, her movements as unselfconsciously sensual as her fruity laugh.

'The reason she got the job, though,' Victor said collecting himself, 'was that hers was the only reply to my ad and that had to be because no *trained* designer would have applied for a job offering the lowly salary I could afford.'

'How long was it before your relationship became more personal?'

'It depends what you mean by personal.'

Bella averted her eyes from the twinkle in Victor's. 'I didn't mean to pry.'

'Given the place you once occupied in my wife's life, I didn't construe it as prying,' he replied, 'and the answer to your question is it wasn't too long before I began dating Gerda and two years later we got married.

'In those days,' he added, 'young people didn't set up home with no thought to how they'd pay the bills, or I'd have proposed to Gerda a month after I met her. I'm what you might call the decisive kind.'

Victor waved to Connie who had just blown him a kiss from beside the bar, then returned his attention to Bella. 'Now tell me about yourself. I was sorry to hear from Connie that you've lost your husband. Was he with you in the business?'

In a manner of speaking. 'Yes, as a matter of fact.'

'Was that why you sold out?'

'Did you feel like carrying on when you lost your wife?'

'If it weren't for my elder daughter, I'd probably have done what you have.' Victor took some snapshots from his pocket and passed one of them to Bella, saying affectionately, 'Lorna has become like my right arm.'

'She must be a great comfort to you,' Bella remarked.

'And this one is my younger daughter, unfortunately the opposite applies to her! Mimi went to art school like her sister, both girls inherited their mother's talent,' Victor revealed, 'but one has her feet on the ground and the other gives me sleepless nights.'

The snapshot Bella was now studying could have been one of Gerda when she was young. Except for her colouring, Lorna bore no resemblance to her mother, but Mimi was the image of her.

'Lorna joined Gerda in the studio the day she left college,' Victor went on, 'and I intend giving her her own label for a more expensive range of hats she's currently designing.'

His elder daughter is the apple of his eye, thought Bella, and Connie won't relish that if she manages to hook him. Nor would she have left him chatting for so long with any of the females present but me.

Victor Lang was a nice man by any woman's standards and his bank balance a bonus for those to whom that mattered, Bella was thinking when Connie appeared beside them carrying an outsize pizza.

'Since nobody shows any sign of going home to eat, I picked up the phone and ordered. Can you do that in England, Bella?'

'I wouldn't know, I've never tried.'

'There you go!' Connie said offering the pizza box.

'Could we get ourselves plates and cutlery?' asked Victor.

'If you two want to be different, go right ahead.'

'What she means, Bella, is when in New York do as the Romans do.'

Bella found herself sharing a laugh with him before they dug their teeth into the thick wedges Connie had thrust into their hands.

Late that night, when all the guests had finally left and Bella and Connie were sitting with their feet up, Connie said, 'If you want Victor, he's yours, Bella.'

'I beg your pardon?'

'I'll make like I've lost interest in him, though if the opposition weren't you I'd put up a fight.'

Bella was momentarily speechless.

'That guy is definitely on the lookout for a second wife,' Connie went on, 'and I'd have to be blind not to see he prefers you to me. I wouldn't be your best friend if I didn't step out. Besides which it will save me the hassle of uprooting myself to London at my age.'

'I sometimes think you live in a fantasy world,' Bella

informed her, 'which could be why you've gone from husband to husband and *I* wouldn't be *your* best friend if I didn't take the opportunity to tell you so. It's time, too, that you stopped thinking money can be a substitute for happiness, instead of letting it be a precondition that rules out less wealthy men who might have made you happy.'

Bella got off the sofa and went to stand with her back to a hearth that couldn't be the heart of a home that wasn't one, the aftermath of the party as depressing as the guests' bantering and laughter had rung false, and the débris they had left behind equating with the broken marriages that were part of Connie's social scene.

'There've been times when I've let my own imagination run away with me,' Bella told her, 'everyone does, but they come down to earth again which you don't, Connie. All that stuff about uprooting yourself to London to marry a man who hasn't proposed to you sums it up.'

'And if the lecture's now over, mine will be a lot shorter,' said Connie, 'in fact it's just a proverb: Opportunity doesn't knock twice, and it's your opportunity not mine we're talking about.'

'If I ever remarry,' Bella said crisply, 'it will be because by chance I've met the right man.'

'Which in my opinion you did tonight.'

Chapter Five

BEFORE BELLA'S RETURN to England her children were informed of their inheritance.

Leonard read the letter from a Toronto lawyer while eating breakfast with his flatmate, Roy Gower, his expression one of disbelief.

'Just chuck it in the box with the other final demand notes,' Roy said through a mouthful of cornflakes.

Leonard rose from the cluttered table, a beatific smile now on his face. 'That's no way to speak to a half-millionaire.'

'Say that again?'

'You heard me the first time. I've come into big money, it's here in black and white.'

Leonard glanced around the seedy kitchen, at the grease-stained wallpaper and the gas stove encrusted with spillage, the grimy windows, and the cracked lino underfoot.

'When I think how I've been living and where . . . But that's all over now, Roy.'

'When shall you buy the mansion, old chap? Today, or tomorrow?' said Roy with a grin that enlivened his equine features. 'Will there be a corner for me in it?'

'I shan't forget my friends now I'm rich.'

'They're unlikely to let you.'

Edith received the information by the second post and called her brother immediately.

'Did I waken you?' she asked though it was past noon.

'I haven't been to bed.'

'From which I assume you were at an all-night party. What a dreadful life you live, Leonard.'

'And you had the makings of a staid matron long before you got married. You've called me about our windfall I suppose. But if you'd had your way, Edith, Mum wouldn't have gone to Toronto and the lawyer wouldn't have known of our existence.

'That's all I have to say to you on the subject,' Leonard declared, 'and I was on my way out when you called –'

'To spend the money you haven't yet got, no doubt.'

Edith slammed down the receiver and turned to find her husband surveying her.

'Can't I talk on the phone with my brother without you creeping up on me, Keith!'

'I'm surprised you bothered calling him, and look at the effect it's had on you. All this has to be bad for the baby, Edith.'

'So you keep telling me.'

She brushed past him and went to pace the living-room.

'You're making me dizzy and this isn't the girl I married,' Keith said from the doorway.

'Then you evidently didn't know the girl you married.'

'And one day her high principles are going to land her in even more trouble than she's already in.'

Keith came to fold his lanky frame into the armchair beside the window, took off his glasses and contemplated them absently. 'Okay, so you don't want the money left you by the grandfather you think was an ogre though you never met him –'

'He *has* to've been an ogre!'

'Didn't anyone ever tell you there are two sides to every story?'

Edith stopped pacing and gave him a frigid glance.

'How you look now,' he remarked, 'reminds me of your mom when she's making someone quail.'

'And were you suggesting that my dad was a liar?'

'Would you please sit down and open your mind, Edith?'

273

'Now *you* remind *me* of my obstetrician, only it isn't my mind he asks me to open! Your approach to what we're discussing is equally clinical, but you can't expect mine to be. I adored my father and I won't have you inferring that he told lies.'

'But isn't it time,' Keith said gently, 'that you asked yourself what he did actually tell you? As opposed to what you grew up assuming?'

'Why are you defending that Canadian mogul!'

'I'm not,' said Keith, 'that's just your interpretation and coloured by how much you loved your dad as everything he said, or didn't say, was.'

Edith picked up a cushion from the sofa and threw it at him.

'I'm lucky the nearest thing to hand wasn't a vase! But nor was *that* the girl I married and if she doesn't take the weight off her feet, I'm going to *put* her in a chair.'

Keith eyed Edith's puffy ankles. 'You were told to rest up, but I don't see you doing it.'

'But it isn't me you're thinking about, it's the baby,' said Edith. 'Nobody thinks about me except Aunt Beth! Uncle Joey's sole concern is that I should patch things up with my mother, and when Aunt Sylvie rings up and asks how I'm doing, that's just the preamble to her subtly suggesting that a girl needs her mum when she's pregnant – a performance if ever there were one, since my aunt is hardly the voice of experience in that respect!'

'Well, you're a close family, aren't you?' Keith answered. 'And I shouldn't think Joey and Sylvie are happy about what they're now seeing. You can't blame them for doing what they consider is their duty –'

'Like you, you mean?'

'I have a *special* duty. To my wife and my unborn child.'

'All right, Keith! I'll sit down.'

Edith plonked herself on the sofa, her expression tight-lipped.

'But you're not going to let yourself relax, are you?'

'How can I relax when all the people I care about are against me? And that includes you!'

Keith came to sit beside her. 'If you go on like this, you'll end up paranoid,' he said brushing a lock of hair from her forehead and surveying her bulging belly, 'and that smock you have on looks about to pop a button! What worries me is you could pop the baby too soon –'

'And you'd say it was my fault.'

'I sure would. If you hadn't called your brother you wouldn't be in this het-up state. You must have known his reaction to the legacy would be the opposite to yours.'

Edith rose and resumed striding back and forth. 'Of course I knew that, but emotionally I needed to speak to him. There's something about being a twin that's hard to explain to someone who isn't one, and times when one needs the other and nobody else will do.

'It was that way for me when I read the lawyer's letter. Did that mogul imagine that leaving a million to my dad's possible offspring would compensate for how he treated him?'

Keith got up from his chair and halted her.

'Let go of me!'

'Not till you do what I asked you to. Open your mind. You're a rational person in every respect but one, Edith. Your father. And I'm beginning to feel that a dead man is ruining my marriage because my wife won't let him lie in peace.'

'That's a terrible thing to say.'

'But I said it and I meant it. Returning to Leonard – and your mom is getting the same treatment from you – what right have you to judge others by your own standards, damn them accordingly, and blame the whole thing on the grand-father you see fit to contemptuously dismiss?

'What the legacy tells me is that he cared about your father and never recovered from losing him,' Keith went on, 'and whatever their fall-out was about it strikes me they *both* suffered on account of it.'

'Have you quite finished?' Edith said coldly. 'If so, please let go of me, you're hurting my arms.'

'I'm sorry.'

'But not for what you've been letting off steam about,' she replied rebuffing Keith's attempt to gather her close, 'and I've certainly learned my husband's opinion of me.'

'To which I may as well add that what Leonard does with his share of the money is his affair, though I heard you make a crack on the phone about his spending it before he's got it.'

'He's welcome to my share too!'

'Hold on a minute,' said Keith, 'I'm prepared to understand *your* refusal to accept it, but it would sure come in handy for your children.'

'Forget it,' said Edith.

'I'm afraid I can't. They'll be my kids, too, and I can't let their mother's principles deprive them of a half-million trust fund.'

'I said forget it, Keith.'

'Properly set up, with the right investments, it would take care of their education and a helluva lot else,' Keith declared.

'And this isn't the person *I* married,' said Edith curtly.

'But he's about to become a father.'

A strained silence followed, then Keith glanced at his watch and forced a smile. 'I promised to eat lunch with Joey today.'

'And my refusal will be written and mailed to Toronto before you get back.'

'Did your parents make unilateral decisions that affected their children, Edith? Because mine didn't and if a partnership isn't what you want, you chose the wrong guy.'

Edith was left to digest her husband's parting words. And who but the mogul was indirectly responsible for this too? A surge of anger overwhelmed her, then she felt the baby stir in her womb and made herself calm down.

Only her father would have understood, she was thinking when the telephone rang.

'I wasn't sure if you would be home from the clinic yet,' said her mother as if she were still part of Edith's life and speaking from around the corner instead of from New York.

276

'I gave the clinic a miss today.'

'Are you not feeling well?'

'Physically I'm fine.'

'I've called several times, but you never seem to be in.'

'I often go round to Aunt Beth's, this place is like a hen coop.'

'Since I haven't seen it, I wouldn't know. As I wouldn't know Tuesday morning's when you go to the clinic if Beth hadn't told me.'

'And whose fault is that?'

'That depends on the viewpoint.'

'If yours and mine were the same, I shouldn't be faced with the dilemma I now am,' Edith replied. 'Was the legacy willed to Leonard and me *should we exist* – and that makes it the more disgusting – mentioned to you in Toronto?'

'Yes, as a matter of fact.'

'You'd have done us a favour if you'd refused it on our behalf, since it will hasten Leonard's progress to decadence and has already caused trouble between Keith and me.'

'Legally I am unable to do that and even were that not so, it isn't for me to decide what's right or wrong for my adult children. Your father's half-brother is very nice, by the way –'

'I don't want to know.'

'You intend going on living in the past?'

'It was a damn sight happier for me than the present,' Edith said stiffly. 'If you're not back before your grandchild is born, one of the family will track you down and tell you if it's a boy or a girl.'

Edith's baby was born prematurely the following night and it was of her mother she was thinking during her labour.

'Our daughter is safe in her incubator,' said Keith when eventually Edith was sipping a cup of tea and he seated at her bedside.

'Would you please call my mother and give her a message from me?' Edith requested. 'I had no idea what she went through to give me life.'

'That's the message?'

'Yes, and I wish there was something I could do to make up for how I've treated her.'

'How about the way you've treated me?'

'Your compensation is in the incubator you mentioned and since she weighed in heavier than most premature babies there's no danger. Did you notice her long legs?'

'I'm more interested in yours,' said Keith, 'though long they're not. I can't wait for you to come home.'

'But you didn't bring me flowers,' said Edith glancing around the ward which resembled a florist's shop.

Keith took the cup and saucer from her and kissed her fingertips. 'I haven't left the hospital since I watched you recede along the corridor on that trolley they put you on, scared I might never see you again, and I thought, Nothing is worth enough to let it come between us.'

'Not even half a million pounds?'

'If you want to turn down the legacy, Edith, the hell with it.'

'I was about to go and mail the letter when a contraction stopped me short.'

'Want me to mail it for you?'

Edith shook her head. 'Arabella's birth has helped me see things in perspective.'

'*Arabella?*'

'I'd have liked her to have my mother's name. Since Jews don't call their children after living relatives, Arabella is the next best thing. We must do something to make *your* mother happy, too, Keith.'

'If I hadn't known I was in a maternity ward, I'd sure know now!'

'She gave birth to the man I love, didn't she? So why don't we also call the baby after her sister who died last year?'

'Arabella Lee,' Keith said contemplatively, 'well, it sure has style.'

A remark they would have reason to remember.

Chapter Six

BELLA'S REUNION with her daughter was joyful beyond her imaginings. She had returned to England immediately after learning of the premature birth, moved by the baby's being called after her if unofficially, and amusedly thankful that Keith had not insisted on a derivative of *his* mother's name too, or the child might have gone through life as Arabella Hermionetta.

Hermione and Lionel Rosenberg were disappointed that Bella would not be joining them in Florida and had urged her to do so next winter. But Bella felt unable to look that far ahead, an alien state of mind for a woman who had always known where she was going though it was not where in her girlhood she would have chosen.

Instead, she remained beset by the restlessness that had dogged her since her husband's death, nor was it just restlessness, but uncertainty too. As though, she thought on the way back to London after a weekend in Oxford, without a target I can no longer function as I once did.

She was still staying with Sylvie and Tess, but could not go on doing so. Nor could family alone fill her life.

'There's another message for you from you-know-who,' Sylvie said when Bella entered the flat, 'it's on the telephone table with all his others! Why are you punishing him for what Gerda did all those years ago?'

'If you knew what it was —'

'I do.'

Bella was taken aback.

'It was Gerda who told me,' Sylvie revealed, 'before we lost touch. I was hurt when it seemed that she'd suddenly dropped me, but how I see it now is that I reminded her of you and the episode she'd prefer to forget.

'You eventually forgave Hal and took him back,' Sylvie went on, 'why can't you forgive Gerda?'

'Would you mind staying out of this, Sylvie?'

'I'd like nothing better, but I'm the one who has to take her widower's phone calls and tell him you're out when you're not.'

Bella averted her gaze from the message pad in the hall and went into the living-room.

Sylvie followed and continued haranguing her. 'I knew you could be hard, Bella, but not *this* hard.'

Bella turned from the window to face her. 'Would you believe me if I told you that when Gerda turned out to be a viper in my bosom something died in me and it's still dead? Trust is what I'm talking about. If Victor Lang weren't who he is, though . . .'

'Yes?'

'I found myself reluctantly drawn to him,' Bella admitted to her sister and to herself.

'Then you're a fool if you *don't* call him back,' Sylvie declared, 'and Connie rang up to ask me for a progress report. I think she's enjoying playing Cupid!'

'And I could kill her,' said Bella, 'for giving Victor your phone number.'

The following morning Bella learned that Connie had also supplied Victor Lang with Sylvie's address.

'You are certainly persistent,' Sylvie said drily when she opened the door and he introduced himself.

'Is your sister at home?'

'Please come in. I'll get her.'

Sylvie left Victor in the hall and strode into the living-room, her brightly hued kaftan lending her the air of a purposeful peacock as she swept through the open French window to the lawn, where Bella was expending her surplus energy with the mower.

'He's here and I'm done lying,' was all Sylvie felt it necessary to say before returning to tell Victor that she must now resume learning the lines for her next role, after which she made herself scarce.

Victor's greeting to Bella was, 'You look very nice in casual clothes.'

'Thank you, but somewhat dishevelled right now,' she said stiffly, glancing down at her checked blouse which she had not bothered to tuck into her skirt. 'Mowing is hard work and it's been years since I last did any.'

'Did your husband do the gardening?'

'Yes, as a matter of fact.'

'In our ménage, Gerda was the gardener.'

'Well, she was an ex-Land Army girl, wasn't she? May I ask what brings you here and unannounced?'

'The second part of your question is easy to answer. If I'd left a message that I was coming, you'd have found a reason to be out. I might find it less difficult to reply to the first part if we weren't hovering in the hall as if I were a salesman trying to sell you a vacuum cleaner.'

'Come into the living-room by all means,' Bella said leading the way, 'but I haven't much time to spare this morning. I've decided to rent a flat in London till I make up my mind what I want to do and I have an appointment with an estate agent at noon.'

'Why don't I drive you there?'

'I have my own car, thank you.'

'Dare I invite you to lunch?'

An invitation couched as Ross Diamond's was in Toronto and Bella almost replied as she had then. But evidently she was capable of seeming formidable and Victor Lang, who had seated himself opposite her, awaited her answer.

If Bella said yes, it would let him into her life and present her with yet another major turning point. She was as attracted to him as he to her and he was too worldly not to know it, riveting her now with that searching gaze.

'I like you a lot,' she told him.

282

'Only you see Gerda standing beside me, how could you not?' he replied. 'But Gerda is dead and you and I are still alive. I have a proposition to put to you over lunch, Bella, and it isn't just marriage. You and I will be a great combination.'

Bella said when she found her voice, 'Given our brief acquaintance wouldn't you say that you're rushing things?'

'I've never believed in wasting valuable time,' he said with a smile, 'how about you?'

'Where are you thinking of taking me for lunch?' Bella asked and it was as though she were letting herself go with the tide, as she had long ago.

But she was now a mature woman and Victor a very different man from Hal. Her judgement, like his, was that together they would weather the storms.

Chapter Seven

THE FIRST STORM occurred when Victor quarrelled on the telephone with his younger daughter, who had refused to come to his wedding.

'Mimi was very close to her mother,' he explained simmering down after replacing the receiver, 'but sooner or later she'll put my happiness before her own feelings.'

From what Bella had heard about Mimi, that was wishful thinking. Lorna, though, had turned out to be the warm, friendly girl Victor had led Bella to expect.

'The way things are looking, we could both have one missing at our wedding,' Victor said tersely. 'How could that son of yours have gone off on a round-the-world trip without leaving an address where you can get in touch with him?'

'I'm afraid,' said Bella, 'that coming into money has done Leonard no good.'

'Has he always been a bit of a ne'er-do-well?'

Bella almost retorted, 'How dare you!'

'If Mimi were male, that's what I'd have to call *her*,' Victor went on. 'When you and I met in New York she was living with some of her arty friends in St Ives and I was sure she'd get arrested for smoking pot.'

Bella told him that she had been through that with Leonard.

'But a man can look after himself better than a girl can,' Victor answered, 'and where is my little girl right now? Travelling the country with some pop singer! My only way of contacting her is by finding out from his agent which hotel he's staying at, in which town, on which night of the week.

'When Mimi said she was taking a job as the show's wardrobe mistress, I thought, Just so long as that's the only sort of mistress she is on that tour!'

'And if you don't stop working yourself up about her,' said Bella, 'you could burst a blood vessel before our wedding day.'

They were spending the evening in Victor's house in St John's Wood, the interior as gracious as the landscaped garden and Bella would have expected no less from Gerda. But it had not been necessary for her to tell Victor she could not live in Gerda's home.

They would begin their married life in a rented apartment, afterwards house-hunting at their leisure and Bella would remain a *lady* of leisure. She had unhesitatingly turned down the part of his proposal that wasn't marriage. Lorna had stepped into her mother's shoes in the business. There was no place in it for his second wife.

A few days before her wedding Bella's new-found peace was again disrupted, when her brother rang up and told her his twelve-year-old daughter had run away from home.

'Hannah's been gone since the day before yesterday,' Joey said, 'I'd hoped not to have to tell you. I thought at first it was just one of her pranks, but now it isn't looking good.'

'Keith and Chris and I have tramped all over Oxford looking for her,' he went on. 'Not an accurate description of how *I* got myself around!'

Bella pictured him dragging himself through the Meadows and alongside the river, and wanted to smack her niece's plump little bottom for putting him through this.

Another picture replaced it: Hannah thumbing a lift at the roadside, her silky black ponytail tied with a ribbon bow and a fetching smile on her innocent face.

Bella blotted that picture out, also what it might lead to and tried to reassure her brother. 'Girls start having boyfriends before they're in their teens nowadays, Joey. Have you enquired if any of the boys Hannah knows has gone missing?'

'Kindly don't add to my anxiety, Bella! We've contacted all her schoolfriends and none of them has seen or heard from her. The police are now in on it, Beth's taken to her bed and I'm going out of my mind. If we don't show up at the wedding, you'll know why.'

Sylvie came into the hall from Tess's studio as Bella replaced the receiver. 'Who have you been talking to? You look terrible.

'How dare that little madam do this to *you*!' she exclaimed when Bella told her. 'If she isn't found before Sunday it will ruin your wedding day –'

'And that would be a pity,' said Bella, 'but it's the least of my concerns. My first, needless to say, is that no harm has befallen Hannah.'

A moment of anxious silence followed, then Bella added, 'Our niece has been spoiled rotten by both her parents, Sylvie, and now they're paying for it. Since Beth never expected to have a child, how she is with Hannah is understandable, but I'd have thought Joey would know better.'

'I don't think it's a question of Joey knowing better,' said Sylvie, 'just that he's so immersed in his work he left it to Beth to raise Hannah and shut his eyes to the spoiling so he'd be left in peace. I'm going to Oxford, Bella.'

'There's nothing you can do there.'

'Only be with my twin when he needs me.'

Bella recalled how they had fought and made up when they were little, and Sylvie's terror when Joey was stricken with polio and whisked away in an ambulance to where she was not allowed to visit him.

It was then that Sylvie had begun behaving badly, but it had taken till now for Bella to understand why and their special closeness had stood the test of time.

Later, when Bella was seated at the kitchen table sketching a hat to keep herself occupied, Tess came into the room and glanced at the drawing.

'For someone who says she can't draw, you don't do too badly, Bella.'

'Thanks, and I mustn't let myself get out of practice,' Bella said drily, 'one day I might get fed up with idling and decide to open a boutique.'

'If I were you, I'd give that some serious thought,' said Tess, 'turning yourself into a full-time housewife is a waste of your talent and I don't see it being enough for you.'

Bella replied as she had to Ezra apropos her becoming a social butterfly. 'How do I know till I've tried it?'

'That,' Tess answered, 'could be said of many things.'

Bella noted her strained smile. 'Have you and Sylvie had a row?'

Tess shook her head. 'But she didn't say where she was going to, just that she probably wouldn't be back tonight.'

'Well, she left in a hurry, didn't she?' Bella answered. 'And I'm here to explain to you that there's been a family emergency –'

'She could have spared the two seconds it took you to tell me that,' said Tess, 'and it was cruel of her to let me think she was rushing off to where she often does these days. Your sister's met a man, Bella, and while that may be cheering news for you, it isn't for me.'

Bella was stunned into silence.

' "How do you know till you've tried it?" certainly applies to Sylvie's giving the lesbian life a go,' Tess went on, 'and I should have said she's met a man capable of taking her away from me, since men cross her path every day and so far as I know this is her first infidelity.'

Bella had long since adjusted to sexual love between women being possible, if not for her, and said gently, 'I'm deeply sorry for you, Tess, and surprised that you haven't thrown Sylvie out.'

'I've always known this could happen, Bella. Sylvie isn't like me, as I told her years ago. If we'd never met, she would probably have followed the usual path without ever discovering she was capable of the alternative. She was just a kid when we met and I had no right to do what I did.'

'It takes two to tango, for want of a better way of putting

it,' Bella answered, 'and whatever comes or goes you've helped Sylvie become the special person she is.'

Tess managed to smile. 'You didn't used to like that person.'

'Nor she me,' said Bella reflectively, 'and there are still things we don't like about each other. Liking and loving don't necessarily go hand in hand, a built-in hazard for blood relatives! I certainly don't like what you've told me Sylvie is now doing, having an affair while she's living with you, and for two pins I'd tell her so.'

Tess went to gaze through the window at the twilit garden. 'Please don't.'

How pathetic she looks, Bella thought with compassion, a middle-aged woman let down by her lover and her feelings no different than had that person been a man.

'There's no such thing as a static situation,' Tess said quietly, 'and sooner or later this one will come to a head. I ought not to have referred to her unexplained hasty departure this evening as cruelty, but in my present position – well, a lot of what I suffer is probably all in the mind –'

'You don't have to explain to me, I'm furious with Sylvie,' Bella cut in.

'But I'd rather you weren't,' said Tess, 'and I want you to know she's been painfully honest with me. Given the length of our relationship and her belief that it would last for ever, she has to be in the grip of confusion to put it mildly.

'If I asked her to leave, she'd understand,' Tess went on, 'but she needs my support no less now than before this happened. There's a good deal more to what we've been to each other than sex,' she added with another wan smile, 'and thank you for listening, Bella.

'I'll make us an omelette for dinner, unless you have other plans?'

'As it happens I haven't,' Bella lied. Spending the evening with Victor was less important than Tess's need for company. 'and I must stay by the phone in case there's news of my niece,' she said, anxiety on Hannah's account returning to her.

288

'Is Hannah the family emergency?' Tess asked while taking butter and eggs from the refrigerator. 'Joey and Beth should have seen it coming,' she declared after hearing the details.

'Since they didn't, how could you?'

'My home life was similar to Hannah's,' Tess revealed, 'my father was a Cambridge don and it was like living in a backwater even in my day, when the world was a much less exciting place for kids than it is in the seventies.

'When occasionally I was taken to London for a treat, I used to wish I need never go home. The Oxbridge ethos is very rarefied, Bella, and while born academics thrive on it, it can have the opposite effect if it isn't your scene.'

Tess began breaking eggs into a bowl, her expression pensive. 'It wasn't my mother's scene and when I think back – well, she seemed to spend most of her time making jam, as if she had to find herself a raison d'être and filling all the kitchen cupboards with jars was it.

'She used to pickle onions, too, though my father disliked them and said so each time she put a dishful on the table, and I've sometimes wondered if she did it to get him to notice her.'

Tess collected herself and whisked the eggs. 'As for what living in academia can do to kids, I didn't do what Hannah has until I was fifteen.'

'You ran away?'

'Twice and my parents yanked me back. By then I'd begun sculpting and saying I wished I lived where the artists did. They knew Chelsea was where to look for me.'

'But there's no clue of that sort for Joey and Beth.'

When Sylvie asked her brother and sister-in-law if they had looked in the late Professor Watson's garden retreat, they told her they had forgotten it was there.

'Didn't the police ask if you had an outhouse?'

'Stop cross-examining us!' Joey exclaimed. 'You've only just walked in and is this why you came?'

'You know perfectly well why I came,' Sylvie said quietly, 'and if you'll let me have a torch I'll take a look in the chalet.'

'If you insist,' said Joey, 'but Hannah's a nervous kid and wild horses couldn't drag her into that place.'

'There's nothing to be lost by looking,' said Beth who had leapt from her bed and rushed downstairs when Sylvie rang the doorbell, her nightdress flapping and her demeanour distraught. 'I want my darling back,' she added pathetically.

'She's my darling, too,' said Joey.

'But when do you spare her a minute? If she hadn't run away you'd still be in your lab with your cohort Chris Bennett.'

'That's a new name for scientists pitting their wits against disease.'

'And what else but that do you care about?' Beth retorted. 'Men like you and Chris ought not to have children.'

'Or perhaps,' said Joey, 'we should make sure we've found the right wife.'

'Like Chris did, you mean, because Helena's a scientist? I'm even sorrier for their kids than I am for my own,' Beth declared, 'days can go by without their seeing *either* of their parents.'

'But none of their kids has run away,' Joey answered, 'and there has to be some significance in that.'

Sylvie was appalled by what she was hearing. 'Will you please stop this and fetch me a torch?'

'Joey wouldn't know where it's kept,' said Beth, 'it's only used when I light fireworks for Hannah on bonfire night and her daddy is never here.'

'If you let her go to the bonfire parties she gets invited to, you wouldn't need to light fireworks,' Joey responded.

Beth had opened an oak chest by the window and was ferreting inside it. 'Hannah must have taken the torch, it isn't here —'

'Then I shall have to stumble through your jungle in the dark,' said Sylvie striding to the door, 'and if the performance you two just put on is a sample of my niece's home life, I don't blame her for running away!'

While making her way to the chalet Sylvie twisted her ankle which did not improve her temper. Compassion took over when she entered the musty retreat and saw the child huddled beneath a heap of blankets on the sagging sofa, the flickering light from a stub of candle casting eerie shadows on the walls.

Forget what she's put her parents through, thought Sylvie, only a desperate kid would put herself through this. An adventure it wasn't, all it would take to make Sylvie flee from here was the hooting of an owl.

Hannah, though, had spent two nights here and that meant she was plucky as well as desperate. Sylvie went to sit beside her and gently removed her thumb from her mouth.

'Sorry to waken you, love, but you can't stay here for ever.'

'I wouldn't want to.'

'Me, neither.' Sylvie glanced at the empty baked beans tins and lemonade bottles on the cobwebbed desk. 'I see you brought your supplies, but they've run out.'

'I thought Mummy and Daddy would find me sooner than you have.'

'Did you want them to?'

'I don't *know* what I wanted,' Hannah said tempestuously, 'but Daddy didn't even look for me here, did he? It was you who did.'

It didn't need a psychologist to figure that one out and it gelled with what Sylvie had learned from the tiff she had witnessed.

'We must hurry and put your parents' minds at rest,' she said straightening her niece's tangled hair.

'I really like you, Aunt Sylvie,' Hannah told her while getting off the sofa, 'and I sometimes wonder how you and my daddy can be twins. You're always so lovely to me.'

'Isn't he?'

'When he remembers to be. Was he like that when he was a little boy?'

'Absent-minded, you mean?'

'If that's what you call it.' Hannah picked up her rag doll and cuddled it, reminding Sylvie of her own attachment to the long gone Belinda.

'Forgive me for bringing you to this smelly old place,' Hannah said to the doll, 'but you wouldn't have wanted me to stay here on my own, would you, Tracy?'

Dolls' names change with the times, Sylvie reflected, but the comfort they are to little girls remains. Belinda was my alter ego, she recalled with a smile, I said what I liked to her and she couldn't talk back, and so it was for Hannah with Tracy.

'I'm glad you and Tracy didn't resort to eating the fungi sprouting from the chalet walls!' she joked en route to the house.

'Mind you don't trip, Aunt Sylvie,' said Hannah lighting the way with the torch, 'and I can tell the difference between a mushroom and a toadstool, though my mummy still treats me as if I'm a baby. Did Aunt Bella treat you like that?'

Sylvie smiled and borrowed Bella's favourite reply. 'No, as a matter of fact.'

It was Joey whom our big sister singled out for that treatment and oh, how deprived I felt! He, though, rebelled against it as his daughter is now doing. Was there a foolproof recipe for raising children? With the sharp exchanges between Joey and Beth still echoing in her ears, and the cause of them clutching her arm, Sylvie was again thankful that her observations of parenthood were secondhand.

Their daughter's return was greeted rapturously by Beth and angrily by Joey, which evoked further acrimony between them reducing Hannah to tears.

'Why are Mummy and Daddy quarrelling?' she sobbed to Sylvie as though she had never before seen them do so.

Nor had she, Sylvie learned from her brother when his wife had taken the child to be bathed and put to bed.

'You'll have to excuse Beth and me for what went on tonight,' he said, 'there's never been a cross word between us and how we behaved has to be put down to our anxiety.'

'If I'm supposed to find that reassuring, I don't,' Sylvie replied, 'and you look as if you could use a drink. Me, too, want me to get them?'

'Don't *you* start trying to save my legs!'

Sylvie watched him drag himself to the cupboard that served as a drinks cabinet.

'If I finish up in a wheelchair, I'll still be able to do my work,' he declared.

'And as Beth said tonight, to you that's all that matters.'

'Beth said a lot of things tonight.'

'You too and what they meant can't be written off as lightly as you dismissed the row itself. Add to it that Beth's contribution came as a shock to you –'

'How the hell could I have known what she's never told me?'

'And you were stung to say to her what you did, implying she isn't the right wife for you,' Sylvie reminded him.

'Here's your drink!'

Joey put himself in the high, wing chair Beth had had made for him and contemplated the whisky in his tumbler.

'Did you mean what you said to her?' Sylvie persisted. 'Or were you just hitting back?'

'My answer to that, Sylvie, is I love Beth dearly and a man can't have everything. And it certainly *was* a shock to learn my wife's been storing up resentments.'

Sylvie said after a pause, 'What you and she reminded me of tonight was that family showdown after Hal's suicide and for me it did some good. Since then I've had what I was never able to achieve, a good relationship with Bella.'

Joey set down his glass on the coffee table, his weary expression matching his tone. 'I don't have time for what you call relationships, Sylvie. Either people get on together, or they don't.'

'Then I fear for yours with your daughter, not to mention with your wife.'

Joey watched her rise and carry her drink to the fireplace,

leaning her elbow on the mantelpiece in one of the graceful poses that came naturally to her.

'It's a pity you gave up the West End stage for that experimental stuff,' he told her, 'you'd have been another Sybil Thorndike in your old age, but this isn't a play, Sylvie, it's real life.'

'Are you staying the night?'

'I'd thought of doing so and taking Hannah back with me. As you'll gather, I haven't a part in our current production, or I'd be working tonight. I could take Hannah backstage tomorrow evening though, kids always find that exciting and it'd take her mind off her troubles.'

'What troubles? And I don't intend rewarding her for her escapade,' said Joey, 'or extending her unofficial holiday from school.'

'You've certainly done a rapid U-turn,' Sylvie said with a smile, 'and a little discipline wouldn't harm her. As for Hannah's having no troubles, that wasn't my impression when I had a chat with her –'

'That's all I need,' Joey interrupted, 'you having cosy chats with Hannah and taking her to stay with you and Tess. Please don't take that the wrong way,' he added when the smile froze on Sylvie's face.

'There is only one way I *can* take it and this has been an educative experience for me in many respects,' she replied collecting her handbag and heading for the door.

'Where are you going?'

'Back to the leper colony and don't bother seeing me out.'

Chapter Eight

BELLA'S REMEMBRANCE of her wedding day was the opposite of perfect.

She and Victor had masked their distress that neither Leonard, nor Mimi, was present. Sylvie had pointedly avoided Joey and a more miserable little bridesmaid than Hannah would be difficult to imagine.

The strained atmosphere at the family luncheon was compounded by Arabella Lee, resplendent in a pink bonnet, yelling her head off even when lifted from her carry-cot and the tut-tutting of Victor's two maiden aunts.

Not a good beginning, she thought drily while dressing for dinner on their eighth anniversary, but it wasn't a portent for our future. Victor's judgement that they would make a great combination, and Bella's that they could weather the storms together, had over the years been confirmed.

With Victor, Bella had learned the true meaning of marital partnership and as the present took precedence the past had largely receded for her.

It was now 1980, more than a decade had slipped by since Hal's suicide stopped her in her tracks. In the interim Britain had elected a woman Prime Minister and America had impeached a President. Edith's family had grown with the arrival of twin sons, Leonard and Mimi had gone from bad to worse, and Bella had got herself back in business.

'Nearly ready, dear?' Victor called.

'But not quite.'

The anniversary was being celebrated in Paris, where tomorrow another boutique would open its doors, enhancing the international image of the designer label Bella's flair and Victor's capital had set on the road to success in the seventies.

It had not taken long for Tess's prophecy to prove correct. Filling in her days while her husband was at the office had soon become a problem for Bella and his being in the millinery trade had sustained her interest in hats.

So sensitive was he to her moods, it had not been necessary for her to tell him of her growing restlessness and he had said to her one evening, 'Now you've had enough of being a lady of leisure, let's talk turkey.'

The result of that talk was Victor's handing over his business to Lorna and afterwards giving his attention to the new venture that had since grown beyond Bella's imaginings.

The company now had branches in every European capital except Madrid, where a suitable location had not yet become available. Would Bella be satisfied when that city too was included?

Probably not, she thought with a smile, a branch in New York, and it would have to be on Fifth Avenue, will be my next goal. Bella had finally accepted that ambition was what made her tick and was able to be at peace with herself.

While she was putting the finishing touches to her appearance, Victor was enjoying the view of the Place de la Concorde.

Though staying at hotels like the Crillon was now part of Bella's lifestyle, there were still times when she had to pinch herself to believe it. How had little Bella Minsky, the haberdasher's daughter, got from that to this?

What seemed like a dream, though, had been in reality a long hard slog and meeting Victor had given Bella the second chance few people got, not just of fulfilling her potential but of personal happiness.

'Did I tell you today that I love you?' he said when she joined him in the drawing-room of their suite.

Not the way he had loved Gerda, perhaps, or how Bella had loved Hal, with a passion kindled in youth. Mature love was something else and for Bella a good deal more satisfying.

'Since I know you love me, you don't have to go on telling me,' she answered with a laugh.

'I *enjoy* telling you and you've never looked more beautiful than you do in that gown.'

'Beautiful I'm not and the credit for the gown must go to Yves St Laurent!'

'What are you wearing for the opening tomorrow?' Victor asked while pouring their apéritifs.

'A simple black sheath – if you think my sixty-year-old shape won't ruin it!'

'A dowager's hump you haven't got. As for the rest of you –'

'All right, you've convinced me,' she said as he reached out to stroke her still-slender hips, 'and we haven't time for what Connie would call an early evening matinée.'

'How many husbands has Connie now had?' Victor enquired. 'I've lost count. And by the way, I was never a candidate.'

'I knew that the minute I met you, and I think this one is number six.'

'Your friend,' said Victor, 'has gone into competition with Zsa Zsa Gabor and has probably had as many facelifts. You on the other hand know how to grow old gracefully.'

'So would Connie,' Bella replied, 'with the right man beside her.'

She helped herself to an olive from the tray of canapés on the antique table and returned to the subject from which they had digressed. 'I decided on the black sheath for tomorrow, Victor, as a background for one of our new range of belts. If I wear one, it'll show my generation of Parisiennes that Arabella Lee accessories aren't designed just for the young –'

'Talking of Arabella Lee,' Victor interrupted, 'while you were taking your bath Edith rang up to wish us luck.'

'And tomorrow she'll send flowers to the boutique like she has for all our openings,' Bella said affectionately.

'Unlike Lorna!' Victor exclaimed.

Suddenly their lightheartedness was gone, an evening both would prefer to forget returning to them.

They had taken Lorna to dine at Quo Vadis, expecting her to share their excitement when told of their business plans, but the smile had disappeared from her face when she learned the designer label was to be 'Arabella Lee'.

'How does Bella's granddaughter come into this?' she had asked Victor coldly. 'It will cost a fortune and you, no doubt, are financing it.'

'Why shouldn't I finance my wife, like I'm giving my daughter my business?'

'You seem to be forgetting that my mother's talent was the reason your business succeeded and without it you wouldn't have been the wealthy man you now are.

'I know my own limitations as a designer, it isn't just loyalty that's kept me at the mass production end of the trade, but my mother –'

'Was a *brilliant* designer who could have gone far,' Bella had interrupted, 'and I too am indebted to her.'

'Then why don't the two of you have the decency to accord her the recognition she deserves? Let "Gerda Lang" be your designer label.'

Lorna was gone from the restaurant before Bella and Victor had time to draw breath, leaving them as if on an arctic island in a sea of bonhomie, so icy was her parting glance.

'We must think again about the label,' Bella said eventually though she doubted she could live with the constant reminder Lorna had suggested.

'Lorna is the one who must think again,' Victor had answered tersely, 'and if she isn't prepared to, that's her lookout. You and I have just begun a new life together, Bella, and forward, not backward, is where we're going to look.'

Despite Bella's misgivings, they had gone ahead with their plans for the label, and Lorna's unspoken ultimatum had resulted in a rift yet to be breached. As Edith's words about my going to Toronto might have, Bella reflected now, if becoming a mother hadn't served to soften her resolve.

But for Lorna, the right man had still to come along though she was now twenty-eight, and Victor might have to wait some time before motherhood had that effect upon *her*.

He was now gazing pensively through the window and turned with an upsurge of anger. 'My daughter should be content with the *marble* memorial I gave her mother and with my making over to her the business her parents built together! Believe it or not, Bella, Gerda's talent alone didn't achieve it, though Lorna seems to think it did.'

'I doubt that she still thinks so,' Bella replied, 'since she's had to cope alone with your side of things.'

'And I've heard she's made a bit of a mess of it,' Victor revealed. 'Rather than come to me for advice! She sacked the factory manager recently for advising her to do things her father's way, he told me when I ran into him in town.

'I now have *two* daughters who seem to have written me off, Bella! At a time of life when I should be getting some pleasure from grandchildren. If I didn't have yours to boast about, I'd have to sit "shtum" in the company of men of my age.'

But except for Edith's annual visit, Bella's contact with her grandchildren was restricted to their chattering to her on the telephone. The fellowship Keith had accepted at Harvard had removed Edith and her family from Bella's scene.

As Leonard's questionable lifestyle had removed him from the solid background in which he was raised. It was no surprise that he had frittered away his inheritance, large though it was, or that he was at present a croupier in one of London's seedier gambling clubs.

'When that look appears on your face, I know who you're thinking of,' said Victor, 'and I wish you wouldn't.'

'I could say the same to you about Lorna and Mimi, but it's easier said than done.'

'Would you still be willing to meet Mimi?'

'You should know the answer to that and who would believe that a couple who have all we have, with the exciting prospect tomorrow's opening is for us, could sit in the midst of all this splendour wringing their hands about their kids?'

'Anyone who is himself, or herself, a parent,' Victor replied, 'but let's begin celebrating our anniversary, be thankful we've got each other.'

'Well, I couldn't be more thankful for *you*.'

'Nor I for you.'

But when later they raised their glasses to toast each other over dinner at Maxim's, the aftermath was still with them and again Gerda's shadow hovered beside Bella, which her daughters had between them ensured.

Victor awoke the next morning beset by a malaise which was not physical. Beside him, Bella lay sleeping, her hair unloosed from its daytime chignon and her face in repose free of the thoughtful frown now so familiar to him.

If he had married a woman content to be companion and lover, how different his autumn years would have been. But he had known when he met her that Bella was the one for him, as he had with Gerda in his youth.

Instinct had told him that her restlessness might erode their relationship if her energy remained unharnessed and her potential unfulfilled. But he had not foreseen the outcome of Bella's returning to business. That their thriving boutique in London would very soon not be enough for her.

She had told him jokingly on the eve of opening the Amsterdam branch that her grandmother used to say she had a dynamo inside her. By then, Victor had not required telling and 'Arabella Lee' was as well known for accessories as for the chic hats Bella had continued designing.

Though she credited Victor along with herself, it was she who had masterminded the achievement, Victor's role in the business he had built with Gerda, but at his age he was content to be the voluntary has-been Bella would never be, he thought as she frowned in her sleep, and keeping her happy has *become* my role.

Victor got out of bed and went to take a shower. Bella would tick him off for not wakening her, but the nights she spent tossing and turning over this business matter, or that, went with the territory and she rarely slept in when her busy schedule allowed it. The Paris opening was a big occasion and she needed all the rest she could get, in order to cope with it.

Cope with it? thought Victor while applying shampoo to his hair. My wife is a born coper, or how would she have survived raising two lots of twins, building the provincial business she had, and her layabout first husband's suicide?

Victor had put together his impression of Hal Diamond from the things Bella *hadn't* said. And her son took after his father! While that frown he had just observed might have been evoked by a bad dream that all would not go well this evening, it might equally well be due to the life Leonard was living.

But Bella had her daughter to compensate. Me and *my* daughters! Victor turned on the shower full-pelt, such were his feelings. When he called Lorna, which he did frequently, it was as if a polite stranger was at the other end of the line. As for Mimi's refusal to meet Bella, she would have resented her mother's replacement sight unseen no matter who the woman was.

Lorna, though, hadn't wanted her dad to be lonely and her initial reaction to his choosing her mum's old friend couldn't have been more reassuring, nor the warmth with which she had greeted Bella when they first met. It wasn't until she learned of the 'Arabella Lee' label that Victor's gentle daughter revealed that she had claws.

After showering, Victor wrapped himself in a robe and decided to have one more try at making Lorna see sense. He would call her while Bella was still asleep and plead with her to get on a plane and be here for the Paris opening.

Lorna's cool response was, 'I've already told you I can't make it.'

'What you mean is you don't want to be there.'

'Why *would* I want to be there?'

'Because your mother is dead and your father is still alive.'

'But I made my feelings clear and it was then up to you.'

'To see it your way, you mean? Though you've made no attempt to view it the other way round? If you go on holding this against me, Lorna, you'll end up an embittered old maid.'

'And if that's what you rang up to tell me, thank you for nothing, Dad.'

In London, clad in her bathrobe as her father was in Paris, Lorna was gazing down at the receiver she had abruptly replaced. There was a time when she couldn't have envisaged anything coming between her and her dad. But those days were long gone – and I now know I'm a disappointment to him on more counts than one.

Though choosing to stay single was nowadays an accepted norm, 'left on the shelf' was how Victor Lang still saw it in relation to his elder daughter and as some sort of disgrace to himself!

As to that bloody label, thought Lorna, how I'm behaving isn't me, but I can't help it. For once, the sensible big sister is being ruled by her emotions instead of by her head, while the little sister, from whom common sense and consideration weren't expected, went on doing her own thing as she always had.

How did that pattern begin in our family? Lorna asked herself while selecting her outfit for lunching with the millinery buyer of a provincial department store – which could have been postponed had Lorna been prepared to play kiss-and-make-up in Paris. It began because Mimi, even as a tiny tot, had dug in her heels till she got her own way, but I always tried not to upset Mum and Dad.

Born to be an elder daughter described it! Being Mummy's-little-helper had come naturally. Lorna could remember rocking the cradle while her mother dipped a dummy in honey and popped it into Baby Mimi's rosebud mouth to quieten her and so it had in effect continued.

Mimi, though, was now a woman and still existing in cloud-cuckoo-land. Not that her present location was that, Israel was anything but, the cuckoo was Mimi herself, thinking that at last she had found what she wanted when she didn't *know* what she wanted and never had.

Unlike me, thought Lorna while donning a green silk suit that matched her eyes, the only feature she had inherited from her beautiful mother. The rest of me is all artifice, make-up carefully applied to give the illusion of cheekbones, clothes that don't draw attention to my hips, the rinse that gilds my mousey hair, and the pretence that I like my life.

Dad wouldn't believe that Lorna Lang, managing director of Gerda Millinery Limited, would without a second thought swap everything she had for the role of wife and mother.

Bella was at that moment hastily consuming a croissant and coffee.

'What's the big hurry?' Victor asked putting down the *Herald Tribune* he was scanning while they ate breakfast.

'You shouldn't have let me sleep late.'

'Why not?'

'I still have a million things to do at the boutique.'

'Would you mind citing some of them?'

'All right, not to do, but to check.'

Victor said after a pause, 'I'm going to give you some advice you won't like, Bella. It's time you learned to delegate responsibility to the staff you've engaged, or you and I will spend the rest of our lives as airline commuters.'

Bella eyed him anxiously. 'Is the travelling becoming too much for you?'

'Not yet, but it will, for you too. An opening is one thing,' Victor went on, 'but thinking nobody can deal with things but yourself –'

'I've always had to.'

'But you don't have to any more and you must shed the one-man-business attitude ingrained in you and conserve your energy to run a big organization the way it has to be run.'

'Am I allowed to go on designing?' Bella said lightly.

' "Allowed" doesn't enter into our relationship,' Victor answered. 'One partner, though, is entitled to advise the other.'

Bella removed the croissants from his reach. 'In that case, don't eat any more of these, you've already had two and with lashings of butter. I have to protect my partner, who's very dear to me, from the effects of too much cholesterol.'

'And I have to protect mine from burning herself out. Will you please think over what I've said, Bella – and while you're doing so, take a nice relaxing stroll instead of hastening to where your presence isn't required until this evening.'

Bella emerged from the Crillon's imposing entrance into the morning sunlight of a balmy May day and stemmed her instinct to take a cab to the boutique. Instead, she strolled towards the Rue de Rivoli – forced herself to stroll! When had she last gone for a walk? Sauntered around without a destination?

All about her was the heady atmosphere that inspired the song 'Paris in Springtime'. The gendarme chatting to a pretty girl on a street corner. The young man hurrying by clutching a long stick of bread. The traffic beetling its way from the Place de la Concorde to the Champs-Elysées, and the flower-stall beside the Métro. Tourists queuing outside the Louvre and afterwards they would perhaps take a boat ride on the Seine, on one of the colourful bateaux-mouches.

Though Bella was by now no stranger to Paris, she had never found time to partake of the pleasures for which the city was renowned. Found time? It hadn't entered her head and the same went for Brussels and Amsterdam and all the other cities in which she had kept her eye on the ball.

As she had said to Ross Diamond in Toronto, habits could be broken – and his reply was that first one would have to want to. An astute observation and as relevant to Bella as to Ross himself.

On the Rue de Rivoli smartly clad women were window-shopping, the aroma of coffee from a pavement café mingling with the sweet scents drifting through the doorway of a perfumery as Bella passed by.

She crossed the street and entered the Tuileries Gardens, an oasis of quietude and in spring a treat for the eyes. Where better to do the thinking-over her husband had urged her to do?

Here, the thrum of the city was muted and nobody in a hurry, an artist was setting up his easel and a couple of young mothers sitting gossiping on the grass, one with a toddler on her lap, the other feeding a bottle to the fat baby she had lifted from its pram.

A man who evidently did not cast a clout till May was out sat wrapped in an overcoat playing chess with a lad who might be his grandson, and a vagrant was sharing a bench with a corpulent gentleman whose appearance was distinctly prosperous.

Whoever said the best things in life are free could be right!

Bella sat down on an unoccupied bench and watched a lady whose apparel brought to mind the phrase 'mutton dressed as lamb' teeter on high heels along the broad pathway, her companion a rhinestone-collared white poodle on an emerald green leash.

When she sprayed herself with Chanel Number Five, or whatever, did she spray the dog, as well? But Bella hadn't taken the morning off to watch the passing parade. A thought that summed up what Victor wanted her to think about, the quality of her *own* life, and designing and purveying feminine fripperies seemed to her no less an empty occupation now than when circumstances had propelled her into it.

Her brother, though, was damaging his health and his marriage for a worthy cause, Bella thought with distress, remembrance of her last visit to Oxford returning to her. Joey in his wheelchair, Beth obese from the over-eating that was her comfort, and their daughter, who flitted in and out of their lives, briefly with them before leaving for a commune in California whose guru was one of the sixties 'flower children'.

Minus the garlands and the ethereal garb, the same thing is still going on, thought Bella, young people searching for something they can't find.

Is it something my generation of parents has done to our children, that ours didn't do to us? Or the competitiveness and the corruptive influences that weren't there in my day?

Thankfully, Hannah wasn't travelling the sleazy road Mimi had, via go-go dancing in a gilded cage, topless cabaret in Frankfurt and all the rest of her dubious jobs, to Tel Aviv and finally an ultra-orthodox settlement on the West Bank. Should time prove religion to be what Mimi had unknowingly been seeking, God's ways were truly weird and wonderful.

Bella glanced at some children playing with a ball on the grass. What had *this* decade in store for *them*? And for Edith's children, though Arabella and her little brothers could not have a more secure home life. Edith was lucky to have found Keith, who but he had helped her come to terms with her father's suicide?

Since that tragic event stopped her short, Bella hadn't paused to take stock of her life and Victor was right to have forced her to do so now. Though he hadn't actually said so, he plainly thought it time for her to slow down. But was Bella capable of slowing down? She was still the person she had always been, driven by that inner dynamo.

Sorrow had briefly halted it, but if I hadn't met Victor, sooner or later I'd have picked myself up and got back in the race, like Gran used to say, 'If there isn't a way, you'll invent one.' But without Victor, what would my personal life have been but the vacuum it was before Fate brought us together.

Fate was kind in that respect to Bella, if not necessarily to Victor. Few men, their own years of striving behind them, would defer as he did to a wife unable to stem her ambition.

Bella rose from the bench to continue her solitary stroll and after leaving the Tuileries again had to stop herself from taking a cab to the boutique.

The manageress and staff were hand-picked and she must leave them to carry out her instructions. Nor was it sensible to fly hither and thither keeping an eye on the day-to-day running of her shops, like she'd gone back and forth between Liverpool, Leeds and Manchester in the old days.

Instead, she would engage a smart young executive and hand that responsibility to him, or her. You've learned your first lesson in the art of delegating, she said to herself, and now you've started it won't stop there. Time, as Victor had said, to stop being a one-man band and adapt to your company's escalating requirements.

Bella quickened her pace and headed towards the Crillon, impatient to set down her plans on paper, the throb of the world's most important fashion centre all about her and in her mind's eye a map on her office wall flagged with 'Arabella Lee' markers in every major city worldwide.

The Paris opening was all that Bella had hoped for, and the presence of some of the Parisian haute couture an accolade to her achievement.

But the sense of unreality that assailed her on such occasions did so no less tonight as she chatted with her guests at the champagne and caviare reception.

It was still difficult to believe that she *had* achieved this. Possibly I never shall, she thought glancing at the stunning display of accessories, to which the diamanté buckles that were her private symbol of her beginnings lent a sparkling sophistication, 'Arabella Lee' silk scarves in a range of brilliant colours threaded through them.

Hats and handbags, gloves and belts, too, were displayed in the elegant and spacious boutique and, as at her openings in other cities, Bella had hired some models, one of them middle-aged, to circulate and show off her wares in the informal atmosphere she considered more suitable for a boutique-opening than presenting a cat-walk show.

'Is it Madame's intention to later include the designer jewellery?' a French journalist enquired.

'And when will New York get an "Arabella Lee" boutique?' asked a woman from *Harper's* magazine.

'On both counts,' said Bella with a smile, 'we'll be letting you know.'

Victor, beside her as always, said when the journalists had gone to replenish their glasses, 'You handled that fine.'

'But I intend engaging a public relations person,' Bella answered, 'who'll deal with the press and clue me up when I have to up-front.'

'And after tonight,' said Victor, 'nobody can say "Arabella Lee" hasn't arrived!'

Though Bella's adrenalin was soaring on that account, the family woman she also was could not but be dispirited by the absence of those she had once supposed would rejoice for her.

The sole evidence that one of them did was Edith's basket of flowers. Joey and Sylvie had forgotten to send their customary telegrams. And Leonard . . .

Bella then saw her son weaving his way through the throng towards the bar.

'I'm glad Leonard's made your day,' said Victor, 'though it will probably cost you, like it did when he turned up at the Brussels opening without a penny in his pocket.'

'There's a price for everything,' Bella replied, 'and though you'd deny it, you're paying one for marrying *me*. Despite what my son's put me through, his making the effort to be here tonight means a lot to me.'

'But instead of rushing to congratulate and kiss you, he's knocking back champagne and talking to that red-haired woman dripping with diamonds who looks as if she could use a good meal!' Victor observed. 'Who is she?'

'Camille Gerard, one of the Paris jet-set,' Bella supplied while exchanging a smile with Yves St Laurent who was appraising the contents of a showcase.

'What Yves and the others don't yet know is that I intend launching an "Arabella Lee" perfume,' she whispered to her husband.

'Thanks for telling *me* and cosmetics will no doubt be next, but at least my wife won't have to sit up all night designing them! Oughtn't we to circulate, Bella?'

'Not until I've had a minute with my son.'

Leonard then disengaged himself and came to hug his mother and shake hands with his step-father. 'I couldn't get away from the lady,' he said with mock chagrin, 'did you notice those rocks, Mum?'

'Who could fail to?'

The painfully thin, but immensely striking woman, now posing for a photographer from *Paris Match*, was smoking a cheroot in a long silver holder, her mass of vermilion hair framing a dead-white face and her gown, a swathe of purple brocade, a backcloth for jewellery that outdid Elizabeth Taylor's favourite adornments.

'I told her I'm your son,' said Leonard watching the models show a range of perky hats, 'and she told me I remind her of Clark Gable in *Gone with the Wind*.'

'Well, she's old enough to remember,' said Victor uncharitably.

'She mentioned that she has an apartment on the Champs-Elysées and a villa in Monaco,' Leonard went on, 'and that she loves having young people to stay.'

'Oh yes?' said Victor.

'What an old-fashioned guy your husband is, Mum,' Leonard said with a grin. 'I was about to add that Madame Gerard could be a lucrative customer for you.'

'I doubt it,' Bella replied, 'she and her pals are just here for the party, getting their pictures in magazines is one of the ways they get their kicks. It happens at all my openings.'

'Then why invite them?' Victor enquired.

'They're part of the necessary scenery, love, photographers wouldn't show up just to flash their cameras at a new boutique.'

Leonard glanced around at the silver grey walls and gleaming black fittings, the framed fashion plates executed in charcoal, and the wrought-iron sculpture that was the shop's centrepiece. 'Is that one of Tess's, Mum?'

Bella smiled and nodded. 'The sculptures are the only thing that makes one "Arabella Lee" branch different from another.'

'When Leonard turned up for the Brussels opening, he was too busy ogling the models to notice the sculpture,' said Victor.

'They were prettier than this lot,' said Leonard, 'though the mademoiselle with the fringe has come-to-bed eyes.'

'It's her hat you're supposed to notice,' Bella jokingly rebuked him, 'and about the sculptures, when I commissioned the second one, Tess refused to do a replica of the first, she's a true artist.'

'Does designing hats et cetera to be reproduced for all your shops bother *you*?' asked her son.

'Since I wasn't born to be a designer, no.'

'But designing for mass production bothered Gerda,' said Victor, 'and Lorna knew it. That could be what she's punishing me for too, not just because her mother's label wasn't the exclusive kind.'

Would the past never stop intruding on the present? 'Lorna still shows no sign of returning to the fold,' Bella told Leonard.

'It's nice not to be the only black sheep in the family!'

'I wouldn't call Lorna eligible for *your* club,' Victor said collecting himself, 'nor does Mimi now qualify, though I'm not over the moon about her joining the one she has.'

'Victor hasn't become an atheist, he just doesn't like religious zealots,' Bella felt constrained to say to her son.

'But some parents are never satisfied, it seems.'

'Here's one who is tonight,' Bella declared.

'And you're looking smashing, Mum.'

'I keep kidding her that she chose a black and silver colour scheme for the shops to go with her hair,' said Victor, 'but she doesn't seem to like it!'

'Mum's had that silver streak since I was a little kid,'

Leonard informed him, 'and it hasn't spread much, nor has the rest of her.'

He gave Bella the smile that had always melted her heart, but right now it didn't require melting. 'I'm so happy you came, Leonard.'

'Me too, but I almost missed the plane!'

Could Bella have foreseen the consequences of his being at her Paris opening, she would have fervently wished that he had.

Chapter Nine

BRITAIN'S SLIDE into an economic recession, which the pundits were forecasting would overtake the whole of Europe and also the USA, cut short Bella's plans to open more branches. Her remembrance of the thirties was that even the ladies who lived in fine houses had thought twice about buying a new hat.

Had her provincial millinery business been up for sale today, she would not have found a buyer. She now learned from Ezra on the phone that it was on the verge of bankruptcy.

Listening to her old friend reel off a list of Manchester shops that had closed down brought home to Bella what the newspapers had told her in cold print, that the north was being hit much harder than the south.

'And needless to say, I'm losing clients,' Ezra added grimly, 'if I moved to London would you have me for your accountant again?'

'Is that a serious question, Ezra?'

'Would my wife agree to move to where her competition is?' he said with a laugh. 'What Doreen would actually like me to do is retire and let her cook lunch for me as well as dinner!'

'Tell her I send her my regards,' said Bella.

'First I'd have to tell her we're still in touch!'

Distressed though Bella was on Doreen's behalf, she had to laugh.

'I keep having this pipe-dream,' said Ezra, 'that you fall out of love with Victor, then Doreen runs away with the milkman and you fall in love with me.'

'A pipe-dream is what it will remain,' said Bella, 'and it's time you stopped smoking opium!'

Victor entered the living-room as Bella replaced the receiver. 'Was that a call from your son?'

'To the best of my knowledge Leonard has only smoked cannabis and what you heard me say – to *Ezra* – was just a figure of speech.'

Bella then noticed her husband's despondent expression. 'What on earth's the matter?' she asked as he lowered himself into a chair and emitted a long sigh.

'Lorna is the matter. The business I slaved to build is the matter!'

Bella poured him a stiff whisky and watched him drink it.

Victor put down the glass. 'I still have a spy in there, as you know, or I'd hear nothing –'

'I don't think your ex-secretary would be pleased to be called that.'

'Okay, so she wouldn't, but in effect that's what she is and it's her concern for Lorna and for the business that's kept her in touch with me. Since the major part of the production is for provincial department stores, and not the high class ones, I suppose this was inevitable, the business has almost hit rock bottom, Bella –'

'And I'm sorry for all the moaning I did when I had to dispense with one of the salesgirls at my Knightsbridge shop.'

Lorna came on a bleak February evening to deliver the news she knew would be even more painful for her father than for her.

'I kept hoping it wouldn't happen, Dad, that trade would improve –'

'But with that woman in Downing Street,' said Victor, 'there's no chance! Her idea of curing inflation is starvation –'

'I wouldn't say that exactly applies to us,' Bella cut in.

'But there are plenty to whom, give or take the degree, it does,' Victor declared, 'and Lorna's going out of business will put another hundred on the breadline.'

Lorna, who had seated herself on the opposite side of the living-room, removed her pensive gaze from the ornamental gasfire and looked her father in the eye. 'A businesswoman I'm not, nor have I ever claimed to be, but what's finally happened certainly isn't my fault.'

Victor replied, 'Did I say it was? I couldn't have saved the business myself, Lorna, and I know how much it meant to you, how hard you must have worked –'

'To keep going what my parents had begun,' Lorna interrupted, 'believe it or not, I never saw what I was doing as being for myself.'

'Unlike your sister!' Victor suddenly flared. 'Who thinks of nobody *but* herself. I thought, since she's still in the bosom of the ultra-orthodox – the longest I've known her stay any place – that she'd do what *they* do, get married and have children, but the nearest Mimi's got to that is looking after other women's children in the kibbutz crèche!'

Lorna managed to smile. 'You can't say that isn't progress, Dad, could you have envisaged Mimi spending her days changing nappies and all that?'

Bella said thoughtfully, 'Though I haven't met Mimi, the impression I have of her doesn't jell with how the ultra-orthodox approach marriage. Theirs are usually arranged even in this day and age, no such thing as waiting for the right person to come along.'

'But Mimi, like me, is still waiting,' Lorna said to her father's astonishment, 'and I shan't be looking for another career to hide behind.'

'Right now,' said Victor, 'you'd be unlikely to find one and all I want, Lorna, is for you to be happy,' he added going to kiss her pale cheek.

'I'd like that, too,' said Bella quietly.

'And I,' said Lorna, 'must apologize for how I've treated my mother's dearest friend.'

A poignant moment for Bella, nor could she find a reply suitable to her mixed feelings.

'Would you and Dad mind giving me bed and board for a while?' Lorna requested.

'You mortgaged your flat to get a business loan?' asked Victor.

'For all the good it did! But even if I still owned a home, I wouldn't feel like living by myself right now.'

'And you're more than welcome here,' Bella told her.

Lorna was still in residence when Ross Diamond called Bella in June and it was she who answered the telephone.

Ross said on learning that Bella was in Paris, 'When a friend of mine had to cancel his trip and offered me his tickets for Wimbledon, I thought I'd give Bella a surprise and invite her to see some tennis with me.'

Lorna replied with a laugh, 'You'll be lucky! Bella doesn't have time to watch the tennis on TV, her evenings are as busy as her days.'

'That doesn't sound like the woman who lectured me about being a workaholic,' said Ross.

'Did you take her advice?'

'I guess not, but like I told her, habits are hard to break.'

'Bella couldn't have achieved what she has without being a workaholic,' said Lorna, 'this weekend, though, she was going to take a country break with Dad and me. Instead of which they've had to rush off to deal with a family matter and I'm sitting here cursing the cause of it!'

'Are you a blonde or a brunette?' asked Ross.

'Does it matter?'

'I'm trying to picture the girl I'm talking to. Why don't I take you to lunch and find out?'

'That's an expensive way of learning what colour my hair is!'

'But I have the feeling it could be worth it.'

Ross would say afterwards that he fell in love on the

telephone, and Lorna that a telegram from Paris had served to change her life.

Bella and Victor went directly from the airport to Camille Gerard's apartment. It was from her that a frightening summons had come that morning.

Victor had said when Bella handed him the telegram to read, 'That sort of woman wouldn't be likely to nurse a sick lover,' and had since kept his thoughts to himself.

He gave his wife an encouraging smile as they entered the palatial apartment building and told the uniformed concierge that Madame Gerard was expecting them.

The man checked on his house-phone and conducted them deferentially to the lift, where an equally deferential porter was waiting to press the button for them.

One would think this was Buckingham Palace and that woman the Queen, thought Bella watching the lift descend behind an ornate brass grille in keeping with the antique luxury of the foyer. But behind the trappings of gracious living decadence sometimes lurked, as applicable to Camille Gerard herself as to what went on in her apartment.

What was Madame Gerard but a predator and Leonard her prey? She had looked him over at the Paris opening, liked what she saw, flattered him with her attention, and the rest, thought Bella, is family history!

Leonard had not returned to England even to collect his clothes. Given his weak character, why would he bother to do so when Madame Gerard was only too willing to clothe him according to her taste as she was to feed and house him.

Bella had visualized his benefactress taking him shopping in the exclusive Faubourg Saint-Honoré and had felt her gorge rise, as it had when she learned from her Paris manageress of the rumours about sex and drugs orgies in Camille Gerard's apartment.

Unlike her initial attitude to Joey's involvement with Beth, the age difference was the least of Bella's anxieties. She had known from the first that Leonard's enslavement could be but a temporary situation, that eventually the woman would tire of him, but his enslavement to the drugs she had doubtless plied him with could be permanent, Bella thought now.

'If I had a gun, I'd shoot Camille Gerard!' her anger exploded when she and Victor were riding upward in the lift.

'But you've turned the other cheek till now,' Victor answered quietly, 'instead of telling Leonard straight when he's met us for lunch on our Paris trips – wearing designer jeans and jackets that *he* didn't pay for.'

'You forgot to mention the Gucci shoes and the Dunhill lighter!'

'Shout at me if it makes you feel better.'

'Nothing will make me feel better about Leonard.'

'That's why I put it the way I did, Bella, that you turn the other cheek for him to go on hurting you.'

'And where did your expressing your opinions to Mimi get *you*?'

'At least I tried.'

'So did I, a long time ago and equally unsuccessfully.'

Bella eyed her chic appearance in the lift's gilt-framed mirror and tilted her hat to enhance it.

'Preparing for battle?' said Victor.

'Since my acquaintance with Madame Gerard is limited to the occasion on which she ensnared my son, that's one way of putting it, though I doubt that a battle will be necessary to remove him from her clutches now.

'It's difficult to believe she has a son of her own,' Bella briefly reflected.

'But God knows what he did to her,' said Victor, 'remember Leonard mentioning that they're estranged?'

'The same goes for you and Mimi, but you haven't consoled yourself by corrupting other men's daughters – and Leonard is by no means Madame Gerard's first in that respect!'

Bella added after calming down, 'About what you call my turning the other cheek, given how family life has changed, strife is the only alternative to letting one's children go their own way. If you hadn't made known your feelings so strongly to Mimi, you wouldn't have alienated her and I made up my mind that nothing was worth alienating my son.'

Victor replied caustically, 'When I alienated Mimi she was a stripper in some dive in Soho! Which respectable father would stand for that?'

'I can't speak for fathers,' said Bella as the lift halted, 'nor for every mother, only for the sort of mother I am.'

They walked in silence to Madame Gerard's apartment, along a wide corridor lined with oil paintings, Bella's heels sinking into the pile of the splendid carpet and her heart thudding with apprehension on her son's account.

'Shall I thunder on the door with that heavy brass knocker, or would you like the pleasure?' asked Victor.

'I have no intention of losing my dignity,' said Bella, 'it's enough that for four years that woman has made me feel I've lost Leonard.'

They were admitted by a maid and conducted to an opulent drawing-room, where they were kept waiting for ten minutes.

'Why aren't you tapping your fingers?' Victor asked Bella.

Mentally she was pacing the room. And recalling the long ago day when she was summoned by Sylvie to London and faced with the dilemma of whether or not to let Hal back into her life and into her children's lives.

Her feelings had overruled her head, but when hadn't they with Hal? And so it was with their son, Bella was thinking when a soberly garbed and bespectacled man entered.

'I am Roland Duval,' he said pleasantly, 'Madame Gerard's secretary. Madame wishes me to tender to you her apologies that she is not here to receive you.'

'I am here solely to collect my son,' Bella replied, 'is he fit to travel?'

'I must leave you to decide, Madame. Monsieur Diamond awaits you on the terrace. His baggage has been packed.'

Camille Gerard prefers not to face me and she can't get Leonard out of here fast enough! thought Bella as they followed Roland Duval to the far end of the drawing-room, through a conservatory stifling with the scents of the exotic plants, to a patio overlooking the Champs-Elysées.

Leonard was seated in a wrought-iron chair, his back towards them and a bowl of black grapes on a table beside him. In his hand was a long-stemmed red rose.

'Super view, isn't it?' he said with bravado when they joined him, 'And Fouquet's, my favourite restaurant, is nice and handy. Have some grapes, they're delicious –'

'Stop it, Leonard!' said Bella. 'Madame Gerard's upfronter has diplomatically made himself scarce and there's no need to put on a show for *us*.' You look like a scarecrow, she silently added, what has that bitch done to you?

A paroxysm of coughing then gripped Leonard, reminding Bella again of his father's illness and its serving to reunite the family. Would this bring Leonard back to where he belonged?

'How long have you been ill?' she asked him.

'I caught a cold in Le Touquet a few weeks ago but I didn't let it get the better of me.'

'It seems to have done so,' said Victor, 'have you seen a doctor?'

'Not until yesterday, there's been too much going on.'

'And what did the doctor say?' Bella enquired.

Again bravado masked Leonard's true feelings. 'That I'd be dead before I'm forty if I don't change my ways! Just my luck that Camille was present when he said it.'

Though Bella still thought of her son as young, he was now thirty-nine and dissipation written on his handsome face. Illness too had taken its toll, his fragility emphasized by the heavy leather jacket slung around his shoulders and his unhealthy pallor was alarming to Bella.

The reason for the peremptory summons was now all too clear – Madame Gerard didn't want a corpse on her hands. 'We must get you home as soon as possible,' she said to Leonard.

'But I haven't a home, have I?' he replied.

'You have one with us for as long as you need it,' said Victor, 'like we told Lorna and she's still with us.'

Leonard hid his gratitude with flippancy. 'All you need now is Mimi descending on you clutching a prayer book. And for me, it's farewell to all that!' he said gesturing towards the view and mustering a smile.

'I'm not too good on my pins right now,' he continued bantering when it was necessary for Victor to help him to his feet, 'and you forgot to give me a kiss, Mum!'

Bella corrected the omission, her dismay increasing when she saw Leonard hold on to Victor's arm. Her son required nursing – would that include his entering a clinic for drug addicts?

Leonard handed her the rose. 'Since I'm not up to tossing it over the balustrade myself, Mum, would you please do it for me? It was on my breakfast tray, Camille must have put it there before she left for Baden–Baden.'

To revitalize herself for whoever your successor will be. 'Without saying goodbye to you?'

'Camille is marvellous at saying things without words.'

And what was Leonard's tossing her farewell offering away but his putting her behind him? Bella flung the rose where she would have liked to hurl Madame Gerard and watched it descend through the still summer air to the Champs-Elysées.

When they arrived in the foyer, the Louis Vuitton luggage awaiting Leonard beside the desk epitomized for her not just this episode in his life, but the transient he was, able to shrug off four wasted years, and learning nothing from his experiences.

On the way to the airport Bella could no longer contain her feelings. 'If you don't want what the doctor said to happen, Leonard, you better *had* change your ways.'

'That doesn't seem to me a good enough reason.'

'Are you saying you don't care if you live or die?'

'Your mother doesn't deserve this,' Victor interceded.

They had left the glamorous face of Paris behind and were journeying through her drab outskirts. Leonard gazed through the window, his expression suddenly weary.

'Mum didn't deserve what my father did,' he answered,

'and he had more to live for than I have, a wife and children, troublesome though one of us continued to be.

'I've tried to forgive him, but I can't,' he said turning to Bella, 'his dad gave him a bad time and I'm sorry about that, but he was lucky enough to meet *you*.'

Bella had not known until then just how scarred Leonard was by his father's suicide. Nothing could have been more unstabling for the lad he then was, already on the way downhill. Edith had had Keith to sustain her, but Leonard had gone on pretending to himself that he needed nobody, frittering away half a million pounds along with his youth in pursuit of the pleasure he had once mistaken for happiness.

Whether he knew it or not, what he needed was the right woman, but would he ever meet her?

Chapter Ten

THE WALL STREET CRASH in the autumn of 1987 wiped out the trust fund Edith had set up for her children, as the repercussions in the London stock market diminished Victor's income.

'There's no such thing as planning for the future any more,' he declared bitterly.

'But "Arabella Lee" is going strong again,' Bella replied, 'and I can't stop now.'

'Would I dare suggest that you stop?' he said with a smile. 'What I *am* going to suggest, though, is that you think very carefully before expanding further at this point. You got away with opening two more boutiques in what we now know was a false boom. Take time to consolidate.'

'Since New York was to have come next, I shall have to. This isn't the time to set up shop on Fifth Avenue, the women who'd be "Arabella Lee" customers are probably queuing up to sell their furs.'

'But they wouldn't find a furrier who'd buy them,' said Victor, 'not in this country, either, with the animal rights campaign that's now going on worldwide. The fur trade has gone what my Canadian son-in-law would call "down the tubes".'

'And I shall soon be an aunt-in-law to your grandchild,' Bella said with a smile.

'Will you go with me to Toronto when Lorna has the baby?'

'Would I trust you on your own?'

Fate had once again played a hand, re-entangling Bella with her first husband's past.

On returning from Paris she was too preoccupied by Leonard to notice that Lorna and Ross were in love and their announcing their engagement before Ross left England had come as a complete surprise. To Victor too. He had not allowed his wife to spend hours at her son's bedside alone when, as she had feared, it was necessary for Leonard to enter a clinic.

A month later Lorna was married and happily setting up home in Toronto.

'When Lorna met Mr Right she didn't waste time,' Victor reflected while Bella poured him another cup of the decaffeinated coffee they drank after dinner.

'Nor did he when he met her.'

'And the same should only happen to my younger daughter,' Victor said fervently, 'shall we watch the *Nine O'Clock News* and see what's happening where she still is?'

Bella and Victor were enjoying a rare opportunity to relax together during the pre-Christmas season, when Bella's presence at all the right parties was part of her business scene and Victor her escort.

Victor, though, would willingly have had them swap places with the proverbial Darby and Joan, he thought watching his trim wife rise to switch on the television set. Only Bella is no Joan!

'Things seem to be getting worse and worse,' she said with distress as yet again the Arab unrest in Gaza and on the West Bank was graphically illustrated.

'Where are you going?' she asked when Victor sprang from his chair.

'To call Mimi and order her to come home,' he said striding to the telephone.

'Don't you dare! Put that receiver down.'

Victor did as he was bid and with a slam.

'This isn't a case for me turning, or not turning the other cheek,' he declared after Bella had switched off the set to remove the alarming pictures from his sight. 'Mimi's safety is at stake.'

'So was Leonard's with that woman and I knew it. The life

he lived with her can be just as much a killer as a bullet or a stone and for him it nearly was. But he wasn't a kid any more and nor is Mimi. You, though, have made yourself like a red rag to a bull to her, which I was careful not to do with my son, or he'd have thought me his enemy, not his friend.'

Victor returned to his chair, his expression despairing. 'All right, so I did the wrong thing.'

'And now it's *my* turn to advise *you*,' said Bella. 'Pick up the phone again and force yourself to tell Mimi you hope things aren't as bad as they look to us on TV. Say we're thinking of taking a holiday in Israel –'

'Since when?'

'Since now.'

'How will "Arabella Lee" manage without you?'

'Our children come first and if you didn't know that, Victor, you've just learned something. Tell Mimi we'll come in the spring, the climate then will be beneficial to Leonard –'

'How did Leonard get into this?'

'He's one of our children, too, in my opinion he still hasn't fully recovered and a change of scene would be good for him. If Mimi still doesn't want to meet me I'll have Leonard for company while you spend time with her –'

'If she still doesn't want to meet you, she needn't bother seeing *me*!' Victor flashed.

'That's the attitude that got you exactly nowhere,' Bella told him, 'and when you call Mimi, don't you dare suggest it might be wise for her to come home. She believes God is protecting her and I hope she's right.'

'And that's twice you've said "don't you dare" to me. Am I married to a fishwife in couture clothing?' Victor answered wryly.

The telephone then cut short their conversation, nor did Victor call Mimi that night. Instead he drove Bella to Oxford.

Chapter Eleven

IT WAS JOEY'S FRIEND and colleague, Chris Bennett, who greeted Bella and Victor when they arrived at her brother's home.

'I wanted to make the phone call, but Beth wouldn't allow me to,' he said as they followed him into the living-room, which nowadays would be called 'shabby-chic' though that term hadn't yet entered the vocabulary when Bella first saw this room and nothing had changed.

'I could barely make out what Beth was saying,' said Victor who had taken the call, 'she was so distraught.'

'And why wouldn't she be?' Chris said grimly. 'But you evidently gathered that Joey's been taken ill.'

'And I'm wondering,' said Victor, 'how many more emergencies my wife will suddenly be summoned to.'

'That's something of an exaggeration,' said Bella, 'my husband is upset on my account, Chris, please excuse him.'

Chris fumbled in his jacket pocket for his tobacco pouch. 'But I shall find it difficult to excuse Joey for what he's done. If I'd known I'd have put my foot down, but of course he kept it from me.'

He took his ancient briar from his mouth, began filling it and stopped short. 'Do you mind if I smoke?'

Bella shook her head. 'Kept what from you, Chris?'

'That he's been using himself as a guinea-pig in our current project. Trying out the drug we're developing. I've sometimes thought, Bella, that your brother is cursed with a death wish!'

Bella was glad there was a chair directly behind her and lowered herself into it, her mind swooping backward to the war. Herself and Gran and the twins sheltering in the cellar. The frightening sounds and reverberations of an air raid. A jar of homemade pickles lying shattered on the floor and Joey wanting to deal with the mess. His yelling that he wished he were dead, when Bella wouldn't let him, and his expression when he glanced down at his frail legs.

'This confirms it,' Chris went on scathingly, 'and he might now *get* his wish. Since Beth called you, he's been taken by ambulance to hospital. She went with him and I waited for you.'

A silence followed while Bella tried to pull herself together, Chris puffed his pipe angrily, and Victor gazed through the window at the gathering fog swirling around the overgrown bushes.

'What we're talking about is side-effects,' Victor said turning to Chris.

'Too true.'

'And God knows what damage gets done these days to people who think they're taking something to help them when the drug is already on the market,' Victor went on with feeling. 'What sort of drug were you and Joey developing?'

'I'm afraid that's still a secret.'

'Does that mean you intend going on with the project?' Victor demanded. 'After what you've told us?'

'Scientists must remain dispassionate,' Chris replied, 'though I'm finding that difficult right now.'

His face crumpled with distress. 'Joey suffered an internal haemorrhage and was undergoing surgery when I called the hospital just before you arrived.'

Later, while her brother hovered between life and death in the intensive care unit, Bella sat in the hospital waiting-room isolated by her thoughts though Beth was weeping beside her, and her husband and Chris seated opposite them.

Was Joey's taking the risk he had born of the death wish he had expressed as a crippled little boy? Since Bella saw him but rarely, she had not paused to consider the quality of *his* life.

To me, he's my brother the brilliant scientist and I'm proud of him. Though I raised him, I had to let him go despite his disability, make what he would of himself, but how painful it is to come face to face, years later, with consequences you were unable to avert.

Sylvie, whom Bella had called from the hospital, arrived ashen-faced and was received acidly by Beth.

'You haven't been to Oxford since the night you found Hannah hiding in the chalet when she was twelve. What are you doing here now?'

Sylvie replied quietly, 'Joey and I had a difference of opinion that night, but he's still my twin and I love him.'

'Yours,' said Beth, 'is a strange kind of love and on more counts than one.'

Sylvie sat down in a corner of the room, her crimson trilby seeming a gesture of defiance in the institutional surroundings and again Bella's mind returned to Joey's and Sylvie's child-hood. When my brother's disability was all I thought about and my healthy little sister suffered accordingly.

Sylvie, though, had disguised her hurt with behaviour comparable to thumbing her nose and the pattern was perhaps set then for how she would live her life, eschewing stardom to employ her talent for purposes other than mere entertain-ment and taking her happiness where angels feared to tread.

She and Tess were still together. Sylvie's brief involvement with a man had ended as suddenly as it began and she had afterwards formed a theatre group increasingly prominent in the Gay Rights scene.

Until then, Sylvie hadn't flaunted her lesbianism. Was the change in her another of the defiances that had peppered her path and evoked maybe by something Joey had said?

Bella hadn't expected their avoiding each other at her wedding to last and Sylvie must be wishing she had made peace with her twin.

It was now 3 a.m. The tea a nurse had brought for them an hour ago had gone cold on the table and Beth seemed unable to drag her gaze from the clock above the door.

Joey died at daybreak without recovering consciousness. The stunned silence that followed the surgeon's delivering the grave news and departing was broken by the sound of Beth slapping Chris Bennett's face when he came to comfort her.

'You were supposed to be Joey's best friend, Chris, and it's a sick joke that it was you who brought him to me and you who's responsible for my losing him!'

'I'm broken-hearted, Beth, and anything I can do –'

'You've done enough, you callous bastard!'

Chris stood his ground, the weal on his cheek livid and his complexion paper white. 'Please believe that I had no idea what Joey was doing.'

'I do! And that makes it worse. It's you bloody scientists to a tee, busy peering into miscroscopes to save lives and not giving a thought to those you yourselves are ruining. Between you, you and Joey have put paid to mine!'

'You still have your daughter, Beth,' Victor said quietly.

'In a manner of speaking.'

'I could say the same about one of mine,' Victor went on trying to console her while Bella and Sylvie sat enveloped in their private sorrow and Chris stood clutching his pipe as if shock had immobilized him.

'I waited so long for a child,' Beth said piteously to Victor, 'and it was Joey who gave her to me –'

'Come on, Beth, we'll go together to say goodbye to him –'

'Not now he's dead, I want to remember him alive.'

'Then we'll take you home. Where's your coat?'

'I don't think I brought one.'

Victor put his coat around her.

'You're a nice man, Victor, and so was my Joey – it wasn't that he didn't care –'

'Just that he didn't have time to,' said Chris, 'and I must now hasten to the lab.'

'To begin figuring out why Joey suffered fatal side-effects!' Beth exclaimed.

'How did you guess?'

'You bloody scientists,' she said again, but this time her tongue was not as if dipped in vitriol.

Joey's funeral fell on a Friday and that evening Bella was surprised to see Beth light Sabbath candles.

'You take your conversion to Judaism very seriously,' she remarked.

'By now it's part of me,' Beth replied, 'and before Hannah left the nest, Friday night was a family occasion in this house. Joey actually came home to make Kiddush and eat supper with us.'

Sylvie had returned immediately to London, allowing Bella and Victor an opportunity to talk privately with Beth before they too returned to their own life.

'Excuse me for not cooking you the usual Sabbath fare,' Beth said eyeing the light supper she had put before them.

'None of us has much appetite,' said Victor, 'and instead of making unnecessary apologies, Beth, tell us what you'll do now you're alone. We're family and concerned about you.'

Bella put it more bluntly. 'How are you fixed financially?'

Beth then revealed that Joey and Chris had over the years turned down offers from wealthy pharmaceutical companies prepared to set them up and pay them well to work exclusively developing drugs for them.

'We could have lived on the shores of Lake Geneva, or in a house with a swimming pool in the States,' she added, 'if those two had been prepared to pick themselves up and go.

'To tell you the truth, I don't think they ever took their minds off what they were currently involved in for long enough to give those offers serious consideration.'

'But that was my brother the scientist,' said Bella poignantly, 'and I can understand your adding the adjective you did to Chris.'

Bella, though, could also understand Joey and the burning thirst for knowledge that had driven him, material things remaining unimportant. Joey wasn't an achiever for achievement's sake, nor might Bella have been had she not been deprived of the chance to follow the path he had. And right now, how empty her own achievement and the affluence it had brought her seemed.

'As for what I shall do,' Beth went on, 'Hannah will be inconsolable when she returns to the commune and gets the message I left for her, and she'll fly to her mother's arms for a brief while.'

Victor helped himself to a clementine and began peeling it. 'There were times when *I* could've been dead and buried and Mimi wouldn't have known till she got back from wherever she was!'

'My husband's developed an allergy to young people, Beth,' Bella said caustically.

'But I've always enjoyed having them around and I shall probably take student lodgers again. The rent money would help me get by financially and you two wouldn't have to worry about me going short or being lonely. I might even resuscitate the Sunday evening gatherings people used to flock to.'

And it would then seem to Beth as if her life was again as it was before she met Joey, thought Bella. How long would it take her to realize that she was no longer the same person and you couldn't turn back the clock?

A lesson Bella had learned when she gave Hal a second chance and nothing but their passion was the same.

Victor, though, was the friend and lover combined that Hal never was and Bella hoped with all her heart that her dead brother and the woman now his widow had experienced together what she and Victor shared.

Chapter Twelve

MIMI'S REACTION to hearing her father was planning a trip to Israel was, 'About time, Dad!'

'You've never said that before when I've rung up to say I'm coming to see you.'

'That could be because it always seemed like a threat to drag me back home, but everything's different now – and what I meant was it's about time you visited Israel. I'll try to take time off when you come.'

'Bella and her son will be with me.'

'From what I've heard about her son from Lorna, he's going to love Tel Aviv and hate Jerusalem.'

'Like you would have once.'

'But now it's the other way round.'

'And if you could bring yourself to meet Bella, it would make your father a happier man.'

'The new me will be pleased to meet her, Dad, and that should tell you what God has done for me. I have to go now, the babies are raising the roof in the crèche!'

The old Mimi would have said 'raising hell' and Victor was left wondering if he would like the new one and if he had lost the high-spirited daughter whom despite her shortcomings he had adored.

'If religion is Mimi's salvation,' Bella said when he relayed the conversation to her, 'you should be glad she's found it.'

'But it isn't her any more.'

'Or possibly it's the *real* her,' Bella countered, 'as Leonard once said of you in your presence, some parents are never satisfied, and in my opinion they're the ones with high expectations for their children. Is it any wonder that some kids get damaged trying to live up to them and others say the heck with it, I'm my own person?'

'You, of course, had no expectations for your children!' Victor responded.

'I taught myself not to have when Leonard began getting poor reports at school, or I'd now be the bitterly disappointed person you are with regard to Mimi.'

'Only a rabbi would be pleased by how Mimi has finally turned out! One of my expectations, and I don't have to be ashamed of it, was for her to have a family life. Now my heart's in my mouth in case she suddenly gets married and has a baby who could get stoned to death by Arabs on the West Bank. How can those settlers go on living there with their children?'

'Their kind of Judaism,' said Bella, 'accepts everything as God's will, including no doubt the dreadful picture you just conjured up about a grandchild you haven't yet got.'

'Including, too,' Victor said with feeling, 'their right to be where they are, on land which the Palestinians believe is rightfully theirs. Mimi could have chosen a less dangerous way of being religious than attaching herself to those fanatics!'

'But on a personal level,' said Bella, 'they're probably happier than people who don't have their faith and Mimi's now being willing to meet me has to mean something.'

Before Bella and Victor left for Israel, taking with them a reluctant Leonard, the Arab unrest was being referred to by the press as an uprising and Lorna had presented Victor with a granddaughter.

'Arabella will be delighted,' Bella said after Ross had telephoned the news, 'and there are now two of them to take over "Arabella Lee" eventually.'

'Now who's letting expectations run riot!'

'I can dream, can't I?' Bella said with a laugh as the telephone rang again. 'If that's Ross calling to tell us what colour the baby's hair is, which he forgot, say we'll fly to Toronto as soon as we're back from Israel, to see for ourselves.'

'Right now, you are certainly putting family before business!'

'Not necessarily,' Bella replied as he went to answer the phone, 'I shall keep my eye open for the right location for a branch there.'

They were preparing for bed and Bella creaming her face at the dressing table.

'If you wouldn't mind holding on a minute, I'll get her,' she heard Victor say quietly and saw him cover the telephone mouthpiece with his hand. 'It's Ezra and he sounds terrible.'

Bella leapt to her feet and grabbed the phone. 'What can I do for you, Ezra?'

'All I want is for you to listen.'

'You have my ear.'

'Doreen has cancer and I'm calling from the nursing home she's in.'

A pause followed and Bella felt the depth of Ezra's emotion as though it were crackling on the line.

'I now know I love her, but it's too late, she hasn't long to live. And what makes it the more tragic is Doreen doesn't believe me, though I keep *telling* her I love her. I could never bring myself to say it when it would've been a lie. Now, she thinks I'm lying because I want her to die happy.'

'I wish I were there to hold your hand, Ezra.'

'My daughter is here to do that. I just needed to tell the only person I *can* tell.'

Bella replaced the receiver, tears stinging her eyes. 'What Ezra rang up to tell me, Victor, can only be described as one of life's capriciously cruel twists.'

'But they're not always cruel,' he replied, 'to prove it, I now have a nice son-in-law who's also your brother-in-law, not to mention the grandchild born today.

'And let's not forget,' he went on, 'me finding happiness with my first wife's old friend who never forgave her for

333

whatever it was she did. Are you ever going to tell me what
it was?'

Bella returned to the dressing table and resumed creaming
her face. 'If Gerda had wanted you to know, she'd have told
you herself.'

'And nobody could say that isn't loyalty!'

Chapter Thirteen

THOUGH EXTENDING her business to Toronto was not yet on the agenda, establishing 'Arabella Lee' in Tel Aviv was high on Bella's list and her intention to combine the holiday with finding suitable premises.

But the family matter has to take precedence, she thought en route from Ben Gurion Airport to the city, she and Victor again crammed into a cab with Leonard, only this time it's my husband the vibes are coming from.

Mimi's agreeing to meet her was a relief to Bella on more counts than one. So edgy was Victor about the reunion he craved, without Bella at his side to kick his ankle and give him warning glances, the opposite might have been the outcome.

Victor called his daughter immediately they were shown to their suite at the Tel Aviv Dan and was left cooling his heels for ten minutes while she was fetched from her work.

In the meantime, Leonard went out for a walk and Bella put the duty free whisky they had bought at Heathrow on the coffee table, lest her husband require it.

'Dare I leave you, to go to the bathroom?'

'What am I, a child!'

'Nor is your daughter and it would be useful for you to bear that in mind.'

When Bella returned to the sitting-room, he was replacing the receiver. 'How did it go?'

'She's meeting us for lunch tomorrow.'

'We can reserve a table here.'

'That wouldn't suit Mimi's new requirements,' said Victor sardonically, 'it has to be one of the restaurants she's specified, the double-kosher kind! When I think how that girl used to enjoy prawn cocktails and ham sandwiches –'

'But don't you dare remind her of that,' Bella cut in, 'or you can forget being friends with her.'

'Like you're friends with your son, but what good is it doing him?'

'He knows he has me to turn to.'

'A man shouldn't need to turn to his mother.'

'But Leonard still does and I have to be there for him. What he said in the taxi, in Paris, scared me stiff, Victor. He's since put the veneer he's worn for so long back on, but what I see when I look at him is what he briefly let me see that day.'

'Turning to *me*, though,' said Victor, 'has never been one of Mimi's symptoms!'

'Isn't it time you stopped thinking of her finding religion as a symptom and accepted that for Mimi it might be a cure?'

Victor turned restlessly from the window and put himself in an armchair. 'I'll believe she's cured when she has a wedding ring on her finger. She has to be the only spinster on that settlement and what the others think of that –'

'Is Mimi's problem, not yours.'

'It could end up, though, with them throwing her out,' Victor declared, 'breeding like rabbits is also seen by those people as God's will.'

'Time will tell.'

'But I'm not getting any younger, nor is she.'

Leonard's return cut short their conversation which to Bella, as always when the subject was Mimi, or Leonard, had seemed more like a debate.

'I think I'm going to like Tel Aviv,' said her son.

As Mimi predicted, thought Victor.

'It seems there's plenty of night life here, which wasn't what I expected of Israel.'

'Tel Aviv isn't Israel,' Victor informed him, 'Jerusalem is here, too.'

'But I don't see myself spending much time there,' said Leonard sprawling on a sofa and stifling a yawn.

'Did you take your vitamins this morning?' Bella asked him, to her motherly eye his recovery was not yet complete despite the passage of time. But nobody could abuse their health as Leonard had and get away with it, and there remained within him the loneliness Bella hadn't realized was there.

'I'm afraid I forgot,' Leonard replied, 'and I can't go on taking vitamins for ever.'

Nor his mother continue mollycoddling him as she has since we brought him home from the hospital, thought Victor, and my step-son is still living with us.

Though that was not strictly correct – Leonard now occupied a flat above the garage intended for the resident help Bella preferred not to employ – his proximity kept him in the forefront of her mind though she rarely saw him. And if she thinks I don't know she flits in and out of there, tidying up and filling the fridge, it's best for our relationship to let her go on thinking so.

This was the woman who repeatedly told Victor that parents must let their children make what they would of their own lives, or words to that effect, and if ever a person was blind to their own behaviour it was Bella in this important respect. Even before Leonard's illness she had got him out of trouble over and over again, thankful that he still turned to her.

My daughter could end up a disillusioned ex-ultra-orthodox kibbutznik and Bella's son an elderly playboy! Victor was thinking with asperity when Leonard told them he had just met a fabulous Israeli girl and she had invited him to a party.

'It hasn't taken you long,' Victor could not stop himself from saying and received a rebuking glance from his wife whose friendly relationship with her son included never saying the wrong thing to him.

Victor, though, had had enough of playing the role she required of *him*. 'I suppose we should be grateful,' he added, 'that the female you just mentioned isn't another old hag.'

337

Leonard was gone from the room before Bella found her tongue.

'What the hell do you think you're doing, Victor!'

'Out comes the fishwife in couture clothing again,' he replied, 'though she only seems to emerge to protect our children who are no longer children – and like some primeval maternal creature with respect to her son.

'What do I think I'm doing, you asked me and the answer is it's time for some *undoing*, Bella, for you to see sense though it could be too late.'

Meeting Mimi was for Bella another transportation backward in time. Though she had seen photographs of her younger step-daughter, Mimi in the flesh was like a reincarnation of the Viennese girl at whose hands she had suffered such painful disillusion.

Bella and Victor, the aftermath of yesterday's confrontation still with them and the cause of it behaving like the injured party, had spent fifteen minutes in the hotel foyer awaiting Mimi's arrival.

Victor was now tapping his foot impatiently while the doorman found them a taxi. 'The dinner we ate here last night was excellent, Mimi, and –'

'And what?' she cut in challengingly.

'It would've been more convenient to lunch here, but we understand why you prefer the restaurants you mentioned.'

'Well, that's a good start,' Mimi replied with a mischievous smile that belied her demure apparel.

But it would've been a bad one, thought Victor, if my wife hadn't pinched my arm and stopped me from saying that pandering to your whim is a damned nuisance! Victor still couldn't accept that this wasn't just another of his daughter's escapades and no less dismaying to him than her baring her breasts in cabaret, if the opposite extreme.

Leonard and Mimi had disliked each other on sight.

She had only contempt for the men who had bedded her

and for herself for letting them. One look at her step-brother in his snazzy outfit had relegated him to a life she had put behind her.

He saw a frumpy young woman, the sort he wouldn't be seen dead with if he could help it, sensible shoes on her feet, and her ankle-length long-sleeved brown dress buttoned to the neck despite the heat of the day. Even her head was covered, and she was eyeing him with condemnation. Who did this born-again religious maniac think she was?

But men like Leonard Diamond, Mimi was now thinking, were responsible for my turning to God and finding peace. When Mimi threw in her lot with those of her religion who lived by His laws, it had equated for her with a Catholic girl joining a Holy Order.

In Judaism, though, there was no such thing, family life was the core and the union of man and wife sacred and essential to the procreation of the race. Since the ultra-orthodox married young, some seeming little more than children when they became parents, Mimi had so far evaded her duty to God in that respect, grateful that in her thirties she was considered too old for the available males, nor were they available for long.

But an elder of the kibbutz had just *become* available after the death of his wife and speedy *re*marriage was also deemed a sacred duty. Even a substantial age difference was not viewed as prohibitive the other way round, illustrated by the young women helping greybeard husbands produce a second family.

Did Mimi love God enough to follow suit? Meanwhile she had to get through this encounter with the woman who had replaced her darling mother, and with that woman's despicable son who probably thought himself as devastatingly handsome as he must once have been.

The conversation over lunch was for Bella like a play for which those around the table had carefully rehearsed their parts. Communicating it wasn't, but for Victor this had to be better than nothing.

Bella had rarely seen Leonard behave with such stiff

politeness and Mimi had barely addressed a word to him. What though, given her sequestered life, could the two have in common?

What, other than Victor, did Bella have in common with this pious young woman who had in effect cut herself off from the real world?

'That's a pretty kerchief you have on your head, Mimi,' Bella remarked over coffee.

'I don't wear it for adornment.'

'Is it holding on your wig?' said Leonard.

'I shall take that rude witticism from where it comes,' she replied.

'Now hang on a minute, I wasn't being rude, I thought your sort of Jewess is obliged to wear a wig.'

'But allow me to inform you,' said Mimi, 'that it's only after marriage that applies. I'm not even obliged to cover my hair with a kerchief –'

'May I enquire why you do?'

'What's it to you!'

A flash of the old Mimi, thought Victor.

Suddenly the conversation has come to life, Bella said to herself.

'Now who's being rude?' Leonard responded. 'And if I may say so, it's a pity to hide your crowning glory when you don't have to.'

'Kindly keep your flattery for women who enjoy it,' Mimi answered, 'I don't play your sort of games any more.'

'I shouldn't think you play *any* sort of games in that place you've put yourself in,' said Leonard, 'and if you ask me, what you're doing is wasting your life.'

'I *didn't* ask you and from what I've heard about how you spend yours, the pot shouldn't be calling the kettle black. I know your scene and decided I'd had my fill of it, you know nothing about mine.

'It might seem a strange way of life to you,' Mimi went on with feeling, 'but one thing it isn't is useless. We don't spend all our time praying, everyone pulls their weight and the

340

kibbutz supports itself. Who, may I ask, is currently supporting *you*, Leonard?'

'Leonard's health isn't too good,' Bella defended her son.

'Balls!' said Victor. 'He just can't hold down a job and why
should he bother to with a mother like you?'

'Thanks for the diatribe,' Leonard said to Mimi.

'It was what you deserve.'

'Who are you to say what I deserve? Everything you know
about me is hearsay. And they should send you out as a
missionary, that was wonderful propaganda you delivered,
designed for the gullible which I'm not. Sorry to disappoint
you!'

'You,' said Mimi, 'are too deeply entrenched in the cesspool
you live in to dig yourself out and give God a chance.'

'That's a new name for the flat over our garage, Bella,' said
Victor, 'and I feel as if I'm at a verbal ping-pong match!'

'Me too, and I'm finding it interesting.'

'But I'm wasting my breath on Leonard,' said Mimi, 'he
doesn't *want* to be saved.'

'From what?' he said feigning a yawn.

'From yourself, but you wouldn't have the guts to try
finding that out, would you?'

'Since I'm invited to a party tonight, I'm not free to attend
synagogue,' he said flippantly.

'It doesn't have to be tonight and it's the kibbutz, not
"shul", I'm talking about. Tomorrow will be soon enough for
the sinner you still are.'

'And am likely to remain.'

'I'm offering to help you save yourself.'

'She can't be serious,' Leonard said to Bella and Victor, 'and
the way she was shouting at me before she reverted to
piousness again, it's a good thing we're in a Jewish restaurant,
where *everyone* shouts, or we'd have been asked to leave!'

The voluble conviviality all around them was to Bella
deafening and she feared that the waitress squeezing her way
between the packed-in tables would sooner or later spill the
food on her tray in some unfortunate customer's lap.

'What Leonard just said,' Mimi told her father, 'is one of the best things about living in Israel. Here, Jews don't have to bother about the impression they're making, we can be ourselves.'

'But where *you* live isn't, according to the map, Israel,' Leonard corrected her, 'and given your personal history I'd suggest you reconsider whether *you're* now being yourself.'

For once, Victor agreed with Leonard, but held his tongue.

'And why do you cover your hair when you don't have to?' Leonard went on.

'If you must know,' Mimi flared, 'I prefer not to draw attention to my unmarried state, though if I had my way I'd stay single for ever!'

'Have the matchmakers been getting busy with you?' Victor enquired.

'Not yet, but they soon will and I don't conform easily.'

'No need to tell your father that!'

'But I'm now trying to do something worthwhile with my life, Dad, which is more than can be said of my step-brother.'

'Are you going to pick up the gauntlet?' Bella asked Leonard. 'Mimi's challenged you to give her way of life a try.'

'Are you out of your mind, Mum?'

When it came to Leonard, Bella always had been she thought surveying his Armani jacket, sleeves pushed up in the current fashion, and charged to her Harrods account. Victor was right, it was time not just for some undoing, but for drastic measures.

'Working in the fields, or whatever, side by side with others for a few days would do you no harm,' she told her son.

'Is that an order?'

'Yes, as a matter of fact.'

'What we witnessed at lunch today,' Bella said when eventually she and Victor were alone in their hotel suite, 'could've been the prelude to another of life's capricious twists.'

'If you mean what I think you do, the mere idea of it scares me to death! You, though, encouraged it with that pick up the gauntlet stuff –'

'My intention was solely to shake my son from his lethargy,' Bella replied, 'and if Mimi and Leonard are destined to fall in love they'll need no help from me.'

'But it will be heaven help them and us.'

'Or might it be their final salvation? Mimi is too like her mother for a love affair with God to satisfy her.'

'Since I was Gerda's husband, how wouldn't I know that?'

Victor went to gaze through the window at the Mediterranean lapping the shore. 'She wasn't entirely satisfied with the *married* love affair she shared with me.'

Bella said after a silence, 'You're telling me Gerda was unfaithful to you, aren't you? But it doesn't surprise me.' At last she could unburden herself of the secret she had kept from Victor.

'That was the reason for the break in your marriage?' he said when she had done so. 'I should've guessed. Yet you took Hal back –'

'It was Gerda I blamed.'

'And no man could be blamed for succumbing to Gerda – which didn't stop me from sacking the best salesman I had!'

'How did you manage to forgive Gerda's infidelities?'

'I knew she loved me.'

'But she didn't deserve you,' said Bella, 'and if my son is as happy with your daughter as I am with you, finding her was worth waiting for.'

' 'Your imagination,' said Victor, 'is running riot again. Mimi and Leonard don't even like each other and the capricious twist you mentioned is one that all concerned could do without.'

Chapter Fourteen

THOUGH THE ODDS had indeed seemed against it, a year later Leonard and Mimi were married and for Bella it was as if Destiny had again pulled the strings.

Watching her son and Gerda's daughter become man and wife, radiant with love for each other, it was of Gerda that Bella thought.

'Like you can't help being you, I can't help being me,' Gerda had once said and at last Bella was able to recall it with a smile, the bitterness she had harboured for so long gone from her.

Leonard had remained at the kibbutz when his mother and step-father returned to England, which Bella had thought miraculous and Victor a good deal more earthly.

Since it can't be God, it has to be sleeping with Mimi that's keeping Leonard where he'd rather not be, was Victor's private explanation.

Bella's was that Mimi was doing what his mother had been unable to do, make a 'mensch' of Leonard, confirming that the right girl was all her son needed.

Leonard had made only one stipulation to Mimi about their future together. He was prepared to give God a chance, if she was willing for him not to have to do so on the kibbutz, to which she had agreed with such alacrity Victor felt vindicated in his certainty that a religious enclave was not the place for her.

She had nevertheless insisted upon an ultra-orthodox marriage ceremony, which took place out of doors as tradition demanded and reminded Bella, as did its clerical participants who afterwards danced the 'kazatski', of the wedding scene in *Fiddler on the Roof*.

Leonard and Mimi, her veil caught by the breeze, stood together clapping their hands in rhythm with the frenetic music and Bella found it hard to believe that the robust and happy man at whom she was looking was the son for whom she had feared.

A year of tilling the fields, which surprisingly Leonard had not eschewed, had contributed to his rehabilitation and Mimi had done the rest.

Arabella Lee Rosenberg, now a college girl, had flown to Israel with her parents and twin brothers to be a bridesmaid, as had little Gerda Diamond there with Lorna and Ross.

Sylvie, despite her commitments, had managed to be present, making a last minute entrance in one of the vividly outré outfits that had become her hallmark, as the distinguished actress Margaret Rutherford had in her day been synonymous with tweeds and a trilby hat.

Beth, though, had not managed to come, her absence heightening Joey's, but Hannah was there with the French doctor she had recently met on her travels. Would it last?

Once again Bella resorted to the useful cliché, Time will tell. How else to approach the vicissitudes of young people prey to the ever more turbulent world in which they lived, one in which the old values were no more, the environment polluted by poisons administered by Man, and even the food they ate no longer to be trusted.

How else, thought Bella wryly, to approach life itself? Time had certainly told that Connie, here with yet another wealthy husband, would never change! Nor had Connie's appearance, her most recent cosmetic surgery must have been what she and her pals called 'the whole shpiel', not just her umpteenth facelift but the rejuvenation too of her sagging curves. How could a woman of seventy look like Connie still did in that clinging white sheath?

Bella's beige silk dress was cunningly draped, camouflage the sole concession to age she was prepared to make. Nor, since Victor loved the woman she was, not the shell, would Bella still be paying so much attention to how she looked were her image not a necessary attribute of 'Arabella Lee', where smart elderly ladies shopped along with their daughters and granddaughters.

Lorna joined her on the terrace, feasting her eyes on the plethora of colourful bushes. 'Who'd have thought Mimi would end up getting married in Jerusalem?'

'The same could be said of Leonard.'

'And Dad's done them proud, giving them a reception at the King David Hotel.' Lorna glanced at her little girl who was romping on the lawn. 'While my bundle of mischief is getting grass stains on her bridesmaid frock, I can have a private word with you, Bella.'

'In which capacity shall I listen,' said Bella with a laugh, 'step-mother, or sister-in-law?'

'Friend,' Lorna replied, 'as you were to my mother and what I want to say is I hope my naming my child after her didn't upset you. Though she never said so to me – well, something went terribly wrong between you and her, didn't it?'

'But it's all come right and I wish I could tell her so. Shall you manage another trip to Israel when we open the Tel Aviv branch?'

'Mimi will kill me if I don't. What a splendid idea of yours it was, Bella, to let her and Leonard manage your Israeli outlet.'

'Your dad isn't so sure!'

'But *I* think those two will make it together in every way,' Lorna declared.

And I that they were meant to find each other, thought Bella.

Victor came to sit with them and helped himself to some of the sweetmeats on the table, his expression pensive. 'I have to keep pinching myself amid the gaiety to believe what's going on in this country.'

The frock-coated clerics were still dancing the 'kazatski' and the hand-clapping of those circled around them ever louder while the violinist played on.

'If Jews had stopped celebrating weddings every time trouble clouded their horizon, kosher caterers would have gone out of business,' said Bella, 'and that, minus the caterers, applied to my grandparents' wedding in a Russian "shtetl" and the Children of Israel who got married in the Wilderness.'

'What I think Bella's saying, Dad,' Lorna put in, 'is our people have learned to laugh and cry at one and the same time and it's helped us survive.'

'With that I agree, but the Palestinians in Gaza and on the West Bank have plenty to cry about this time around and Mimi has now admitted to me that, like many Israelis, she doesn't believe it's God's will for Jews to stake their claim to those territories.

'I don't envy Mimi and Leonard beginning their married life in the political turmoil that's all around them and could tear this nation apart,' Victor went on. 'There's also how Israel is currently being viewed by the rest of the world – and Jews everywhere are as usual caught in the flak!'

'Have you finished, Dad?' said Lorna. 'This is supposed to be a party.'

'And oh to be young again!' he replied as the 'kazatski' finally ended and Mimi and Leonard began dancing the Horah with their friends. 'And when I think of the changes I've lived through – If anyone had told me when I was a lad that if and when our people finally got the land promised them in the bible, forty years on they'd be daggers drawn among themselves, I wouldn't have believed it.

'In more personal matters I have no complaints,' Victor added giving his wife and daughter a smile.

'But you and Bella should think of taking a real vacation,' said Lorna.

Victor answered drily, 'With "Arabella Lee's" New York opening scheduled for next year and the perfume soon to be launched on the market? Your father, Lorna, is married to a lady-tycoon.'

Which Gran had foretold Bella would one day be. The years between then and now could be likened to a long and winding road, among its milestones all the hats Bella had designed along the way, wide-brimmed straws and velvet toques and turbans, boaters and berets, sequinned cloches and leather caps, floral confections and peach-bloom felts, all of them distinguished from their kind by what Amelia, Bella's first salesgirl, had called 'the Bella touch'.

'Though I still can't draw for toffee, I could design a hat in my sleep!' she said with a laugh.

'Run a business too,' said her husband.

'But neither was what I wanted to do.'

'And you're crying all the way to the bank,' said Lorna, 'like my better half who wanted to be a concert pianist. How did you and Dad enjoy dining at ten Downing Street?'

An occasion on which Bella had again asked herself, 'How did little Bella Minsky come to this?' Margaret Thatcher, though, had doubtless stopped asking *herself* a long time ago how the grocer's daughter from Grantham had got where *she* now was.

'Your dad found a lot in common with Denis,' she told Lorna.

'That doesn't surprise me. Women like you and Maggie need the right consort and that isn't an insult to Dad, it's a compliment,' said Lorna wafting a wasp away from the cream cakes a waiter had just brought to the table.

'But I wouldn't say bracketing me with Maggie in any respect but one is a compliment to *me*.' Bella exchanged a smile with her husband. 'And what you just called your father, Lorna, is less than what he is to me.'

It was Victor who replied when Lorna asked if Bella was looking forward to receiving the Businesswoman of the Year Award, an honour awaiting her on her return to England.

'She'll take it in her stride.'

That's the story of my life, thought Bella, and she still wasn't sure if she was the victim or the beneficiary of her own personality, only that she could be no different if she had her time again.